# BRING ME TO LIFE

Back to Love Duet

Charlotte Frances

*To anyone who has ever let someone else make them feel unpretty; this book is dedicated to you.*

*You are beautiful*

*x*

# CONTENTS

Title Page
Dedication
Warning     2
Spotify Playlist     3
Epigraph     4
Prologue     5
Chapter 1     13
Chapter 2     26
Chapter 3     36
Chapter 4     43
Chapter 5     50
Chapter 6     61
Chapter 7     72
Chapter 8     83
Chapter 9     96
Chapter 10     106
Chapter 11     112
Chapter 12     123
Chapter 13     133
Chapter 14     142
Chapter 15     149

| | |
|---|---|
| Chapter 16 | 157 |
| Chapter 17 | 171 |
| Chapter 18 | 184 |
| Chapter 19 | 188 |
| Chapter 20 | 196 |
| Chapter 21 | 206 |
| Chapter 22 | 214 |
| Chapter 23 | 222 |
| Chapter 24 | 233 |
| Chapter 25 | 243 |
| Chapter 26 | 250 |
| Chapter 27 | 259 |
| Chapter 28 | 270 |
| Chapter 29 | 284 |
| Chapter 30 | 294 |
| Chapter 31 | 305 |
| Chapter 32 | 312 |
| Chapter 33 | 322 |
| Chapter 34 | 333 |
| Chapter 35 | 343 |
| Chapter 36 | 348 |
| Chapter 37 | 355 |
| Chapter 38 | 360 |
| Chapter 39 | 367 |
| Chapter 40 | 375 |
| Chapter 41 | 381 |
| Chapter 42 | 388 |
| Useful Contacts | 393 |

| | |
|---|---|
| Authors Note | 394 |
| Acknowledgement | 396 |
| Back to Love Duet | 398 |

Copyright © 2022 Charlotte Frances

All rights reserved. No part of this book may be reproduced or used in any manner without the prior written permission of the copyright owner, except for the use of brief quotations in a book review. All versions of this book are registered and protected with Copyright House, London.

Cover Image by Vitalii Matokha/Shutterstock.com
Chapter Subheading  Graphic Designs  Canva
Published by Kindle Direct Publishing
Proofread by C. Smyth
Edited and formatted by C. Smyth
Charlotte Frances Logo Design  Canva

For permissions please contact:
charlotte.francesauthor@outlook.com

This is a work of fiction. Any similarity to actual persons, living or dead, or actual events, is purely coincidental. As this is a contemporary novel, certain long-standing institutions, businesses, celebrity personalities, and popular culture references are mentioned, but all of the characters involved in this story are wholly imaginary.

# WARNING

This is a new adult, contemporary romance. The main characters are 18+.

At times, this book features scenes of bullying, explicit language, assault, and sexual content. It also deals with suicide, the loss of a parent, and mental health issues.

Please note there are also brief conversations relating to FGM, rape, and forced child marriage.

If any of these are triggers for you then please proceed with caution or do not read.

Know your limits.

# SPOTIFY PLAYLIST

**Hate Me (With Juice WRLD)** Ellie Goulding
**Antisocial (With Travis Scott)** Ed Sheeran
**Top Dog** AJ Tracey
**100 Letters** Halsey
**What You Know** Two Door Cinema Club
**Heatwaves** Glass Animals
**Toxic Pony** ALTÉGO, Britney Spears, and Ginuwine
**Quit Playing Games (With My Heart)** Bodybangers, Stephen Oaks, Just Mike
**I Wish I Knew** CAGGIE
**Hate You, I love You** Arz
**Lean on Me** Cheat Codes, Tinashe
**Summer of Love** Shawn Mendes, Tainy
**Wait** Nao
**Three Little Birds** Bob Marley & The Wailers
**Whole** Sam Topkins
**Bloom** The Paper Kites
**Breath** James Arthur
**Sweet Baby** Macy Gray ft Erykah Badu
**Is Everyone Going Crazy** Nothing but Thieves
**24/5** Mimi Webb
**Hallucination** Regard, Years & Years
**Devil's Side** Foxes
**Don't Delete the Kisses** Wolf Alice
**Little Lion Man** Mumford & Sons
**Even If** Ella Eyre
**Bring Me to Life** Evanescence

# EPIGRAPH

*There is no grief like the grief that does not speak.*

- Henry Wadsworth Longfellow

# PROLOGUE

## Faith

*August 2018...*

"Junior year Faithy, are you excited?" Dad asks enthusiastically, spreading way too much butter onto my toast for my liking.

"Of course, I'm absolutely thrilled at the prospect of two more years at school, what gave it away?" I retort sarcastically. "I think that's enough butter, Dad, thanks."

He frowns at me and continues spreading.

"You're not worrying about your weight, are you sweetheart? Because you know you're perfect as you are, don't you?" He asks with casual concern. I let out an annoyed breath and roll my eyes.

"You have to say that because you're my dad!" I stand up from my breakfast stool, taking only one of the slices from the plate. "I gotta run, Dad. You know how excited I am to get back to school after all," I add, offering a saccharine smile as I'm halfway towards the door.

"Faith, you've still got twenty minutes before you need to leave, finish your breakfast at least?" He calls after me looking at his watch, but it's too late. I'm already out the door, ignoring his plea. It's not that I want to be at school early, or that I'm in a hurry to catch up with friends. I don't even have any friends. I just need to get there before *they* do. First day back I'm always fair game, so if I can avoid them all by going in early then I will.

I jump in my car and throw on my favourite Britney Spears CD. Yeah, my car is way too old for Bluetooth. Hey at least it's a CD player, the 1985 Jeep we use in Africa only takes cassette, so this is all out modern technology to me.

I flick through to find my favourite song, *'Toxic'*. I'm gonna need to channel all my inner Britney to get through today. I sing my heart out for the entire drive, but as I approach the gates of the school I turn the music down. They wouldn't understand because apparently, they aren't Britney fans. I roll my eyes again at the thought. Whatever, she's a total babe in my book. Anyone who doesn't love '... *Baby, One More Time*', is a freakin' liar.

The coast looks clear, and I can't see that infamous pink convertible anywhere. There is however a totally rad pick-up truck I've never seen before, parked opposite me. It looks more expensive than any of the other cars I've ever seen parked up in the school lot. It's black, with huge-ass wheels that look bigger than me, complete with the most polished, jet-black rims I've ever seen. Not a scratch on them. My car has so many dents and scuffs. I guess I'm not exactly the best driver.

This has to be a dude's car, it screams big dick energy. The windows of this are black, the interior looks black, even the grille is a glossy black.

All black everything - check.

I notice there is someone getting out of the driver's seat. He looks young, and potentially hot too, it's hard to tell from way over here. Is he a new student?

Another car pulls into the lot, signalling to me that it's time to move; *she* could be here any minute. I grab all my books and head over to the main entrance. I'm just at the steps when I see the pink car I was dreading come rolling in. In my haste to get out of her line of sight I walk straight into the door, dropping my books all over the floor. Shit on a stick.

"Hey, are you alright? That was pretty gnarly. Here let me get that," says a boy's voice. A guy's hand reaches down into my personal space and drags me up from picking up my own books. He leans down, and with his big ol' boy hands, manages to gather all my books in one swoop. He straightens out and holds out my books, and I get to see the mystery stealth truck boy for the first time.

The most beautiful boy I think I've ever seen. He's got wonderfully soft, curly dark blonde hair, with golden brown eyes that look like they hold a thousand secrets. He smiles an awkward smile at me, still holding my books, and I realise I'm gawping at him like a fish.

"You know, I tend to find doors seem to work better if you open them first," Mystery Boy offers, his smile still not quite reaching his eyes. His accent is a little off. It sounds more east coast but has a twang to it I can't decipher. Wow, he has really kissable lips. "Umm, thank you, I guess? I was actually thinking yours are pretty kissable too! Is your head okay?" He says with a confused smirk. Holy crap, did I say that out loud? Oh God.

"Oh, yeah, my head. Erm, I'm okay thank you. I'm sorry, I'm just in a hurry," I retort nervously, skimming over my slip up. *Way to be cool, Faith. He said you had kissable lips too, why would you ignore that?*

Damn, why did I ignore that? I glance across to the Barbie-mobile knowing I'm running out of time.

"Why the hell are you rushing anyway, class doesn't start for another ten minutes? What are you, like a hall monitor or something?" he laughs, and opens the door for me. He stands there holding it open and I notice that he is wearing a St. Edmund's Academy uniform. He *is* a new student.

I hear laughter coming from *her* direction, and I know the others must be here now too. I've really gotta go, but this boy is new. A beautiful new boy, and he is talking to me, right here in front of everyone. Maybe he will give me a chance, maybe we could be friends? *Let's be honest Faith, you wanna be more than his friend with that pretty face.*

Okay so maybe that's true, but however nice he is to me right now, I know it won't last. Give it until the second period and he will know who I am, and what everyone says about me. Then he won't want to be near me like this again. He moves in front of the door to stop it closing. For whatever reason he frowns at me, making me feel all kinds of self-conscious. I pull my books close and wrap my arms around myself.

"You're not very talkative, are you?" he asks, another slight smirk playing on his lips. "What's your deal?"

My deal? What's my deal? Like I said, give it till second period, then he will know exactly what my deal is.

"Uh, sorry. I just... I mean... I'm just..."

"SLUT!" Someone coughs as they barge past me, pushing me into Mystery Boy. Oh wow, he is solid like a wall and is that him that smells so good? He catches me and holds me firmly against him in a protective stance. I actually feel myself getting hotter at his closeness but I can't bring myself to pull away.

"Hey! What the hell, man? Fucking moron!" He shouts, still holding me tightly against his chest. Why does it feel so good? I don't know why, but I feel so safe. Is he mine? *Don't be an idiot, Faith.*

I realise I am clutching at his shirt so I immediately loosen my grip. I have an inexplicable urge to wrap my arms around him and hold on as tight as a can. He takes a deep breath in. Wait, is he smelling me?

I don't wear any perfume, or use fancy shampoos, just a vanilla soap bar made from natural, cruelty free ingredients. Bunnies before beauty I always say. He will probably think I'm as boring as my soap now. Great.

"Are you alright? Who is that asshole anyway? Do you want me to kick his ass?" Mystery Boy adds, straightening me out before my arms have a chance to snake around him like they'd threatened to.

"I don't know?" I say shaking my head. I can't even look him in the eye now. As if he would ever be mine. Although, he did just offer to kick that guys ass for me.

"Yeah well he's a fucking tool! What's your name anyway?"

Truth is I honestly don't know who that was, it could have been anyone. Practically everyone here treats me that way, so who knows who the hell it was. Pretty soon this guy, this beautiful curly haired Adonis, is going to treat me the same way too. Either that or he will act like I don't exist. It's inevitable. There are two types of people at this school. The ones who see me, and the ones who choose not to see me.

"Hey, are you sure you're okay?"

"I- I don't know, I'm sorry. I've gotta go," I say, fighting to hold back the tears that are burning my eyes. "Thanks for your help!" I add, gesturing to my books, before running through the open door.

"Hey! Hey, wait up!" I hear him call, but I don't answer. I already hear *her* sickly voice calling out to him and I know its game over. I've lost him.

I get to the end of the hall before I'm brave enough to look back. What I see breaks my heart. My beautiful mystery boy is still there at the door holding it open, but he's not looking at me now, he's forgotten me. Now he's looking at *her*, McBitchface. She puts her hand on his chest and laughs. The same chest that just made me feel safe.

My place. Mine.

I feel angry. He looks down at her and says something and she laughs again. McBitchface takes him by the hand and leads him away, just like I knew she would. She takes everyone away. She will get to him and he will hate me now, just like they all do. I shake away the tears threatening to fall and head to class.

I don't even know him so I don't know why this hurts so much. He's just another guy. Just another asshole to put me down. I try to console myself in the knowledge that at least the bitch and her minions didn't see me, so there's that small victory. Why do I wish she had shown her true colours before she could get to him. Maybe he would have been in my corner?

As I get to the end of the hall a big hand wraps around my throat shoving me into the janitors closet and I fall straight on my ass. Oh shit, it's him.

Shane Frost.

"And just where do you think you're going, Pork Chop? Didn't think you could miss our first day back catch-up now did you?" An evil smirk sits on his ugly face.

"You look a little dirty, Porky. I think maybe you need a wash?"

"Oh no, please don't!" I plead, trying to stand up, but he kicks me back down.

He pins me down by pushing his weight into a heavy boot pressed high on my chest, making it hard to breathe. He grabs the dirty mop out of the bucket and with a sinister look on his face, he shoves the soaking filthy mop straight into my face. I try to squirm away but he rubs it all over me, until I'm choking.

"There now, that's all better. Can't have you showing up on first day looking all cute, talking to new guys, forgetting your fucking place here, now can we? You're a fucking ugly pig! Why don't you say it so you remember, hmm? Say it, say you're an ugly pig!" He screams down at me, his boot still pinning me down.

"Fuck you!" I manage to choke out, spitting the remnants of dirty mop water out from my mouth. He bends down and pulls me up to my knees by my hair. Pain burns through my scalp as I try and fight my way free of his grip.

"The fuck did you just say, Pork Chop? You think you can speak to me like that? How about I shove my fucking dick down your throat huh, teach you a fucking lesson you'll never forget?" With one hand, he pulls out his dick and he's already hard. He presses himself into my face, and I instinctively close my mouth firmly shut. I try and move my face away but his grip is so tight I think I will lose what hair I have left.

"Come on Porky, don't be like that. Open up for Daddy!" he laughs, slapping my lips with his dick. I want to curse him but I'm afraid to open my mouth to speak. The bell rings and the sound of students roaming the hall fills the closet. He still has my hair bound tight in his hands, and all I can do is cry because it hurts so badly.

He takes out his cell, and tells me to smile for the camera. I squeeze my eyes closed and he laughs a sinister laugh before he finally let's go, shoving me down to the floor again.

"Hope you had a nice summer, you fat filthy whore, because I'm about to make you wish you'd never been born!"

# CHAPTER 1

## Faith

*The following April...*

You know what I hate the most in this world? Pigs! People think that they are cute and all, what with being pink. But pigs? Pink, hairy, spawns of Satan that will eat anything and everything, including an actual person. Have you ever looked into a pig's eyes? I'm pretty sure, if you look, you can see right into their deep, dark, evil souls.

Ever since I was thirteen and I found out that a pig could eat an entire human body, even their clothes, I've hated the very thought of them. I've even had a recurring nightmare about being eaten alive by pigs. It doesn't help that I've been called a pig every day by my tormentors for almost three years now either.

Today, I discovered that there are worse things than being thrown to the mercy of pigs. Like when the boy you've been secretly in love with for the past eight months finally acknowledges your existence, only to find out that it was all just a setup for you to be brutally humiliated. Tonight, when I was literally thrown to the pigs, he stood there smiling. Not with his usual sexy as hell smile that sets my whole world on fire. No, this was a smile of pure satisfaction at my humiliation.

Eight months since our first encounter, and I've not even been a blip on his radar since. I have absolutely no idea why he would suddenly want to hurt me. My heart aches from the loss of the boy who I thought he was, the boy who I thought I was in love with. My mystery boy.

I wish I could say that was the worst thing that's happened to me tonight but it wasn't. The worst is why I'm here, sat waiting in the emergency department for some sort of news.

See, after being tricked by Ryan into getting into his big badass truck; Mystery Boy, Ryan, that's his name. After being tricked by him, alarm bells weren't even remotely ringing in my head. I was too caught up in the fact that Ryan Scott, the hottest guy in school, not only was he talking to me again in the first place, but he was also asking me if I wanted a ride home.

I mean he lives all the way out in Calabasas, so this was a big deal. He was going out of his way for me. I was so happy that it didn't even occur to me to ask why he was suddenly talking to me after eight months of radio silence. Nor did I think to ask where his McBitchface girlfriend was. Yeah, she's his girlfriend now.

Her name is Mia Chase, but I personally find McBitchface suits her so much better. One, because no joke, she is a total bitch, and two, because I hate her. She's been an absolute cow to me ever since freshman year.

It all started when she discovered her gynaecologist was my dad. Don't ask me why a fourteen-year-old needed to see a gynaecologist, I didn't ask, nor did I care. A girl's lady garden is her own damn business. Not that my dad would ever break patient confidence with me anyway, but I saw her at his office one day and she put two and two together from our names, and since then, made it her life's mission to make my life hell.

Gum in my hair, spreading rumours I was sucking dick for cash, and then there's the fat jokes. I'm not even that fat, not really. I mean, I'm not skinny either. I'm just a little chubby in places, you know.

Anyway, I hate her, she's the ultimate bitch. I never understood why Ryan was with her in the first place. I mean I get it, she has the whole big tits and blonde hair, head cheerleader vibe, and well he is a guy. Dudes love that crap. What I didn't get is they are two very different people. Although he was popular, he was quiet, and really smart. He mostly focused on soccer, but he was always a genuinely nice guy that literally everyone loved. At least, I thought he was a nice guy, until now.

When Ryan first walked into the halls of St. Edmund's Academy eight months ago it was the beginning of Junior year. Ryan arrived and instantly became top of the food chain. Within mere minutes Mia had staked her claim on the gorgeous newcomer and within a matter of weeks they were officially the school's 'It couple', both equally beautiful and wanted.

Turns out Ryan had transferred here from some exclusive prep school in London. The Scott family are from old east coast money and they have always lived in New York. Apparently, after his mother died Ryan's father, Eamon Scott, remarried a young actress slash ex-topless model, Melody Masters, now Melody Scott.

At just turned twenty-two, Melody is only a few years older than Ryan. It was apparently quite the scandal of Manhattan, or so I heard through the rumour mill at St. Ed's. Okay, so I may have read the gossip pages online too. Mr. Scott decided to move their lives right across the country from an exclusive penthouse on Manhattan's Upper East Side, to an eight-bedroom, fourteen bath, bespoke mansion in California, to be with his new young wife. Why does anyone need fourteen bathrooms?

Plus, and I don't know why now considering Ryan was in London for another two years after his mom died, but when his dad remarried, he decided to bring Ryan home to the US to finish school here in California at St. Edmund's, and no one knows why.

Also, Ryan should have been a senior this year, he turns eighteen in the summer so he should be graduating, but for some reason St. Edmund's decided he must join as a junior, even despite his excellent grades. I've heard it's either something to do with how the academic system is in the UK, or something about him being a late summer baby, but that all sounds like bullshit to me.

Not that I'm one to talk. I am eighteen in the summer too, so technically I should also be graduating. I was homeschooled until I was fifteen when I was invited to join St Edmund's on a scholarship, but only if i started as a freshman. My parents thought it would be for the best, so I reluctantly agreed, which is why I'm still only a junior.

Ryan is only a couple of weeks younger than me, but his birthday is in July before school starts back up. Plus, he has a 4.0 GPA so it's not like he doesn't have the grades, so he should definitely be a senior. Not that I made it my business to know everything about him or anything. Whatever the reason, they wouldn't accept him as a senior, and he agreed to repeat. Who in their right mind wants to spend a whole extra year at high school when all their friends are going off to college.

My guess is that he is putting off going to college for

as long as possible because he doesn't want to go back to New York where his mom died.

From what I hear, familial tradition dictates that after St. Ed's, Ryan will attend Columbia University in New York, like his father and grandfather, and all the previous men in his family before him. After which he will join the family business, before taking over as CEO from his father when he retires.

The Scott family business deals in infrastructure and large-scale real estate. They are super mega-bucks billionaires, I'm talking about the richest of the rich here in California, and there are some really rich people.

The thing is, from what I see, that's the last thing Ryan would want for his life. He wants to play soccer in London, and he could too, he is really good. Before he joined the school, no one cared about soccer. We had a team but there wasn't much school spirit for it. Now not only is the school soccer mad, but so is the entire district, all because of Ryan.

Anyway, after being tricked into leaving my shit heap car at school and getting a ride in his sexy black beast, we talked and he actually laughed at my jokes, which was saying something because I'm really not one bit funny.

Conversation felt easy, unlike our first little tête-à-tête where I barely spoke. I can only guess that I was correct in my assumption that by second period, he had been filled in on what a social pariah I was, and to stay the hell away from me. After what I like to refer to as our 'meet cute', he hasn't spoken to me since. *You haven't spoken to him either though, you just stare like a moron.*

Okay, so that is true. Ryan smiles at me though, all the time actually. Those smiles get me through the day. I'm embarrassed to say I've thought about Ryan a lot since that first day. *Literally every day.*

I can't seem to help it, something draws me to him, I'm like a moth to a flame. My mystery boy was kind to me that day, but yet, after sticking up for me that one time, he has never done it again. I mean, he hasn't ever joined in until now either, so I guess I foolishly hoped that one day we would just pick up where we left off. I *thought* that day was today, but turns out I couldn't have been more wrong.

Wow, he was so beautiful. With his wavy, dirty blonde hair that seemed like it was completely untameable, but in a deliberate way. It had gotten some natural highlights from exposure to the California sun. Total surfer hair. If I had to guess, this guy had never been on a surfboard in his life but my god, did he have the look. The West Coast definitely suited him. He had lightly bronzed smooth skin, and a body that should be illegal for an almost eighteen-year-old guy. God, I just want to run my fingers through his hair, and maybe lick his abs too. He was such a babe.

It wasn't until he suddenly pulled over I realised we'd been going completely the wrong direction for my house. In fact, we were apparently in the middle of nowhere. How is it possible to be in the middle of nowhere in L.A? I don't know, but apparently here we were.

As soon as we stopped, two guys got out of a pick up on the other side of the road, which was not nearly as expensive as the one Ryan was driving. As they headed towards us I recognised them as Ryan's friends, Levi and the devil incarnate, Shane. My defences automatically shot up at the sight of this pair of douchebags. Ryan might be a nice guy, but these two most definitely aren't.

These two are bullies and both right up there on my shit list with McBitchface, especially Shane. He has bullied me since day one of high school, although I have no idea why. It got progressively worse once Mia joined in. I thought once she got with Ryan, they might lay off me, but they haven't.

In fact, I expected things to get a whole lot worse now, since I saw Shane having sex with Mia in the girl's locker rooms yesterday. They both saw me too so they know I know. I'd received a nice death threat, along with a used condom in my locker this morning letting me know what would happen if I talked. So gross.

Levi and Shane are both fairly big guys, both having played a lot of football. Shane usually has dark hair, although not as dark as mine, but he bleached it during spring break, and what with his pale complexion he legit looks like Eminem back in the day. Or maybe I should say he looks like '*Stan*' with that shitty home bleach. Great, now I got the lyrics to that going off in my head, and I'm definitely wondering why I got out of bed.

Levi has dark hair as well, but his is long and wavy which he wears in a man-bun type style. They both look like total tools in my opinion.

"You don't mind me picking up the guys, do you baby? Only they wanted to hang with us tonight. It's cool, right?" Baby. Woah! He'd flashed me an awkward smile that as usual didn't quite reach his eyes, but now for some reason, that made a lump form in my throat.

"No, I mean, it's fine I guess," I lied, not knowing what else to say. I hated the idea, it didn't feel right to me. Plus, I just wanted to be alone with Ryan. This was my first chance to spend time with him and they would ruin it. Didn't he know that Shane bullies me?

Also, now I was reminded about what I'd seen yesterday and my stomach suddenly felt like an empty pit. I'd spent this whole time talking to Ryan, when I should have told him what I saw when I first got in the car. God, I'm so self-absorbed. Before I could even think about saying anything else the next thing I knew, Shane was already at my door. He yanked it open harshly, forcefully pulling me out of my seat, scaring the cookies and cream out of me.

"Ouch, what the hell? You're hurting me," I screamed at him and tried to pull myself free, but he slapped my face hard before grabbing my arms and pulling them behind me.

"Shut the fuck up, you ugly bitch. We can do this the easy way or the hard way!" Man that hurt, my face was burning. I was sure Ryan was going to lose his shit over that, but he didn't speak. I turned to Ryan for help, but he was just watching with a raging fire burning in his eyes. He shook his head and turned his face away.

Shane wrapped a strong arm around my chest before pulling my head back by my hair with the other. I could feel his hot wet breath against my face as he spat his words out. Had he been drinking?

"You didn't honestly think you had a chance with Ryan now did you, Pork Chop?" He spews, his breath reeking of liquor. I remained silent, not taking my eyes off of Ryan who still remained in the driver's seat looking impassive.

"Oh, you did! Ha, this is gonna be funnier than I thought, you bet on the wrong frog, Miss Piggy, he's not going to help you. He wants to see you squeal just like the filthy pig that you are!"

Shane pulled my arms tighter behind my back and started binding them together, the cable ties pinching at my skin. No, no, no, this isn't happening. Tears were already falling down my face. I thought Ryan liked me, I thought he was a good guy. I couldn't take my eyes off of him. Remorse flashed quickly across his face, but just as fast it was gone.

"Stop fucking around and get on with it!" Ryan finally spoke angrily, as if he had somewhere else better to be. Who was he? As if he'd heard my thoughts he replied

"Sorry Pork Chop, but you had this coming," he said bitterly, breaking my heart in the process.

Pork Chop. Not from him. No, he is supposed to be my safe place.

Out of nowhere Levi pushed a dirty old sock in my mouth and taped over it so I couldn't spit it out, then he pulled a dark black sack over my head while Shane finished tying my hands behind my back. I gagged at the sock, I just knew it had to have been used by one of these bastards.

"Hurry up, asshats! Throw her on the back of the truck and let's get out of here, Mia's waiting… and watch my fucking paintwork!"

We were only moving for maybe five minutes before coming to another stop. I felt the blow of a large boot in my ribs as I was shoved hurtling off the back of the pick-up, my face and right shoulder taking the brunt of the impact with the ground. Jeez that hurt. I could already feel blood running down from my nose and I felt winded from being kicked in my side.

My school skirt had also risen right up in the process exposing my big white granny panties for all the world to see. Great. Could this get any worse? Something told me this was just the beginning.

I felt a hand grab on my ass. What the hell, asshole? I tried to squirm out of his touch but whoever it was, he just laughed and gripped it harder.

"Nice fat peach you got there, Porky. Maybe I'll fuck you in the ass if you want, as long as you keep the bag over your head!"

Shane.

He ran a disgusting finger along the line of my panties slowly tugging them down. I screamed out for him to stop but it just came out muffled due to the balled-up sock taped inside my mouth, and the bag over my head. I squirmed as hard as I could, but my hands were tied and I was in agony from the kick and the fall. Hot tears of shame, mixed with warm blood rolled down my cheeks.

"The fuck, dude? Get your fucking hands off her now! Pull up her fucking panties and cover her up, I'm not into that shit."

Ryan. My safe place. *No not safe, Faith! Not safe. He got you into this mess, remember? He might be covering you up but he isn't letting you go, remember that.*

I felt his hand brush against me as he rushed to cover me up and whilst I was mad as hell at him, I was grateful, as tears continued to stream down my face.

"Just having a little fun, bro. It's not like the whole school hasn't already seen her filthy cunt," Shane jokes like the bastard he is. He knows that's a lie!

"I couldn't give a fuck if she's shown her beaten blue pussy to the entire fucking state, you still don't fucking take what's not offered! What are you, some kind of pervert? For fuck sake!"

"Ryan's right man, we get plenty of easy pussy. Besides, that one is probably infected, don't want to lose your dick," Levi added. Hearing them talk that way in front of Ryan breaks me more than it should. I know he's probably heard it all before about me, but I could pretend before. With each smile he offered up to me freely, I could pretend he didn't know. *No more pretending. He knows, and this time he hasn't come to bat for you, he's joining in!*

Ryan is sitting close to me, his body next to mine, almost protecting me from Shane. I know it's him, I can feel him. *Why are you still pining after him, God, you're pathetic!*

Inner Bitch was raging, but apparently, she was angrier

at me than anyone else. I could barely breathe with the bag over my head, and the blood in my nose. I was in a bit of a daze from the shock of being kicked off the truck, but I was soon brought back to reality with the sound of McBitchface's whiney voice cheering on.

"Finally, you're here! Let's get this party started bitches! Get this Pork Chop up and take her to meet her new friends!" She shrieks with excitement. Jesus, what does that mean?

After being pulled up and quickly dragged along the ground so fast I was tripping over my own feet, I was picked up again by strong arms. It was Ryan, I was sure of it. I recognised his coconut scent because it's my favourite smell. *Please get a grip girl, this douchebag is screwing you over big time.*

Inner Bitch was right this time. Something bad was about to happen and Ryan no longer felt safe to me. My stomach was in bits, my face was blooded and here he was carrying me to my fate.

I was swiftly dropped back to the ground on my ass. This asshole dropped me? Mother fucker. This was bad whatever they were planning, but at least the drop wasn't as harsh, and the ground was a lot softer. Urgh, it was softer because it was wet and God it stank. What on earth?

I could hear laughing and what sounded like grunting, and I could feel people touching and prodding me all over. I swear to god if anyone tried to take off my panties again, I was ready to kick them in the ball sack.

What in the name of Britney Jean Spears was happening? What the hell was I lying in, and who keeps touching me, what the heck?

All of a sudden, the bag was pulled off and even though my eyes were blurry from all the tears and blood, I saw them. Not people. Pigs! Right in my face, freakin' pigs everywhere. I could hear muffled screaming. I tried to move to get away from them but I couldn't move my arms were still tied behind me. I realised the muffled screaming was me, I was still gagged.

All around me I saw faces laughing and cheering but I couldn't make out what they were saying. Mia, her minion friends Madison, and Hayley, and then the guys, Shane, Levi and *him*. Now the newest douchebag at the top of my shit list, Ryan Shithead Scott, breaker of lonely hearts.

Whilst the others were all laughing at me he just looked at me with pure hate in his eyes. The girls kept throwing buckets of old food over me causing the pigs to keep coming at me. I was so humiliated I could feel the hot tears streaming down my cheeks. I was thrashing my legs about trying to keep the pigs away.

Everyone knew about my fear of pigs from freshman year, when we had to write an essay on our biggest fear. This dick called Trevor thought it would be hilarious to steal mine and read it out to the entire class. For about three weeks after that people would make snorting noises every time I passed, or they would put pig stuffies with fake blood around their mouths in my locker. At least I hoped it was fake blood.

Suddenly someone shouted to run, and everyone began running away leaving me alone in the pig pen. Everything else is a bit of a blur after that.

Apparently, I was at some sort of petting farm. God only knows where. The manager had heard the commotion and came out to see what was going on. He had helped me out of the pig pen, and after giving me a towel and helping clean up my bloody face, he generously gave me a ride all the way back to school. He offered to take me home or to the hospital, but I didn't want to have to explain to my dad why I didn't have a car, and no ride to school in the morning. It was bad enough he might see my bruised face and bloody shirt.

We must have been pretty far out because it was dark by the time I got in my car and back to my house. I walked indoors praying desperately my dad wouldn't be around to see me like this. But it turns out he was home. That's when I found him face down on the kitchen floor covered in so much blood that at first, I honestly thought he was dead. He was badly beaten and unconscious.

I'd called for an ambulance. They said he had a pulse, but my dad didn't regain consciousness. They rushed him straight to the hospital and now here we are in the emergency room and I'm waiting for the doctor to tell me what's happening.

Truth is I would gladly climb back in with the pigs again if it meant my dad was going to be ok. Please God be ok.

The sting of Ryan being the one to trick me hurt me more than what they actually did to me. They wanted to break me tonight, and honestly, when Shane pulled down my panties, I thought they had. At the very least they almost broke my nose.

But like I said, there are worse things than being thrown to the pigs, and now all I want is justice for my dad.

# CHAPTER 2

## Ryan

*July...*

What in the fresh hell is this? For fuck sake I've got myself into some shit situations before but I've definitely outdone myself this time.

When my dad suggested we spend the summer in Africa, I'd assumed he meant safari's, cocktails and sandy beaches. Definitely not me volunteering at a medical centre as a French speaking interpreter, while he goes off with his asshat business partners on a three-week big game hunting trip. Yet here I am in my hot as hell, basic-ass hotel room, with no air conditioning, a two drop a minute shower, and a bed with what feels like rocks for a mattress. Fuck. My. Life.

My father had expected me to join him with his buddies and their sons, that's why he brought me over here. When I'd politely declined the hunt, he took that as an opportunity to teach me yet another lesson in humility. His kind of humility that is.

See, when he says he wants to keep me humble, what he really means is keep me obedient. He wants to remind me at every opportunity that the life I was born into is a privilege, bestowed upon me only by his good graces. This was his way of showing me that if I don't play by his rules, he can cut me off. Maybe he will now that his beautiful young wife is pregnant with a boy. I guess I am just as easily replaced as my mother was. Who knows, and who the fuck cares? Certainly not me.

All I know is that I'm not about to start killing animals for sport. Especially magnificent ones nearing extinction. I might be an asshole, but that's a whole new level of douchery in my opinion. So like I said, I declined his offer and he swiftly dropped my ass here, telling me he would send for me in three weeks. Send for me, what kinda bullshit is that? Gave me some crap about looking good on my college applications as if we both don't know that I'm already a sure thing for Columbia. Whatever.

It's so fucking hot here I'm sweating my ass off. I can't sleep. I know even if I do somehow manage to fall asleep, I'll only end up having another one of my usual fucking nightmares. I guess now is as good a time as any to check my messages, it's not like there's anything else to do.

**Mia** - Shane came on to me, it was just that one time I swear baby. It's always been you and me. X

Delete

**Mia** - I love you, Ryan. Please answer me. X

Delete

**Shane** - Ryan, we need to talk. I wanted to tell you but it just kept happening. Look, Mia's with me now and you're just going to have to accept that. Don't make this a thing.

Delete

    My girlfriend cheated on me with my so-called friend by the way, in case you didn't get that.

**Levi** – I swear I had no idea about those two assholes. Stay safe in Africa, bro! Watch out for snakes.

    Fucking needed to watch out for snakes in my own backyard apparently. Delete.

**Hayley** - Hey gorgeous, you want to hang out this summer? We don't have to tell Mia or Lev. Call me!

    Hayley is Levi's ex, and Mia's best friend. So fucking shady. Friends' ex's and ex's friends; both off limits in my book. Delete.

**Madison** - Heard about you and Mia. If you need a shoulder to cry on, or a warm mouth to suck your dick, then let me know.

    Another of Mia's friends. She is hot though, I'd probably go for the blow. I mean I won't, I'm not *that* guy. Like I said some people are off limits, but I'll save the mental image for the self-care bank. The message I'll delete.

**Mia** - Hey baby, I miss you. How's Africa? Have you seen any tigers? X

Tigers? Seriously? This chick, honestly. I used to find that playing dumb shit cute, now it's just annoying as fuck. De-fucking-lete.

**Dad** - Don't embarrass me with Dr. Asher.

Dele...

    Wait what? Dr. Asher? The fuck now? Surely not the same Dr. Asher I'm thinking of?

**Ryan -** Who the hell is Dr. Asher?

**Dad -** Dr. Malcolm Asher. He has a private practice in Beverly Hills. He and his wife are heading up the clinic over here. His daughter goes to St. Edmund's, you probably know her. Faith Asher? She's volunteering at the clinic as well. Anyway, he is a respected member at the country club and I won't have you embarrassing me in front of him.

**Ryan -** You mean that guy who had Peado sprayed across his front door? You do know he's a pervert, right?

**Dad -** Those rumours were completely unfounded. He is a good man and you will show him respect. Like I said, don't you dare embarrass me or there will be consequences.

    What the actual fuck? Faith Asher is here, and with her sicko father. Ha, and my dad is what, best friends with the guy? I'm gonna lose my fucking shit. I grab a bottle of water from my bag and take large gulps until I've practically drained the bottle. It's warm, well that's just great.

    Fucking Pork Chop, of all people! Faith didn't show her face at school for the rest of the semester after the pig incident. Not surprising after what we did to her, but it's not like she didn't deserve it. *Yeah, keep telling yourself that, bro. Maybe one day you will believe it.*

    What? She did deserve it! Her dad made my ex-girlfriend show him her vagina when she was only fourteen. When Faith found out she threatened Mia to stay quiet to protect her scumbag father, and then she'd bullied Mia ever since to make sure she didn't talk. When Mia finally found the courage to tell me about what happened to her, she wasn't ready to go to the cops. So, I handed out my own justice, to Faith and her father.

After the pig party, I drove straight to their house and beat the ever-loving shit out of that bastard for what he did to my girl. Who knows how many other girls there have been. He deserved every hit I gave him. Hell, he deserved worse. He's lucky it was just one crack with my baseball bat before I used my fists. He's even luckier it was just a regular bat and not a barbed wire baseball bat like in *'The Walking Dead'*. That shit was gruesome, but effective as hell. I just didn't much like the idea of doing life behind bars.

It wasn't supposed to happen. I mean, I didn't plan that part. We were only supposed to teach that bitch Faith a lesson with the pig prank, but after she gave me her address when she thought I was giving her a ride home, going around there to deal with him was all I could think about. I wore my hood up, with some creepy-ass LED mask that I'd had in the back of my truck from last Halloween, just to make sure I couldn't be identified. I'd have gladly shown him my face but like I said, fuck doing jail time for that prick.

Fuck, Faith was so easy to get in my car. She was practically salivating just looking at me, so it wasn't hard to sweet talk her into trusting me. She was nervous at first, but I smiled and laughed at a few of her jokes, and soon she was talking so much shit she didn't even notice I wasn't driving anywhere near her house. I might have even been smiling back, but inside I was raging.

I've caught her staring at me countless times in class. She's either fucking weird or dick desperate, I can't tell which. I'm pretty sure I could have gotten her to suck my dick if I'd asked. But fuck that, I'd rather stick my cock in a cheese grater. Although, I can't deny the idea doesn't cross my mind every time I look at those sinful lips of hers.

When I first met her, I thought she was a doll. Like literally she looks like a fucking doll. She reminded me of one of those anime porno cartoons, with her wide eyes, and cute face. Her dark hair, a contrast to her milky porcelain skin. She also has the prettiest pink lips that are so full, they were just made for sucking dick. Women pay good money to have lips like those, but even then, they don't come close to hers.

I've never seen anyone who looks like her before, and at first, I can't deny that I wanted her. A total fucking peach. She was weird as fuck though that first day, well every fucking day for that matter, and I was kinda intrigued by her. After she ran off, Mia told me what a slut she is and to stay away from her. At first, I thought it was just typical girl jealousy crap, but I heard the same story over and over from everyone I spoke to.

Apparently, her mom is in prison for being a crack whore, but they lie and say she works here in Africa. Although my dad did just say she was here too, so I guess I'll find out who's actually lying. Everyone says Faith sucks dick for cash, probably for crack too, and from what I've seen written in the guy's bathroom, most of the guys at school have been serviced. I even heard she let some guys from the basketball team run a train on her in the locker rooms, but I don't know how true that is. Either way, she's trash, and her dad's a fucking sick bastard.

Don't get me wrong, I'm usually a pretty chill guy. I would never normally get involved in anything like what happened on Pork Chop day. I won't lie, some of what happened that day made me feel really uncomfortable, and I actually feel pretty guilty about some of it. I hated the fact she got physically hurt. All that blood on her face, especially at a guy's hands, well that didn't sit right with me. When Shane tried to take off her panties I was raging. I mean, perverted shit like that was the whole reason we were getting justice in the first place.

When I told him off again later, Shane's argument was

'what about all the shit Faith put Mia through? What goes around comes around'. Not really my style but I let it slide. I think about it a lot though. I know that type of shit isn't right and I hope to God he hasn't ever tried anything like that with other girls before.

Personally, I would have preferred we just went to the police, but Mia had a plan, and because I wanted justice for her I went along with it all. Even now after what Mia has done with Shane, I still feel sick to my stomach at the thought of what that bastard and his bitch daughter did to her. No one deserves that, especially not my girl. Except fuck, she's not my girl anymore is she. Fucking hell, I'm such a loser right now.

I didn't even get a chance to process what happened the other night before I was on a plane, halfway across the world. Shane was having a party. I'd already told them I couldn't make it because I had an early flight, but I changed my mind and thought fuck it I'll go for an hour, just to be with my girl. It didn't even occur to me to question why my girlfriend would rather be at the party than spend my last night home with me, I'd just accepted it like a chump. Then there I was, the one chasing after her to the party. Pathetic right?

I got there and couldn't see her anywhere. I went upstairs to Shane's room. I figured it would be quiet enough for me to call her and see where she was. Instead when I walked in, I found them going at it, and I mean going at it hard. She was face down, ass up, panties at her knees, with her dress pushed around her waist. My girl was totally taking it like a pro. He was pounding into her from behind while she moaned his name and begged 'harder baby'.

You know it's funny, whenever I've tried to fuck dirty like that, she's always shut me down with her 'let's make love instead' bullshit. Sure, at first she was all too eager to drop to her knees for me, but that soon died a death. Now that I think about it our sex life was boring as fuck, but now I guess I know why, huh.

Shane's filthy hands were firmly gripped on her ass like he owned it, and all I could think was, cool bro, you can fucking have it. It clearly wasn't their first rodeo, that's for damn sure. I wondered how many times I'd dicked down after he'd been in there, and fuck if that's not enough to put me off her for ever. Thinking about her now, it's fucking gross, I don't think I've ever been so turned off in my life, hell I'd rather fuck Pork Chop.

I stormed out with a half-dressed Mia chasing after me, but fuck if I could face talking to her right then. I jumped in my truck and got the hell out of there. I hopped on my flight and ignored them all ever since. I'll deal with that shit when I get back, but for now, I'm here, and so are The Ashers. Figure I can take my shit out on them until I get back. Maybe I can fuck with Porky some more? All of a sudden, this trip just got a lot more interesting.

*** 

The sunlight streams into my room, and I'm woken up to the sound of a loud and extremely irritating buzzing. I don't know what time I finally fell asleep but I can't have had more than a couple of hours, I feel exhausted. No way can I sleep in this bed for three weeks.

I found the source of the offensive noise and it was my phone. Missed-call from Levi, he must be heading to a party or something. Blows my mind that it's last night back home right now. Lev says he didn't know about Mia and Shane, but I don't give enough of a fuck to go over any of that shit. He will just have to wait.

I take a cold shower and get dressed. Seeing as I'm not sure what the dress code is I go for some smart but casual navy shorts, and a plain white tee-shirt. I leave my hair messy, grab my hoodie and my *Ray-Bans,* and head outside to wait for my ride. The pack my father left me had an itinerary for my time here, showing all the days I'll be required to work and when I'll have free time. Yes, there was an actual pack. Fucking tool.

It includes an itinerary, emergency contacts, emergency credit card and currency, and details of an apparent safe house my dad arranged in case, and I quote, 'of emergencies only'. This guy, seriously. What sort of emergencies are we talking about here? This shit hole not having aircon or like *Hotel Rwanda* type trouble?

Wouldn't surprise me if it was one of the many luxury properties he owns all around the world, in which case it would be a helluva a lot better than this dive I'm staying in. I wonder why he wouldn't just let me stay there? Another fucking lesson. I make a mental note to go and check it out the first chance I get.

First on the agenda, pick up outside the hotel at 8 a.m. with FA who I now know to be little Miss Blowjob Lips herself, Faith Asher. I make sure to be ready at 7.55 a.m. sharp. I debated coming out late to piss her off, but I decided I'd have more of an upper hand if I was already waiting outside with my game face on. Cue smouldering stare.

Twenty minutes later and I'm still waiting. My game face has been replaced with my annoyed, don't-you-know-who-I-am scowl. A rusty old Jeep comes rolling into the parking lot and I see her. She's so flustered she doesn't recognise me at first. She's cursing the medieval car and already rambling some apology about why she's late. I don't hear a word she says though. I'm too busy waiting for the penny to drop. *Five, four, three...*

"... And that's when he finally managed to move his goat out of the way. I mean I felt sorry for the guy, his goat was dead.

Poor little goat. But anyway, I'm here now... Oh." And there it was.

To my enjoyment, she totally just shit her pants. Not that I let my amusement show. I got in the car without saying a word or changing my facial expression. She just sits there speechless with her mouth wide open, before painfully grinding the jeep into gear and pulling away.

First round to me, Pork Chop. First round to me.

# CHAPTER 3

## Faith

**S**hit on a stick, it's him. Ryan, former love of my life, the gorgeous heart-breaking bastard, Ryan. He is here! *Okay chill out, Faith, jeez.*

So maybe not the love of my life, but still, I definitely did love him. I adored him. But apparently, I didn't even know him. *You were an idiot.*

Okay, so I was an idiot. Who seriously believes they are in love with someone they haven't even had a real conversation with anyway? Me, apparently. When he tricked me that day with the pigs, when he sat by and did nothing as his friends hurt me, my heart completely broke. It's been broken ever since.

Why isn't he talking? He hasn't said a word, not even hello. Awkward turtle. Why does he look even more beautiful than I remember him? Shit, I'm going to have to speak first, sweet Britney Jean. Okay, here goes...

"So, erm... Hi?" Why did that come out as a question?

Why do I have to be so lame, he hasn't even looked at me let alone responded to my greeting slash question. Dickwad. "So, I'm sorry I was so awkward back there, but I was a little shocked to see *you* standing there. What are you doing here?"

He takes a sharp, loud, frustrated breath through his nose, turns his head to me slowly as if he's not remotely interested in me, or conversing in any way for that matter. He pulls his sunglasses to the tip of his nose so I can now see his warm brown eyes, flecked with beautiful golden secrets.

*"Je suis le traducteur... Côtelette de Porc."*

Pork Chop. Wow, doesn't sound any less brutal in French.

I don't know why I wasn't expecting him to call me that, but I wasn't. I feel a huge lump in my throat, but I swallow it down and try my best at giving him a sarcastic smile.

"The translator, right..." We sit in silence for a beat before I decide to call him out. "... And I know you called me Pork Chop. Bitch."

He smirks as he pushes back his sunglasses and turns back to face the road.

"I know."

That's it. That's all he says, with a shit eating grin on his face he doesn't even try to hide. Is he seriously going to be a dick to me the whole time. I'm honestly not sure I can take that. I'd much rather go back to him not even knowing I exist, at least then I could pretend.

When my dad told me there was a young American guy my age coming for a few weeks to volunteer as a French speaking interpreter, I was a little excited, but nervous at the same time. He failed to mention he went to my school or that I might know him. Thanks for the heads-up with that, Dad!

I've never really been confident around guys, especially this guy right here. But as much as it would be nice to have a summer romance, or hell even just a date, what I really hoped for was for someone who could be a friend. I could really use one of those. I guess that's not gonna happen now.

Sure, I have Ade, a local joker from the town who helps out round the clinic sometimes with transport and supplies and stuff. Then there is Greg, well Dr. Larke really. He's only twenty-three, fresh out of med school in England but he's doing a volunteer summer here, before starting an internship at a research hospital in London.

They are both great, and Greg is really funny, but they are a little older so they see me as an annoying little sister more than anything. I couldn't tell them girl related things, or talk about my problems with my mom. Now Ryan is here, I'm guessing he is going to bring a whole heap of other problems into my life for the next three weeks. Great.

I decide if he wants to be like that then he can go suck it. After all, he was the one who was a dick to me for no reason. Why should I be nice to him? I turn on the stereo and of course Britney comes on. Ryan instantly snorts his displeasure and that makes me smile.

"You don't like Britney?" I laugh. He groans out a sharp "No!" before taking off his glasses. He turns to me, as if waiting for me to turn it over, while I keep my eyes on the empty road, pretending not to notice. "Well it sucks for you, because this is her greatest hits album soooo..." I don't even try to hide my smirk, which clearly pisses him off.

"Yeah, well I guess you'd know all about sucking now wouldn't you, Pork Chop? Exactly how much do you charge anyway, you know, in case I need a service while I'm here?" My smile drops and his smile widens.

He leans in close. I can feel my palms sweating against

the wheel under his scrutiny. I feel his eyes as they lower down my body. I'm not wearing anything to show off my body shape, just my usual yoga pants and baggy slogan tee-shirt combo. Today's one is white, and says '90s Baby' in hot pink writing across it. I was actually born in 2001, but i'm totally a '90s baby at heart.

I keep my eyes on the road, waiting for what's coming next.

"You know, I usually like to watch a whore choke when I blow my load, but with tits like that I'd definitely prefer to paint you a pretty picture, baby."

My stomach twists at hearing him call me baby. I know it was meant to patronise me, but hearing it on his lips along with the image conjured by his dirty words sends heat to my core. My cheeks burn with shame. I've never even come remotely close to kissing a guy, let alone the things I've been accused of at school. He leans back in his seat, smugly satisfied with his brutal retort to my seemingly innocent Britney remark.

"Oh, and by the way, the '90s called, they want that ugly-ass shirt back! You realise you weren't even fucking born!" He says rhetorically, looking away like he's suddenly become disinterested in the conversation. "How far exactly is this place anyway? I'm not listening to this crap much longer."

Woooah! Shots fired. I bring the car into the track that leads down to where The Old Farmhouse Clinic is, and slam on the brakes. I put a saccharine smile on my face.

"Well it so happens, it's right down this track. You'll have to walk from here though, I have somewhere else to be." Now his smile is the one to drop, as he looks at me confused.

"You gotta be shitting me? I can't walk, how far even is it? I can't even see anything down there?" He says straining to look for a sign of life.

"Don't be a baby, it's only about a half a mile down this track, you'll be perfectly safe. Now get out and get moving or you'll be late."

He huffs, thinks for a minute and then he storms out of the car, and without so much as a thank you for the ride, he starts walking away down the track.

"Watch out for snakes!" I yell after him, trying not to laugh. I don't feel too bad, I know my father had a drinking water pump placed halfway along the path for patients who arrive on foot, so at least he can have a little drink on the way.

I laugh at my now potential total badass status. After a couple of minutes watching him strop towards the end of the track, I throw the Jeep into gear and carry on up past him, being sure to flip him off as I drive past. Take that, McDickface!

***

I stand leaning nonchalantly against the Jeep as I watch him stroll casually towards me exactly nine minutes later. He may have slowed his pace, but I can tell he is raging inside by the look on his face. He's still beautiful even when he is angry.

I gotta say I'm feeling this outfit on him. He is now holding his hoodie, his white shirt, now a little sweaty, showing off his lean muscular biceps. His hair is messy in a sexy, just rolled out of bed look that only certain boys can pull off. He is wearing shorts, showing off his toned soccer player legs. His face is a bit red now after his walk, and although it wasn't far, it is hot. Shit I hope he didn't get burnt, my bad.

"You think that was funny? I'm sweating my balls off now, what the fuck?" Oops, he is definitely pissed. Good, he's a jerk, but feeling a little guilty about the red face, I hand him a fresh bottle of water I'd just grabbed for him out of the kitchen.

"Look Buster, you can insult me all you want, but let's get one thing straight; Nobody talks smack about Britney! Nobody! Especially not in my car, you got it?" He reluctantly takes the water, but raises a questioning eyebrow like he thinks I'm crazy, which he confirms when he speaks.

"You're fucking crazy, you know that. Crazy and weird. What's with you anyway? Always fucking staring at me like some pathetic bitch in heat." He gets right up in my space, looking at me like he just stepped in something. "Even now you're looking at me like you want me. Get it into your head. I don't like you, Pork Chop.  I'll never fucking like your skank ass. You think I'd ever go near someone who has let the basketball team run a train on her? You think I need to put my dick in the mouth of a whore when I can get any girl I want to suck it for free?"

Well shit.

I knew he must've heard all the rumours about me, but hearing them from his lips like accusations really stings. My eyes burn with the need to cry, but I fight them back. I have no words right now to address what he just said to me. I know if I try I'll just end up a blubbering mess, so I decide on my classic, ignore-it-and-store-it approach for now. It takes all my effort to pull a smile back onto my face.

"Unless you want to walk every day, you better start appreciating '90s pop. I got two cassettes on rotation, one is Britney, the other is a '90s mix. Shania, Backstreet Boys, Céline. Deal with it. I mean there's also an afrobeats mixtape that Ade left in there, but I'll reserve that party for good behaviour, which you my friend have failed on miserably today!"

He waves a dismissive hand towards me, with a scowl on his face like I just ate his M&Ms.

"See, fucking crazy. Whatever you say, sweetheart. Just tell me where I need to be, and then stay the hell out of my way!"

Now I know he meant to patronise me again with 'sweetheart', but God, it sounded good. Damn it, what the heck is wrong with me. He literally just screamed how much he doesn't like me. But then why the hell not? Why can't I just ask him what his problem is, why am I such a coward.

One thing's for sure, I'm not gonna let him fool me again, no matter how gorgeous he is on the outside, he is ugly as hell on the inside.

# CHAPTER 4

## Faith

I reluctantly show Ryan around. I take him to the main farmhouse which now operates as the clinic. It's right by the shoreline of a huge lake. It's simple yet beautiful.

It has a basic waiting area, with two small consultation rooms, and two larger treatment rooms. Towards the back is an office, a storeroom, and a small kitchen and bathroom. We are very lucky to have an indoor water supply, many here don't. Then there is also a private room where patients who have travelled a long way, or those who are incapacitated after treatment can stay overnight if needed.

Outside there are five residential cabins. They are all single rooms, except my parents who have a larger cabin that has a main room and two bedrooms; one room was mine from back when I was too young to have my own space.

They are pretty basic but comfortable cabins. They each have a bed, a small sofa, a small kitchen area, and their own washroom, but that's just a sink to have a basic wash and space to change in private. If you want to shower or use the bathroom, you have to use the communal ones across the yard. There are only two showers, and two toilets, each male and female, but they are tiled, and have relatively good water flow, and the toilets have a flush, so we are lucky.

My parents have the big cabin, then there is Charity, a local woman who works as a nurse in the clinic, she has another, then Greg has one, and then I have my own. This is the first year I've been allowed my own cabin. The last one is empty right now. Well it's not empty, it's currently full of supplies. According to my dad, he offered it to Ryan, but Ryan's father declined in favour of the hotel so he didn't bother to clear it out. Not good enough for their expensive tastes I guess.

Anyway, my parents bought this farm in 2012 converting it into what is now The Old Farmhouse Clinic. I lived here with them for four years before Dad and I went back to live in Santa Monica, but I've spent every summer here since. Don't get me wrong, I love it here, but after college I really want to go to Europe. Paris, London, Rome, Vienna. I've never been anywhere like that.

My whole life I've spent on the road with my parents, going from place to place, helping people where they need it. South America, South East Asia, Africa, you name it. We would always go back to Santa Monica in between places though, before this became our permanent home.

My mother grew up in L.A and went to St. Edmund's herself on a scholarship. She met my father in med school and they have been together ever since. I know they'd both love for me to be a doctor as well, but that's really not what I want. Don't get me wrong, I love that they help people, and I want to help people too, just in other ways.

We walk through to the office where Dad sits waiting for us. I introduce Ryan to my father, and I can't help but notice Ryan's face hardens, but as he shakes my dad's hand it softens just as fast.

"Dr. Asher, it's great to finally meet you. My father has told me so much about you and your wife's work here. My French isn't perfect, but I hope it's good enough for me to be of some help," he offers a sweet smile. To anyone else it would appear sincere, but to me it just seems like an act.

"Please, call me Malcolm. I'm only Dr. Asher in front of patients. Your father tells me you are applying to Columbia? That's a great school, son. I went for a couple of semesters myself before I transferred over to Stanford. You must have some pretty good grades under your belt? Can I ask why you had to repeat junior year?" Wow. Dad actually went there. Let's hear Ryan sweet talk his way with this one. Wait, I didnt know my dad ever went to Columbia?

"Yes sir. You see, the grading system is a little different at home in the States than it is back in London. Principal Meyers thought it would be best if I repeated to avoid any confusion over my grades, but I've maintained being top of my class." Ryan doesn't miss a beat in replying. My father smiles, clearly impressed, and why wouldn't he be. Ryan is super smart. Smart and beautiful, some people have all the luck.

"That's fantastic. Faith has her heart set on University of Michigan, but I'm trying to persuade her to apply to Stanford, being alumni myself, and I definitely think she has the grades. You never know, right kiddo?"

I frown as Ryan nods in agreement. The whole thing just seems way too fake to me. Ryan doesn't seem himself at all, not even the original nice version of himself everyone loves, this dude is fake as a snake. Is that a thing? *Or maybe the guy you always thought he was is the real fake?*

Sensing my scrutiny of him, Ryan looks at me and smirks knowingly.

"I completely agree, sir. Always strive for the best you can be, that's what my father always says." Why does he keep calling Dad 'sir'? What a brown-nosing douche canoe. He turns back to my father and carries on. "Stanford is a great school. I'm sure Faith has all the credentials to impress the admissions office. From what I know of her reputation at St. Edmund's, she certainly enjoys a lot of extracurricular activities, and she always works real hard."

He looks back at me and I know he was referring to the rumours. He wants to make me feel uncomfortable, as if he somehow has the upper hand because he is talking to my dad with loaded statements about me. Honestly, be more of a dick.

"Dad, don't start, okay. I wanna go to Michigan, it's a good school," I say ignoring Ryan's comments and he smirks again, thinking his work is done.

"Okay, okay. We'll leave it there, for now," Dad offers with a smile that tells me he really does only mean 'for now'. He's not going to let this drop.

"So today, Ryan you're with me, we have a couple of appointments that I know are coming in, nothing too gruesome if you'd like to stay for treatments. Please don't feel like you have to if medicine isn't for you. I mainly just need you for the consults. Faithy, you're heading into town to help Ade with supplies?" I nod. No pressure for Ryan to consider medicine as the only possible career choice then.

"Yeah, I think we are going to stop by the school first, Ade said my package has arrived so I want to take them all the new supplies. Ryan, did you bring anything over with you?" Ryan looks at me confused.

"Was I supposed to bring something?"

"Well yeah, rich boy, this is a developing country. Usually people bring stuff with them to donate, you know like stationary, kids' shoes, sanitary products that sort of thing? I mean you gotta be some kinda asshole not to bring *anything?*"

His face drops and he seems genuinely upset that he has shown up empty handed. For the first time since I picked him up he lets his mask slip, and I see the real him again. Mystery Boy.

"Jesus, I'm so sorry, I didn't even think. Please, give me a list of what's needed and I will arrange to have some stuff sent over straight away."

He does seem really sincere and I don't know why, but now I feel like the one who's being an asshole. But why should I? He's the one who's been a dick all morning. He's the one with the billion-dollar trust fund but can't seem to spare a few bucks to buy some pencils!

"Faith! Don't be so rude, and watch your language young lady!" My father reprimands curtly. "Ryan, that's very kind of you, but it's really not a problem, and it can take weeks, if not months for things to arrive from the States. Don't worry about it. I'm going to grab a drink, why don't you catch up with Faithy, then meet me out front in ten minutes to open up?"

Ryan nods and my father gets up and walks out of the office leaving Ryan and I alone. He stares at me and cocks his head, like he's trying to work me out. I put my loose strands behind my ears, not knowing what else to do with him looking at me like this.

"Why don't you want to apply to Stanford, 'Faithy'?" I shake my head, not answering, it's none of his business. I don't like how he called me Faithy either. Everyone around here calls me it, but for some reason, it doesn't sound right on his lips. "It gets pretty cold in Michigan you know," he adds patronisingly. The nerve of this boy.

"So what?" I don't tell him I want the cold, but it's not

the weather in California that puts me off. "It also gets pretty damn cold in New York, as I'm sure you well know," I continue matter-of-factly while he walks right into my space again.

He smells so good, even after his sweaty walk I can still smell the sweet coconut. He scowls a little at my mention of New York, confirming my suspicions he does not want to go there. "Anyway, what about you, huh?"

"What about me? Why on earth would I apply to Stanford? My family go to Columbia, everyone knows that."

I roll my eyes, he knows what I meant.

"Who cares if your family all went there, that doesn't mean you have to? Just like I don't have to go to Stanford just because my parents did. You're your own person, and I know you don't want the life your father has mapped out for you, so why not stand up for yourself, huh?"

He gives a small laugh through his nose.

"Tell me, 'Faithy'. How exactly would you know what I want, hmm?" He takes a loose strand of my hair and plays with it between his fingers.

"Because I see you. You don't even want to be in America, you want to be back in London. Sure, you're the most popular guy at school but you miss your real friends back there. Levi and Shane? They aren't your friends, you just got stuck with them by default because of Mia, but they're nothing like you. They're bullies, especially Shane, but you, well you're kind, and funny, and smart. Except for recently that is, you've become a helluva lot more like them nowadays."

He carries on playing with my hair, but raises his eyebrow at my statement. "You're a fake, and you're a coward. I know you don't even want to go to Columbia, you want to play soccer, don't you? You're good enough, you could go pro, but your father won't let you continue after high school, am I right?"

He screws up his nose and I know I've hit another nerve. Although his face shows his annoyance, he still doesn't speak, so I continue. "You said it yourself that you've noticed me watching you. You knew I liked you, didn't you? That's why it was you who was the one to trick me into a ride? You knew how I felt and you used it against me, but what I can't work out is why?" My voice starts to crack and I try to swallow my emotions down.

"Why Ryan? Why do you hate me? That first day, you were nice to me. You're not like them, I know you're not, so tell me what I did?" He puts one hand on the wall beside my face caging me in, and then with his other hand that's still playing with my hair, he brings the hair to his nose and smells it. His eyes flash black and I can't tell if it's because he likes or dislikes what he smells.

"You shouldn't have been there that day, it's not who you are," I whisper sadly as a tear drops down my cheek. He drops my hair and brings his face even closer to mine. I can feel his breath on my lips. He is so close, that for a minute I genuinely question if he is going to kiss me, but he doesn't. Instead he wipes my tear away harshly with his thumb, before shoving my face away from his in a move of disgust. He brings his thumb to his lips and tastes my tears.

"Don't let your guard down around me, Pork Chop. You have no idea who I am or what I'm capable of."

With that he pulls away and turns to walk out, leaving me feeling more alone and confused than ever.

# CHAPTER 5

## Ryan

It's almost 5 p.m. and I'm so ready for this day to be over. I've been in a shitty mood ever since Faith made me haul-ass the last half mile in the dry morning heat. Kudos little Faithy. I can't believe I fell for that. It was sneaky and she got me fair and square. Round two to Pork Chop.

In hindsight, I'm surprised she didn't have my balls considering what I said to her about sucking my dick. I was also a little harsh with some of the things I said to her afterwards too, but hey, if the shoe fits. Still, the look on her face, like I stole her puppy or something, did get to me a bit.

See contrary to what you might think, I'm not the kinda guy who gets his kicks from upsetting girls. Faith was right in her analysis of me, I've never bullied anyone in my life, and I'll be honest, I never really thought of what we did to Faith as bullying before, it was supposed to be justice. But I couldn't shake the sting of what she said.

Faith was also right about me knowing that she liked me when I asked her if she wanted a ride. She did stare at me a lot, and Mia was always complaining about it, telling me she must want my dick.

I know that Shane, and even Levi, can both be assholes sometimes. Especially to the younger kids, I've seen it. I guess I just shrugged it off as a part of the school hierarchy, which sounds like a cop out I know, but it wasn't my business.

What happened with Faith was probably the first time I've ever seen Shane be violent like that though. I gotta admit that's really not my vibe at all. Don't get me wrong, if I need to fight I can handle myself, but I usually prefer to talk things out rather than resort to violence. I've probably been in about two fights my entire life, although that's not including what I did to Dr. Dickwad. That was different.

Dr. A was nice enough today, all his patients seemed to like him, but I know what's behind his mask. He has a basic understanding of French having spent so much time over here. Turns out he mostly only really needs me to help translate for him, because whilst he understands some of it, he can't speak it.

He was right though, nothing too gruesome, so I actually did stay for the treatments, especially when Nurse Charity was doing them. What a badass she is. She seems the kind of woman who would only have to give you a look and you know you're in trouble. Total no bullshit kinda lady, and I got a lot of time for that. Besides, I'd prefer the company of hyenas rather than the child abusing doctor, so I jumped at the chance to be elsewhere at every opportunity I got.

I noticed that I didn't get a response to my comment about his wife, and she is nowhere to be seen, so I'm guessing the rumours about her really are true too. I did briefly meet another doctor, a young British dude doing an internship over here. He seemed pretty cool so I'll be sure to try to actually be nice to him, as well as Charity. There's also a Dr. Pierce, who I haven't met yet, who's a paediatrician that's been out in the villages most of the day.

Faith hasn't been back here all day either, and I was surprised at the good doctor's lack of concern for his teenage daughter. I didn't get to meet whoever this Ade person was she mentioned, I'm assuming it's a local guy. I don't know why the thought of her spending the entire day with another dude irks me, but it does. *What is that about?*

From behind his desk, Dr. Asshat breaks my trail of thought as if he knew what I was thinking about.

"Faith and Ade should be back soon. The school finishes around 2 p.m but I know Faithy likes to walk some of the kids home and say hello to their families, and make sure they are all okay. She cares very deeply about the people here, she has a big heart." He gives me a knowing look. Does he think that I like her? Ha! Big heart, yeah right.

We hear a car arriving outside and some modern African music blaring from the speakers. I walk out to the main door to see what's going on, leaving Dr. A-hole to continue his paperwork.

A tall guy helps Faith from the Jeep as they dance to the music. He is young, probably only a few years older than us. He's taller than me and I'm 6ft. He is wearing a vintage looking Manchester United shirt that's a little short. It's well-worn and says 'Cantona 7' on the back. Jesus, that is old. I'm pretty sure he hasn't played for United since '97.

Nurse Charity appears from somewhere with another lady, a patient maybe? Both join in with the dancing, and soon Greg, the British doc, is out there as well. Wow, considering he is only young, that guy has some serious dad moves.

As they all dance energetically, I notice Faith does actually have good rhythm. She moves her body so perfectly to the music, and for a minute I imagine how she would feel, her hips in my hands while she moves her ass like that against me. Fuck yes.

Apparently, I'm not the only one to notice her, as I see Ade is also watching her attentively. He dances closer into Faith's space and whispers something in her ear to which she laughs and blushes, as she playfully pushes him away. Are they flirting? I can't help but wonder if he's fucked her, a thought that for some reason pisses me off.

With all the stories about Faith at school, I can't say I've ever actually witnessed her offering it up to a guy before. In fact, now that I think about it, I don't think I've ever even seen her talking to anyone at school for that matter. I guess she doesn't have a lot of friends. Why would she, everyone knows she's a tramp.

Let's be honest, no guy is going to openly pursue the school whore for a girlfriend. Again, something about that thought makes my stomach knot. Then again, I'm the idiot who didn't even realise his girlfriend was sleeping around, so who the fuck am I to judge.

I'm so caught up in my thoughts I didn't hear someone appear behind me.

"Why don't you go and join them? It's a Monday tradition around here, we all like to dance together and let off some steam. Ryan isn't it?" A woman's soft voice speaks, making me jump a little.

"Yes ma'am, Ryan Scott, and uh, it's okay I don't dance. Dr. Pierce, I presume?" I offer my hand to her as I haven't actually met her until now. Instead of shaking it she takes it in both of hers, holding it tightly like it's precious to her. A motherly show of affection that twists something in my gut.

"Please honey, call me Lorrie. We are so happy to have

you here, it's such a nice change for Faith to have one of her friends around. She talks about you so often back home, so I'm glad to finally meet you." Wait, back home, is she Faith's mother? I wonder why everyone said she was in prison. "Faith's never mentioned anyone else, we were beginning to think she didn't have any friends."

She's got that right, but why does it piss me off that it has taken them three years to even suspect their daughter is a loner. Lorrie looks at me expectantly. Does she actually think Faith and I are friends?

"Well I'm happy to be here," I say sounding lame as fuck, but I have no idea how to respond to that. Lorrie said Faith talks about me all the time, what the hell does she say?

"Will you join us for dinner tonight? It's nothing fancy, but we'd love to introduce you to everyone properly, and I know my daughter would especially like it if you could join us?"

Daughter, so she is Faith's mom. She has a real kind face, although she looks absolutely nothing like Faith. Lorrie has long blonde hair and blue eyes. She's tall, with a slender and athletic frame, although she looks like one of those skinny chicks who are actually hella' strong. The complete opposite of Faith's dark hair, and shorter, curvier frame. I'd never pick her out as being Faith's mother.

Now that I think about it, she doesn't look much like Malcolm either?

Whilst I couldn't think of anything worse than socialising with these people right now, I don't have the heart to turn Lorrie down, as she actually seems really nice.

"That would be lovely, thank you Lorrie." Thankfully, she offers to have Faith run me back to the hotel first so I can wash up. I'm happy, not only because I really need a shower, but also because I get to break up whatever this shit is between Faith and Ade that's pissing me off. Although why I care, I'm really not sure.

*\*\*\**

A few hours, and two silent car rides to the hotel and back later, we've all eaten, and both Lorrie and Malcolm are regaling us all with tales of baby Faith. I particularly enjoyed the one about the time she apparently stripped down to her underwear during a family wedding and refused to put her dress back on, so spent the entire evening reception wearing her father's dinner jacket.

I gotta hand it to Lorrie, she's put on a great dinner. A large pot roast type stew consisting mostly of vegetables and pulses that had a slight spicy kick, with the most amazing home baked bread I think I've ever tasted. She invited everyone who works at the clinic, as well as a few of the locals, and there was plenty of food to go around, with even some leftovers that Lorrie potted up to be taken to the school tomorrow. There is a real community feel here that I really admire.

I also discovered that Lorrie goes by her maiden name, Dr. Pierce, to avoid the whole 'which Dr. Asher do you mean' confusion. Makes sense. Turns out the other lady with Charity earlier was Blessing, Charity's sister, and both are Ade's aunts. It turns out, Ade only volunteers here now and again with maintenance, transport, and deliveries and stuff, he actually works as a maintenance man in the city most of the time.

Apparently, he got mixed up in some sort of gang when he was a kid, but when he moved here, the Ashers helped him start over.

I don't know why I'm so pleased to hear he isn't always around. He actually seems like an ok guy, and I definitely feel like I could get along with him given his love of soccer, or real football as everyone here refers to it. He is also a pretty funny guy, but I can't help but feel annoyed every time he makes Faith laugh. Again, what the hell is that? I need to get my fucking head straight.

Everyone here is actually so welcoming and friendly, it's easy to forget the truth that I know. I was undecided if Lorrie knew about it, but after spending time with her tonight, I feel like there is no way she would sit by and do nothing if she knew the truth about her husband, so I assume she doesn't know. Which makes me even angrier about the whole situation.

Then there is Faith. What a fucking enigma. First, she can barely get two words out when she speaks to me, other than to tell me I have kissable lips that is. Then she doesn't attempt to say one more word to me for the entire junior year, and now all or a sudden she's feisty as fuck? Why the hell does her sass make my dick twitch?

"So Ryan, how'd you enjoy your first day, mate? Sorry I didn't get to spend much time with you but I actually speak French, unlike this old twat." I'm broken from my thoughts at Greg's statement, for which he receives a playful clip around the ear from Dr. Dick.

"Hey, I might be a twat but less of the old, kid!" Malcolm ruffles Greg's hair like he's appraising a child.

Greg is what some might call Emo-geek chic, with black, thick rimmed glasses, and brown wavey hair that's even wilder than mine. He has a lip ring piercing on the side of his bottom lip. He's wearing some band tee that I've never even heard of, with black skin-tight ripped jeans. He has a whole bunch of brightly coloured cotton bracelets that look like the little friendship type kids make around one wrist. His arms are covered in some pretty rad ink as well. Not your typical doctor look, that's for sure.

Greg speaks with an accent that suggests he comes from money, but he is either trying to hide it, or has spent a lot of time away from it. His accent now sits somewhere between cockney, and Lord of the Manor.

"Okay Grandad, whatever you say. But mate, you were old enough to buy a pint to see in the millennium, so you're bloody old. Plus, you were also old enough to…"

"Alright, alright, please don't continue. I'm old, and I accept it. How did you enjoy your meal, Ryan? Faithy makes great bread, doesn't she? She is famous for her brilliant baking skills around here."

"It was great, thanks," I say, not really paying attention. Dr. Asher gets up from the table and starts clearing some plates. Faith is still talking to Ade. I can't hear what she's saying but she's talking animatedly and he seems to be hanging off her every fucking word. Dick.

"…He's right though, Faith makes the best bread. She makes amazing cakes too, she's like Betty bloody Crocker that girl. So you went to school in London, right? Where abouts?" Again, I'm pulled from my thoughts about Faith by Greg. Why can't I stop thinking about this girl? Wait, did he say Faith made the amazing bread? That's impressive.

"Erm, yeah. I boarded there from age eleven. It's in Primrose Hill. It's not sign-posted, so unless you knew it was a school, you'd probably walk right by it thinking it was just another historic building turned office space." I say, glad to have a distraction from Faith's tempting porno lips. Greg nods knowingly.

"Ah, Camden! Some bloody great pubs around there. I'm from West London myself, Chelsea originally, but I live over the other side of London in Stratford now. So, are you an Arsenal man then?" he asks, referencing a London soccer team.

"Hell no bro! More like your new address, I like West Ham. 'Come on, you Irons'!" I say the last part in my best cockney accent, while Greg shakes his head and roars with laughter. I guess West Ham aren't the most successful team in the Premier League, but they hang on in there and I always appreciate an underdog. Although I guess it could also be my attempt at the accent that has him howling. I may have spent six years in London, but my accent is still mostly New York.

"Mate, I thought you might know a thing or two about football, turns out you're no better than that dickhead over there in his Man-U shirt!" That statement peaks the interest of both Ade and Faith. Ade kisses his Manchester United Badge before throwing a peace sign to Greg that I'm certain would have been deuces had his aunts not been sat right there.

"It's vintage, brother. Be worth a goldmine in a few, no? Ooh-aah, Can-to-naaaa!" Ade offers energetically, and Greg howls with laughter again. It's actually Faith's reaction that surprises me the most.

"Well actually Greg, Ryan is an incredible player. He was the top goal scorer and MVP at his previous school for five consecutive years, and he single-handedly took St. Edmund's to win state for the first time in the school's history. He was even scouted by two major London teams before he came back to America. He could teach all of you a thing or two about soccer." She says matter-of-factly, as if she's reporting for ESPN.

"FOOTBALL!" Both Greg and Ade roar in unison which actually causes me to laugh too. Fuck, when did I last laugh?

I wonder how Faith knows so much about me? Same as earlier, she hit the nail right on the head when she mentioned how much I miss London and my real friends. Then again, she also said I was kind. How on earth can she think of me like that after everything I've done. I guess she doesn't actually know the full extent of my sins, but still, what she does know is bad enough, so I have no idea what leads her to think I'm kind.

"If that's true mate, you want to get your arse over to the school and give the kids a lesson or two. They love football out here," Greg suggests.

"That would actually be pretty awesome, I know the kids over there would love that," Faith offers in a quiet voice with not nearly as much confidence as she had a moment ago. She smiles an unsure smile at me, and then dips her head in embarrassment. Same old Faith, I guess the confident chick who sassed me earlier was just a fluke.

Blessing says something to Ade, and he repeats the conversation we just had back to her in French, and she laughs. She then looks to me and basically reaffirms what Faith just said to me, but also in French. I politely agree to make sure I find the time to go over there at some point.

I'm still feeling pretty shitty about not bringing anything over with me for the kids, so it's the very least I can do. I emailed our head housekeeper on my break asking him to urgently ship some bits over for me. I hope that old fucker sorts me out, he usually only responds well to my father for some reason.

It's getting late when Faith offers to drive me back to the hotel but as much as I hate her, it doesn't sit right with me to have her then drive back alone. Luckily, her father agrees and offers to take me back himself. As much as I don't want to spend time in his company either, I'd suffer it, to prevent Faith from driving alone at night. *You didn't seem to care when you left her stranded two hours from home, bound, gagged, and dumped in a muddy pig pen, asshole.*

The fuck is wrong with me tonight? So apparently now I feel guilty? Fuck that, she deserved it. Well she did, didn't she?

She said she sees me, and I'm starting to think maybe she

actually does. God, why am I still fucking thinking about her. Do I fucking like her?

Okay I definitely need some sleep, I'm doing my own head in today. Maybe tomorrow I'll have some fresh perspective. I grab my stuff and say my goodbyes, making sure to especially thank Lorrie for the lovely food. I deliberately avoid saying goodbye to Faith, which works to my advantage because she's clearly upset about it, although she tries to act indifferent.

If I'm going to survive three weeks here I need to get my head in the game fast, and that means avoiding Faith Asher at all costs.

# CHAPTER 6

## Ryan

I successfully managed to stay away from Faith as much as possible for a couple of days. Each morning she picked me up, but she was late every time. However, she no longer tried to regale me with wild tales of dead goats, and '90s pop princesses, she just drove. I don't know why, but that pissed me off more than her deliberately being late.

Faith would arrive with a smug look of self-appraisal that she tried to hide, but couldn't. For some reason I found that endearing, I actually liked her spunky side. After all, I was the one being a dick, so I deserved it. The silent treatment annoyed me. Although I was doing all I could *not* to talk to her, so why I was pissed at her lack of conversation back is beyond me.

After work, every afternoon at 5 p.m. on the dot she would ask me if I was ready for a ride back. Every journey was sat in silence, not even any music playing. Fuck I'd even take Britney back over this. To be honest, I'm confusing the fuck out of myself, but the awkward silences were probably on me. Okay, so they were definitely on me. I don't need her thinking we can become friends, because we can't.

I can't believe I actually almost kissed her that first morning too. I don't know why, but like I said I just found her sass toward me strangely appealing. I guess I'm not really used to that. Chicks usually either throw it at me on a plate, desperate to suck my rich dick, or they are too fucking shy to even speak to me. Until recently that was exactly how Faith was. Hell, she barely said two words to me that first day, so her giving me a bit of spunk out of nowhere was definitely an unexpected turn on.

She also smells amazing by the way. It intrigued me that she didn't have any scent of tacky perfume like most girls seem to layer on thick. Faith just smells really clean, like old fashioned soap. There's a hint of something else though, something sweet like vanilla and brown sugar. Also, she does have very kissable lips herself, in my defence. Team those with her creamy soft skin and big cartoon eyes, I still find her a total fucking temptation.

I don't know what came over me though. I put my temporary lapse in judgement down to the fact I hate Faith. They say there is a thin line between love and hate right? *Wait, what?*

Not love, definitely not love, but you catch my drift. I figured that seeing her happy with Ade is annoying me, because why the hell should she be happy after what she's done. Now Dr. Asher on the other hand, he doesn't really seem happy at all actually, but that's for me to work out another day.

I mean I could just leave, why don't I? Yeah, my father would be pretty pissed, but seeing as how we're pissed at each other about ninety percent of the time I really couldn't give a shit. It's not like I actually need the extra credit for college either, but I can't bring myself to quit. I may hate Dr. Ass-wipe, but even I can admit it's actually pretty decent what they are doing here. I figure that would make me some kinda dick to just up and leave. Plus, I find it cool helping out. Mom would be proud of me for doing it, and that's really important to me. *She wouldn't be proud of anything else you've done lately though, would she?*

Whatever. See here's the thing. It's now coming to the end of day four and I'm bored as hell. Not so much the work at the clinic, but the rest of the time when I'm not busy. Every night, Lorrie and Malcolm extended me an invitation to join them for dinner again, but I politely declined as part of my stay-away-from-all-things-Asher routine.

After being dropped straight back to the hotel at 5p.m. sharp every night, I've spent all evening alone in my room, with nothing to do and no one to talk to. I still haven't spoken to Mia or Shane, or even Lev for that matter. I can't say I'm overly cut up about it, now I've had time to think about everything. Don't get me wrong, I cared about Mia but I wouldn't say I was in love with her. When you have a heart as black and broken as mine you learn to accept that you aren't capable of love anymore, but I did care about her.

The more I think about it, the more I know Faith was right about Shane and Levi. They were my friends by default, because they were already the most popular guys in school. They were on the school football team, American that is, not soccer. Whilst the team was pretty dog dump, they were still revered as Gods among men. That was until I came along, and then soccer became the school's number one game. They even gave up football halfway through the season and joined the soccer team just to stay on top. Not that they were much good at that either.

Fact is once I arrived, they were only top dogs because I said so. I was crowned King as soon as I landed in L.A. Not that I wanted it, but I tend to spark a lot of interest, mostly because of the Scott name. In Manhattan, the Scott's are a powerhouse. Wherever I went I was addressed as Mr. Scott before I'd even introduced myself. L.A is all about money and fame. It's full of plastic people and plastic relationships. So much so that my reputation had preceded itself before I'd even stepped foot inside St. Edmund's Academy.

My father was sure to build the largest, and in my opinion, most vulgar house in Calabasas. He also bought a secluded beach house in Malibu, as well as a penthouse apartment in Beverly Hills for his wife to use while she was working. Everyone lapped up our arrival with everything from fruit baskets to exclusive party invitations. It was even posted on the gossip pages, apparently. Pathetic.

In London though, it was different, I wasn't that special because everyone there was from some serious money. Old money too, and I mean really old. England is full of wealthy aristocrats, Lords, Earls, Dukes, you name it. Manhattan has its fair share of old money too, but even they would be considered mere pups in comparison to the lineage of some of the families in England. So over in London, the only place I was considered special was on the pitch. I was popular enough, sure, but was I walking around as if I was ruling the school like I do now? Hell no. I really didn't give a shit about any of that, and I still don't.

I had my friends, Tom, Alex, Spencer, and Kat. My crew. They would be shocked to see me now. It was a co-ed school, although we took segregated classes. From what I hear, Spencer is an unusual name for a chick to have in England, or for a 'bird' as they would say, but It suited her. She is absolutely beautiful and she rocks it, although she was bullied a lot for being overweight.

Kat was Tom's twin sister, but also my best friend. When Mom died she was my rock. The five of us were pretty solid, but for some reason I only felt comfortable enough to talk about my mother in front of Kat. The other guys respected that. They always let me know they were there for me, small gestures and such, but they never pressed me and I appreciated that.

I haven't spoken to any of them in a while. Months even. They have called a lot, sent a ton of messages, but I've responded with the bare minimum back. I guess I've been avoiding telling them about what I did to Faith, and Dr. A-Hole. I did what I had to do, but I know they won't understand, and I don't want to face their judgement. I fucking miss Kat, I miss them all. I miss my mom. I miss my fucking life.

It's not like I can sleep here either, because I'm pretty sure a bed of nails would be more comfortable than that pile of shit in my room. So instead of heading straight back there with Faith today, I decided to head over to Greg's cabin to see if he wants to maybe have a kick about or something. I brought a change of clothes just in case.

Unfortunately, I bump into Faith on my way outside. Awkward.

"Hey, how was your day? Are you ready to head back?" She says, wrapping her arms protectively around her midsection while looking out the window. Her eyes are red and puffy and she looks distracted. I look out the window to see Ade getting into his van. Faith turns her head away from the window, shaking it, blinking a lot like she's fighting back tears. Has he upset her? Why the fuck that pisses me off I have no idea. *Dude, you just said she doesn't deserve to be happy?*

"Is everything alright, you seem upset?" She looks up at me, surprised by my concern. I'm a little surprised by it myself, in all honesty, I really shouldn't give a shit.

"It's nothing! Are you ready or not?" She snaps back. Wow, touchy.

"Actually, I was thinking of heading over to see if Greg wanted to hang out for a bit. Being alone at the hotel all night is lonely as hell." Faith looks a little annoyed at my statement, but I have no idea why she would be.

"Whatever asshat, suit yourself," she scoffs as she turns and storms out, literally slamming the door open against the wall as she leaves. I probably shouldn't, but I follow after her, annoyed and confused by her attitude.

"Hey! What the hell was that about? Is there a problem with me hanging around for a bit?"

She comes storming back to me with fire in her eyes. She's furious about something, and I gotta say, it's hot as hell.

"Why would I have a problem with you wanting to spend time here? It's not as though my parents haven't been asking you to join us every, single, night, but hey, apparently you'd rather spend time alone in your hotel room than be around us?" She's a firecracker when she's pissed. "Or maybe it's just me? Do you really hate me so much that you'd rather be lonely than spend time with me?" Her voice cracks at the end and I can tell she's fighting back tears. I lower my head, not knowing what to say to that. *Coward.*

"Yeah, that's what I thought. I mean it's not like anyone else ever wants to spend time with me either, so why would you be any different?" She says with complete desperation. It's then that I *see* her for the first time. She's lonely. She's dying inside, and she is screaming for someone to notice. A feeling I know all too well, and fuck if it doesn't make my chest ache. I watch as she wipes away tears that are now streaming down her face, before she turns and runs towards her own cabin, shutting herself inside.

I guess she has a point, I have been a little rude. I make a point to myself to apologise tomorrow, at the very least to Lorrie. Maybe I'll even suck it up and stay for dinner if she asks.

I go over and knock on Greg's door. He opens it dressed for a run.

"Alright Ry-Man, what's happening, fella? You need a lift back into town or something?" This guy is clearly anything but cockney, but he tries nonetheless.

"Actually, I was going to see if you would put your money where your mouth is. Wanna have a kick about? Only, I don't have a ball so I was also kinda hoping you might?" He laughs and takes off his thick rimmed glasses. He grabs a hair tie from the counter and somehow manages to pull his untamed hair back into a top knot.

"Well, I don't have a ball either but how about this, you come with me for a run tonight and we can source a ball over the weekend. Perhaps we can get some of the young lads involved?" He starts lacing up his shoes and stretching.

"Okay, let me just get changed real quick and we'll head out," I reluctantly agree, knowing I haven't run properly in weeks and how much I'm going to regret it.

***

We get back from our run and I'm sweating my balls off, not to mention exhausted. Turns out that Greg, the little asswipe, forgot to mention he runs ultra fucking marathons for fun. He is currently training for Marathon des Sables to raise money for an AIDS charity back in London. Apparently, that's why he chose to volunteer over here, so he could train in the climate and be ready. I remind myself to donate to his fundraiser as soon as I can get some Wi-Fi. Fucking sneaky bastard.

Whilst he wasn't hard to keep pace with, he just kept going and going, until we had run about eight miles out, which of course meant a painful eight miles back. He tells me that tonight was more like a short run for him, he can run thirty to forty miles in one session some days. Who the fuck knew?

When we got back the sun was setting, Faith was out

in the yard alone doing yoga. She was actually pretty good at it from what I could see, she's obviously been doing it a while. Maybe that's why she's always wearing yoga pants.

"What's the deal with you two anyway? Faithy says you hate her, but I'm not sure I can believe that for a second. I mean, who could hate that adorable little kitty cat?"

I raise my eyebrow at Greg. Why does it piss me off that Faith spoke to him about us? And why does it really fucking kill me that he also calls her Faithy like her parents? As if reading my thoughts, he speaks again.

"Don't give me that look mate, Faith is far too young for me, and far too much oestrogen if you catch my drift. But I do care about her a lot, and so does Ade, we all do round these parts. If you've got beef with her, you got beef with everyone, do I make myself clear?" He raises a serious eyebrow. I nod but continue to scowl. He doesn't know fuck about my situation with Faith. He can't even see who she really is. *Do you see who she really is?*

"By the way, you can stop giving Ade the stink eye as well while you're at it. He's a great guy, but Faith isn't exactly his type either." He wiggles his eyebrows at me suggestively, and I cotton on to what he is saying.

"You and Ade? Seriously?" He winks at me confirming my suspicions. "Wow, I did not see that coming." He pulls me up and pushes me down the small space between two of the cabins for privacy.

"Look, don't make it a thing alright. It's not exactly accepted around these parts so don't go shouting your mouth off, okay?" Fuck, I didn't realise. It's ridiculous that people still have to live in fear of who they are in this day and age. There sure are a lot of pricks in this world.

"Hey, look I'm sorry, of course I won't say anything. It's

completely cool with me, honestly man." I hold my hands up in a surrendering gesture. "I definitely thought Ade was into Faith though, I won't lie. He flirts with her a lot!"

He smirks and shakes his head, then pushes me back out into the yard. I sit down on the steps to his cabin as he goes in and quickly passes me a bottle of water and an orange before sitting down next to me.

"Listen, Ade see's Faith as a little sister. Or more of a very distant cousin I guess, because you're right he does flirt with her. Only because he has watched her grow into a beautiful young woman, but she doesn't have an ounce of confidence, that girl. She has no idea what a salty little potato she is, and well, he just tries to boost her confidence by teasing and flirting with her a little. But that's all it is."

He gives me a stern look like he thinks I'm the reason for her lack of confidence. Am I? Faith is such a fucking mystery. From what I've seen of her here, I would totally agree with what he is saying. She doesn't seem to have a shred of confidence. Like what's with her hugging her waist all the time. Then there is Faith back home. She is far too full of herself, she's a bully and a slut.

Why do I find it hard to believe that they are the same person. Which one is real?

"See me, I just like boys. Tall, dark, and bloody gorgeous ones. But Ade, he is a free spirit. For him it's all just about relationships. But he would never be inappropriate with Faith, he loves her and her family too much for that." He continues as he takes a sip of his drink. "The Ashers are well respected around here, not just for The Old Farmhouse, but for just being good people. Now are you gonna answer my earlier question about your beef with Faith, or what?"

I shake my head. It's my turn to smirk as I turn to watch Faith. She moves effortlessly from Warrior II pose, to

Sun Warrior with perfect form, the low sun behind, giving her silhouette a soft glow. She moves into a perfect Dancers pose, and I have no idea why, it's probably just the sunset, but I feel compelled to take a photo of her on my phone.

"Flexible little thing, isn't she," Greg says jokingly, catching me staring at Faith. He playfully ruffles my hair before he slaps me around the back of the head as he stands up. "Whatever your shit is with her, stop being a twat and sort it out. Faithy is an absolute rocket. Anyone with eyes can see you fancy her, you'd be an idiot not to. You gotta be a real sort of bellend to let her get away over some bullshit issue that no one else seems to know anything about, eh? Get your head out your arse, Yankee Doodle before someone else snaps her up, and trust me, they soon bloody will and you know it!"

With that, he goes over to join Faith in her session. I feel a little pissed at his assumptions. I do not 'fancy' Faith. *Sure. Keep telling yourself that, man.*

The issue between us isn't just some bullshit, and it's not going away any time soon. But even I have to admit it's pretty draining keeping up with it, so for now, I decide to call a temporary truce as I head over to join them both. I expect Faith to object but she doesn't. She doesn't acknowledge me at all as she carries on leading us through a slow, and at some points painful, routine.

I have a sneaking suspicion that she deliberately pulled some difficult moves to try and piss me off, but it actually just amused me, even if I did fall on my ass a couple times in the process. Faith is really good, and it was definitely what I needed to loosen up after that run.

After we finished, Greg took a selfie of the three of us and posted it on the page for the clinic. He has tagged a couple of photos of me this week, hoping that some of my two million or so followers might put their hands in their pockets and donate. From what I hear, each time he posted a photo of me the clinic has had a surge of donations. I make a note to tag the clinic in all of my photos when I finally get around to posting them.

I take some photos myself of all of us, mostly geeking out using funny filters. The three of us sit around for a bit, talking mostly about London. Faith talks excitedly about all the places there that she wants to see, the usual tourist traps. Hearing her talk about it though, I remember how exciting London really is when you experience it for the first time. It's like nowhere else in the world.

I don't know if it's the chill vibe tonight, or the maybe it was the 'namaste' offered up at the end of the session, but I'm left wondering if maybe we could extend this truce. By the time we got in the Jeep to head back, the mood was a lot lighter than it had been all week. I'm not sure if it was Faith trying to sass me again with her difficult moves, or if it was watching her bend in ways that my dick truly appreciated, but either way, when I finally got back to the hotel that night the bed wasn't the only thing hard as a rock.

# CHAPTER 7

## Faith

It's Friday afternoon and it's super-hot. My hair is so frizzy I've had to throw it up after I spent all that time last night trying to make it look cute. I've had a busy day with Greg doing a walk-in minor injuries clinic, and we are both ready to call it a day, but I'm waiting to help my dad with a patient coming in from a few towns over. She's a young girl, only thirteen years old, so my father needs a female to chaperone.

The thought twists in my gut because I know that usually means she needs to be examined, and that's likely to mean she has had serious complications from being cut. That or she is either pregnant or been raped, or both. I fight back tears that burn in my eyes.

This kind of thing happens all too often here. Usually my mother would do these types of exams, but she's out of town today with Charity doing some maternity checks in some of the more remote villages. It's unusual for women to be allowed a male doctor here, especially to have him do an exam on a female, but sometimes they allow it as long as there is a family member to chaperone. My father will always insist on having his own chaperone as well, just to be safe.

I notice Ryan outside greeting an elderly gentleman in French, as Ade helps him out of his van. Why does the French language make everything seem romantic? This guy is here to have an abscess drained, yet hearing Ryan talk to him in French hits me right in the feels. I've barely seen Ryan all day, and after how things seemed to thaw a little between us last night, I'm desperate to see how he is going to be with me today.

The first couple of days were a little awkward. He either didn't speak to me at all, or if he did he was short with me. He seemed curt with my father at times too. Funny thing was he was always really friendly to my mom, and he seemed to get on really well with Greg too. Maybe because they remind him of things that he has lost?

I don't actually know how his mother died, that was never really spoken about at school. In fact, most people only really referred to his step-mother as his mom, which is really weird considering she is only a few years older than he is. There were also plenty of rumours he was having an affair with her, making it even more weird. Kinda gross, actually.

After yoga last night I drove Ryan back to the hotel as usual. He wasn't very happy at the thought of me driving back on my own at night, but I assured him I would be fine, it's a ten-minute drive, but he insisted Greg jump on the back and come with us.

### *Last night...*

"Just as long as you two love birds don't start snogging, I really don't wanna see that," Greg teased. My cheeks flamed and Greg howled with laughter.

"I'll be the perfect gentleman I promise." Ryan holds his hands up in a submissive pose. Why does that feel like rejection?

"Just get in both of you, I need to get back to wash, I stink." *Nice Faith, way to be sexy.*

"You need to wash? This clown tricked me into running sixteen miles tonight, I don't think I've ever sweated so much in my life. We did see a huge snake though, that was pretty awesome!" Ryan smiles and runs his hand through his messy sweaty hair. How is it possible he looks even hotter when he is all sweaty? I can't help but conjure images of sweat beads dripping down his perfect abs. To my embarrassment, Ryan notices me checking him out and he smirks at me. Apparently, Greg has noticed too.

"Hey, eyes on the road Faithy, I'm too pretty to die, and snakes are not cool. They are the devil's work! Nothing but sneaky, slithering bastards," Greg says in his distinctively British timbre. Ryan laughs as Greg sits back and pulls his hood right down his face, covering his eyes.

"What about you? Are you scared of snakes?" Ryan says playfully, taking me by surprise. After all the nasty things he has said to me this week, Ryan is actually speaking to me and it's not an insult. Wow.

"No, I'm good with snakes. Well, actually no, I'm not overjoyed at the thought of them to be honest, but they aren't what scare me." A slight smile forms on Ryan's lips and I can see the cogs turning in his head.

"What are you scared of, Faith?"

Faith. Not Pork Chop. But then I guess he probably doesn't want to insult me with Greg in the car, it doesn't mean anything has changed. I shake my head. Of course, nothing's changed.

"Don't do that. Don't pretend you don't know." I barely whisper. He raises an eyebrow.

"How would I know?" He asks innocently. Is he serious? Is he deliberately trying to piss me off, because it's working. I remember all the bullying and taunting back at school and then I think about the stupid pig pen I'm sure he was the one to throw me into, and I start to feel panic. "Are you okay?"

"PIGS!" I scream, startling everyone, myself included. I don't know why I shouted that, but I'm angry at him. Why is he still trying to taunt me. Greg, shoots up wondering what's happening.

"I'm scared of pigs," I add at a more civilised volume. Ryan shakes his head and then lowers it in what appears to be shame. He must have known, how could he not, everyone knows. "I mean that's why you did it, isn't it?"

"Okay, what's going on here? Am I missing something?" Greg questions, as an awkward silence hangs thick in the air. After a beat I decide to respond, I don't want to start anymore drama.

"It's nothing. I just *hate* pigs, okay. Did you know pigs can eat an entire human body? Bones, clothes, and everything? It's a legit fear alright, I hate them. I've hated them since I was a kid."

Greg raises a questioning eyebrow, clearly not satisfied with my answer. "Look, I was teased a lot about it at school and I'm a little sore about it, that's all."

Greg frowns at me in the mirror.

"Teased by who, this dickhead?" he says protectively as he gestures towards Ryan.

"No!" I cut in. "It was before he started, look just drop it. Please?" I catch Greg's eye in the rear-view mirror silently pleading with him to drop it, and he reluctantly does. But he gives me a 'for now' look similar to that of my father's.

"Don't lie for me, Faith. I don't deserve your protection. I didn't know that you were afraid of pigs, but I've still been an asshole to you. I'm sorry." A silent exchange passes between Ryan and Greg that I can't decipher. Ryan looks sincere, and I wonder if he really didn't know. Mia was a top-class bitch and I wouldn't put it past her to have manipulated him into being involved that day, he was never involved before that.

Part of me wonders why am I making excuses for him. Surely he must have heard the stories about the pigs, it's not like he hasn't heard all the other stories about me. *He reminds you often enough.*

"Don't worry about it". I say curtly, unable to look at him. Jeez, why don't I have any backbone when it comes to this boy.

"So, I think I was pretty good at yoga, I might join you again sometime, if you don't mind? You make a pretty decent coach," he says enthusiastically after a deafening silence, trying to lighten the mood. I laugh a little at that.

"You are welcome to join me, but not because you are good, but because you definitely need more practice," I tease, making me laugh a little more. It feels good to laugh, even if it's not whole heartedly. It was funny watching Ryan try and do some of the more advanced poses I snuck in. He fell on his ass a bunch of times, but he always tried again, so I'll give him his dues.

"What the hell? I was good! I was at least better than Greg, he didn't even try to do the last few poses!" Ryan shakes his head but smiles a warm smile knowing how much he sucked, and for some reason it warms my heart.

"Yeah because I'm not an idiot. I *know* I can't do that shit,

I wasn't gonna end up on my arse like you, you big tosser!"

Ryan and I smile at each other, and I feel all kinds of excitement in my belly. Is this what it could be like if we were actually friends? All too quickly though we are back at the hotel, and Ryan gets out of the Jeep, leaving me silently pining a little.

"Thanks for tonight, I actually needed this more than I thought." He passes me his phone. "Here, put your number in, let me know when you get back safe, please?"

I enter my number, confused and ecstatic at the same time, trying my best to ignore Greg's teasing how he already had Ryan's number on day one. Such an A-hole.

"Goodnight 'Ry-man'. I'll see you in the morning, 8 a.m. sharp," I say sweetly, knowing how late I was this morning. Ryan shakes his head and chuckles, his golden curls dropping across his eyes. Damn it, why is he so gorgeous. I've been late every day. The first time wasn't my fault, there was this goat, but anyway the other times I deliberately took my sweet ass time just to piss him off. Not that it seemed to work.

"We'll see," he says unconvinced, as he turns to give Greg a fist pump, before heading inside the hotel. Greg climbs up front and we get back on the road.

"Anything you wanna share, Faithy?" Greg teases, pulling me out of my sexy, California coconut induced coma. I shake my head. I don't want to ruin the chance of Ryan and I being friends by dragging up the past.

"Suit yourself baby girl, but ah, you have a little drool on your chin just here… " He leans over and tickles my chin before he switches on the stereo. It's still the '90s compilation, and *Spice Up Your Life* by Spice Girls comes on. To my surprise Greg is here for it, and we both sing along enthusiastically until we get back.

Mom is outside my cabin when we pull up, so I say goodnight to Greg and head over. What could she want? It's not like her to show any interest in my life.

"It's pretty late, Faith. You missed dinner, where have you been?" Seriously, now she's concerned.

"We just dropped Ryan back, he stayed around for a while to hang. How was your day?" She stands up from the step, but instead of waiting for me to open up so she can come in, she goes to leave. Same old Mom, nothing changes. Heaven forbid she actually spend any time with me.

"It was fine. Listen, your father and I need to talk to you, but it's too late tonight. Go wash up, I put some leftovers out for you inside. We will talk tomorrow?"

I already know what they want to talk to me about anyway. I overheard them arguing this morning. She moves like she is about to hug me, but changes her mind and gives my arm a rub instead. Honestly, I've seen her be more affectionate with Ryan in the few days he's been here, than she has ever been toward me in my entire life.

I shrug her hand off like it offends me and I don't miss the hurt in her eyes at the gesture, but I can't be fake. We just don't get along anymore. Not since I found out the truth. She doesn't even try and talk to me about it, she just smiles a half smile and leaves. Whatever.

Before I go get in the shower I bravely drop Ryan a message to tell him I'm back safe. Well he did ask, and my inner Britney seems to have her red latex catsuit on tonight. Yep, I'm feeling fierce as hell.

**Faith -** Surprisingly, we made it back without being attacked by any sneaky, slithering bastards. Or pigs for that matter :)

I finish my shower and throw on my baby blue #ItsBritneyBitch shirt with a pair of clean white bed shorts, and I walk back across to my cabin. My parents won't let me wear the shirt in public so I just use it to sleep in, but I think it's cute. Well if they think this one is bad, wait until they see the *'If You Seek Amy'* one I ordered back home. I wonder if they will get it? Not that I would ever wear it in public, I'm definitely not that brazen.

After adding some curl cream, I tie my hair into eight small braids so that it's nice and wavy tomorrow. As I climb into bed, I check my phone to see if he replied. My tummy turns over a few times when I see that he has.

**Ryan -** I'm glad to hear it, *Ma Foi*! Thanks for the late ride, and the yoga class.

He has attached the photos he took of the three of us, but the last one is just of me holding Dancer's pose. I wonder why he took that? I save my favourite one of the three of us as my screensaver on my phone, before re-reading the message again. *Ma Foi*? My Faith? I have to Google it, not confident in my French, but I know I'm right. My heart leaps at the thought, even though I know I'm definitely reading into it way too much. Before I can reply, another text comes through.

**Ryan -** I actually had no idea you were scared of pigs. I know it probably seems like I did after everything that happened, but I swear I didn't. That whole night was a fucking shit show. It didn't go down how I thought it would, and I'm sorry for my part in it. All of it. x

I never thought I'd ever get an apology for that, but all I can focus on is the little 'x' he put on the end. What the hell does it mean? It's probably just a habitual thing, a lot of people put one at the end of a message. It doesn't mean anything. Right?

**Faith** - Wow, an apology, are you feeling alright? I think all those vinyasas had too much blood rushing to your head, Ry-Man :)

I decide against adding one myself, and go for a friendly smiley instead.

**Ryan** - I am capable of being nice now and again. Shockingly. I'm not sure I like 'Ry-man' coming from your pretty lips. I'll have to think of something else that you can call me instead ;)

See, no 'x'. Wait, pretty lips? Is he flirting? He used a wink emoji, that's flirting, right? Should I flirt back? *God no. You don't even know how to flirt.*

Urgh, that is true. I don't have a clue how to flirt. What if he isn't flirting at all, what if I'm reading this all wrong? What if this is some other way to hurt me? Why are boys so hard to read? You know what, I'm gonna do it. I'm gonna flirt.

**Faith** - I know you are a nice guy, that's not what's shocking. What's shocking is when your pretty lips say mean things to me all the time. Especially when I'm not sure I even deserve it? What would you have me call you then? I'm not sure I'd want to call you douche canoe to your face.

Okay so I have absolutely no game. Shit on a stick. After a long silence I figure my attempt at flirting sucked even more than I thought, and he's not going to reply. I contemplate sending a text to Ade, but I decide against it. I'm still upset about what happened with him earlier, I completely humiliated myself.

I must have started nodding off because my phone vibrating wakes me with a shock.

\*\* **Ryan -** I'm honestly not sure you deserve it anymore either. x

Okay, confused.

\*\* **Ryan -** And yes, I meant to add the kiss.

> Well, hit me baby, one more freakin ' time! Just call me the queen of flirty texts. One text and he's sending me kisses? Well, a kiss. Singular. But he 'meant to send that kiss', that's what he said. But why, that's the question. Does he want to kiss me? Please God, please kiss me. That would make my entire life.
>
> What in the name of sweet Britney Jean does this all mean? How on earth am I supposed to sleep now? Well quite easily it would seem, because I soon drift off with thoughts of Ryan's kisses filling my dreams.

***

*Back the following day...*

> I rush outside, wanting to catch Ade before he leaves. Ryan smiles at me as he walks past with his patient. I smile back but I don't stop. I need to speak to Ade. Yesterday he told me that he had an offer of an apprenticeship in London and that he was going to head over there with Greg when he heads back home in October. I was devastated. I always knew Greg was only here temporarily, but Ade has always been here with me, and without them I won't have anyone.
>
> Earlier yesterday I had overheard my parents arguing because my mother wants to move back home to California. Ha! So now my dad and I are done there, *now* she wants to move back? We finally got back together as a family and she wants to break us up again, she always does this.

I have a mother who can't wait to get away from me at every chance she gets. Ryan can't decide if he can stand the sight of me or not, and now Ade, the first and only real friend I've ever had in my life, tells me he wants to leave me as well. My head was all over the place. I felt totally rejected by everyone, and I didn't want to lose Ade as well.

I don't know what came over me, but I made a move to kiss him. He pulled away as soon as I touched his lips with my own, telling me how I was just a kid. I'm not a kid, I'm a woman. He is only three years older than me and I wanted to show him that, so I pulled off my shirt, exposing my plain white bra that in hindsight, screamed 'I'm too young'.

I tried to kiss him again but he pushed me away and stood up so as not to look at me. I've never felt so humiliated. I've always known my body wasn't very attractive, but to show myself to a guy and have him not even want to see me, hurt more than I thought possible. Am I that really that hideous? I grabbed my shirt and ran the hell out of there. He called after me, but I was too embarrassed to even look back. Now I think I may have lost one of the only people who ever cared about me.

# CHAPTER 8

## Faith

Ade stands by his van waiting for me. I guess he wants to talk to me too, which is a good sign.

"Hey pretty gal, you okay?" He offers me his rogue smile, and I feel a little better already. I nod and smile back nervously. "I've been worried about you, Faithy. I'm sorry. I just… I was not expecting… What I mean is, I'm sorry Faithy. I just don't think of you in that way. That doesn't mean I don't care about you, very much, because I do!" He looks very sheepish and uncomfortable.

Ade is very attractive. He is tall and lean, with dark, coffee brown eyes. He has a very chiselled body, and silky-smooth dark skin with no visible imperfections. He is a flawless diamond. Ade is twenty-one, but his face is very boyish, he could easily pass for a high school senior. Honestly though, I don't really think of him that way either. There was a time when I might have had a little crush, but that's all it was. I was just upset and confused about Ryan, and I was angry with my mom. I don't really want to tell Ade any of this though, but I do want my friend back.

"No, please I'm sorry. I was just upset about you leaving, I didn't mean to embarrass myself like that," I say shamefully, and I wrap my arms around myself like I always do. When he pulls me in for a hug, I let him.

"Faithy, please don't worry, I should be the one to be sorry. I think you are a beautiful girl, I really do, but I haven't been truthful to you. See, I have been seeing someone for a while now, so I didn't want to take advantage of you, but I also didn't want to be disrespectful either."

Wow, this is news to me. I wonder who she is, I've never seen him with anyone like that before. I pull out of our hug but he continues to hold my hands.

"Wait, if you are with someone, then why are you going to London?" He gives me a frustrated look that tells me he isn't happy with my line of questioning. I pull away from his hold; either he is lying to save my feelings or he isn't telling me the whole story. I suddenly feel pissed off. Why does everyone treat me like a child.

"I thought we were friends?" I question and he shakes his head.

"We are Faithy!"

"Then why are you lying to me? You flirt with me all the time; don't you dare say that you don't! Then you treat me like I'm a child, patronising me the next? I put myself on a plate for you. I literally threw myself at you, and yeah okay, so it turns out you don't like me that way, even with all the flirting. That's fine, I get it, you don't need to be an asshole about it, I can handle the truth."

Someone clears their throat announcing their presence. It's Greg. He stands there with a serious look on his face that is highly unusual for him. Crap, did he overhear about me coming on to Ade? As if this situation wasn't embarrassing enough. Just kill me now. A silent exchange passes between the two of them before Greg looks back to me, and finally speaks.

"Ade is coming back to London with me, Faithy." I look between the two of them confused as to what's going on. I know that part, Ade already said. Greg looks to Ade before speaking directly to him

"We can trust her!" He says to him, but then turns back to me and continues. "Faith, you're our friend, and we both love the arse off of you, sweetheart, you know that. You aren't a child anymore, so you must know what this could mean for us if this got out?"

Greg raises an eyebrow waiting for me to catch on but I'm still a little confused. "I hope you understand why we kept it from you and I hope I was right to trust you with this?"

I look back to Ade who has a look of shame on his face. I look back to Greg who is also now looking at Ade, but Greg just looks hurt if anything. Greg shakes his head, clearly upset by Ade's reaction. He rolls his eyes and turns back to talk to me again, but I'm still trying to work out what in the hell is happening.

"Faithy, your old man wants you inside, his young patient is here." Greg strops off, barging past Ade in the process. Ade looks on after Greg, he goes to speak but nothing comes out. Finally, the penny drops and I've pieced everything together. Ade notices the moment understanding hits me. "I'm sorry," is all he says.

"No. Don't apologise, don't ever apologise for that. Not to anyone! I love you Ade. I just want you to be happy, and I love Greg, he's great. Honestly, I was just upset yesterday, that's all. I didn't mean to do what I did, I just didn't want to lose you. You're my best friend." I pull him back into me for another hug. He squeezes me, before slapping my ass like he usually does when no one else is around.

"You are beautiful, baby gal. I want you to know that. I think your heart belongs to someone else anyway?" He gestures with his head over to where Ryan is sitting on the doorstep. Looks like he is taking a break over the other side of the yard. Wow he is looking moodier than usual. Guess his good mood didn't last. He takes a sip of his drink, his eyes not leaving mine, and I wonder how much of our exchange he witnessed.

"He already knows. Greg told him about us last night." Ade shrugs and I grimace, wondering if Greg knew last night about what had happened between Ade and I. Guess I might owe Greg an apology too. I give Ade another hug before heading over towards Ryan. He looks pissed. Jeez, what could I have done now?

"Hey, busy day, huh?" *So lame Faith.*

He doesn't respond, instead choosing to take another gulp of his drink. "So, we're back to this now? Just so I know?" No response again, just another sip of his drink. Such a dick. "Okay. Nice chatting with you, bro!" I turn on my heels, knowing my dad is waiting.

"I'm not your fucking bro!" He spits angrily. "I guess some things never change, huh?" I turn back and he is still sitting on the step, looking like he is contemplating war.

"What exactly is that supposed to mean?" I've barely gotten my sentence out before he is shooting up out of his seat moving into my space, so I have no option but to step back against the wall. He cages me in like he did last time. His eyes are black and filled with hate.

"It means, Pork Chop, that once a slut, always a slut!"

Ouch.

This guy is giving me whiplash. One minute he is sending me kisses via text, next we are back to Pork Chop again? I can't keep up. "What, all the guys you've been through at school weren't enough for you?" He says bitterly, leaning right into my face again. Our noses are not even an inch apart. Just like last time, he makes me feel like he might kiss me at any moment.

"Such a sad little whore. You really should have fucking stayed in that shit sty I dumped you in. At least you fit in there with all the other greedy pigs!" So, it *was* him who put me in there. He doesn't give me any chance to respond, he just keeps going. Keeps attacking. *He wants to see you bleed.*

"Did you kiss him? He's supposed to be your friend, how pathetic are you? Are you honestly that desperate for cock? Hey, because if you are, let me know, I could use a quick fuck? You'll have to take it in the ass though, because no way am I sticking it in your filthy, used up cunt!"

"Please don't do this!" I plead, turning my face away from him, bitterly hurt by his words. Ryan slowly turns my face back to him, smirking at me, letting me know he won't stop until he breaks me.

"Well? Answer the fucking question, did you?" He seethes as if he was expecting an answer to his barrage of insults.

"Did I what, asshole?" What does he want from me?

"Did. You. Kiss. Him?" He says slowly, in a low voice, accentuating every word. His face is still so close to mine. Is he Jealous? The thought sends a flash of heat straight to my core. Surely not, why would he care? Feeling a little bolder than the last time we were here, I push his face away, out of my space.

"That's got nothing to do with you! I don't have to justify myself to you or to anyone else. You clearly don't know the first thing about me if that's honestly what you think of me, so I'd appreciate it if you stay the hell out of my business!" I push his whole body away this time and storm off back towards the clinic. I pass by Greg, who looks furious, like he was clearly watching what just happened. He raises a questioning eyebrow, but I don't want to talk.

"Just don't!" I snap at him, as I walk straight past him back inside.

I head into the treatment room with my dad after apologising for taking so long. Dad explained to me that this young girl was a child bride. As soon as she had her first period her husband had intercourse with her, resulting not only in severe trauma to the little girl, but also pregnancy. I feel sick to my stomach. I'm so angry, not just for her, but for all the girls this has happened to.

The girl is lying in the bed, and a woman I assume is her mother, is sitting next to her. I reserve my judgement of her, because I know it is more than likely that the same thing happened to her when she was young. Sadly, it's the reality for a lot of young girls in these parts. It's one of the many reasons my parents started this clinic, to help vulnerable women and children here. Sure, they help with minor medical needs for all the locals, but their main focus is on maternity and women's health, to make sure there is a safe place for these women to come.

Over here, nearly half of all girls are married before they're eighteen, and have experienced some form of physical violence and abuse. The reality is this girl will go back to her husband. My father will report it to various charities to try and get some official intervention for them, but he can't stop them from returning back. At least she has the clinic to help her through this pregnancy as safely as possible.

My father is almost through with the exam when the door opens and in walks Ryan. He is supposed to knock and wait, but he never seems to remember. He doesn't notice me or the girl's mother to the side of the room, he just sees my father. He looks freaked out at first, then before anyone knows what's happening he lunges for my father.

"What the hell is this? Get the fuck off of her, you disgusting prick! I'll fucking kill you with my bare hands, I swear to God!" Ryan pulls my father up from his stool like he weighs nothing, and throws him across the room. He lands two punches, one in his stomach and one square in his face. The girl on the bed starts screaming, and so does her mother, yelling 'what's happening' over and over in French. I run up to Ryan and grab his arm before it can land another punch on my father.

"Stop it Ryan, please stop, you're hurting him. He is still recovering, please stop. RYAN, PLEASE!" I scream as I tug on his arm. He suddenly swings around catching me hard in the chest with his elbow and I'm knocked back. He comes to a quick realisation that he's hurt me, and drops my dad on the floor. Only then does he breathlessly take in the scene around him.

He finally notices the girl's mother, now cradling her sobbing daughter, who is desperately trying to cover herself up. My dad coughs trying to stand up, but he is winded.

"I... I... I'm sorry. Please, *je suis désolé*. I'm sorry." Ryan apologises to the girl and her mother, before he storms out of the room.

I grab some dressing and some sterile water, and rush over to help my father.

"Daddy, are you okay? You might need a stitch on this eyebrow!" I say wiping the blood from my father's face.

"I'm fine, are you alright?" He visually checks me over but I'm fine.

"I'm okay. I don't know what that was about. He's not

normally aggressive like that, I've never even seen him fight before."

We try our best to calm the young patient and her mother down. My father and I have basic French at best, but between us we managed to explain that they were safe so that my dad could finish the exam, once we cleaned up his face. While the patient gets dressed my father pulls me to one side.

"Faith, please go grab Dr. Larke. I'd like to make sure they are both okay with what's happened, and I need someone to explain a few things about the pregnancy. Then maybe you should try and find Ryan, I think he will be upset about what happened."

Ryan must be upset, is he kidding? I am so angry and confused right now. I know this has something to do with what happened to my dad back in California. Ryan must have heard the horrible rumours that were sprayed all over our front door. That must be why he has been so off with my dad this whole time. It's taken Dad months to recover from what happened to him, this is bound to set him back, but yet here he is, more concerned about Ryan than himself.

"Sure, I'll be right back," I reluctantly agree. I run straight over to Greg's cabin and explain what's happened as quickly as I can.

"Oh bloody hell, Faithy. Little Ryan's got himself in a whole heap of dog shit hasn't he. What a dickhead! First, he lays into you in front of me, then he takes a hit at the boss man? He's not the smartest tool in the box, is he."

I shake my head, too upset to joke right now. "Look, I'll go help Dr. A, you go find that little arse-wipe and give him what for, yeah? You can tell that little prick I meant what I said to him earlier as well!" He says matter-of-factly as he rushes out. I have no idea what he said to Ryan earlier, but it's clear he definitely overheard our conversation before about me being the school slut. Crap, I hope he doesn't tell my parents.

I run around the back of the yard to the Jeep. I'm thinking Ryan couldn't have gotten very far on foot, so I'm surprised when I find him sitting down beside the Jeep.

"What the hell is wrong with you, asshole?"

"What the hell is wrong with me, what the hell is wrong with you? What the fuck was going on in there? Faith, why was your father examining a child like that, huh? What possible reason could he have for needing to see a child in that way, unless he is sick. He's fucking sick Faith, and you keep defending him. What the fuck is wrong with you?"

"Because she is pregnant, you ignorant bastard!" I shout so aggressively I'm almost spitting in his face. I probably shouldn't have broken a patient's confidence like that, but seeing as how he works for the clinic I guess it's okay. He looks at me, letting what I've said sink in.

"What? She's a child, how can she be pregnant?"

"She's thirteen, and she was a child bride, like millions of girls here are. She was cut, and then raped by her forty-year-old husband, and now she is pregnant. Pregnant with a child, that if it's a girl, will more than likely suffer the same fate as her. Is that reason enough for you? Jerk!"

He looks genuinely shocked. Who wouldn't be, and the realisation of what he has done is now sinking in. Guilt and regret creep across his face.

"I didn't know. I just saw... I just thought..."

"You really have no idea, do you? The people here? They lead very different lives to you and I. Maybe if you took your head out of your rich ass for a minute and stopped listening to all the bullshit rumours and lies, you could educate yourself on what's actually going on around the world!" I don't mean to sound condescending, but I'm just so frustrated with his recent behaviour.

Why can't I have my mystery boy back. My safe place.

Ryan's face is full of remorse and I start to feel bad for him. He seems genuinely sorry for what's happened, but he needs to fix this.

"You've pissed a lot of people off today, me included. I suggest you think about how you're going to make up for it," I warn, but internally I cringe at how patronising I still sound. I get into the Jeep. He stands up, but he doesn't move.

"Are you getting in or what?" I don't mean to be so short, but I am still worried about my dad. He swallows, and brushes his hands over his face and through his hair. He doesn't get in though, instead he comes around to the driver's side and opens the door. He takes my hand and gently pulls me out of the car.

Ryan leads me up the small dirt path that goes down to the waterfront. He hasn't spoken so I have no idea what's happening, but I follow him anyway. We come to a stop when we get to the water. It's private down here as there isn't another property around for at least a mile or so. He takes his shoes off and gestures for me to do the same. I take them off and fold up the bottom of my pants, and we walk a little into the water, just enough to cool our feet. He takes my hand again.

"I'm so sorry. I jumped to conclusions, I saw the girl and I just saw red. I've been doing that a lot lately. I saw her and I wanted to protect her, that's all, but I lost control. I didn't assess the whole situation." He shakes his head admonishing himself. His soft, wild curls bouncing across his sad eyes.

"I'm really sorry *Foi*, I truly am. I really do want to be here, I want to learn so I can help. I know I don't deserve it, but can you please forgive me?" He puts a hand on my chest where he elbowed me, but then awkwardly realises he is now touching my boobs, and embarrassed, he pulls it off quickly. Hmm... Not so smooth, is he nervous?

"Forgive you for what? What just happened with my dad, or for being an asshole in general? You said some pretty shitty things to me earlier."

"I was an asshole earlier, all week in fact, I know that. I'm fucked up, and I wouldn't blame you for not wanting anything more to do with me, but *Ma Foi*, the thought of you sending me away kills me." He picks up a loose strand of my hair again and puts it behind my ear. He looks so sincere. My heart doesn't miss how he called me *Ma Foi* again. *My Faith*. Do I even want to be His Faith?

How can he keep switching from one extreme to the other each time I see him? One minute I'm a slut he couldn't bear to touch, next I'm 'His Faith'? If I hadn't seen it with my own eyes, I'd swear the boy standing here in front of me could never have been the same boy that just beat on my dad. Or the one who deliberately hurts me with his hateful words.

I shake my head. Why am I so weak for him? *Because you're still in love with him. You know it's only one sided, right?*

I shake off the thought. I don't want to believe that, although in my gut I know it's true. Ryan has had my heart since the moment he held me so protectively, tight to his chest, like I was the most precious thing in the world. Funny thing is, it turned out I was anything but precious to him. I was nothing to him. My heart was nothing, and he shows me how little I mean to him every time he beats me down.

"Listen Faith, I am sorry about what happened before, the things I said. It really is none of my business who you kiss. I do know that, but when I heard you talk about it, I didn't like it. I shouldn't have lashed out at you like that, I can be a dick sometimes. Well most of the time actually, I know that too, but I am trying not to be."

He doesn't like it? It stung a bit to hear him say it wasn't any of his business, but then he said he doesn't like it. Is it the thought of me kissing Ade he didn't like or the thought of me kissing anyone? What does that mean? *Why don't you just suck it up and ask?*

I reach deep into Inner Britney to try and find my lady balls. C'mon Faith, *work* bitch!

"W-why didn't you like it?" I tremble as I speak. He looks at me, and his eyes are black, but they are different to before. He still has a hold of my hand, and I feel his grip tighten slightly, before loosening. Something tears inside of me when he eventually let's go, and I instantly miss his touch.

"I honestly don't know, but I'm trying to figure it out." He walks back a few paces and sits down on the shoreline, his feet still on the water's edge. He looks so beautiful with the late afternoon sun illuminating his face. He closes his eyes and drops his head slightly. His hair is hanging over his eyes a little in that sexy way that does something to my insides, and all I want to do is run my fingers through it.

"I'm actually trying to figure a lot of shit out lately. Like why do I fucking hate the thought of another dude kissing you? Why am I such a dick all the time now? Why do I find it easier to spit venom, rather than just say how I really feel?" He opens his eyes and looks at me as I sit down next to him.

"So many fucking questions. Why did my girlfriend cheat on me with my so-called friend, and why don't I seem to give a fuck about it? About either of them. Why haven't I spoken to any of my real friends back in London for months? Why am I applying to spend four years of my life in New York, when I'd rather be anywhere else in the world, except there? Why doesn't my father give a shit what I want? Why doesn't he care that my mother died? Why did Mom have to go and…"

His eyes turn a little glassy, but I can tell he isn't going to let his guard down any more than he already has. "Fuck it. It doesn't matter." He takes a deep breath and so do I, the scent of him filling my nose. "It's just a fucking lot going on in my head right now. If you and your family want me to leave I get it, I'll be out of here by tomorrow, but I'd rather stay. I want to try to make amends for what I've done?"

I don't know what to think of all the information he has just given me. It is a lot and I don't know how to even respond to half of it. I take his hand back in mine and pull us both up to stand before pulling him in tightly for a hug. It's all I can think to do, and to be honest as angry as I was, I can't help but think he needs one right now. My father was right to send me after him.

"I accept your apology," I say quietly, breathing him in again as I hold him. I'm sure I feel him doing the same to me as his hold on me tightens. I grip his shirt, just like that first time, I don't know why but something tells me he needs me to hold on to him as tightly as I can.

"Why didn't you send one back to me?" he barely whispers. Huh?

"Send what back?"

"A kiss…"

I'm a little taken back by his question, but for the first time I don't think about my answer, I just say what I'm feeling.

"Because when I kiss you for the first time, I want it to be a real one." With that I pull away. He looks at me, and half smiles, totally bewildered. I have no idea where the confidence to admit that came from, but yep, I'm a total badass.

Keeping hold of his hand, I lead us back towards the clinic. Ryan hesitates when we get to the door, but I gesture with my head for him to go inside. If he wants to stay here, he needs to prove it, and he can start by apologising to my dad.

# CHAPTER 9

## Ryan

The clinic isn't open on Saturdays, so I only had to come in for the morning to help Charity do some inventory, but now, finally it's my day off. After my sixth night of trying to sleep on a bed of rocks, I think it's about time I head over to see this "emergency" apartment that my father has stashed away. Serves him right for not defining what constitutes an emergency. Personally, I'd say being on the brink of putting my back out through lack of a decent mattress is sufficient enough for me to go see what's up.

I'm hoping there might be some Wi-Fi over there so I can hit up Greg's fundraising page, and chase up our house keeper for the packages I asked to be shipped over. The Old Farmhouse does have internet but it's on limited data, and it's pretty unreliable anyway so I've waited to see if there is any at the mystery pad.

I need a ride though, and plus I have no idea how to get there so I'm heading over to Faith's cabin to see if she will drive me. I know it's a bit rich me asking any sort of favour from her after the shit I've pulled, but I'm hoping whoever this new and improved Faith is nowadays is as forgiving as she seems, and does me a solid. *Is it really her who's changed, or is it you, asshole?*

I'm so fucking tired, and confused. After that bullshit yesterday with Dr. Asher with that little girl, my head is all over the place, and now I don't know what to think. I saw red when I walked in and saw what he was doing. I immediately thought he was hurting her. What was I supposed to think?

I was in a haze of anger, I didn't even notice Faith or the kid's mother were also in the room. All I could think about was Mia and what that bastard had done to her. There was no one to protect Mia, so I wanted to protect this little girl. If Faith hadn't pulled me off I don't know what I might have done, the rage inside me had completely taken over. I felt even angrier than I had done when I beat the shit out of him the first time.

I don't even recognise myself anymore. It took a minute for me to even notice Faith was pulling on my arm, screaming at me to stop, and I feel terrible for catching her with my elbow like that.

When she ripped me a new one for jumping the gun, I'll admit I felt like a total tool. I knew things like that went on in the world, but it didn't occur to me for a moment that I would ever come across anything like that in my lifetime. I'm so angry with myself. If anything, I was the one who had scared the little girl and her mother, and I made what was a nightmare situation for them ten times worse. Yep, I'm a grade A prick, but honestly who could blame me for jumping to conclusions, knowing what I know?

I briefly apologised to Dr. Asshat for what I'd done, but I felt sick inside doing it. He might have been innocent then, but he is still accountable for his past crimes. Luckily for me, he was so busy having his eye stitched up by Greg, that he was distracted enough to think my apology was sincere. He even said there was no need for me to leave.

He did ask me if I was sure there wasn't anything else I wanted to talk to him about, which was a little weird. I wondered if Greg had told him about the exchange he witnessed between Faith and I earlier, but he promised he wouldn't say anything and he looked equally unsure of what Malcolm was asking. When I'd said no, Malcolm seemed a little disappointed, but told me we would have a proper chat over the weekend about it. Great, can't wait for that.

I actually had no idea he was a gynaecologist up until yesterday. For some reason it just never occurred to me to find out what kind of doctor he was in California. I guess back home I just assumed he was another asshole plastic surgeon persuading rich housewives, and desperate side pieces, into bigger tits and smaller noses.

I mean over here, well of course, I've seen him do actual doctor things you know, like check-ups and treat infections and shit like that. Obviously, I didn't think he was over here giving free cosmetic consultations, I'm not that much of a dumbass. I just didn't realise the clinic was just a front to help abused women and children. It's not like anyone told me any of that when I started.

Faith said they work with charities who refer people to the clinic, whilst at the same time giving free minor medical care to those who need it. What I can't get my head around though, is why he would be helping so many people, when he is guilty of the same abuse himself? Is it guilt, is that why he does it? I don't fucking know what to think.

Truth be told, if I didn't know what I already know about him, I'd actually think he was a pretty stand-up guy. Like, he was pretty cool yesterday accepting my apology. I'm surprised he didn't have me out on my ass, tapping my father up for a payoff.

Or like the other day, he was telling me about the time he and Lorrie spent volunteering down in New Orleans after Katrina, even with a young Faith in tow. God, my mom would have loved him. As soon as he mentioned Katrina, I knew she'd have been sold, being from Louisiana herself.

Apparently, they only settled in California when it was time for Faith to start high school. They thought she'd have a better chance at getting into a decent college if she graduated from St. Edmund's, but she'd been home schooled before that. They've taken her with them all over the world, teaching her as they went. It's no wonder she's so protective of her dad, she's never had a chance to make any real long-term friends, it's mostly been her and her parents. Explains why she's so awkward sometimes too.

On paper they all sound like good, salt-of-the-earth people, but I can't forget the things I know. I don't trust him, and I refuse to let my guard down with any of them. Although it's easier said than done with Lorrie, where she is so nice all the damn time, and as for Faith, who the fuck knows.

As I come to the door of Faith's cabin, I can hear her singing *'That Don't Impress Me Much'* at the top of her voice. Shania Twain, seriously? This chick needs a serious overhaul of her playlist. I open the door to find Faith dancing around the room wearing nothing but a black sports bra, and a pair of the biggest black granny panties I've ever seen. Her comfy undies I assume.

A mixing bowl under one arm, and a wooden spoon in her other hand which she's using as a microphone in between slapping buttercream from the bowl haphazardly onto a cake. Although this scene is not one bit sexy in theory, I'm instantly frozen in place at the sight of her.

Faith's body is just, wow. This chick has some seriously sexy curves, comfy underwear or not. Everything is jiggling in all the right places. She bounces around the kitchen not giving a fuck, and she's totally oblivious to me standing there. I know I should probably announce myself but I can't seem to speak. I don't think I've ever been rendered speechless by a girl before; the fuck is wrong with me?

I watch her some more, mesmerised as if I'm seeing her for the first time. She's happy. I don't think I've ever actually seen her so carefree like this. This girl actually looks like fun, where has she been hiding? *With Ade, no doubt, he always seems to have her smiling.*

I don't know why that thought guts me, but it does. Greg told me Ade isn't into her that way, so why am I jealous. Do I want to be the one to make her smile, is that it? I haven't stopped thinking about her all week, and jealousy creeps in every time he's around. I need to figure shit out fast.

She looks amazing like this. Where has she been hiding these delicious curves. Every time I've seen her she has on an old baggy slogan tee-shirt over yoga pants. Even her school uniform is at least two sizes too big, now that I remember it.

I gotta admit I've noticed her toned legs and peachy ass plenty this week. I may not like her all that much, but I am still a guy. It's hard not to notice when she's in those tight pants, especially the other night when she was actually doing yoga. Fuck, she looked insane in some of those poses. She still had a loose vest on though, so this is the first time I'm seeing the whole package, and damn baby. I gotta admit I'm feeling it.

I actually never really got the whole calling her fat thing anyway if I'm being honest. She's not fat at all, it's just Mia kept calling her a fat pig, and then Shane called her Pork Chop, and I guess it kinda stuck. It was a dick move carrying it on over here, I know.

Watching her move she's unbelievably sexy, and she has no idea, which makes her appeal even greater. I forget myself for a minute and start picturing myself throwing her up on the counter, ripping that ugly as hell bra right over her head letting her perfect looking tits bounce free. I bet they are perfect as well. I wonder if she would moan out my name if I sucked on them a bit, or is she the type that would bite her lip and hold it in.

Fuck, I'd make sure she had my name on her lips, over and over again. The way she's moving her ass around, I imagine how it would feel pressed against me. I wonder what she tastes like? Sweet as that vanilla frosting I bet.

As I watch her I think about sliding a finger or two inside of her. I'd be sure to make her come on my fingers just so I can watch her suck them clean. Then I'd pull those big ass panties off, and pound myself into her over and over, while she wraps those thick creamy thighs around my waist. I can almost hear her begging me to fuck her harder. Fuck, and now my dick is responding.

The song ends abruptly, bringing me back to reality, and I manage to adjust myself just in time before she notices me, and my rogue dick. I can't help but enjoy the look of pure horror on her face when she realises I've been watching her prance around. Good. I hope she is embarrassed.

I don't know what I was just thinking. Surely, I would never fuck this girl even if she did beg for it? I mentally scold myself for entertaining those earlier thoughts. But who am I kidding really. I definitely would. As soon as she wraps her arms around her waist like she always does, it causes her tits to squeeze together. I can't help but picture them in my mouth again... What the hell is wrong with me, do I actually want this chick? *Umm, duh! She's hot as fuck, whoever says different is a lying asshole.*

Okay, so I guess the truth is I do know I've been feeling something for her, something that I can't seem to shake. She doesn't seem to be who I thought she was before, and I'm definitely confused about who she really is. I can't help but wonder if maybe she's changed. Fuck that, people don't change, not really. I decide to go cutthroat, not only to remind myself who she really is, but to remind her what I think of her.

"Nice moves, Pork Chop. You think you could put some clothes on, some of us just ate!" *Woah, you are such a prick sometimes. Aren't you the one who came here to ask her for a favour?*

The words leave a bitter taste in my mouth and it feels a lot like regret. I'm such a fucking tool, why did I say that? Faith is already rushing about the room in a panic, I assume looking for her clothes, but I don't miss the hurt on her face at the sting of my words. Shit, I'm an asshole.

"Oh no, oh no, oh no, please God, no! Fuck, where the fuck is my shirt, it was right here! Fuck, fuck, fuck!"

Faith shrieks out, losing her shit. I think that's the first time I've ever heard her curse like that, now that I think about it.

She's frantically looking around now, with one arm still across her stomach as if trying to hide it, the other tossing things around looking for her clothes. She trips over her own feet while she rushes around the room. At this point I don't know why she doesn't just go to the closet and grab something else but she seems to be getting herself too worked up to think straight. Wait, she's breathing funny, is she hyperventilating? Fuck.

"Look, calm down *Foi*. It was just a joke, okay. Trust me, there is absolutely nothing indecent about *those* panties. Besides, I'm pretty sure plenty of guys have seen you wearing a lot less, so chill out!"

She freezes, straightens up and then turns to me, putting both arms around her middle now, hugging herself protectively. Why does she keep doing that? She doesn't look up at me, she looks down, as if she can't bear to look me in the eye. For some reason that thought feels like a punch to my fucking soul.

"I can't find my shirt," she says breathlessly, her voice breaking. She's still struggling to breathe right. "Please don't tell anyone about this," she whispers. Tears start rolling down her face, and she desperately tries to calm her breathing down. Fuck, I just wanted her to be a bit embarrassed, I didn't want to make her cry like this. Now I really do feel like an asshole.

I tear off my hoodie and wrap it around her, and she flinches at my touch. What the hell, I'd never hurt her. I might hate her but I'd never physically hurt her. Well not on purpose anyway, and she said she knew yesterday was an accident. So why the reaction?

It's then that I remember Shane did hurt her, deliberately. He slapped her hard around the face, and he kicked her in the side sending her tumbling off the back of my truck. When we took the hood off, her face was covered in blood from the fall. Fucking dick. What kind of lowlife lays a hand on a girl that way. A girl who has got a bag over her head with her hands bound at that. Even if she is a total bitch, that's disgusting.

I should've fucking told him off properly at the time, now she probably thinks that I'm down with it and I think that kinda shit was acceptable. Fuck. Nothing about that night was acceptable, none of it. Whatever she has done, it doesn't make any of what I did okay.

"Look Faith, I'm sorry. I didn't mean to upset you, I wasn't spying on you, I just came to ask for a ride." I say taking a step back, trying not to scare her more than I already have.

She pulls the sides of my hoodie around herself tightly like a security blanket, and looks up at me with pained eyes. My hoodie swamps her, coming down just below her ass. She looks so small right now. I watch as another tear slowly falls down her cheek and I start to realise what's actually going on here. She's not embarrassed that I caught her dancing around and singing, she's hiding her body because she's ashamed of it.

Why on earth would she be ashamed, I have no idea? She's smoking hot. I start to think about all the times I've called her Pork Chop, and instantly feel a twist in my stomach. *Maybe that's why, asshole?*

Mom would be so mad at me right now. Knowing I've made a girl feel insecure about her body this way, I know she would tell me she was ashamed of me, and that fucking kills me.

I feel so confused. All I want to do now is comfort Faith, tell her she's actually so fucking beautiful and beg for her forgiveness. But a big part of me, the part that hates her for what she did to Mia, wants her to feel this way. I wanted her tears, like I wanted her father's blood. I wanted to see her covered in pig shit that day, so what the fuck does that make me?

I surprise myself when my hand seems to come to her face of its own volition, and wipes away her tears. "I'm sorry," is all I can get out. *Coward.*

She goes to pull away, but before I know what's happening I've pulled her into me, and my lips are crashing down on hers. She did say she wanted a real kiss after all. Faith is frozen at first, and doesn't respond to my lips, so I tease hers to part with my tongue. She allows it, and I immediately claim her mouth with my own. Slowly, Faith begins to respond, meeting my tongue with hers in a delicate dance.

I slow my own frenzied kiss to meet her gentle pace, and it's dizzying. She tastes like sugar and buttercream frosting, exactly how I imagined. I'm presuming that's from the cake she was making, but she's fucking delicious in a way that I did not see that coming. I'm surprised at how right this feels.

You might be surprised to learn I haven't actually kissed that many girls. I'm not your typical man-whore, but I can honestly say, this kiss is already the best fucking kiss of my life. I want more of her. I need more of her.

My hands drop to her full round ass and I squeeze it greedily, before pulling her tightly against my body, showing her exactly how worked up she has gotten me. As soon as she feels my dick she pushes me away and breaks our kiss. Shit, did I read this wrong? I'm barely getting my breath back when she slaps me, right across my face. The fuck?!

"Get out! I don't know what game you're playing now, or why you constantly want to break my heart, but I won't ever let you fool me again. I am not a pig, Ryan. I'm not a fucking pig. You're a pig! YOU'RE THE FUCKING PIG! Now get the fuck out!" She screams like a banshee, her eyes filled with an insane fire I've never seen in her before. I am in fucking awe.

Why is an angry chick telling you off just sexy as hell?

Faith storms into the bathroom slamming the door behind her, leaving me with a red face, blue balls, and a shiny new crack I wasn't expecting in my already shattered black heart.

# CHAPTER 10

## *Faith*

Arrrrgh! What the hell was that? Of all the people to see me dancing half naked it had to be him. God why? Why do these things always happen to me? Of course, he had to be a complete dick about it too.

"*Put some clothes on, Pork Chop, some of us just ate,*" I say out loud in my best bratty voice. Such a dick.

Argh! I feel a familiar lump form in my throat at the sting of his words. Am I really that disgusting to him? Back to Pork Chop again as well. That hurts every time he says it. That was always Shane's thing, and I could ignore it because he was just some asshole I hated anyway, but now when Ryan says it, it kills me.

I throw the cake I was making in the fridge before the buttercream melts. God, I hate him now! I wish he would just go back home to California. Or even better, London!

Except of course, I don't. I wish I could hate him, but I can't. I've loved having him here every day, even if he has been a total dickwad. I wish I didn't feel this way about him, he's clearly *not* a nice guy, not to me anyway, but I can't help it.

I've thought about what it would be like to be kissed by him since the first day I saw him. Fantasised about being his girlfriend.

I imagine myself looking all cute, wearing his shirts or his letterman jacket. Ryan would wrap his arms around my waist and kiss my neck, telling me his shirts all look better on me anyway. You know, just like how guys do on TV. I've thought about that a lot, even after the pig incident. I'd imagine he would tell me how sorry he was for being a part of it all that day, and how he would kill his friends if they ever tried to hurt me again.

I know I'm being foolish. I guess things like that probably do only ever happen on TV.

Plus, you know, he hates me, there is that. But then, he *did* kiss me, and he was hard, I felt it. Can a guy fake that? Kissing him was everything I imagined it would be, but why did it have to be like that, right after yet another insult. Did he know he was taking my first kiss, is that why he did it? No, that can't be it. I know he's just like the rest of the guys at school, he thinks I'm a slut. He basically just called me one when he told me plenty of guys had seen me naked. Ha! Yeah right.

Even if I told him I was still a virgin, he would never believe me. He believes all of the lies. I just wish I knew what I had done to deserve any of this. My heart twists and I feel a familiar burn behind my eyes, but I'm done crying. No more tears for you, McDickface!

I finish getting dressed and I have half a mind to go find him. I want answers and it's about time he gave them to me, starting with the day of the pigs. I grab his hoodie and throw it back on. I figure why not, it's the least he can do. Plus, it smells like him, and I want it, so why the hell not. *God you're pathetic.*

He smells like the ocean, or more the warm evening breeze off the beach, with of course that delicious coconut fragrance mixed in. He really is a California dream. Yep. Definitely still love him. Sweet Britney Jean. I start to hear the song *'Toxic'* in my head, the lyrics actually seeming really appropriate right about now. I've had one little taste of his toxic freakin' lips and just like Britney said I would be, I'm seriously slipping under.

I head outside with a purpose to my step, but I'm stopped in my tracks when I see him standing there leaning against the Jeep, frowning as he looks at his phone. Now that I have his hoodie, he is wearing a fitted black tee that shows off the strong muscles on his arms, with some low hanging, light grey sweats that match the hoodie he gave me. What is it about a boy in sweats, totally hot right?

He is so gorgeous, it hurts to look at him right now. Jeez, there goes Inner Brit with that song again. He spots me and moves to put his phone away, offering me an awkward smile.

"Just updating your friends, I take it? 'Guess what guys I just saw Pork Chop half naked and she's hella' fat'. Newsflash dickwad, I'm pretty sure they already know that. What do you want anyway? Haven't you humiliated me enough for one lifetime?"

He frowns again and pushes off the Jeep putting his hands in his pockets sheepishly.

"Listen *Foi*, I don't really know what to say. I'm really sorry about what happened, but I promise you there is no hidden agenda. I was honestly just coming over to ask for a ride, which I still could really use by the way?" He flashes me a little grin, silently pleading with me to agree. I stare at him, trying my best to hold my face in indifference. If he wants anything from me he's going to have to try harder than that. I fold my arms for added effect. *Faith Asher, Boss Bitch.*

"Look, I know we haven't got off on the best foot, and I

guess that's my fault. Well actually, it is totally my fault, but uh, maybe we can start over?" Now there's an understatement. Is he nervous? He lowers his head but continues looking at me through his gorgeous hair and I instantly feel my resolve start to slip. Damn it, my weakness for him starts with his beautiful curls.

Inner Brit pipes up again, but this time I can't help but smirk. He *is* a toxic bastard and he knows it, and I am severely addicted to him. He must see the slip of my mask because he gives me a brilliant smile, the kind that hits me right in my granny panties.

"Listen, my dad has a place somewhere nearby. I wanted to go check it out, but I don't know how to get there. If you did me a solid and gave me a ride, maybe I could repay the favour?" He takes my hand and pulls me closer, and my tummy somersaults thinking about our kiss. "I really am sorry. You have actually been really nice to me, even though I didn't deserve it. I guess what I'm saying is, maybe we could be friends? Start over?"

Friends. Why does that burn more than it should. He didn't mention the kiss; does he regret it? Is he back with Mia, is that who he was texting? *Calm down girl, just be normal for once.*

"W-what sort of favour?" I say, hoping desperately that he wants another kiss. *Unlikely.*

"Well, I'm guessing you like my hoodie, seeing how you're still wearing it?" he says, tugging at the sides pulling me even closer. Is he flirting with me? "How about I let you borrow it for a while? It looks better on you anyway."

Woah! Hold the friggin' phone. Did he just say that. For real?

"Okay sure, yeah, I'll give you a ride!" How those words

came out of my mouth, when in my head Inner Brit is still singing *Toxic*, I don't know. I wanted to make him squirm some more, but apparently, offer me your sweater for a few days and I'm yours.

"You gotta swear you won't tell anyone you saw me in my underwear, you hear me? Forget it happened!"

"I promise," he says offering up a Scout's honour sign. "I won't say anything to anyone, and I definitely wasn't messaging anyone about it just then either. I swear." Ryan offers me his pinkie. I can't help but smile and join it with mine. He's pinkie-promised me now.

"I'm not sure I want to forget it just yet though, I kinda enjoyed the show," he winks at me. The bastard winks at me. Not sure if he is actually flirting with me or making fun of me I continue, ignoring his joke.

"Also, you can stop calling me Pork Chop! Or any other pig related names. My name is Faith, got it?"

"Yes ma'am, of course. Faith. I got it. I've been a dick for that. I heard it one day, and it just stuck in my head. But I won't say it again, I promise!" This time he crosses his heart. He offers me a big warm genuine smile, teeth and all and I find myself fully thawed to him once more. What was I even mad about again?

"You actually have a great body, *Foi*. I don't know why you hide it. I gotta say, I thought you looked pretty hot back there wearing just my hoodie. I'm going to be dreaming about that later, that's for sure."

My cheeks redden as I look at him and raise my eyebrows.

"Oh please. I've already agreed to give you a ride, you don't need to butter me up!"

He laughs a proper belly laugh and it throws me off guard. Not knowing whether to trust him or not, I decide why not. I've got another two weeks with him, I may as well give him a chance. I'll be keeping my walls firmly up though. *Yeah right, sure you will, ha!*

I put on my seat belt and turn on the stereo and as if the music gods are speaking for me, *'Quit Playing Games with My Heart'* by the Backstreet Boys comes on. He groans out loud as he also buckles up, and then it's my turn to laugh.

He said I have a great body, and whether it was bullshit or not, I'm gonna take it as a compliment. Feeling like an empowered badass, I pull my shades on and drive. I only move us a few hundred feet before telling him matter-of-factly,

"By the way, I'm keeping the hoodie, it's not a loaner!"

He laughs again at that and it's beautiful.

"It's yours *Mon Bébé*, so long as you let me borrow it now and again."

My Baby.

I love that.

Sweet home Kentwood, Louisiana; now I'm definitely in trouble.

# CHAPTER 11

## Faith

We drove for about twenty minutes along the coast of the lake. The breeze feels so good and whilst it makes my hair blow out like crazy, it only serves to make Ryan's windswept curls even more attractive.

After what happened this morning, I expected the journey to be awkward as hell, but actually it was great. Ryan even made me laugh a few times, like actually laugh out loud, laugh. It was the most relaxed that things had ever been between us, and my embarrassment from earlier had long disappeared by the time we got there.

When he gave me the address I recognised it straight away as being a rich, private complex on the lakefront. I don't know why I feel disappointed, but I do. This place is the epitome of white privilege and exploitation of local people. With their high walls and armed security, the land was bought for a pittance from the local people. It was turned into a golf and spa complex, with a small boutique hotel, cutting off access to that part of the lake for the locals in the process.

Each of the private bungalows on the estate sold for over four million dollars. Can you believe that? The things that sort of money could do around here, it makes me sick. We pull up to the electric gates, the high walls and trees not giving any hint to what's inside.

A large muscled guard comes to the gate and I gotta admit I shit my pants at the sight of his equally large gun. Sensing my unease, Ryan gives me what I'm sure was intended as a reassuring touch on my thigh, but actually causes butterflies in my tummy and my cheeks to flame.

"Hey, wait here I'll go talk to him," he smirks, noticing my reaction to his touch. He winks at me again as he gets out of the car. Bastard.

He takes out his wallet and hands the guard a pass of some kind. The guard looks at it and back to Ryan, and I'm literally dying inside praying he doesn't decide we are trespassing. The guard starts pointing and gesturing off towards the other side of the complex. Ryan shakes the guard's hand and heads back towards the Jeep.

"All sorted baby, drive in!" Baby again? This is giving me anxiety, maybe Pork Chop wasn't so bad after all.

I drive in and follow the road all the way to the back, to the largest of all the bungalows. We pull up and start to head in. There's a big sign over the front door and I read it out loud.

"Bungalow 21? Sounds like some sort of nightclub or something."

"It's tacky as fuck, but that's my father for you." Ryan presses his finger print to a panel on the side of the door and it opens.

"Okay, finger print entry to a beach house? Now that is tacky as fuck," I add, even though I actually think it's pretty cool.

"Ladies first!" Ryan smiles at me, as he holds the door open for me to walk in first. I don't know why, but this small gesture gives me butterflies again. My mom always says there is nothing more attractive than good manners and a kind heart. Ryan definitely has great manners that's for sure, but does he have a kind heart? Guess I'll find out soon enough.

"My dad has them installed at all his properties. I've never even been to half of them, but it's all linked to the same security system so I can access any of them if and when I wanted."

"Holy shit, look at this place!" I walk inside and I'm completely stunned. Whilst I'm sure this is by no means the sort of luxury Ryan must be used to; with his fourteen bathroom's and all, but compared to the way the local people live, hell, even compared to our house back in California, this is a freakin' palace. Albeit an all-white, minimalist, open-plan, palace. There's a whole lot of white. Reminds me of a dentist room actually.

Ryan looks around disinterested, he's not one bit impressed, but then he is used to luxury I guess. He opens some French doors leading onto a deck, and wow, what a view. The lake is right outside and I can't help but walk out to appreciate it.

"Just give me a minute will you, I have something I need to do. Feel free to look around. Wherever you want, there's nothing personal here," Ryan offers as he heads back inside.

It's beautiful out here. The sound of the birds on the lake fills the air, it's so peaceful and romantic. I can understand why someone would want to be here, but what I can't understand is how they can ignore what's happening on the other side of the wall. After about ten minutes Ryan comes out and joins me with two glasses of orange juice in his hands.

"Sorry, I just had to go online real quick so I could donate to Greg's fundraiser." He says casually, offering me a glass that

I happily accept. "Can you believe the entire fridge is stocked? I guess my father knew I'd end up coming here. He will get an alert that I've activated the door, so if he didn't, he does now," he adds, raising his eyebrows playfully like he is breaking some rules by being here. I gladly take a large sip and enjoy the sweet sugary taste.

"Mmm... thank you, this is delicious. That's really nice of you. I'm sure it will mean a lot to Greg. He trains really hard."

"You're telling me. My whole body felt like it was on fire yesterday, I don't think I'll walk right for a week." Ryan makes a show of trying to loosen himself up by stretching, with the same innocent smile on his face he wore earlier. "He said that was an easy run for him too. Sixteen miles is an easy run, what the hell? He's gotta be so determined, and physically strong. To push himself like that in this heat? I respect that a lot."

Ryan seems genuinely in awe of Greg as he speaks about him which warms my heart. We haven't known Greg all that long but he is already like family. I'm going to be so proud of him when he races. "He's actually a great guy. He sure thinks highly of you by the way," Ryan continues. He certainly is chatty when he lets his mask slip. It doesn't surprise me what he said about Greg, he tells me all the time how much he 'loves the arse off me'.

Ryan looks at me a little more seriously now. "You know he heard everything yesterday, right? Man, was he pissed at me. I deserved everything he said to me, threatened to 'kick my arse' if I ever upset you like that again. I respect that too, to be honest. I'm glad you finally have someone at your back. When I met you that first day I thought...? I don't know what I thought. I don't know what happened since then, everything is so fucked up."

Ryan looks out to the ocean, his eyes full of regret. He seems so real right now, not that fake guy in my Dad's office a few days ago. Not the guy who keeps calling me Pork Chop. This is the real Ryan, the Ryan I fell for. As much as I hate this place, a part of me never wants to leave while he's back to being himself here.

"It's beautiful, isn't it? The water? It's amazing," I change the subject, trying to lighten the mood.

"You know we live right near the beach, right. The Pacific Ocean? It's nothing special." I look at Ryan, confused by his blasé attitude.

"You don't like the beach?" If he says no he will break my heart because everything about him reminds me of the beach. He smirks and brushes his hand through his curls. His hair looks salty from the drive. It's slightly lighter in parts, the sun giving him some natural highlights. The beach suits him, he has to love it.

"Yeah, of course I like the beach, and this is pretty enough, but my idea of a beauty spot is like mountains or forests. I love being outside in nature. When I was at school in London, I went to stay at my friend's house in the Scottish Highlands for a weekend. Now that's what I call breath-taking scenery," he says enthusiastically, his face lighting up as he speaks about it. I love seeing him like this.

"Wow, I bet that was amazing, I've only ever seen pictures but it looks fantastic! I love the beach though, the sounds of the waves and the smells, it's my happy place." I refrain from telling him he smells like the beach to me, and that's one of the reasons why I love it. "Forests and mountains, I've never been anywhere like that, but it all looks so beautiful. I'd love to go someday, especially Scotland, wow. And snow! I'd love to see snow!"

"Wait, you've never seen snow? Seriously?" He looks at me like I'm an alien.

"Well, no. I've been to a lot of places with my folks, but they have all been hot mostly, or like wet and humid. I've never been anywhere cold enough to have snow. Did you know you can actually go to Lapland to meet Santa? Freakin' Santa dude, can you imagine? Husky rides, reindeer, the Northern Lights. Seriously cool. Now *that* is a place I'd love to go to one day, that's right on the top of my bucket list." I say excitedly, enjoying this new relaxed vibe we have going on.

"That does sound pretty awesome," he responds, smiling a genuinely warm smile and it makes my insides flip.

"Let's do it *Foi*, you and me. I mean I'm not sure I've been on the nice list for a while now, but hey, let's go see the big man in red and find out?" He says, sounding sincere. The bastard winks again, sending all sorts of signals to my lady junk. What is it about a guy winking at you that makes you feel all giddy? This boy definitely knows what he is doing to me, judging by his smug grin.

"Well, you'd have to promise, we will do it together or not at all, no cheating! I don't trust you to go without me, you'll sneak me on that naughty list for sure," I say playfully. I know he was just teasing me about us going together, but I feel a lump the size of an iceberg form in my throat at how much I want that.

"Okay, I pinkie-promise. You, me and the big man in red." Another pinkie-promise. Does he really mean that? We walk back inside and he starts to refill our glasses.

"Well, I hear he wears green actually. Ooh and can we do Paris as well? Oh and London too, now that would be amazing! Do you miss it?"

"London? Desperately." He says sadly, passing me a second glass of the deliciously sweet orange juice. "You were right before, I do miss my friends. I only have a select few, but they are solid gold. It's not the same with Levi and Shane. Well, I guess you know about Shane and Mia, but whatever. I really miss the soccer vibe there too. Like, it's okay at school and everything, but in England they live and breathe it all the time, you know."

I'm too afraid to sit on the white couch so I stand in the middle of the room like an idiot looking around. The air becomes thick as Ryan stalks over to me and sets our glasses down on the counter.

He takes both my hands as he leads me to the couch. He pauses for a moment, to see if I'm comfortable, and I guess he takes my not slapping him round the face again as an invitation. He sits down pulling me into his lap wrapping his strong arms around my waist and burying his face in my neck. Holy shit.

He doesn't speak or do anything at all, except breathe me in. I instinctively turn towards him and wrap my arms around his neck, and finally I get to run my fingers through his wonderfully soft coconutty curls. Although, now I've moved, his head is now leaning on my chest, his face is right at my breasts, but it doesn't feel awkward. If anything, it feels right, like it's his space.

He still doesn't make any moves on me, he just seems relaxed so I carry on lightly brushing his hair. This feels so nice, and I'm silently begging for him to kiss me again, but he doesn't. As usual my brain goes down a rabbit hole of panic, and burning questions are brought to the surface.

"What are we doing, Ryan? I thought you hated me?"

Silence. He still doesn't move or respond, so after a couple of beats, I do. I pull away and stand up off his lap, not looking back at him. He doesn't try to stop me, which stings a lot. I don't miss how he didn't deny that he hates me either. I'm such an idiot.

I walk back over to the French window and look outside not wanting to face him. "So, do you think you will move in here?" *Seriously, Faith? An idiot and a coward apparently.*

He clears his throat as if he was lost in thought and now coming back to reality.

"I don't know, it's a bit far out from the clinic. But honestly, I'm not sure I can spend another night in that room, the bed is killing me, and the shower sucks."

I hate the thought of him staying here. This isn't him, at least I don't want it to be him.

"Please don't stay here. This place, it's poison, you do know that, right? It does nothing to support the local community, even the people who work here, the guards, the gardeners, none of them are local people. This place, it's unethical."

I can see the cogs in Ryan's head turning as he takes in what I'm saying. "Could you really stay here in this luxury, knowing that a couple of villages over people have no access to clean water? People who have to walk for miles just to get to it? People are working fifteen hours a day just to earn enough to pay for one meal? The money this place cost, could have paid for a clean water supply, all of these bungalows could take entire villages out of poverty!"

He shakes his head and stands up, walking over to me. He takes my hand and my skin pricks with the electricity in the air.

"It sucks that there are people here living that way. I gotta admit I've never really given it much thought until now, which is pretty ignorant of me I know. I guess I'm pretty naive to the world compared to you. Tell me how to help, Faith, and I will? But you know this isn't my house, or my money for that matter. I don't get much say in how it's spent."

"Maybe not, but one day it will be yours, right? I'm not saying you shouldn't enjoy your wealth or that you should feel guilty about spending it. Definitely not. Your family has worked hard to earn it, so why shouldn't you enjoy some luxury in life. Just maybe not right on the doorstep of people who have nothing?" Ryan nods like he sees where I'm coming from. His face is full of guilt, which I hate because that was not what I wanted.

"Hey," I rub his arm and move back into his space like I belong there. I wish I belonged there. I wrap my arms around his waist, and to my surprise he puts his strong arms around me. A hug. This is an actual hug, with a boy. Not just any boy, Mystery Boy. Holy crap.

"All I'm saying is if you have it, and you have all of your nice things, and there is nothing wrong with that. But, if you still have a ton of money left over, why not do something positive with some of it? Or at least try and make ethical choices when you do spend it. Places like this, they shouldn't be here." He stares at me, a slight frown appearing on his eyebrows.

"Do you think I'm spoiled, Faith?"

"No, of course not. I think you're actually a really sweet down-to-earth guy. Well I used to think that, but then for some unknown reason you changed, and became *this* royal douche canoe!" I gesture up and down his body when I say the last part, and he laughs again, sucking me back in.

"See, you can call me a douche canoe to my face, it wasn't so hard!" He beams a full smile at me, and I get lost in the moment and touch his face. He doesn't stop me, so I stand up on my tiptoes and plant a small, chaste kiss on his cheek. As I pull away he is still beaming from ear to ear. He touches the spot I just kissed, whilst never breaking eye contact with me, as if he can't believe I just did that. To be fair, I can't believe I just did that either, I have some serious lady balls lately.

He is so gorgeous it hurts. For a minute we are lost, both drifting into the unknown depths of the other. Is he mine? My heart seems to think that he is, that's for sure.

I clear my throat breaking the spell, and I regret it as soon as the moment is gone.

"Look, I know you want to help so listen, next week I'm heading north with my mom to some remote villages. I will be helping out at the schools, and if it's okay with Dad, maybe you should come with us? I think it will be good for you to really help people while you are here, rather than just translating, what do you think?"

He looks down sheepishly, putting his hands in his pockets. Is he nervous?

"How could I be of any help to anyone? I mean, besides with my wallet?" Wow okay, an insecure Ryan, there's a first.

"The fact you even need to ask, that shows you have no idea what it's really like over here. Of course, you can help, you can teach, you can build, you can play soccer. Do you have any idea what that would mean to these kids, someone like you teaching them skills? I'd really like it if you came with us, please? And look, if I stay with my parents for a couple of nights then you can sleep in my cabin. How about that? Then while we are away, my dad can get the last cabin ready for you? He did offer to clear it out for you before, but he said your dad insisted you'd rather stay at the hotel?"

He sits back on the couch, and pulls me back into his lap, but this time he pulls me into a straddle position. He wraps his arms around my waist once again, but he loops them through the inside of his hoodie so there is only my tee-shirt between us. His touch feels like fire to my sensitive skin, even with the shirt in the way. My body is screaming at me to move against him, and it takes all my willpower not to.

"Why doesn't that surprise me. My father is a dickwad who wants to teach me a lesson, although fuck knows what this one is." His wandering hands begin to run softly up and down my back, but on the way down they drift a little lower each time, until they are no longer on the small of my back, but firmly on my ass. Once they are there, he stops and keeps them there. I have to admire his confidence. Does he want me right now?

"Hmm, a favour for a favour. Is that how our relationship is going to work, Asher?"

Relationship. Not friendship. I nod my head, unable to speak. "Okay, then we have a deal, but on one condition?" God, what's he going to ask?

"Please don't make a dick sucking joke right now dude, I swear to God." He lets out another belly laugh and its music to my ears.

"How did you guess? Now you've ruined all my fun," he chuckles, and for a minute I swear he is going to kiss me again, but he blinks, and I can tell he has changed his mind. He smiles a knowing grin at me like he is up to something. "How about you let me cook dinner for you tonight instead?"

Well damn.

# CHAPTER 12

## Faith

I couldn't believe that Ryan offered to cook me dinner. I don't know if I was more surprised at the offer or at the fact he could supposedly cook. But here he was in my cabin, well his cabin for now, serving me up homemade fried chicken that looked and smelt amazing.

After what happened earlier it feels like we've finally called a truce to whatever the hell this bullshit issue was between us. Although now I feel more confused than ever, because I still don't know what caused it in the first place.

For the first time since he arrived, he seems relaxed and he actually looks happy to be here. He even seems more like my mystery boy from before, and if he keeps it up with all these gorgeous smiles, I can see myself catching all the feels.

I take a piece of chicken off of my plate and tuck in, trying to distract myself from keep staring at Ryan like he's the snack. Wait, oh my God, what in the name of Kentucky-fried-heaven is this. This is the best chicken I think I've tasted.

"Mmm... Ryan, this is so good. I had no idea you could cook?" I take another large mouthful of Ryan's homemade chicken, not even attempting to be graceful now. This is way too good for etiquette.

"Okay firstly, you moan my name whilst licking your lips like that again, I'm going to have to eat *you* tonight rather than the chicken," he says casually, wiggling his eyebrows suggestively. Of course, my traitorous cheeks pink up, causing him to actually laugh out loud again.

What a beautiful sound it is. It's these brief moments where he lets his mask slip away that I'm reminded just how handsome he really is.

I still had no idea why he suddenly became the angry person he is these days, but it's like right now, when he seemed to forget he was supposed to hate me, he was wonderful.

I honestly can't remember the last time that I was genuinely happy, and that was in part, because of him. I couldn't blame him for the stuff that happened to my dad, or my failing relationship with my mom, or for any of the crap Shane and Mia have pulled. I could however, blame him for my broken heart, that was all on him. I can't help but turn my face away, as a familiar lump forms in my throat. Sensing the sudden change in mood he continues.

"Secondly, are you kidding? My momma was from The South, so of course I can cook, and not just fried chicken either!" He says proudly. This catches my attention.

"I thought all your family were from New York?" I questioned, taking another bite.

"They are mostly, but my dad was gifted my mother as his bride as part of a business arrangement between my two grandfathers', but her family were from Louisiana."

Louisiana? My girl Britney is from Louisiana. Wait, what?

Gifted!? What the hell does that mean?

"What, like an arranged marriage? Do people in America still do that?" The feminist in me getting personally offended.

"It's actually not that uncommon, especially on the Upper East Side where everything is kept exclusive. Imagine the scandal if some young rich debutante was to fall for the charms of some street performer from Brooklyn?" He fakes a shocked expression and smirks. God he is sexy as hell.

Tonight, he is wearing some faded black denim shorts, with a white linen shirt. He has left a few buttons undone, revealing a necklace underneath. It's a black rope, with a silver circle pendant. Inside the bottom right of the circle is an elephant, and above the elephant, to the left of the circle, is a stone that is an unusual shade of blue, and it gives the effect of being the moon. It's simple, but it's beautiful.

"Selective breeding, I guess" He shrugs, running his fingers through his unruly hair. Seriously, so gorgeous when he does that. "Anyway, Mom loved to cook and she loved me to cook with her. She started teaching me as soon as I was old enough to hold a spoon. I used to stand on a chair up at the counter next to her and do the basics." He smiles again, but this time it doesn't reach his eyes.

"You miss your mom, you guys were close?"

"Every day. She was a great mom. So down to earth you know, not one bit impressed with my father's wealth, or her own. Her family are pretty wealthy too, they own a large plantation down there. My Gramps is just like her though, always looking for new causes to give it all away to." He moves his fork around his plate, not really interested in the food anymore.

"She always taught me how to do things for myself even though we had plenty of help. 'The staff are there to help us be independent, not to wait on us hand and foot'. That's what she used to say. Hell, she would whoop my ass if she caught me leaving something for the maid to do. Only verbally of course, she wasn't ever physical with me, that wasn't her way."

His mood has turned sombre and I wonder if it was a mistake to ask him about her. Something tells me he needs to talk about her, so I listen. "She taught me to respect everyone from all walks of life, not just rich people. She was kind and beautiful, and she loved to dance. I always remember her dancing, even when there wasn't even any music. She would say you can always feel it in your heart if you listened carefully. It's why I play the guitar as much as I can. It's like sometimes I think I can feel her there, dancing."

He swallows down his emotions, and I could tell he was now well aware he had shared more than he wanted to with me. "Sounds dumb, I know," he says dismissively, trying to shrug it off, and I hate that he doesn't feel comfortable showing his grief.

"No it doesn't, not at all. She sounds wonderful, and it's amazing you still have a way to connect with her. I'm so sorry she's gone. I can't imagine how hard that must be. Do you mind me asking, how did she die? I mean, if you don't want to talk about it you don't have to tell me that's fine too, it's completely up to you?"

He looks at me with an expression I can't read. He seems to be having a silent argument with himself about something. He stands up and starts clearing the table so I do the same. He pauses and thinks for a moment before taking a deep breath out through his nose, his eyes closing for a beat as he does. He opens them and starts filling the sink with water.

"Your mom, Lorrie, she seems nice. Are you guys close?" Hell no. I'm guessing he doesn't want to talk about his own mother anymore, so I allow the change.

"Yeah, well, we get on. I mean, it's difficult because I've

spent a lot more time with my dad over the past three years. I've been through some stuff and she hasn't been there for me. It hasn't been easy dealing with things without her around. It's partly why I'm going with her next week, my dad thinks we need 'quality time' together or something. Whatever."

Ryan doesn't respond, and I realise I must sound like an asshole, talking about my mom that way when his own is gone, but he doesn't know the whole story. "I'm close with my dad though. He's great, he's like my best friend," I say enthusiastically, trying to lighten the mood. Apparently, it's done the exact opposite as Ryan's face hardens, and I could tell instantly that his mask was back on. Oh crap.

"You don't like my dad?" He turns back towards the sink, his back to me and starts washing the dishes vigorously. Okay, awkward. I take a towel and start drying.

"I don't know him. My dad is a prick, I guess I assume all fathers are, until proven otherwise. According to my father, both our fathers are members of the same country club. Everyone I've met so far from that club seems like a total A-hole, so figured your father is no different." He continues washing aggressively, clearly angry about something, but what? What could he possibly have against my dad? I suddenly feel very defensive.

"Maybe if you'd actually talked to him or tried to get to know him this week instead of being so rude you would know already that my dad is not an A-hole. Nor is he some rich prick from the country club. He's amazing, and funny, and generous, and he's only a member at that stupid club to raise financial support for the clinic!" I feel so angry. What's this guy's issue? Seriously?

"I don't know what your problem is, with me or my family, but we have been nothing but welcoming to you since you got here, even despite what you and your friends did to me!

Which I haven't told my parents by the way, in case you were wondering!" That was true.

I hadn't told anyone about that day. After what happened with my dad that day it didn't seem important at the time, and now it just seems childish to bring it up after all this time, just because Ryan has shown up here. "... And just so you know, my dad is a brilliant doctor. You don't think we could be rich pricks too? If he and my mom had focused on private practice they could have earned a fortune by now, but they didn't."

Again, that's true. They have always dedicated their lives to helping vulnerable people, and the only reason he did any private practice was to pay for our home. Luckily, I have a scholarship at St. Edmund's like my mom did, there is no way my parents could afford it otherwise.

"Dad works his ass off every week not only at his job, but he volunteers three nights a week seeing people at a free clinic downtown. That's without all the work both my parents have done over here in Africa. My dad is the best OBGYN in California, and he deserves some respect! Well, he was the best in California, we won't be going back there anymore now."

Ryan stops what he's doing and puts the dish down, turning to speak to me.

"What do you mean you won't be going back to California? Where else would you be going?" he demands. Why exactly does he care?

"We aren't going anywhere, we are staying here. There's nothing left for us there anymore, especially after what happened to my dad, his reputation is in ruins."

"Bullshit! So, what, you're just dropping out of school and your parents are fine with that? I thought that was the whole point of you being in California in the first place?" Is he actually angry about this?

"If you must know, no, I'm not dropping out. I finished last semester online, I don't see why I can't do the same for the entire senior year. I already have plenty of credit. I have consistent grades, I've already spoken to Principal Meyers, she said all I'd really need to do is maintain my grades. I've got to go back at the start of school for three weeks just to make sure it's what I definitely want, but she understands and agrees it shouldn't be too hard."

There's a fire in Ryan's eyes now I can tell he's getting pissed off, although I'm still at a complete loss as to why.

"What about senior year? What about graduation, homecoming, and prom, and all of that other right-of-passage crap? What about your friends?" He genuinely seems angry about this, but he knows no one wants me there anyway.

"Ha! Friends? What friends? I don't have any friends! Thanks to that liar Shane, and your McBitchface girlfriend deciding to lay all her bullshit problems at my door." Ryan's eyes turn black with rage but I'm too angry myself to wonder why. He stalks closer into my space, staring me right in the eye. I feel the hairs on my arms rise up, the familiar feeling of fear creeping in. *He isn't Shane.*

No, he isn't Shane, so why do I feel like this? I'm just being irrational, I tell myself trying to find my lady balls. I continue with what I was saying, albeit at a quieter, less confident pitch. "In case you hadn't noticed, guys aren't exactly queuing up to take me to prom, and why would I give a crap about some stupid graduation ceremony when I'm probably going to get heckled or booed off stage. Again, all thanks to your girlfriend, so I'm pretty sure I won't be missed by anyone! Why do you even care? You hate me, remember?"

He continues to stare me out, breathing heavily through his nose as if he is biding his time, waiting to strike. "What, am I supposed to feign surprise when you and your bitch girlfriend make Prom Court? Don't you want me to miss the kick ass Valedictorian speech I'm sure you've already gotten prepared? Don't worry, I'll catch the highlights on YouTube, along with all the videos of your twenty-two-year-old step-mom rubbing her fake tits!"

He slams his fist down on the counter, making me jump and back away from him. "Shit on a stick, why did I say that? That wasn't cool, I'm sorry," I say as sincerely as possible. That was way out of line, and I really hope I haven't messed this up.

Ryan steps even closer towards me, still staring at me like I'm vermin. My hairs rise up again, and this time I don't feel so irrational. Please don't let him hit me, we can't come back from that. *Shane hits you, other guys have been rough with you, why wouldn't Ryan too?*

He steps closer still, and I hold my breath waiting for what's coming. I wince expecting another slap from yet another guy, but instead he puts his face right in front of mine. His breath is bouncing off of my lips like before, only this time I'm not turned on, I'm scared. *Ryan isn't your safe place, when are you gonna get that, Faith?*

"Her bullshit problems? Are you for real? Do you actually fucking hear yourself?" He rages, his voice louder than I've ever heard it, causing me to jump out of my skin. "Melody might have rubbed her fake tits a few times for cash, but people actually paid big bucks to see that. You know why? Because she is a prize, a fucking unobtainable diamond, men can only dream of touching. Men jerk off to women like her, because they know they can never have her." He seethes, and I wonder if he too has been one of those men.

Melody is a very beautiful woman. Don't get me wrong, I'm a modern woman, and women can do whatever they want with their own bodies, certainly no judgement here. I only said that to hurt Ryan, like he always hurts me. I guess I'm just not very good at throwing insults, because I've messed this one up badly.

"You on the other hand, are a filthy little cunt. You have sucked and fucked most of the school, and for what, huh? Who knows? For a fucking hit? Are you a crack whore, Faith? Or maybe you just love cock, is that it?" He says grabbing his crotch and although I know he is just trying to antagonise me, I'm instantly transported back to that janitor's closet with Shane.

"Please stop it," I cry. I turn my face away but he gently pulls it back holding me in place.

"You are nothing but a dirty little whore, and you're right, no guy in their right mind would ever fucking want you. Why the fuck would they? The only reason guys fuck you, is because we all wanna see how many names we can get on the hit list by graduation." He laughs a sharp sinister laugh through his nose.

"So yeah, please come back for senior year or my fucking bet was way off base, baby."

"Fuck you!" I scream shoving him off me. "I can't believe I actually fell for you." I say softly, as tears roll down my cheeks.

"I can't believe I ever fell for *your* act, more like," he says, completely missing what I actually said to him. "And to think I had decided to give you a second chance!"

A second chance? When did I have a first chance, and what did I do to make me need a second?

"I thought for a minute you were actually a pretty decent girl, that maybe you'd changed, but no, you're still the same ugly fucking cunt you always were, apparently you just got better at hiding it."

What. The. Fuck?

"You wanna know why you haven't got any friends, Faith, it's because you're a bully and a bitch. You act like a pig, you look like a fucking pig, you are a disgusting pig! No one fucking likes you, Pork Chop. Well, except maybe when you're on your knees taking a cock down your greedy throat, and even then, I've never heard anyone say it was a decent fuck, so who knows?"

I've heard enough. For the second time today, I slap him across his face. I can't take his cruel words any longer, but he has just crossed a freakin' line.

"I told you NOT to call me a pig ever again! You promised, asshole, and not even a day has gone by before you broke that promise! You crossed your fucking heart..." my voice trails off as more tears burn in the back of my eyes. I try to compose myself but I'm so hurt, and so angry. It may not have meant anything to him, but to me a promise is a promise, a person's word, and the betrayal of him breaking it stings more than his hurtful words.

"That was the last time, that I can promise you! Don't ever talk to me again! You pinkie-fucking-promised!" I run out of the cabin as fast as I can, leaving behind all my things, including the hoodie he gave me, and several pieces of my broken blooded heart.

# CHAPTER 13

## Ryan

I'm so fucking mad right now. I can't believe she actually said that about Mia, or Melody, what the fuck. I've been a complete idiot today, letting my dick rule my brain. Took one look at her sexy curves, and her crocodile tears, and completely forgot who she really was. Well that shit ends now. I won't be fooled twice.

I can't believe I actually felt guilty for all the bad shit I've said and done to her as well. I'm such a prick.

After she broke away from our kiss this afternoon and slammed the bathroom door in my face, I gotta admit I felt pretty fucking shitty. That kiss was so amazing and I spent the rest of the day desperately wanting to kiss her again. I had waited outside for her, remembering the look of shame on her face that I'd help put there, and I felt sick with regret. I knew I had to try and make things right. Maybe she was sorry for what she'd done to Mia, maybe she had changed?

The way she flinched when I wrapped her in my hoodie, like she genuinely thought I was going to hurt her had my stomach in knots. I was already feeling all kinds of guilt about what I allowed Shane to do to her that day. It had played on my mind a lot since then anyway, but after seeing her so vulnerable like that, half dressed and scared, it was all I could think about.

I've never wanted to raise my hand to a girl before. Hell, not even when I saw Mia taking another dude's dick, but tonight, when Faith started spouting about how great her dad is and how Mia's abuse was the only reason she wasn't popular, I admit I nearly lost it. I slammed my fist on the counter and she flinched again, but this time she actually stepped away from me. It was then that I could see it, the fear in her eyes. She genuinely thought I was going to hit her and she was trembling.

I guess if you're a bully, violence is all you come to expect.

I was so angry, that for a split second, I enjoyed her fear. I thought maybe Shane had the right idea. I know, I know, I'm a total dick for even thinking that, even for a second. I mean I'd never actually do anything like that, *ever*! Just so we're clear.

I saw my dad slap my mom once when I was nine, and I swore he would never do that again, not if I could help it. If he did, then I never saw it happen after that, but I promised my mother I would never lay a finger on a woman that way, and I meant it. My guilt over allowing Shane to do what he did on pig day was temporarily dispersed, albeit for a moment. It's back now of course, tenfold, because I have the added guilt of thinking it was acceptable for a moment. Fucking hell.

Yeah sure, she slapped me twice today, but they didn't exactly hurt, and I deserved them both. Hell, I've deserved a whole lot more, the things I've said to her tonight and this past week. In my book, there is a big difference between a chick slapping a guy when he has disrespected her, to a guy laying hands on a girl to teach her a lesson.

Seeing her tremble in fear made me feel sick, and I feel even shittier about the whole thing now than I did before.

I don't know why, but for some reason I couldn't stop spitting venom, it was like I wanted to see her cry. I needed her tears, but she kept holding them back, so I just kept on at it. What's wrong with me?

When she finally let her salty tears slip, all I could think about was kissing them away, which pissed me off even more. So, I just kept pushing and pushing, even though she was crying, I was saying all those awful things. What kind of an asshole does that make me?

I'm more annoyed with myself for opening up to her about my mom. I never talk about her to anyone, not even Mia. Not that Mia really asked. She seemed more interested in my step-mom and what A-list celebrities she spends time with. Faith was actually the first person to even ask me if I missed her. Not even my father has reached out to see if I'm okay. In fact, he hasn't mentioned my mother since her funeral. It's as if he seems to think because of how she died, she doesn't deserve to be remembered. My father acts like her life, and her death, are just skeletons that needed to be buried firmly in the back of our family's closet.

Okay, so now not only am I literally raging at Faith, I'm now seriously pissed at my dad again for old sins. Great.

I get up and go to my bag, and pull out one of the bottles of whiskey I swiped from the bungalow before I left. My dad always keeps his apartments fully stocked with his favourite liquor, so I knew it would be there. I pour myself a large glass and take it down in one, enjoying the familiar burn.

I go over everything that's happened this week in my head. Faith seemed so beautiful to me today. Before this trip I wouldn't have said I found her attractive. Well no, that's most definitely a lie. She's hot as fuck and on more than one occasion I've jerked off thinking about her fucking mouth wrapped around my dick.

Usually shy girls don't do it for me, but this girl had something about her that drew me in from day one. I actually thought about her a lot in those first few weeks, now I've let myself remember it. When I first heard the rumours about her, I found it hard to believe they could be the same timid girl who ran face first into a door that day. The same girl who clung to me like I was her life source after being shoved into me by some asshole.

That day I held on to her for a bit longer than necessary. She was so wired, and I felt her hands grip at my shirt, so I held on to her until I felt her relax. Then she ran off and didn't talk to me ever again. If I saw her in the hall she would turn and walk the other way.

What with Mia in my ear about what a freak she was, and all the smack written about her in the guy's locker rooms, I realised our first encounter must have all been an act. I was quickly put off and she became unattractive to me.

That didn't stop me from thinking about her in the shower from time to time. I mean, I had no idea what she was hiding under those baggy clothes. A lot of chick's think guys only like skinny girls, and yeah some do, but a lot of guys appreciate all sorts of different body shapes. Plenty of guys like a girl with little meat on the bone, me being one of them, and this girl has some jelly in all the right places.

Not that a smoking hot bod makes up for being ugly on the inside. Thing is, over the past week I've slowly seen parts of her personality that I had no idea existed. Now when I look at her I see that shy girl again, the peach who held onto me tightly. My little mystery girl. Except she's also so much more than all of that.

Faith has self-confidence issues, sure, but she's anything but shy. She's brave as hell, and speaks her mind. It's like the person I thought she was, is not the same person I've been around over here. Nothing seems to fit anymore, and I honestly can't imagine *Ma Belle Foi* being mean to anyone, let alone doing all the fucked-up things she was supposed to have done to Mia.

Ha, My Faith. Since when did she become 'My Faith'? I have no idea, but I know that she is. The moment I kissed her I knew she was meant to be mine.

*Ma Belle Foi*. Mine.

I think back to all the nasty shit I spat at her earlier. God, I'm such a fucking prick. I don't even believe any of that crap anymore, so why did I say it? Earlier, when she actually laughed with me, her face just seemed to transform into this beaming ray of sunshine, lighting up her beauty to me. Why haven't I seen her laugh like that before now?

Sure, I've seen her laugh around Ade, but I realise now those laughs were hollow; she was going through the motions, laughing when she should. It's as if she's been dead inside, and now all of a sudden, she feels alive again. For the second time, she's made me feel like I'm her life source, but doesn't she know, I'm dead inside too?

Today was the first day I even noticed the colour of her big beautiful eyes. I thought they were blue but they are actually grey. The colour of a storm, like a fierce tornado, tearing through your soul, urging you to run for cover. You don't usually see chicks with eyes that colour, but I guess she is different in more ways than one.

She has dark brown hair, almost black, cut off at her shoulders that hangs in natural looking soft waves, framing her heart shaped face.

She smells like one of those old-fashioned white bars of

soap that old people use, but there is always that little hint of vanilla. It's like she washes her entire hair and body with the same bar, and I was surprisingly intoxicated by it. I first smelt it that first day at school and I was just as intrigued then. They say smell is the strongest of the senses for triggering a memory. I instantly remembered when I got close enough to her after she'd made me walk to the clinic that first morning. I couldn't resist breathing her in. She smelled exactly the same, and I've found myself becoming addicted to it.

Her lips are so full and look so perfectly pink next to her milky porcelain skin. Now that I've tasted them, I want more. I can't help but imagine them wrapped around my dick, teasing me slowly like she did with our kiss. That fantasy brings me back to the rumours about her at school. The fucking thought of her doing that for another guy twists my gut. The thought of her being with other guys in any sort of way makes me feel sick with fucking jealousy. I literally wanna kill any bastard that's even looked at her. What's that about?

When Mia was with Shane, I didn't even say anything, I just walked out. I was completely switched off from her in an instant. As far as I was concerned she was now Shane's, he could have her. Yet Faith isn't even my girl, and all of a sudden, I wanna beat the ever-loving shit out of anyone who has ever touched her? I've lost it I swear.

I go across the room and lay down on her bed, which doesn't help because the bed smells like vanilla frosting, reminding me of our kiss. Again, maybe that's from her actually baking a cake earlier I don't know. I wonder what happened to the cake?

All I know is that up until a few months ago, I didn't even really notice her, and then when I did notice her, I hated her. Now I can't stop thinking she's the most beautiful girl I've ever seen. Truth is, if it wasn't for the rumours about her, I know for a fact most guys would gladly chop off their left nut to be with her, and I fucking hate myself for the way I've been treating her, especially the way I just spoke to her.

Even now while I'm angry with her, and confused as fuck about this whole situation, I still want her. I desperately want to go and comfort her even though I'm the one that hurt her. Should I go and find her and apologise for what happened?

I was a complete prick for calling her a pig again, especially when I'd already apologised for it earlier and promised I wouldn't ever say it again. Faith was right to be mad about that. She probably thinks my word means shit now anyway, and I wouldn't blame her.

Maybe I should talk to her about what happened to Mia. I know that's what I need to do. Sexual attraction aside, I really like Faith, and she deserves a chance to explain her side. I don't know why I didn't just give her that chance right from the start, now that I think about it? Why did I listen to what everyone else said about her when I knew deep down I didn't believe a word of it? I'm broken out of my thoughts when my phone goes off.

**Mia** - Hey Ryan, I really miss you. I made a mistake, please, let's talk about it? School starts back up soon, don't you want us to be together for senior year? Xoxo

Urgh, hell no. When will this chick fucking get it already, I'm not interested! Delete.

I notice I also have some unread messages on my group chat so I read them too.

**Alex** - Yo! Fresh Prince, what's with the change in relationship status, are you single now?

**Spencer** - We miss you Ryan, when are you coming home to us x

**Kat** - Please God, be single. No offence babe, but your bird looks like a stuck-up bitch. Sorry not sorry.

**Kat** - P.S. I miss you so fucking much, why don't you ever answer us you little dickhead!

**Spencer** - Well I just checked, and that bitch already has a new fella! Looks like she's with that blonde twat Ryan is friends with?

**Tom** - Not that fucking tosser who bleached his hair? Kid looks like *Stan*!

**Alex** - That bleached blonde twat looks like the type who wants to fuck his own sister. #Justsayin

**Tom** - Truth. Seriously though bro, reply once in a while yeah? Stop being a wanker.

**Alex** - Wanker!

**Kat** - Such a wanker!

**Spencer** - Still a babe though!

**Tom** - Right, someone delete Spence!

I throw my phone down, not knowing what to say back. I am a fucking wanker.

I see a phone light up with another message, but it isn't mine. It's Faith's. She must have left it here when she stormed out. I'm not usually the type of guy who would invade someone's privacy but curiosity, or possibly jealousy, gets the better of me when I pick up her phone to see who it is. It opens up straight away. Who doesn't have a code on their phone these days?

**McBitchface** - Stay the fuck away from Ryan, bitch, I saw the photos of you all cosy with him in Africa! Fucking stalker! Exactly how desperate are you for his dick anyway? I swear bitch if you tell him anything, Shane will cut your fucking throat next time!

What the actual fuck?

# CHAPTER 14

## Ryan

I know I shouldn't, but I read back through other messages. They go way back and all of them are Mia, Faith never replies. The messages are all much the same. Calling her fat, calling her a whore, Mia laughing about some shit going down that I had heard about, but when I heard the story, it was Faith supposedly doing it to Mia, not vice versa. What the hell?

There are threats about not telling me something. She mentions Shane a lot, as if he was in on it all too. Did Faith know about the two of them?

I feel like shit doing it, but I need to know. I check her other messages and sure enough there is much the same from Mia's minions, Madison and Hayley. There are also messages from unsaved numbers, lots of them. All propositioning her, offering her cash or drugs for a blow. There are guys asking for everything, from a fucking finger bang to a gang bang. What. The. Fuck.

Faith hasn't replied to a single message. Guys have even sent dick pics, as if that's going to help their plight. This is so fucked up.

Then there are guys not asking, but telling her they are going to fuck her, describing in great detail the depraved things they want to do to her. The level of sexual harassment this girl has had to put up with is sickening, and this is just what's on her phone, I dread to think what she's had thrown at her in real life. *You already know what's been said to her in real life, you've heard it all year and done nothing about it.*

I'm so angry right now. I'm angry with all of these pricks. I'm angry with Mia, but mostly I'm just so angry with myself. Why did I ignore it all? I knew it wasn't right. Whatever she did, it wasn't right the way people spoke to her. The way *I've* spoken to her. Hell, the things I've said to her this past week are just as disgusting as these messages. God, I feel sick.

One of my best friends was bullied, and I always had her back. As realisation of how fucked up this is hits me, I remember all the things I've let slide when it came to Faith. All the digs, the snide remarks, all the groping, all the graffiti. No matter who I thought she was, I knew it wasn't right, any of it. A girl can have sex with whom ever she chooses, that doesn't mean there is an open invitation for guys to say and do whatever they want.

Why didn't I ever protect her? I mean, I know full well why, I just didn't care enough. It wasn't my problem. I haven't cared about anything for a long fucking time, but that's no excuse.

Truth is I'm fucking ashamed of myself, and I know my beautiful little Spence would be so mad at me if she knew how differently I had dealt with Faith's situation compared to her own. Especially with all the fat comments, when I know first hand how badly that type of shit can affect a girl. Kat, the guys, my mom; none of them would recognise the person I've become, they would be ashamed of me too.

To punish myself, I keep reading. Even Levi has sent a trail of messages, practically begging to fuck her. He isn't real nasty like the others though, and never offers cash. In fact, going by the way he talks, I think he genuinely wants to take her out on a date or something. Does he like her? He was definitely with Hayley when he sent some of these messages, what the fuck?

Then there is Shane. The things this sick bastard has said to her are disgusting. If I thought him tugging at her panties uninvited was bad, he has threatened way worse. Fuck, has he done worse? I'm filled with pure rage at the thought. I see further back there are even pictures. Often just of Faith lying on the floor, her face bloodied, her shirt torn. I am raging at this point, seeing how often he seems to have hurt her.

I eventually come across a photo that has me livid with a type of anger I've never felt before in my life, and that's saying something because I've been pretty fucking pissed off for years now.

He has her on her knees, his hand fisted tightly into her hair, and she has tears streaming down her dirty face. She is wearing her school uniform but her shirt is all wet and filthy. It's dark and poorly lit, I can't see anything that gives away where they are. The worst part is this asshole has his dick pressed at her mouth like he's trying to force it in, while her eyes are squeezed shut.

He has taken this picture from above, and although his face isn't in it, I know it's him. The disgusting commentary that followed in the texts after were enough to confirm it was him. Whatever the fuck is going on in this picture it's clearly not consensual, and I can promise one thing for sure, that Shane Frost is a fucking dead man. Touching what's mine? I swear to God, he will pay.

I can't stop thinking about what might have happened.

It was sent right at the beginning of school, it's no wonder she was so fucking evasive after I met her. What the hell else was she dealing with? Did she know he was after her, is that why she was so on edge that morning? I feel so fucking sick it hurts, what the fuck did he do to you, *Ma Belle Foi*?

Her reaction to me earlier makes a little more sense now, and I wonder how many times he might have forced himself on her. Fuuuck! My sweet vanilla frosting girl, what has he done to you, baby? My stomach twists, wondering what's actually been going on this whole time. I've been deceived in a big fucking way, of that I am certain.

Was Mia lying to me this whole time? Was it really her bullying Faith, and if so why? Was it because of what Faith's dad did to her, or was even that a lie? Fuck no. Surely not? No that must be it. Mia was lashing out at Faith because of what Dr. Asher did to her, that has to be it, surely. Although that doesn't explain Shane and the rest of the bullshit. There haven't been any new messages for months, until now. Then again, Faith hasn't been around for months. The last one from Mia before tonight makes me feel even more angry than I already do.

**McBitchface** - Not coming back to school then? Hopefully now you've finally got the message. PS If you haven't already, please go and hang yourself.

Go and hang yourself. Those words vibrate in my head over and over. Why would anyone say that?

Go and hang yourself.

I honestly don't know who this girl is anymore. How could I have been so fucking blind? This bitch is dead to me now. The text right before that has my gut filled with dread. It's dated on the night of the pig party.

**McBitchface -** Heard your dad got his ass beat for being a child abuser? I wonder who started that rumour? I told you to watch your back bitch, now stay the fuck away from Ryan.

I race to my own phone, and dial Mia's number. She answers straight away in a sickly-sweet voice that has me wanting to vomit.

"Hey baby, how are you? I've missed you so much. How's Afri…"

"Shut the fuck up!" I interrupt her, before she can spew anymore bullshit. "You lied about Faith and Dr. Asher, didn't you?" There's silence and I instantly know the truth, I feel it in my whole body.

I've been fucking played.

"Answer me, Mia! I saw the messages you sent to Faith!" More silence before she finally speaks, her voice filled with panic. Yep. I've definitely been played.

"I don't know what she's told you, but she's a liar, you can't believe her!"

What the hell does that even mean? I'm gonna lose my shit I can feel it.

"How can you say she's a liar, but then say you don't know what she's told me? Which is it, Mia? What do you think she has told me? What's the real secret here, because you sure as hell have been the only one lying to me?" She starts crying, or fake crying I don't know. I don't give a fuck. "Start. Talking. Mia!"

She immediately stops crying and talks in a perfectly normal voice, showing me even the tears were fake.

"Dr. Asher did look at my vagina, but it was because he was my doctor. I never *actually* said he forced me, you assumed. I mean, I just wanted to teach that pig bitch a lesson. She's always fucking staring at you, and you were always smiling at her! What the fuck, Ryan? It's not like I told you to go beat him half to death, in fact I *specifically* told you to leave him alone!"

The fuck? Is this bitch trying to turn all of this on me? This is so bad. I'm in deep shit and I know it.

"He was your gynaecologist? What the hell, Mia? Why would you deliberately let me think he had abused you? What possible reason would you have to do that? You're fucking sick Mia, no wonder so many actual victims of abuse don't ever come forward!" She scoffs at that, but before she can speak I continue. "If I ever hear about you so much as giving Faith a dirty look I swear to God, I will make sure everyone knows what you did. Delete my number, you vapid bitch!"

With that I hang up. I open Faith's messages and re-read them all again, at least twice. I forward the entire conversations from both Mia and Shane to my own phone. Then I delete every last message. She should not have to look at that shit ever again.

Fuck this is so bad. I could go to prison for what I did to Malcolm. Mia is right, she did tell me to leave it, but she also said she wasn't ready to go to the police, confirming there was something to go to the police for. This was no misunderstanding. This was manipulation, and for what, because I smiled at Faith? And what the hell does any of this have to do with Shane?

I've always known that there was a possibility I could go to jail for what I've done, but I would have gone gladly, knowing he got what he deserved. But he was innocent. This whole time he was innocent, and so was Faith. What am I supposed to do now?

How can I possibly make this right? Malcolm will never

forgive me, and neither will Lorrie. I can't bear the thought of the look on their faces when they find out the truth. Worst of all though is Faith. How can I ever earn her forgiveness? How will I ever deserve her now, even if she forgives me for all the shit this week, that won't excuse the past things I let slide, or what I did to her dad.

Feeling like the lowest of the low, I go back to the scotch and pour myself another large glass. I down it, then pour another, and another, and another, until the bottle is empty inside, and so am I.

# CHAPTER 15

## Ryan

I wake up the next morning to a thumping noise. Urgh, it's my head, it's pounding. How much did I drink last night? *Bang, bang, bang...*

Wait, I don't think that's my head. I reluctantly open my eyes and adjust to the light. *Bang, bang, bang...*

"Open up Ry-Man, you lazy little tosser!" The fuck? Is that Greg? Last I saw him he was pretty fucking pissed at me. Does he know about last night with Faith?

The thought he might be coming to make good on his promise to kick my ass makes my stomach twist. Not because I'm afraid, I very much doubt he could actually kick my ass, but because I really like Greg. I'd hate to lose his friendship, even if I haven't known him that long.

"We know it's your birthday, West Ham boy. You can't hide from us!" Ade's voice joins in. My birthday? Shit, it is my birthday. How the fuck did they know?

I grab yesterday's sweatpants and throw on my hoodie,

swallowing down the ache that Faith left it behind last night after I told her she could have it. It smells like her where she wore it all afternoon. I quickly brush my teeth and then go open the door.

"SURPRISE!" They yell. It's not just the guys, it's everyone. The Ashers, Charity and Blessing are here, and even a few of the locals who I have met at the clinic this week are all here with their families. Some of the kids from the school are here with their teacher too, reminding me what a dick I am for not bringing them anything.

They have set up the yard like a mini football pitch, they have even spray painted the pitch lines. There are two goals at either end made from fishing nets and plastic pipes, and there is bunting along the side of the wall, and a banner that has 'Happy 18th Birthday West Ham Ry-Man' crudely painted on it. I take it Ade and Greg were responsible for that. Art is clearly not their strong point.

There is a table set up at one end where most people are sitting for breakfast waiting for us to join them. There is even music playing. I am speechless and completely taken back by how kind these people are to someone they barely know.

"Give me a minute please," I say as I close the door again. I feel my heart racing with anxiety. My birthday. I haven't celebrated my birthday since before my mom... Well, it's been a while. Can I do this?

I check my phone real quick, although I don't know why because I'm not surprised when I see there is nothing from my dad. Dick. I do however have a bunch of messages on the group chat.

**Kat** - Happy bloody Birthday, you little shithead! Love you, miss you, call me back sometime! X

**Alex** - Happy Birthday mate! Can't wait to party when you're back in town. I'm talking full on boats and hoes! The parentals just bought an insane yacht that is just crying out for some debauchery. Boats and Hoes, baby!

**Spencer -** Happy Birthday gorgeous, we love you. x

**Tom -** Just see a bunch of photos of you online. Are you volunteering in Africa? Kept that bloody quiet?

**Kat -** Asshole keeps everything quiet these days. Bloody wanker. Boats and hoes, baby!

**Tom -** Truth! Call me back you bloody wanker! Oh, and Happy Birthday. Boats and hoes, baby!

**Alex -** Wanker!

**Kat -** Wanker!

**Tom -** Wanker!

**Spencer -** You're such a babe for volunteering, but yeah, you are a bloody wanker! Boats and hoes, baby!

Absolute morons. I can't help but smile, even though there's an ache in my chest.

**Ryan -** Boats and hoes, baby!

I throw on my shoes to the sound of my phone buzzing repeatedly. I know it's the guys, all surprised to see that I've finally responded. I chuck it in my bag, I won't reply anymore. What else is there to say? I grab Faith's phone and step out. All the kids start to cheer and chant songs, and everyone starts dancing around the table. Some of the kids come rushing up to me, each one tying a friendship band around my wrist just like Greg's.

I think back to all the expensive gifts offered up to us

over the years by perfect strangers, just for the chance to get on our radar. A Scott photographed wearing your designer clothes could send your sales through the roof. Some send expensive gifts in the hopes of sealing that lucrative deal with my father's company, but there is nothing that's been given to us that we couldn't have bought ourselves a hundred times over.

Someone even sent me a Porsche 911 once. Me. A fucking Porsche. I wouldn't mind but I didn't even live in America most of the time, and who the hell drives themselves in Manhattan anyway? My dad actually wanted the business with them though, so he soon had me flown over for a few courtesy shots sitting in the car. It's actually in the garage in L.A. somewhere. I've used it once or twice but I prefer my truck so I let Melody, my Dad's wife, have it.

Just like that.

My life is such that I can just turn away the gift of a Porsche, simply because I don't want it. Wow, I sound like a rich prick.

These bracelets though, they mean everything. These kids, they don't even know me. They don't have much themselves. Yet here they are giving me these special gifts on my birthday. I've never been made to feel so welcome in my life, I'm truly fucking humbled.

I begin to feel sick to my stomach that all of this generosity is severely misplaced. I don't deserve any of this, especially after what I've done to Malcolm and to Faith. Man, I treated her badly last night, I'm such a maggot. I can't believe that even after all I've said and done, she's still here with a smile waiting for me, albeit she's back to her awkward half-smile whilst looking anywhere but in my eye. Her eyes look red and puffy, like she's been crying. Something in my chest burns knowing I'm the asshole responsible. Last night I wanted those tears, but now they feel like acid to my soul.

She looks like an angel today. She's wearing a short, loose flowery dress that shows off her amazingly toned legs, and she has a big orange flower in her hair. She looks so fucking beautiful. I notice she is standing near a cake that's sat in the middle of the table covered in buttercream frosting, and decorated with the same flower on the top like the one she has in her hair. Shit, that cake she was making was for me?

I suddenly feel completely overwhelmed and before I can stop myself, I fall to the ground and everything goes black.

*** 

"Is he awake? What's wrong with him, Dad? Please, I want to see him!" I hear Faith's worried voice as I begin to open my eyes. This girl. How can she still care about me after everything I've done?

"He's fine, Faithy. He just fainted. He is a little dehydrated, but by the smell of him, I'm sure alcohol has a lot to do with that." Oops, busted.

I offer as much of a smile as I can muster towards Dr. Asher as he notices I'm waking up.

"I'm so sorry," I croak out. Lorrie comes over with a cup of water. She raises her eyes above me, drawing my attention to the IV hanging there.

"Just a small sip to wet your mouth, that's just a banana bag to help with the hangover," she says knowingly.

"Thank you," I say before taking an awkward sip. "I'm sorry, I guess I got a little carried away. I can't believe I fainted, I'm so embarrassed. I'm never gonna live that down with the guys, huh?" I say with a little more enthusiasm, trying to lighten the mood.

Dr. Asher comes over, with Faith starting to follow, but he

turns back to her, blocking her path to me.

"Faithy, can you wait outside for a minute please, I need to speak with Ryan." Faith looks like she's about to protest, but before she can, Lorrie is already there, ushering her out the door. I swallow a big lump in my throat before looking back to Dr. Asher. Here goes…

"Son, is everything okay? Is there something you want to talk to me about?" A shit ton actually, but seeing as how I'm not quite ready to be shipped home and sent to prison, I decide against spilling the tea and shake my head. He looks back at me, disappointment sitting heavy on his face.

"Look, I haven't had a chance to speak to you properly about what happened the other day. I know you were upset by what you saw. I'm guessing by your reaction, you might know about what happened to me in California? The graffiti sprayed on my door?" I nod like a coward, not knowing what to say. "All I can do is assure you that I have never been inappropriate with a patient, adult or child. I have a daughter, so I know how I would feel if I thought someone was abusing young girls. I would probably want to 'kill them with my bare hands' as well, but I promise you I have never hurt anyone in that way," he says sincerely.

He waits, looking at me expectantly. Fuck, does he know it was me? I was wearing that creepy-ass LED mask; how could he know?

I clear my throat, awkwardly at first, meaning I have to do it again to clear it properly. *Such a tool, what's wrong with you.*

"Yeah I know. Look I'm sorry for how I reacted, and for my attitude all week. I know that I've been a little off with you, and well, I guess I did know about all of those rumours. I definitely had my doubts about you when I arrived, but I was wrong and I'm sorry."

He stares at me for a minute as if he is waiting for more from me. I can't help but cringe internally at my continued cowardice. Malcolm blinks away whatever he was thinking and shakes his head.

"Very well. On another note, did something happen between you and Faithy last night? She seemed extremely upset when she got in from your dinner?"

Well that's a whole other issue. I'm not about to admit to my girl's father that I kissed her while she was standing in her underwear, before later calling her an ugly cunt and a filthy pig. I don't have a death wish. *Your girl? She's not your girl asshole.*

No, she is not. Not yet anyway, but she will be. I decide I need to try and own what I've done, well to some extent at least.

"Yes sir, unfortunately it was me that upset her. I'd rather not discuss the details, but I am deeply sorry for hurting her, and I intend to apologise and make it up to her right away. I promise." Please God, don't let him press for details.

"Well you better had. Faith is a good girl with a lot of love to give. If you don't want or deserve that love, then I'd appreciate you staying away from her," he says, raising both his eyebrows. Wow, go Dr. A. If I hadn't already kicked his ass twice, I might be slightly intimidated. This is the first time I've seen him actually fight Faith's corner, and even though it's toward me, it makes me happy for some reason.

"Okay, that's all for now, but I don't ever want to see tears in my daughter's eyes that belong to you again, do I make myself clear?" I nod again. Why the fuck am I such a pussy right now? This would be the prime opportunity to confess my sins, but I just can't seem to get any words out. He disconnects the empty banana bag.

"It's all thanks to Faith that everyone is here for you today, she arranged all of this for you because she cares about you so much. You might want to bear that in mind when you speak to her. Now go wash up before you come back out, because no offence son, but you stink!"

# CHAPTER 16

## Faith

Ryan finally comes back outside and I rush over to him. I'm not even thinking about how he might react to me after last night, I just want to make sure that he is okay. I know I might come across like a doormat after the way he spoke to me last night, but I'm worried about him, so right now I couldn't give a crap about appearances.

I know he won't be nasty to me in front of everyone else at least, but he might tell me to leave him alone. The thought sits in my throat like a huge lump but I swallow it down. I just need to see if he is alright.

"Hey, how are you?" I ask nervously, desperately trying to stop myself from wrapping my arms around his waist and breathing him in. What I'm not expecting is for him to open his strong arms and pull me into a tight hug, but he does. I guess he is sorry about last night after all.

Now, I know what you're thinking. Don't be such a push over Faith, and I get it. It's just, after crying my heart out last night I really thought about everything that he had said. None of it made any sense.

The only thing I could focus on was what he had said to me the day before at the lake, about how he always says mean things instead of saying how he really feels. I took some comfort in that, and hoped that last night maybe he didn't mean the nasty things he said about me. Not that it's an excuse to speak to me that way, but I'm guessing something else was on his mind. After all, we had spoken about his mom, and he was clearly upset about that. I don't know, I guess I'm hoping he will offer up some kind of explanation for his behaviour last night.

It feels so good in his arms. Safe. Even after everything, why does he feel like home? He smells like his usual coconutty self, but it's mixed with stale whiskey. Somehow, I still can't get enough of it. Enough of him.

Neither of us speaks, we just breathe each other in. I don't know how long we stay like that, could have been a minute, could have been a week, but the sound of everyone heckling and wolf-whistling brings me back to reality. I realise someone is even singing Backstreet Boys, *'I Want It That Way'*, badly.

We both turn to see Ade, and now Greg too, singing into a bread roll come microphone. It sounds funny in his accent, and he gets most of the words wrong but he has a rough idea of the words from how many times he's heard me play it. Apparently, Greg was an avid BSB fan as he seems to know all the right words. Ryan and I both laugh at these clowns. He leans into me.

"How are you still here for me?" He barely whispers. "I'll never deserve you," he adds, planting a gentle kiss on my neck. He pulls me in tighter before pulling away, and I immediately mourn the loss of him. My Inner Brit works of her own volition, and before I know what I'm doing, I've taken his hand in mine. To my surprise, he holds my hand tightly as if it belongs in his, and we walk over to join the others at breakfast.

"You alright, mate? You had us worried there for a second, you little attention seeking bastard!" Greg holds a hand out to shake Ryan's, giving me a quick wink in the process. I'm on Ryan's left, so he doesn't need to let go of my hand to shake Greg's, and when he doesn't let go, it warms me.

To say I'm confused at his apparent one-eighty is an understatement, but this is heaven to me, and I'm not going to question it right now. He and I have a lot to talk about before everything will be alright between us, but for now, I'm just happy.

"I'm good thanks bro, it's so weird. I just took one look at your ugly-ass shirt and hit the deck!" Ryan jokes, and Ade howls with laughter. To be fair, Greg is wearing an awful black shirt covered in what could possibly be golden birds, or maybe they're flowers, I can't tell? Wait, are they cats? I literally have no idea, but in his defence, he is pulling it off.

He's wearing his usual black skinny jeans, and he's left the shirt open over a black vest. He has folded up the sleeves to reveal his impressive forearm tattoos. On one arm, he has a *Harry Potter* slash Dementor themed sleeve covering his entire arm, with what I think is a quote from the book. Something about finding happiness in dark times. So cool.

The other arm is a raven gripping an old-fashioned pocket watch in its claws. The glass of the watch is cracked, the clock frozen in time at ten minutes past six, and it's dated in the British format 21.07.14. All around the watch are dark clouds and there are different lyrics from the song *'Wonderwall'* hidden in each of the clouds. I've asked him about it, he says it's for his older brother who died, but he didn't say anymore.

"Oi, this is vintage *Versace* I'll have you know." Greg retorts, feigning offence. Ryan laughs and moves on to greet the next person at the table. Ade.

"He says *Versace*, but I'm pretty sure it's his mother's old drapes. Happy Birthday brother!" Ade holds out his hand, and for the first time Ryan seems to warm to him. He takes Ade's hand but pulls him into a dude hug.

After saying hello to everyone on the entire table, taking me with him the whole way around, we sit down to eat. The kids get up and perform a traditional dance and song in honour of Ryan's birthday, to which Greg and I attempt to join in and learn the moves.

After breakfast, which is now more like lunch, the guys get down to the important business of football. They put a ban on the use of the word 'soccer'. Each team has eight players, as there aren't enough players to have the full eleven on each side.

One team is made of Ade, Greg, and Ade's cousins, Samuel and Remy, as well as four of the kids. The other team consists of Ryan, Dad, and six of the other kids. Apparently, they thought Ryan was worth two extra adults.

They asked me to referee, seeing as I'm the only one left who has any sort of clue about the rules, but I'll be honest, I only really know the basics, and even then, that's only because my interest in the game started right around the time Ryan came to school.

After about ten minutes of play, it was clear Ryan was doing all he could to set up the younger players for all of the glory, be it on his own team, or the little ones brave enough to try and take him on. He would put on a show of dancing around them with the ball, but eventually he would always let them take it from him.

It was a different story when it came to the adults though. If any of them had the ball, it was game on, and he took no prisoners. He scored and assisted some beautiful goals, and it was 4-2 at half time. Greg was in goal for the opposition, and he spent the entire first half of the game cursing, to the point I gave him a yellow card. Apparently, it's not a yellow card offence, but hey, I'm the ref and there's kids around. Sue me.

At the end of the game, Ryan's team had won 6-4. All the kids run straight to Ryan to celebrate, even the ones not on his team. They are all dancing and cheering around him when he picks up one of the youngest boys, Joseph, and throws him on his shoulders dancing around like he's having the time of his life.

Afterwards, Ryan starts showing the boys a few tricks he can do with the ball, and one of the older boys suggests starting a keepie-uppie contest. Turns out my dad is surprisingly good at keepie-uppie. Ryan has literally had a look of pure joy on his face all day. He looks so handsome, wearing a smile I've never seen before that lights up his entire face.

Ade puts on some of his own music, and the whole yard comes alive. The kids go wild doing some new dance craze they all seem to know the moves to. So does Ade, and even Charity is joining in. Dad is dancing with Mom and it's easy to forget for a moment how much they have been arguing lately. Greg is on the side-lines taking some photos, he has a pretty decent camera and he loves to take pictures for the clinic's socials.

"Come on, *Ma Foi*, you're not getting out of it that easily!" Ryan says, pulling me over to join in the dance. We each take one of Joseph's hands, and the three of us dance and laugh together until our feet won't hold us up any longer, and it's honestly the best fun I've had in a very long time.

*\*\*\**

Later, Ryan decides to give a little speech and stands up from the table. He speaks in French and it sounds so romantic.

I don't fully understand everything he says, but I feel giddy, like I have a crush on him all over again.

"I just wanted to say thank you so much for today. I am so amazed by your generosity and kindness, I can honestly say I've never experienced anything like this in my life." He switches to English as emotions start to come through in his voice.

"I'm sorry about passing out earlier. I haven't celebrated a birthday for a few years, and to be honest I forgot it was even my birthday. I have no idea how you knew?" He looks right at me when he says that. Erm, I know because I've shamelessly stalked you for nearly a year now, can I say that?

"I guess I was just a little overwhelmed to see you all here for me, but I'm so thankful. I haven't been the most gracious guest here at times, and I'm sorry for that, truly I am." I can hear the sincerity in his voice and there is clear regret in Ryan's eyes when he speaks. He really does seem genuinely amazed by the fact everyone is here for him. He seems a little lost for words, as a sadness appears to creep over him.

Recognising he might need a moment, Greg stands up and starts singing a soccer chant, taking the attention off of Ryan, who offers him an appreciative nod, before walking away. I'm not sure if it's the right thing to do, but I follow him.

He walks down the dirt path towards the lake again. He sits down at the shore, and starts to skim stones into the lake. The late afternoon sun is hot, but luckily, he's sitting under a tree for shade. Sunlight trickles through the leaves, hitting his face in the most beautiful way.

"I know you're there. You may as well come over, rather than stand there spying on me, you naughty little pervert." My cheeks redden, but I go over and sit down.

"Are you okay?"

"Why are you always so nice to me, Faith? Like seriously, I don't deserve it, I never have? I'm awful to you, and you let me get away with it over and over again, why?" He says, seeming a little annoyed. It feels like a rhetorical question, and he doesn't look to me for an answer, so I don't respond.

"Don't let anyone treat you badly, Faith. Especially a guy. Especially not me!"

My chest aches. He is right, he is awful to me, and I do deserve better. But I know he has a good heart, I can feel it. I just wish he would tell me the truth.

"Why do you hate me? What did I do? Please be honest with me because I'm sorry, but I really don't know?" I grimace as I await his response.

"Nothing. You didn't do anything." He skims another rock and I watch it bounce along the water. I let out a loud breath, frustrated he didn't elaborate. "Today is just a hard day for me, that's all. I haven't celebrated a birthday since I lost my mom. Her anniversary, well it's a few days away. It never felt right celebrating, you know. But today, man she would have loved today. I'm pretty sure she was here, I could feel her."

I put my hand on his back but he shrugs me off, and I can't ignore the sting of it. "Tell me about Mia?" He asks quietly.

"What about her? She's your girlfriend!" I snap. I didn't mean for it to come out so bluntly, but it did nonetheless. He frowns, and throws another stone, but it's way too hard to skim, so this one just sinks straight to the bottom. All I can focus on are the ripples it makes. Is he pissed at me?

"She's not my girlfriend. She cheated on me, remember?" He skims another before turning to look at me. "She told me that you bullied her, in the past. That's what the pig thing was about. She wanted to get revenge and teach you a lesson, and honestly, so did I after the things she had told me. She lied to me and I believed her, which seems dumb as fuck now. As if anyone would believe you could be a bully. Ha, what a joke! My only defence is that I didn't know you, and I thought I knew her."

Another rock goes bouncing in.

"Did you know? About Shane and Mia, did you know?" Oh crap, I'd forgotten about that. Now I feel like shit. I guess I have to be the one who's honest now.

"Yes," I confess. "I saw them together. It was the day before the pig incident, they were having sex in the locker room," I admit as I hang my head. I'm not sure why I feel this way, I didn't do anything wrong, but I can't help feeling guilty all the same.

"They used to be a thing, back in freshman year. Mia decided one day she hated me, and that was it. Her and Shane, they made my life hell. All the rumours about me, they aren't true. You ask any guy in school and I bet you won't find one guy who could say they have actually slept with me. Sure, they will tell you that they know someone who did, or they heard about a thing, but it still won't be true. It was all Mia and Shane, and their lies." I watch his Adam's apple bob as he swallows. He knows it's the truth.

"Did Shane ever hurt you before that day?"

"Yes. He's hurt me a lot. Shane has slapped me before a few times, he has even punched me in the ribs once, I had bruises for weeks. He has kicked me, pulled my hair, all sorts of stuff." Ryan's features harden. He doesn't like that, but then he still sat there that day and let it happen? "How did you know? Last night you were so mad at me, you were certain I was still the bully by the way you spoke to me, so what changed?"

His face turns full of guilt as his eyes flicker from side to side. He reaches into his pocket and pulls out my phone, tossing it to me.

"You left it behind. I'm not a stalker I promise, it's just, well it went off, and I saw 'McBitchface' light up the screen. I was curious, I'm sorry, I shouldn't have invaded your privacy like that." He can't hide his smirk at the revelation of my name for Mia.

"What did it say?"

"It doesn't matter. You don't need to see that, so I deleted it. She knew you were with me, she must have seen the photos Greg posted, and I guess that pissed her off. I saw all the other messages, what the hell, *Foi*? Mia, Shane, Levi, all the fucking assholes chasing you? I deleted all of them too!" He throws another rock, angrily this time. I swallow down my embarrassment of what I know he must have read.

"I called her up and told her to stay the hell away from you, and from me. She's a nasty little bitch and I'll ruin her if she comes for you again! As for Shane? That scum will get what he deserves, mark my words!" His eyes have a fire in them I've never seen before. They are filled with anger, but there's something else I can't decipher. I'm furious he went down my phone, and deleted my messages, but at the same time I can't help but be happy he finally knows the truth.

"That thing he did with your panties? Did he ever force himself on you?" His eyes are black now, and his mouth pressed in a hard line. I know he must have seen the picture from the janitors' closet.

"No. He threatened to, a lot. One day, he almost did. Right after I met you, actually. First day back is always pretty rough, it's like they spend their summer breaks thinking up new ways to torture me. That's why I was rushing that morning. I was trying to get to a safe place before they got to school, but I was too late," I say quietly.

I attempt to shrug it off casually, trying to stop myself from showing how much this all affected me. He stares at me, silently demanding more details.

"You were talking to Mia, right after I left. I looked back and saw you with her. I was upset, and when I ran around the corner, I didn't see Shane waiting for me. He grabbed me, and forced me into the janitor's closet. He tried to force his dick into my mouth after assaulting me with a dirty mop. If it hadn't had been for the bell and all the students filling the hall, I doubt he would have stopped!"

Ryan breathes heavy, loud breaths through his nose. He is really mad, I've never seen him like this before. Last night he was angry, but this is different. It's like he wants to kill someone to avenge me.

"I saw the picture. That piece of shit is gonna pay, I promise you that! That was right after you spoke to me? Was it him who fucking barged you?"

"I honestly don't know who that was, but yes it was right after. You were with them all the time after that, so I couldn't trust you. I avoided you like I avoided them, but I was drawn to you. I couldn't stop thinking about you after, like how nice you had been to me. I needed to know if you were different, so I watched you. I was a bit of a stalker actually." I admit, lowering my head, cringing to myself. He doesn't even blink at my admission, which probably means he already knew I watched him. Oh crap.

"You seemed different to them, nice. Of course, you were really pretty to look at too, so that didn't help." Sweet Britney Jean, please stop talking. Ryan can't hide his smirk on hearing that, and I giggle nervously. Why do I feel so exposed right now? I'm so nervous. "Mia didn't like that though, me looking at you. if she caught me looking at you, she would make me pay for it."

There's a moment of silence, as the truth sits heavy between us, and my earlier nerves are replaced with anxiety, knowing I need to tell him more.

"My hair used to be long, you know that? One day I saw Mia at my father's practice. I had no idea why she was there, could've been a whole bunch of reasons. I didn't ask and Dad would never tell me anyway. She didn't leave me alone after that. One day, they put so much gum in my hair, I had to have it cut out. It went from being half way down my back to my shoulders. But that wasn't enough for them." He skims another stone.

"The next day, I was forced into the guy's locker room. Shane had two guys from the basketball team pin me down, while he took a knife to it and hacked off a big chunk of what was left, while Mia and Hayley threw the contents of my bag in the shower. Then they held me down while they smeared red lipstick all over my lips and then smudged it to look like I'd been, well you know, up to no good!" I grimace, remembering it all. I was totally humiliated that day.

"They ripped open the top of my shirt and then they threw me under the shower, still in my uniform. I had no option but to walk out into the packed hall in my wet clothes and see-through shirt, my face and hair a mess." Ryan's face is hard as stone, as if he is hearing this for the first time. How did he not know any of this until now?

"The next day everyone was saying that I got caught letting the basketball team take turns with me, and that someone's girlfriend went crazy on me for it. I guess you heard that rumour, huh?" I say in a tone more sarcastic than I intended it to be, and he looks away, guilt all over his face.

"Somehow the rumours evolved over time, and before I knew it I was the school slut, but the funny thing is no one would go near me after that, even if I'd have wanted them to.

Even girls stayed away not wanting to be associated with me. There was always another rumour, something worse than the last. Even the guidance counsellor called me into her office for a chat!" I laugh out, pretending my eyes aren't stinging from going over it all. My voice weakens as I continue.

"I've seen the boy's locker room. The graffiti about me? It's the same in the girl's too. I know why you think the way you do about me, but the truth is I've never, well you know, been with anyone before. Never." I drop my head, cringing at my own confession. He's never going to want me now. He stares at me and the silence is deafening, making me feel even more exposed than I already did.

"I'm pathetic, I know. I hadn't even kissed a guy until yesterday, so you were my first. Except, for trying to kiss Ade the other day, but he didn't kiss me back so that doesn't count. He couldn't pull away fast enough actually... "

I'm broken from my speech by his sudden lips on mine. It's different than before, this is a slow and gentle kiss that has my tummy doing somersaults. He cups my face as he kisses me tenderly. It might be slow but it's still filled with his need for me.

Now *this* is a kiss.

Yesterday was great but this, this is how I imagined it would be. Gentle, romantic, filled with passion.

We finally break for air and I can't help but smile from ear to ear.

"Fuck, I hope that was a better kiss than yesterday's. I'm sorry *Foi*, I would never have acted how I did if I'd known that. Fucking pushing my dick onto you like that, I'm such an asshole."

I continue to stare at him like a deer in headlights after being rendered speechless by his whimsical kiss. He offers me a nervous grin that makes a similar one appear on my own lips, and he takes that as an invitation to kiss me again, and it's so amazing.

I greedily climb onto his lap, and run my fingers into his hair. He moves his hands to my waist but doesn't try to move any lower. It's all very PG, aside from the fact I can feel him harden beneath me. We both ignore it, choosing to lose ourselves in our delicious kiss. Although I have to admit, for the first time in my life, the feel of him beneath me makes me feel sexy.

We carry on like that for a while. We talk, we kiss, we laugh, we kiss some more. I don't know how long we spend like that, but when we finally realise the sun has gone down, we head back up to the yard to see everyone else has gone home. We say goodnight with another spine-tingling kiss, and head into our separate cabin's to try to get an early night, we will be leaving with Mom first thing.

I'm so giddy when I go inside, I'm already debating whether to text him or not. I decide what the hell. He's had his tongue in my mouth all evening. I'm sure he knows I like him by now.

**Faith** - I really enjoyed today. I realise I didn't actually say happy birthday yet, so Happy Birthday douche canoe! I know we still need to talk about a lot, but I really like you, I always have. X

He doesn't reply straight away, although I see that he's read it. I assume he's gone for a shower, so I spend some time with my parents discussing the day's events. I leave out the part about the kissing marathon. By the time I have gone and showered and gotten into bed there is finally a reply waiting for me.

**Ryan** - I think maybe we should just be friends. I'm sorry.

# CHAPTER 17

## Ryan

To say things are frosty the next morning is an understatement. Faith hasn't spoken to anyone the entire journey, and Greg keeps giving me the stink eye because he clearly knows something's up. I know what you're thinking, I deserve the cold shoulder, and I do, I'm an asshole. But hear me out.

Yesterday was amazing, the whole day was the best fun I've had in a long time, and I know Faith was the one to thank for it. I've decided Faith is like a lioness. She's brave, and magnificent, and she loves fiercely.

I still don't know how she seems to know all this shit about me, but she had to have been planning it all week. Since I've been nothing but a dick to her for most of that time, I have no idea why she would have gone to so much trouble. I mean, she was already baking me a cake before anything happened between us. Even more confusing is why was she still doing it, after I beat her dad?

Malcolm was right, she does have a big heart. He said to

me yesterday, that if I didn't want or deserve her love then I should stay away from her. Well after spending the rest of the day yesterday just kissing Faith, talking and laughing about silly things, I know that I definitely do want it. Man, do I fucking want it. Do I deserve it? Abso-fucking-lutely not.

See, I figure it's bad enough starting a friendship built on a foundation of lies, but I'd be some next level ass-wipe to get involved with her, knowing what I've done. When she texted me and told me she liked me, I knew it would be wrong to let her fall for me when she doesn't know the truth, especially after her confession yesterday about still being a virgin.

Urgh. It's not like I can just tell her the truth either, because then I'll not only lose her, but I'll be arrested for sure. I'm not sure a charge of aggravated assault will look good on my Columbia application. Scott family name or not, I'm pretty sure I'd struggle to get into any school if the truth comes out. I'll be lucky to escape jail time.

I'm damn sure my father won't be bailing me out either. He would bury it so that no one would ever find out his name had been tarnished. He would likely say I'd gone abroad to study. He would pick some prestigious school somewhere obscure, so as not to get caught out in his lie. He would never admit the truth publicly, but he would teach me a life lesson and make me do my time nonetheless.

The truth is I really do want her beautiful lion heart, and I would gladly give her mine, if I had any of it left to give that is. I'm pretty sure upsetting her a little now is better than the alternative of breaking her heart further down the line. It's too late to worry about mine, about a thousand fucking days too late to be precise.

I told her I wanted to be friends, so for now I'll let her be angry with me, and then hopefully she will come around. It sucks though, because I already miss her. I know she's sat right there in the front of the Jeep, but I miss her.

Walking back up from the lake last night I genuinely had butterflies. I know, right? I don't think I've ever felt so excited and nervous with a girl like that, ever. Not even when it was my first time, especially not with Mia.

Up until I was about fourteen, I didn't get all that much attention from girls. Let's just say I was a late bloomer. Once I turned fourteen though, girls started to notice me. I guess the three solid years of intense soccer training helped a little with that.

I actually had my first kiss with Spencer when I was thirteen, but that's a whole other story for another time. My second kiss was a year later at a Halloween party. The girl was dressed as a ballerina with fake blood smeared all over her huge tits, and seeing as how I have no fucking idea what her name was, she will be forever referred to in the history books as 'Ballerina Girl'.

I went to the party in the rival school's soccer kit, with the words 'R.I.P. next season' crudely written on the back. Everyone loved it, especially Ballerina Girl, because she even let me finger bang her too. True story.

My third kiss, and first official girlfriend, was a girl named Harriet behind the bike shed, as *cliché* as it sounds. She was pretty cool and I actually liked her. We weren't anything serious though, we never got past second base. We were only together a couple of months before it was summer break and I had to go back home to New York. Then, after what happened that summer, I completely fazed her out.

It wasn't her fault, I just wasn't interested in her anymore. I wasn't interested in anyone.

I guess she didn't take to kindly to that, because pretty soon I had this reputation of being a fuck boy. Funny thing is

I really wasn't. Girls just seemed to flock to me though, once that rumour was out. I guess what they say is true, girls love a bad boy. But like I said, I wasn't interested in anyone anymore, so they didn't get very far with me.

Faith and I, we just kissed, neither of us tried to take it any further. If I'm honest I was happy just to take things slow. Mostly because I was enjoying the kissing and the new butterfly feeling she was giving me. After hearing I was her first kiss, I knew she needed time, and I'd never rush a girl into anything anyway. The night was perfect as it was.

Reality hit me when I got back to my cabin though when I saw I had a text from Mia, wishing me 'Happy Birthday'. Seriously, happy fucking birthday, as if the conversation the night before never happened? Crazy bitch.

Hearing all the awful shit Mia and Shane have done to Faith made my blood boil. I swear to God I'm going to kill Shane when I see him. If he thinks he can get away with hurting a girl like that, my girl, he's in for a big surprise. *Yeah, still not your girl, ass-wipe.*

\*\*\*

We've been on the road for about four hours when Lorrie pulls over so we can all have a drink and bite to eat. Things have definitely gotten a lot more rural. At one point we drove for a good half an hour before we passed another person. We actually did see some really cool birds though, and I even saw some buffalo, which was rad. Not quite the safari I was hoping for, but still awesome. How Dad and his douchey pal's go hunting over here, I'll never know?

So anyway, it turns out the clinic hasn't got many appointments this week so Malcolm asked Greg to come along with us. I got the impression it was because he wanted Lorrie back sooner, but what do I know. We also have another larger vehicle with us carrying all the supplies, which is driven by Ade's two cousins I met yesterday, Remy and Samuel. Apparently, although they are brothers, they aren't Ade's actual cousins, but they refer to each other as such because they grew up together. They are both travelling with us as chaperones as apparently it can be unsafe to travel alone, especially for aid workers who are often robbed or kidnapped for ransom.

The thought makes me feel glad that Faith invited me along, I'm not sure how comfortable I would have been staying back while Faith and Lorrie are out here potentially at risk. How Malcolm can just let them go off without him, I don't know, but then I suppose they have spent their whole lives moving around in dangerous places. I immediately noticed that Ade's 'cousins' were armed. I'm not sure if that brings me comfort or anxiety, but none of the others seemed phased. I guess that's why they invited them.

Apparently, they will also be acting kinda like roadies, setting up camp, and making sure all the supplies are kept safe, which is cool because I don't know the first thing about pitching a tent, and I'd be very surprised if Greg did either.

We pull over on the outskirts of a little village at what appears to be a sort of restaurant. I guess you could call it that. It's a small place, more like an open front hut, with decorative but heavily worn rugs on the floor to sit on. The place serves plantains and potatoes with a local beer, and to be honest, although the food was great, I was more psyched about the beer.

There is a bathroom out back, well actually it's more a shed with no real plumbing, just a bucket to flush out the wooden toilet after. There is a clean water pump outside for filling the bucket and for washing up afterwards. After eating I use the bathroom. I splash my face with the water from the pump, and run a little through my hair. It's another hot day, so after checking that it was ok to drink, I fill up everyone's water bottles for the rest of the journey. I'm just putting them back in the crate when someone clears their throat announcing their presence, and it's Faith. Oh fuck, she certainly looks pissed.

She's back to her yoga pants and oversized tee-shirt look again. Today's shirt is black, and in white writing it says 'Kiss my Calabasas' on it which I'm guessing is for my benefit. Shit, now I'm actually thinking about kissing her sweet ass. Or biting it, whatever. I smirk to myself that she's completely missed the mark on getting her point across. She scoffs, noticing my smile creeping in, as if she knows exactly where my wandering mind has taken me.

I gotta say, a pissed off Faith is a big turn on. I feel like being annoying to her, just to have her sass me some more.

"Hey, erm, I was just, err, filling up all the water bottles." *Or you could just be lame as fuck dude, whatever.*

Why does this girl make me so nervous?

"Cool story, bro. Did you carry a watermelon too?" She says quickly in a bratty voice, wiggling her head from side to side to emphasise her attitude. She even has her hand on her hip. I raise my eyebrow. Trying to stay as cool as possible

"Yeah, erm, I don't get that reference, *Baby*. Sorry, but I'm sure it was real funny though?" I rub her arm in a deliberately patronising gesture. I do get it, but I won't tell her that. You don't grow up having chicks as best friends and not know a *Dirty Dancing* reference. *Touché, Ma Belle Foi.*

Faith rolls her eyes and winces as she shrugs off my touch and I can't ignore the cut that slices through me.

"Ha! Well I can't believe that for a second, but apparently you don't like it when the joke is on you, huh? Whatever. Let's just pretend you *don't* get it. Cool. Are you done here, *Bobby Bushey?*"

See, sass. I can't help but laugh at that one, and for a split second, I see her mask drop as she tries to stop a smirk creeping in at her own joke. I take my chances at thawing the ice.

"Looks like nobody's gonna put you in a corner, hey?" I smile at her and she scoffs back a laugh. "Listen *Foi*, I meant what I said, I want us to be friends. I wasn't trying to piss you off, or hurt you. I was just trying to be honest about how I feel. I don't want to fight with you, I really do like you, but that's all I can offer. I'm sorry." As the words come out of my mouth I watch as her face speaks a thousand words. She's clearly hurt by what I'm saying but I don't know what else I can do for the best.

If I tell her the truth I'll lose her for good. At least this way I get to keep a part of her, even if it's not her lion heart.

"It's fine, I know I'm not good enough for you, but I thought we had a connection, I thought you felt it too?" Her voice breaks as she looks away from me, and something in my gut aches.

"Not good enough for me, are you crazy? If anyone's not good enough here it's me. I don't deserve you, I doubt I ever will!" She shakes her head but won't look at me so I move into her space and push her chin up toward me. "Please Faith? We do have a connection, but I've just gone through a break up, I just found out my ex-girlfriend manipulated me into hating you all this time, and I just don't want to rush into something with you. I'm sorry. I want to be friends, but it's definitely not because I don't want you, believe me." *Pussy. Just tell her the damn truth. She won't want you anyway when she knows.*

She straightens herself up and raises her chin slightly and I can tell instantly she's about to put me in my place. Yep, my girl is definitely a lioness. *Still not your fucking girl.*

"I'm in love with you, Ryan, don't you see that? I'm not sure I can be friends with you, because I want to be more than that. I want to be the one you kiss, all of the time. I want to be the one you wrap your arms around just so everyone knows that I'm yours and you're mine." She wraps her own arms around herself like she always does. "I want to wear your sweater because you love to see me wearing it, not because you traded it for a stupid ride. I want to be your girl so badly, it's all I've ever wanted."

At this point she drops her head back down, as if she used up her daily allowance of balls, and makes herself small again, and it pisses me off to see her that way. "I don't want to fight with you either, so I guess we can try the friends thing, if that's what you really want." She shrugs and gives me a half smile before she walks away. I haven't even had a chance to process what she's said let alone respond. She's in love with me? What the hell? I chase after her needing an explanation.

"Faith!... *Foi*, wait! What do you mean you're in love with me, how can that be, it's only been a week?" She looks down at the ground again, like she's embarrassed. How can she switch from lion to mouse in an instant?

"It's been almost a year, actually."

What the hell does that mean? I put my hands on each of her arms and gently run my hands up and down.

"Talk to me, *Ma Foi*?"

"Stop it, stop calling me that. I'm not *your* Faith, you don't want me as your girl, remember?" She fiercely shrugs out of my touch, and my fingers burn with the need to reach back and grab her again, to shake her and scream at her that she *is* mine. Mine. But I fight it.

Her skin is so soft, probably where she hasn't spent years applying crap to it. Just a cute little handmade bar of ethical vanilla soap is all. I know because she left a fresh one out for me at her vanity sink when she let me use her cabin. It came in a little burlap pouch, all tied up with a yellow ribbon that had a label on it, all about the independent store where she bought it. It even had a request to send the pouch back so they can re-use it, instead of sending it to the garbage. Adorable, right?

As soon as I smelt it I realised that's where the hint of vanilla comes from. My vanilla frosting baby. I made a mental note to order some as soon as I get back to L.A.

"Are you kids ready, we're about to head back out?" Lorrie interrupts us and I'm left wondering how much she's overheard. Faith seems to have the same thought as she looks back at her mother, mortified.

"I was just about to use the bathroom," Faith says quickly, running back towards the shed.

"Is everything okay, Ryan? You don't seem yourself? I know Faithy can be a little difficult to get along with sometimes, but she always means well." Lorrie gives me a motherly back rub as we walk back towards the Jeep. Wait, what? She thinks Faith's the problem here? Surely, she should be checking that Faith is alright, not me.

"Faith's not difficult to get along with, she's the complete opposite. It's me who's the problem, I'm the one who's an asshole!" Lorrie looks at me, surprised by my bluntness, but also a look I can't quite decipher. It's almost like pity?

"You've been through so much, Ryan. Losing your mother the way you did at such a young age, no one could blame you for being a little pissed at the world."

How would Lorrie know anything about my mother? She gives me a warm smile and gets into the Jeep just as Faith comes walking back with Greg, who's carrying the crate I left behind. Where did he come from? Faith has thrown her hair up loosely and a few rogue strands are left framing her face. She's so natural, her beauty is effortless. Why did it take me so long to notice how beautiful she really is?

"I hear you filled these up, mate. Cheers, *Water Boy!*" Greg says beaming at his own joke. Faith can't hide the smirk at hearing him repeat a version of the joke she made.

"Nice try, wanker. Faith already used that joke." I thought he would appreciate the English slang, and he does, going by the roaring laugh he offers in return.

"My delivery was way funnier too!" Faith chirps up as she climbs into the Jeep, offering me an awkward smile. I can't help but give her one back, and whilst I don't intend for it to be, I'm pretty sure my smile is just as awkward. I'm still taken back by her confession; how can she be in love with me?

Hearing her say she wants to be my girl made something flip inside me. Do I want that? Hell fucking yes.

It's weird, because I don't feel like I've had enough time to get to know her properly, but yet I know with every fibre of my being that she is meant to be mine. I've never felt this way about a girl before, not Mia, not even with the chick I lost my virginity with, and not even Kat.

There was a time after my Mom died, that I confused Kat's friendship as something more. We kissed, and fooled around a little. It was great, though something about it didn't feel right to me, but I carried on with it anyway because I needed it. I used her. We were best friends, and as much as I cared for her, I had never wanted to kiss her before that.

Don't get me wrong, Kat has always been smoking hot, I just didn't look at her in that way. To me she was more like a sister, it just didn't feel right. The next day I knew it was a mistake, so I avoided her and acted like an asshole. Two days later I ended up losing my virginity to some random girl in the upper-class called Liv.

Liv was eighteen and getting ready to graduate, while I was still barely fifteen, although she didn't seem to mind the age gap. She lived off campus and had a car. She flirted with me one day, and then just full blown asked if I wanted to go eat her pussy somewhere. I had never done anything like that before. Sure, I'd fingered a couple of girls, but I'd never taken it any further than that.

So, I got in her car, and she drove us right out to some industrial place on the outskirts of the city somewhere. It looked abandoned, lots of windows were smashed and there was no one around.

Liv reached over and took my cock out of my pants and started sucking me off. I wasn't even hard yet, but that didn't seem to deter her. It didn't take long for me to get hard and swiftly blow my load down her more than eager throat, having been so inexperienced at that point. When she was finished she made a point of licking her lips before sliding off her scarlet red, G-string panties. She passed them to me and said I could keep them, before she got out of the car and sat spread eagled on the hood waiting for me to hold up my end.

I did, but she didn't get off, again due to my lack of experience. After I fumbled my way around down there for a while, she pulled me up and wrapped a condom over my dick before guiding it inside of her. I wasn't expecting it, but it happened, and it felt good. So, I went with it. I fucked her, hard and fast, in the middle of a dirty abandoned warehouse yard.

I felt nothing being with her. Sure, she was hot, but there was never any real emotional connection. Afterwards, I didn't even feel phased that I'd had my first time. I didn't care. Nothing mattered, and I didn't want to feel anything anyway.

I made her my girlfriend, although I never actually asked her. I chose instead to make a very public show of it by accepting her request for the title on my social media. I allowed her to post several photos of us together in compromising positions, in the hopes Kat would get the message.

I know, it's a fucked-up way to treat your best friend, but my only defence was that I wasn't really thinking straight at that point. In my head it all made sense, even though I knew I was hurting Kat. I carried on ignoring her for a few weeks, which in turn meant ignoring my whole friendship group.

When the others found out what I did and how I'd treated Kat, they weren't very pleased with me, especially Tom. They all voluntarily ignored me back for a while too. Alex was pretty pissed, he's always been very flirty with Kat, but I'd often suspected he really had eyes for Spencer. For whatever reason he was confused about that, and he flirted with Kat to deflect from his real feelings. What the hell do I know though, as far as I know he has still never made any real moves on either girl.

Talking of Spencer, now she was hella' mad, though fuck knows what her issue was. Girl code or something.

Anyway, I was fucked up, and the only person I spent any time with was Liv, and all that really involved was sex. Nasty sex too, like a quick fuck while she was bent over in the backseat of her car. Or I'd have her on her knees for me in one of the school supply closets, taking my cock as far down her throat as I could get it. I took everything out on her, giving it to her brutally every time.

She lapped it up, telling every chick in school what a great fuck I was. I even had girls propositioning me after every game, but fuck if I gave them the slightest bit of attention. For all intents and purposes, Liv was my girl and I'm not a cheater. Besides, what would've been the point. Liv was an easy lay, and she didn't seem to give a shit that that's all it ever was. We both got what we wanted from it; she wanted to get off, and I wanted to forget.

It was a couple of months later when Tom came and beat my ass, before dragging me off to speak to Kat. After actually talking to her, I finally came to my senses. Luckily, we were both on the same page, and it wasn't a big deal. She knew it was just about comfort for me, and she only wanted to give me that.

We were friends, that's it. She understood why I acted out the way I did, even though it hurt her. I apologised and she accepted, saying she was just worried about me and only wanted her best friend back.

See, best friends, no need for drama. But it was a big reality check for me, and I realised how lucky I was. I would have hated to lose the friendship we have.

Had. I guess I did end up losing it anyway, because I sure as hell haven't been a good friend to her, or to any of them for a long time. Shit, I really need to sort that out. Only problem is, they will tell me I need to be honest with Faith if I ever want to be with her.

It's a rock and a hard place, tell her the truth, or give her up. As much as I agree with that, I'm just not sure I wanna do either.

# CHAPTER 18

## Ryan

After two more silent hours on the road, we finally get to the first village we will be staying in. It's on the outskirts of the jungle, and I'm told by Samuel that if we are lucky, we might see some bonobos, forest elephants, or even gorillas, but it's rare to see them so close to the village.

About two miles out was a well, and we filled up a bunch of large water tanks to bring into the village. Apparently, each household in the village has to make several trips a day, carrying heavy containers of water on their backs, in order to have enough water for their families. Here I am complaining about the shower pressure every morning. What an asshole, talk about first world problems.

We are welcomed into the village like honoured guests with most of the villagers coming out to greet us. Lorrie is known here as she's visited before during an Ebola outbreak. It's also thanks to the Ashers that every home in this particular village has mosquito nets. Something cheaply supplied that saves so many lives.

A lot of the locals seem to think Greg is a famous rock star, and I can see why they would think that with his black skinny jeans, tattoos and wild dark hair. They couldn't believe it when they heard he was a doctor.

I'm not sure how, but they already seem to know that I play soccer, and several of the kids drag me off to have a kick around. They call me Ryanaldo. Hey, Ronaldo is one of the most successful players of all time so I'll happily take that as a compliment.

I'm not usually one to show off. But the kids love to see some ball skills, so I dance around with the ball, flashing some of my best moves much to their enjoyment. I even managed to teach a few of them some of my tricks. We play penalty shoot-outs for a while before I deliberately shoot one wide for the kids' amusement. I fall to the ground like I can't believe my bad luck, and half the kids come and jump on top of me in a dog pile. I haven't laughed like this for a long time. This was definitely the light-hearted distraction I needed.

"Come on up, *Ryanaldo,* it's time to start earning your keep around here!" Greg stands over me smiling offering his hand to pull me from the ground. "You've got some talent when it comes to balls mate," he winks at me suggestively, but I know he is only fooling around. "Are you seriously not going to pursue a professional career?" Greg continues, as I dust myself off.

"I thought about it. Faith was right, I was scouted a couple of times, but my father would never allow it." I shake my head knowing how pathetic that sounds. I high five all the kids before I head back with Greg.

"Listen mate, I get it. It's all very well Faithy saying 'who cares what he wants', but she doesn't come from that life," Greg offers knowingly. "But she's not wrong. You can make your own choices, walk away if you have to, that's what I did. Life is too short not to live it your own way." So I was right, he does come from money. Wonder what his deal is?

"I come from a long line of Scott men, who are born and raised for the sole purpose of becoming CEO, making even more money, then marrying a bride from a pre-approved list, just to produce the next heir in line. I can walk away from that, sure, but it's walking away from everything, including my family. My father might be a dick but he is still my father. His new wife is nice enough, and their new baby, he will be my brother. I might be eighteen years older than him, but fuck if I'm not going to be the best big brother I can be."

Greg gives me a supportive smile, silently telling me he understands. "I don't want to go back to New York. Whether I play soccer or not, I could still think of about a hundred other things I'd rather do than spend four years of my life back in New York."

We get back to the village and we can hear a woman screaming. We rush over to a small house, where Faith is standing outside with tears streaming down her face. I instinctively pull her into my chest as soon as I reach her, while Greg rushes inside the house to see what's going on.

"What's wrong, *Ma Belle Foi*? Tell me what happened?" I demand, as she trembles in my arms.

"H-he was just a baby. It's not f-fair, it's not right." Faith's words are barely legible through her sobs, so I walk her away from the house. We walk towards the edge of the village where there is a small camp set up for us to stay in, kindly pitched by Sam and Remy.

Man, these guys work fast. They have somehow managed to pitch up three tents and set up all the supplies, and now they appear to be making dinner. Two of the tents are for sleeping in and a third for Lorrie and Greg to work from, but seeing as how Greg and I are last minute extras on the trip, we will need to share the third tent to sleep in at night.

I take Faith inside the third tent. I sit on one of the cots and pull her into my lap. She snuggles into my chest like she belongs there, and honestly, I think that she does. She wraps her arms around my waist tightly burying her face in my neck, like she's afraid to let me go. The thought makes my chest ache. Please don't ever let me go, no matter what happens, I silently plead.

I wrap my arms around her tightly, and hold her. I have a strong inexplicable need to protect her, and I feel a rage burning inside me. I intend to destroy any bastard who ever puts tears on her face again, even if that bastard happens to be me.

# CHAPTER 19

## Faith

I don't know how long Ryan holds me on his lap, but he has a big wet patch on his shirt from my tears. I can still hear Sam and Rems outside talking and making dinner, but I haven't heard Greg or Mom come back yet. As much as I don't ever want him to let me go, I reluctantly begin to explain my hysterical behaviour.

"There was a baby. He was sick, and they couldn't get to a doctor. They thought it would be ok because they knew Mom was coming, so they waited. They didn't know it was Malaria. They have nets, but there was a small hole in the one the baby was using. He deteriorated really fast. Mom said it was too late, he was too advanced, she gave him what she could but he...he...he was only a year old." My voice breaks as a tear falls down my cheek and Ryan moves to wipe it away.

"It's not fair, Faith, I know that. Nothing about this place seems fair. How can my family have so much, and yet millions of people here have nothing? It doesn't make sense, any of it. Just the thought of my father's bungalow now makes me feel sick." Ryan shakes his head in disbelief. "You were completely right about that place. I want to be better, Faith, better than my dad. I want to do some good in this world. I don't want to be the man who wasted millions of dollars on an eyesore mansion. Who the hell needs that many bathrooms anyway?"

I laugh a sad laugh, because I literally used to say the same thing, but then I start sobbing again uncontrollably. Ryan rubs his hand across my thigh. I'm sure he didn't mean anything by it, it was just a comfort thing, but we both feel a spark ignite at the gesture. I look up into Ryan's gorgeous gold flecked eyes and they seem laced with desire, but I must be imagining it? He said he just wants to be friends?

I put my hands on his face and he doesn't stop me. He remains completely still as I run my thumb over his bottom lip.

"You feel that too, right?"

"Yes," he says, seeming barely able to speak.

"Do you want me?" I ask bravely, and I feel my heart racing. He keeps the same intense look on his face as he moves his groin around beneath me, rubbing himself up against my core, showing me without words that he definitely does want me, or at least, his body does.

"Yes," is all he answers again, his face giving away the fact he is battling some inner demons. He wants this, but he is holding back. A voice inside of me tells me he doesn't want me because I'm a virgin. *You know that's not the reason, Faith, just be cool.*

I'm not expecting what comes next when yet again I find myself taking off my t-shirt for a guy, for the second time in a few days. I don't know who the hell I think I am lately. Unlike Ade though, Ryan doesn't turn away, he stares, his big brown eyes now black with need. He licks his lips. Does he actually like what he sees?

Keeping the momentum going I move to straddle his waist. I'm wearing a lilac bra that's not really sexy, but it is cute, and the colour looks good against my skin tone. I thank God I'm not wearing my boring white one, or my sports bra like the other day.

He puts his hands on my hips and watches me. He seems mesmerised, watching as my chest rises and falls. His touch on my bare skin sends goosebumps all over, even though it's hot. I decide that it's now or never to be completely honest. It might scare him off again, but if I don't get this out now I feel like I might burst.

"I've felt a connection to you since the moment you came to our school. I know that sounds crazy, but I thought you were so beautiful. You are really smart, and funny, and everyone thinks you're great. You are the most popular guy because you're a great guy, and you're nice to everyone, not just the popular kids." He gives me a soft smile that reminds me of the reason I fell for him in the first place.

"I saw you a few days later in class, and you gave me the warmest smile. You used to smile at me all the time, did you know that? I know that might seem a small thing to you, it's just your good manners I guess. I knew deep down it didn't mean anything, you probably didn't even realise you were doing it, but it meant everything to me." He frowns, and I can tell he is trying to remember.

"You don't know what it's been like for me there. Everyone hates me, I don't have any friends, I don't have anyone. When you smiled at me, and you helped me out that on that first day, I thought maybe you might give me a chance. You didn't talk to me anymore, but you didn't hate me either, and I loved you for that." I admit honestly. I did love him, he was mine. I began to live for those smiles.

"You really are gorgeous when you smile. I mean you're

gorgeous whatever your expression. I especially like your brooding scowl, but you were definitely made to wear a smile." He gives me another smile, but this time it's a cocky one, and he even adds a wink that sends heat straight to my core. That bastard. He laughs, sensing my reaction to him. Why does his laugh make me want to kiss him? *His laugh, his hair, his wink. What doesn't make you want to kiss him?*

"I guess that's why I always watched you, because I didn't want to miss it if you did look at me. I'm pathetic, I know." I shrug and look down, starting to feel exposed. He still hasn't spoken but his hands are gripped firmly on my hips while ever so slightly rubbing his thumb up and down in the gentlest of motions. "Even when you did hate me, I still couldn't find it in me to hate you back. I still hoped you would tell me it was a mistake."

I suddenly feel overcome with need. I want Ryan to be my first. I want to tell him that, but I'm afraid he won't want me. Inner Brit starts singing loudly in my head. Okay Inner Brit, we got this. I take a deep breath.

"I've thought about this for a long time. I want you, Ryan. I want you to be more than just my first kiss, I want you to be all my firsts. All of them. W-would you want that too?" Something burns inside me. His thumb movements are driving me crazy and leave my whole body aching for more.

I cautiously put my hands back on his face again and I'm not sure when he put them there, but his hand's are now sitting heavy on my ass. He squeezes it possessively, before he slowly leans in to kiss my neck. He starts peppering tender kisses all over my neck and shoulders.

"I do want you, Faith... *kiss

"I don't hate you... *kiss

I let out tiny whimpers in between kisses and he growls

in response, letting me know that I'm making him just as crazy as he is making me.

"I don't deserve your firsts... *kiss

"But I want all of them... *kiss

"I want you to be mine... *kiss

Wait, what? Did he just say? Oh God. He bites and sucks on my shoulder, and I let out a loud sound of pleasure I didn't realise I could make.

"*Ma Belle Foi*. Mine!" He practically growls out and we both lose it.

I pull his face up to mine and my lip's crash to his in a brutal kiss that's filled with a raw passion I've never experienced before. He meets my pace, before taking control. He pulls me firmly down into his lap as if to make sure I can feel his rock-hard dick straining against his shorts. To my own surprise, my body moves against him of its own volition, as if my body knows what it needs.

I slowly grind my hips and I feel him press back hard against me. He pulls at my bra, revealing my full breasts to him as they bounce free. His eyes darken. This is the most exposed I've ever been but yet I don't feel nervous, I just feel alive.

Seeing this look on his face, he can't hide how much he is enjoying my body and I feel empowered. I've never felt beautiful or sexy before, but right now, with him looking at me like this, I feel like a goddess. I want more.

Ryan waits for a beat to see if I object before he runs his finger's gently over one of my nipples, teasing it between his thumb and finger. God that feels so good. I let out another of those loud moans before pressing myself into him, letting him know that I need what he's offering. He doesn't need any further invitation as he leans down and takes my other nipple into his mouth.

I throw my head back as he sucks and nibbles on my sensitive buds. My fingers are wrapped in his thick hair and I can't help but tug on it as he drives me wild with pleasure. He growls out a low growl each time I do it, a sound that for some reason is only intensifying my own desire.

I feel a wetness in my panties as he slowly starts to run his fingers along the waistband of my yoga pants, his eyes fixed on me as he does. He looks down at the waistband and back to me for approval, and I nod.

"Please Ryan, I need you." I beg unashamedly. He doesn't waste a moment before he stands me up off his lap and pulls down my pants. He takes a minute to appreciate my matching lilac thong. He leans in and kisses my soft tummy, which makes my cheeks heat with embarrassment, but he just smirks up at me.

He tugs off my pants and pulls me back onto his lap and kisses me again, his hands roaming freely around to my ass. He grips both cheeks possessively, and lets out another low growl that I catch, passionately with my mouth. He squeezes my ass hard enough to leave marks as I rock myself against him. He takes the hint and pulls my panties to the side with one hand, and slips his finger's gently between my soaked folds.

Oh. My. God.

He lets out another sexy low growl at discovering my wetness, before biting my shoulder like a wild animal. I move against his fingers, it feels so good, I can hardly breathe.

Ryan reaches up with his other hand and runs his fingers into my hair. He grips it, tight enough to send shivers through my body, but not so tight that it hurts. He pulls me in for a gentle kiss, completely contradicting his savage bites.

He increases pace, with his hand and his tongue in a

synchronised dance, and pretty soon I'm panting with need. He continues kissing me, claiming all of my moans with his mouth.

I can't hold on much longer as I feel my orgasm building. I move against him faster and he presses harder against my clit before sliding his finger up inside me. I gasp at the sudden invasion. Ryan chuckles, but gives me a minute to adjust. Still gently rubbing me with the palm of his hand, he slowly slides in a second finger. I take a deep breath as I get used to the feel of his fingers inside me.

"Just relax, *Ma Belle Foi*, let me take care of you," Ryan says in a low voice, as he begins to move his fingers gently in and out of me.

My body, apparently now a slave to Ryan's command, immediately relaxes, and the need from before returns. There is a fierce fire burning inside me that I know only he can put out. His eyes blacken as he hears my silent plea. He moves his fingers in and out a little faster, and I begin to move with him.

"That's right, baby. Do you like that?" He asks, his low voice sounding sexier than ever.

"Oh God. Ryan, I'm so close, please…"

He lets out a chuckle.

"I got you, baby!" He grips me tightly with his other hand, holding me firmly in place while he begins to thrust his fingers harder inside of me. He curls them forward, hitting a spot I didn't even know existed inside of me, and I throw my head back.

"Yes, I like that. Ryan, God yes!" I'm suddenly seeing stars. I must have let out a loud cry, as he chuckles again, pulling me back in for another heart melting kiss, continuing to thrust in and out of me until I'm completely spent. I stay still against his chest, unable to speak or move. I've never felt this way in my whole life, I feel like I'm floating on a cloud. Sure, I've sorted myself out from time to time, but nothing like this.

"Hmm... Can I just sleep forever now, please?"

He laughs and I feel it vibrate inside his chest. I listen to his heartbeat and it's racing. Should I do something for him now, is he waiting? Oh God, what if I'm not any good at it? Before I can get too deep in my own head, he takes his fingers away and my cheeks burn with embarrassment when he puts them in his mouth, sucking them clean, then making a show of licking his lips after.

"Vanilla frosting, baby; my new favourite flavour." He gives me the most gorgeous and heartfelt smile he has ever given me and I can already feel question after question burning inside me.

"What does this mean?" *Woah! Way to kill the mood. What the hell is wrong with you?*

I'm mortified at my own bluntness, but I can't hide how I feel, it's not who I am. I'm sat here, naked and exposed, literally and figuratively, and I need something back from him. I know what we just did should be enough, but he's still fully clothed, with all his feelings safely tucked away. I need words from him right now. What? I'm insecure, sue me.

Just as I've convinced myself he is about to freak out or tell me it was nothing, he goes and surprises me. He wraps his arms back around my waist, setting his hands firmly back on my ass in a possessive claim. He owns it now.

"It means, Faith Marie Asher, that you're MINE."

Okay, those were words. Just not the ones I was expecting. I'm too shocked to say anything but I don't need to because he pulls me in for another delicious kiss.

# CHAPTER 20

## Ryan

I knew she would be perfect, and she really is. That purple bra next to her creamy skin was sexy as hell, even better once I pulled it down over her beautifully perfect tits. A little more than a handful, with pretty pink nipples. Did I mention that she was perfect?

The thong was a real nice surprise too, sexy little minx. Her ass feels too good in my hands. A full peach, ripe enough to bite. The thought of watching it jiggle as I pound into her from behind has me hard as a rock.

Her hips are wide and her waist is smaller, forming that perfect figure of eight. She's wonderfully soft all over and I can't help but imagine how good she will feel beneath me. So fucking sexy, how did I miss her this whole time?

Whilst I am desperate to see more of her, literally salivating with a need to taste her, I'm also all too aware that we are in a tent, with Sam and Remy just outside. She deserves a lot better than that. She deserves a lot better than me actually, but the selfish bastard in me doesn't seem to be able to stop though. I didn't intend for things to go as far as they have, but this girl literally just bared her body and soul to me, the least I could do was appreciate it.

Watching her come undone at my hands was the best fucking thing I've ever seen, I've never been so turned on in my life. She makes the sexiest little whimpers that we're driving my me crazy. I wanted nothing more than to just rip off her cute purple panties and fuck her into oblivion. But like I said, she deserves better than that.

Faith is definitely a lioness, so fucking brave the way she completely opened up to me about how she feels. A lot of people would be afraid to make themselves vulnerable like that, but not *Foi*, she puts herself out there and from now on I'll give her the respect she deserves.

When she moves to undo my pants, I stop her.

"It's fine *Foi*, this was about you not me. I can wait." I know I said this morning that it was best if we were just friends, and whilst I stand by that statement, I decided I'm just going to go with it now and see what happens. She wants me and I really fucking want her, so what's wrong with that? *It's not like she would be offering what she is if she knew the truth though, is it?*

I guess the selfish part of me is hoping she won't ever find out the truth.

"It's okay, I want to touch you too. I want you to have a good time with me," she says, looking at me all wide eyed. Her cheeks are still rosy with her post orgasm glow and she looks gorgeous. It would be so easy to take her up on her offer right now. She's trying to be as confident as she can, but I can tell she's nervous as hell.

"I *am* having a good time. *Ma Belle Foi,* I'm having a great fucking time. Trust me, this is perfect, I don't need anything more right now. Just kiss me again, that's all I need."

She smiles at me but I can see the cogs turning in her head. She's doubting herself. Or maybe she's doubting me? Either way she does kiss me, and as *cliché* as it is, it just gets better every time. I feel like I'm fucking floating on a cloud with this girl. Nothing else seems to matter at this moment, it's just us. Even my demons are silent.

Turns out my concerns about the lack of privacy weren't wrong as we are brought swiftly back to reality by Greg walking in while we are making out, Faith still pretty much naked in my lap.

"Woooaaaah, Fuck! Okay guys, I did not want to see that, bloody hell…" He says covering his eyes and walking straight back out. I can still hear him cursing outside, to which I can't help but laugh.

Faith climbs off me and rushes around trying to get dressed. She bends over to collect her pants from the floor giving me a full view of her ass, and fuck if my dick isn't screaming to get out. I take a moment to adjust myself, before I change my mind about wanting to give her better.

"Shit, shit, shit!" She panics, just like she did in her cabin that time. I immediately get up and pull her back into me and hug her tightly.

"It's okay, baby. Don't worry, it's not a big deal."

"Easy for you to say, you weren't the one naked. Greg saw me naked! What if he tells my mom?"

I draw lazy circles around her lower back with my finger to try and calm her, and it seems to work.

"Faith, listen, I meant what I said. I want you to be mine, but we do need to talk." I feel her tense in my arms. Greg was right, this beautiful girl doesn't have an ounce of self-confidence, and fuck if I'm not going to help her get some. She's fucking badass and she needs to know it.

"Don't freak out. I'm not going anywhere, I promise. I just want you to be sure about me, and who I really am. I've done things, some bad things. Things I'm not sure you would feel the same way about me if you knew. I've been awful to you, and I desperately want to make that right, but we don't need to rush into anything." I gently kiss her forehead. "This is a precious gift you only get to give once, and I'm not sure I will ever deserve it. But I want to try to earn it, if you'll let me?"

She puts her hands on my face again in a comforting gesture that's starting to become my favourite thing in the world.

"Ryan, I forgive you for the pig thing. You said Mia lied to you about me, and honestly, it's not like you were the only one who believed her lies. I meant what I said though, you won't ever call me a pig again, I swear that was the last time. You do that again there won't be any more chances for you!"

"I know, and I wouldn't expect anymore. I'm a lucky bastard just to have been given this one, I know that. I realise my promises don't mean shit to you now, but I swear, I will never speak to you like that again." I promise, knowing full well how I can be at times. I say things in the heat of the moment that I don't mean. I regret them the instant they leave my lips, but I know Faith won't put up with my bullshit anymore.

"Let's just forget about it, it's done. Fresh start?" She gives me a warm smile, and I'm suddenly reminded of all the times I used to catch her staring at me. Now that I think about it, she was always smiling at me. Did I always smile back or was I the one who smiled first? Why can't I remember? "Ryan, what's wrong? Talk to me, please?"

I seriously consider for a minute just telling her everything. How can she be so brave to put herself out there how she did, yet here I am keeping something from her. Can I ever truly earn the right to be with her if I'm keeping something like this from her? I know it's the right thing to do, but I don't want to lose her now that we finally have this amazing connection with each other.

I swallow down my guilt as I decide to continue with my earlier plan of ignoring it and hoping she never finds out. *Such a fucking pussy, dude.*

"It's nothing. Look I don't think Greg would say anything to Lorrie, he's cool. But we should probably go out there and deal with him anyway just in case." She doesn't look convinced but I take her hand and lead her out before she can protest.

***

Greg is sitting on his own next to a campfire, with a hip flask in his hand, looking sombre. He tells us that Sam and Remy have gone back into the village to take some food to Lorrie and the grieving family. They have left some aside for Faith and I, so Faith goes over to grab our mess tins and a couple of forks, while I take a seat on the floor opposite Greg.

My phone vibrates in my pocket, when I check it it's Spencer. She's called me four times today, and just like the other times, I choose to ignore it.

"Here you go mate, you can drink legally now in my hometown, so knock yourself out." Greg offers me the flask and I take it gladly. It's tequila. Not my drink of choice but fuck if I don't take another sip just to feel a burn.

"The curse of tequila mate, it makes a bloke happy. Didn't you know?" Greg adds, noticing my grimace, referencing a weird song from the '90s. What is it with these people and the '90s?

Faith joins us and I pull her down to sit between my legs. While I don't think Faith would want any, my manners dictate that I should pass the flask to her anyway. I gotta say I'm surprised when she not only takes it, but she shoots it without so much as batting an eye. Greg takes it back from her equally impressed, raising up a toast to her, before taking another shot himself.

"It's fucking dogshit. The things that happen for no apparent reason, and the way the world works. Why do some people have to fucking die before their life even begins?" He takes another sip. I can see the cracks in his armour now he has let his mask slip. The jokes, the bravado, the weird ass shirts. He is carrying some heavy shit just like the rest of us. I guess that explains the dark tattoos.

"I'm a doctor, I should probably get used to death, right? I don't think I will ever be ok with losing a kid. It will never make sense to me."

Faith leans forward and rests her forehead against his knee. I'd forgotten for a moment how upset she was before. This has hit both of them hard. I realise this probably isn't the first time they have experienced loss like this. Sadly, things like this are a harsh reality here, and each time it chips away at them.

I see things really clearly now. They do all they can to help as many people as possible, but it's never enough. It will never *be* enough, and when you realise that, it is a hard pill to swallow.

"Here's to you two lovebirds anyway, finally making a go of it, ay?" Greg raises up another toast before taking another sip. Faith sits upright with a grimace on her face.

"God Greg, I'm so sorry. I'm so embarrassed. Please don't tell my mom." He offers Faith the flask and she takes it, taking another easy sip just like before. I can't help but wonder how she's come to find it so easy.

"I'm no grass, Faithy. Like I said, you're old enough to make those decisions. As long as it's consensual, what you choose to do with your own body is your business. Just hang a sign-up next time; If the caravan's a' rockin', don't come a' knockin', eh? Just don't tell your old girl I gave you booze, alright. And while I think about it, let's not mention ever again, ever, that you were naked. Ever! Bloody hell, I didn't need to see that. No offence."

Faith's cheeks turn a pretty shade of pink that has all the blood rushing to my dick. So cute when she gets embarrassed. She passes me the flask and I take another generous mouthful. Seems like we are all trying to punish ourselves tonight.

"So, come on then. What's your baggage?" The silence that follows makes me realise Greg's question is aimed at me. Faith is looking at me too, and I figure they are waiting for me to talk about my Mom.

"My mom died. What's yours, Dark Lord?" I counter, gesturing to his tattoos. I'm not willing to share any more of that story yet.

"AIDS." He says matter-of-factly, and both Faith and I are taken back. "AIDS is my baggage mate. My older brother Michael, well, Mickey everyone called him. He was ten years older than me but he was my hero. The best big brother a boy could want.

You'd think being a teenager he wouldn't want some snotty nosed five-year-old hanging around with him, but he always did. He took me everywhere, always had time for me no matter what. Unlike our parents, fucking pricks they are. Always off somewhere doing whatever the fuck they wanted, forgetting they had two kids at home." He takes another drink. His eyes are black with buried emotions, burning to get to the surface. I know that feeling all too well.

"We were rich. I mean like fifty million-pound Chelsea townhouse, as well as a thousand-acre Surrey estate, just for the weekends, type rich. We had this Nanny, Nanny Eleanor. Sounds stuck up, but she was actually a fucking joy to be around. More of a mother to us than the bitch that birthed us that's for damn sure." He laughs, even though he clearly doesn't find it funny.

"Mickey, he used to be the one to tuck me in at night, and read a few chapters of *Harry Potter* to me every night. I didn't understand half of it, but I just loved listening to him read to me," he adds, seeming to become a little more emotional with every detail he shares.

"Thinking back now, I wonder how he managed it, considering he was fucking wasted most of the time. He was my whole world, until one day he wasn't. I was eight and he was eighteen. He left home without looking back, and spent the next ten years on the streets. Ten years of sleeping rough, taking drugs, and doing fuck knows what, just to get another needle in his arm."

Shit.

I wasn't expecting that. Greg blinks a few times, holding his emotions at bay.

"He would come to my school from time to time, in rare moments he was half sober. I'd bunk off to spend time with him. He would even bring me the next *Harry Potter* book when one came out. I suspected he most probably stole it, but still, it meant a lot that he never forgot it was our thing. I would beg him to come home, I didn't understand the reasons for any of it until I was older. Turns out he was already using drugs before he left home. He'd been hooked on heroin for two years by the time my parents kicked him out!" Greg adds solemnly.

Fucking hell. Sixteen and taking heroin? How does that even happen?

"He told me years later that he had been abused, but he would never say who by. I came to suspect it was probably my father, but I can't be sure. That's why he got into drugs in the first place, because of the abuse." Greg adds as if he read my mind. "He turned eighteen. He had been ill for some time, he had some routine blood tests and that was it. He was diagnosed as HIV positive, at eighteen. Instead of getting him the help he needed, my father kicked him out and cut him off. Said he didn't want any 'dirty boys' in his family. Ironic, huh?" Again, he laughs, but his eyes are glassy.

"Mickey was on the streets, he wasn't receiving any treatment, just taking more and more drugs. In and out of prison for things people do to get drugs. So, when he finally ended up being moved from prison to hospital ten years later they said he was dying. My parents refused to go and see him, even though he begged for them to come… " He swallows, unable to speak for a minute. Fucking hell this is bad.

"I was eighteen, watching my big brother cry because he was scared shitless, and our bastard parents wouldn't show up for him when he was dying. That was the single worst moment of my life!" Greg shakes his head, remembering the pain of that moment. "I remember thinking how addiction reminded me of the Dementors from *Harry Potter;* Sucking every ounce of joy from a person's life until there is nothing left but darkness."

I shake my head, knowing that feeling all too well.

Addiction. Disease. Mental illness. Loneliness. Guilt. Grief. We all have a soul sucking demon living above our heads. Mine sucked the light from my life years ago.

"In less than a month after being moved to the hospital, he passed away. I haven't seen or spoken to my parents ever since. They didn't even go to his funeral. Sod them and their bloody money. I hope they burn in fucking Hell." He takes another large sip. When the flask is empty, he reaches into a bag underneath the chair I didn't even notice before, and pulls out the remainder of the bottle. "What the hell, we may as well just use this now."

Faith has tears in her eyes as she gets up to her knees and wraps Greg in a tight hug. He allows it, as a lone tear streaks down his face. I immediately feel inclined to do the same. I wrap my arms around both of them and the three of us stay there like that for a few minutes. Faith is the first to break the silence.

"I think my parents are getting a divorce!"

# CHAPTER 21

## Faith

It's no secret I don't get along with my mom like I do my dad. She is always running away from us. Away from me. It's like she can't stand to spend too much time with me because all I do is remind her of the child she lost.

See my parents had a child before me, Toby, but he died before I was born. He had leukaemia, he was only two years-old. After Toby died, Mom didn't want to have any more children. That's when she decided she wanted to go work in places like this, helping other people. Dad said she never stopped, even for a moment, just to grieve Toby. Instead she just kept herself constantly busy, wrapping herself in other people's problems. Even now she never talks about him.

"Me and my dad, we just got back here, but my mom, she wants to go away. She thinks our work is done here, can you believe that? She wants to go back to California. After everything that happened to my dad, she wants him to go back there. Apparently, she's ready to go 'back to reality' as she called it."

Ryan and Greg stare at me waiting for more information. Ryan's face flashes with something, but it's gone before I can decipher it. They both get along great with my mom, more so than my dad. They are bound to take her side.

"Dad said he isn't going back there, not to live anyway. He's coming back at the end of summer to sort out the house and whatever but that's it, he's done with it there. We both are." I don't miss the hurt on Ryan's face and I instantly regret my choice of words.

I hadn't considered how he might feel about me not going back to school now. I hadn't actually considered how I would feel now either for that matter.

Could I go back there if we were together? Could I stay here without him? But then, are we even together? Would he really want me to be his girlfriend? He didn't actually say those words, but he did say he wants me to be his? *His little secret probably, he would never tell anyone at school.*

I swallow down my paranoia.

"He told her if she leaves us again, he wants a divorce. You know what she said? 'So be it'. That's all she said. 'So be it'. She doesn't care about either of us." I still can't believe she said that. Well actually I can, because she's a selfish bitch. Okay so she's not, not really. She wouldn't be here doing the work she does if she was. But she doesn't care about me, she never has. She didn't want me, and she made no effort to hide it from me.

"Are you sure there's not more to it? I mean, I don't know your folks that well, but that doesn't sound like Lorrie? Maybe there are some problems between them you don't know about?" Ryan questions, his eyebrows pinched.

"You would say that. You get the nice Lorrie. The motherly, caring Lorrie. The Lorrie who is still over there now with that poor mother, taking care of her and her family. The Lorrie who my dad fell in love with. But me? I get Lorrie 2.0, and trust me, when I say that this is exactly like her." I know it's not Ryan's fault. It's true she is great, she's kind and smart, and she really does spend her whole time caring for everyone. Everyone except me.

"It's her way or the highway, it always has been. My entire life, everything has been dictated by her. Where to go next, how long we stay. When I need to be sent away to school, where I should go, what sports I should take. I wasn't ever going to go to St. Edmund's, then out of the blue I got an offer for a full scholarship and bam, my mom's mind was made up. I didn't even apply for it, so who did, huh? Three guesses." I'm practically shouting, but I'm so angry.

"You wanna know why I won't go to Stanford? Why I *don't* want to be a doctor? Because I'm sick and tired of being told where to be and what to do. For once in my life I want to be the one to make a choice, I want to be the one who decides! I want to feel cold, I want to see snow. I want something new, and exciting. I know how selfish I sound, but I want something that's just for me. Surely you of all people can understand that?" I don't know why I feel angry at Ryan now, but I do. He should get it.

Greg stands up and applauds my little outburst.

"That was bloody brilliant, little Faithy. But listen, I walked away from my life because I fucking hated my parents, but that's not you. You love your parents, both of them. Just have a conversation with them, I'm sure they will understand. You only get one life, you have to do what's right for you." He holds his hand out for a fist pump before passing me the tequila.

I take another large gulp that I know I'm going to regret in the morning. I already feel half wasted. I notice Ryan looking at me and I can't read his expression.

"Why are you looking at me like that, do you disapprove?" I offer him the bottle and he takes it, giving me a run for my money.

"I don't disapprove, *Ma Belle Foi*, I'm just wondering how you came to be a girl who can, what, down her third or fourth shot of tequila and not even feel the effects? I also stand by my earlier statement that there must be more to it?"

"So what, you think I'm lying?" I snatch the bottle back and down another shot. I offer it back to Greg who holds his hands up submissively and sits back in the chair like he's about to watch a showdown. Ryan snatches the bottle back and takes another shot himself.

"No, I don't think you're lying, but I do think you're only telling us half the story. What are you leaving out, huh? What's the deal with you and your mom?"

"She didn't want me!" I shout a little louder than I intended. "Yes, she's taken care of me, and done all the things she should as a mother. Maybe she's even grown to love me, but I know in my heart that if she could give me up to have Toby back, then she would!" My eyes are burning with the need to cry but I honestly have no more tears left to give today.

Ryan wraps his strong arms around me and I wrap my own around his waist.

"Who is Toby?" He whispers. I forgot I hadn't told them that part.

"My mother went to St Edmund's on a swimming scholarship. Did you know that?" Ryan shakes his head and his messy hair falls slightly over his eyes. "She was a big deal there, she was head of the swim team and she was on cheer for a while too. She was the most popular girl in her class, she was even Prom Queen. If you look in the trophy room you will see her name all over. 'Loretta Pierce' - winner of absolutely everything, class of '91!"

Ryan pulls out of our embrace enough to look at my face and raises a questioning eyebrow.

"Lorretta Pierce? Like as in The Loretta Pierce Hall, where the pool is?" I can see him remembering seeing her name around and piecing it all together.

"Yep, that's her. The school's most successful athlete of all time. So good, they renamed an entire sports facility after her." I roll my eyes and he smirks at my childishness.

"When I started, my mom insisted I try out for the swim team, and for the cheer squad. I mean, can you imagine? Me, on cheer? Obviously, *that* didn't happen, but I did show up for swimming. Coach Hibbert was my mom's coach too. She pulled me aside after trials, said she was disappointed and that she'd had high hopes for me considering who my mother was. Then she suddenly apologised, and that she had forgotten. I was totally confused. She then freaked out even more and told me to forget she said anything, and how she was going to be in so much trouble if 'they' found out. I went home and told my dad about it and he told me I was adopted. They aren't my real parents. Neither of them."

I feel Ryan hold me a little tighter as he takes a sharp breath. "You know she didn't even come back to California to be with me when I found out. Not to comfort me, to make sure I was okay, nothing. She stayed here. She spoke to me on the phone, but it wasn't the same. I needed my mom, and she wasn't there. I don't think things will ever be okay between us again after that."

Greg let's out a low whistle at that revelation, and Ryan lets out a hard breath. He is pissed.

"I'm so sorry, baby. That's not right. I know what it's like to not have your parents there when you need them, and it sucks. I'll always be there for you, *Foi*, I promise. Whenever you need me."

I give him an extra tight squeeze. I can't believe he is really here with me saying these things. I just pray that they are really true.

"I couldn't even ask Coach Hibbert what more she knew, because she literally disappeared. I heard she retired and moved away. Mom, she lost a child before I was born. He was sick with cancer, and he died. She didn't want any more children after that, she wanted to focus on her career. Then one day my father just came home with me, like I was a fucking take-out or something." True story he literally just showed up with me in his arms, right out of the blue.

"Right after their son died, a women from out of town came to see him for an appointment. She said she hadn't realised she was pregnant until she was almost full term. Sounds unlikely, but apparently it happens all the time. She told him she wanted to give me up for adoption, so my father offered to adopt me privately. He paid her to stay in town for a few weeks until she could have the baby and give it to him, without involving the authorities. Not even sure that's legal, but it's what happened."

My birth mom was a Polish immigrant called Lena Lewkowicz. She was in America illegally, and she had been working as a high-class prostitute for the Russian mob, but I don't tell them that part. For some reason, I don't want them judging her for that.

Lewkowicz - It means lion, I looked it up. I guess I just needed to know something about her.

"I think about her a lot, what she was going through, what her life is like now. I don't even know if she's alive. Her number was disconnected right after, and her apartment abandoned. Apparently, they had a deal where he would keep in touch and send updates, but after she handed me over to him and took the money, he was never able to contact her again."

Dad said he thinks she used the money to escape her life as a prostitute, which in turn would mean she would have to hide from the people she worked for. That's probably why she didn't come back for me, right? I don't know why I take comfort in that, but I do. Some of the alternatives as to what might have happened hurt too much to think about. I just pray every night that she is okay. I'd much rather she was safe, and just didn't want to know me, than for her to have been hurt by the people she was running from.

I didn't realise I was crying until Ryan moves to wipe away my tears.

"What a fucking revelation that was, Faithy. Jesus. I'm sorry you had to deal with that." Greg says, clearly astonished by my story, which brings me back to the reality that I've now completely made everything all about me. I'm a shitty friend. *No wonder you don't have any.*

"I'm sorry Greg, I feel really awful. You just told us this really personal story about your brother and I've just turned all the attention on to me and my problems. I'm such an asshole, I'm sorry."

He waves a dismissive hand.

"Don't worry about it, it's a night for sharing. We've all got our monsters in our closet, it's important to air it out once in a while, or they will fester."

Ryan shakes his head and closes his eyes. He breathes in and out slowly and deeply like the way I showed him during our yoga session. I can't tell if he is psyching himself up, or calming himself down.

I don't know what monsters are buried in his closet, but whatever it is, he is clearly afraid to talk about it. He told me he's done some bad things, things that would make me feel differently about him?

All I know is if we are going to be together, then whatever it is he is hiding, I need to find out.

# CHAPTER 22

*Ryan*

I don't need to look to know that they are both waiting on me to speak. Fuck if I'm airing any of my own shit tonight. Let it fester, my heart is already rotten anyway.

"Not tonight…" I close my eyes and let out a sharp breath. I pray to God they don't push it, because as much as I don't want to lose my shit with either of them, I will. I'd rather cut off my fucking arm that talk about that day.

"It's alright mate, I get it. I've had bloody years to deal with my shit. You take as long as you need, but I will say this. Don't dwell on past shit and forget to live your life. You know where I learnt that?" He raises his arm gesturing to his tattoos. "You might laugh about the tattoos, but there is a lot of wisdom in those bloody books!" Greg slaps my back and ruffles my hair.

Forget to live.

"How can I possibly forget to live, when every fucking day it hurts so much just to breathe? Every breath I take fucking burns, just reminding me that I'm alive, and she's not."

"Mate, there is a big difference between being alive, and living your life. Your bullshit will always hurt no matter how long you try and bury it for, trust me. I won't press you, but I'm here. I won't pretend that my shit is anywhere near the same as yours, but loss is loss. You've lost someone, Faith's lost someone, and I've lost someone. I'm here for you brother, I'm here next week, I'm here in ten years time. Whenever you are ready, I'm here. We both are." He gestures to Faith.

Her eyes are glassy, and her face is full of empathy. Usually I can't bear to see it on most people, but on her it feels sincere, comforting almost. I've not been able to silence the monsters that live inside of my head for three years now, but Faith seems to have found the off switch. It's only temporary though, they still seem to haunt me when I'm alone.

"I hear you, man. I just can't right now, it's too much. When she died, I was there. I still haven't processed what happened in my head enough to be able to talk about it. I appreciate what you said though."

I offer Greg my fist and he pumps it with his own.

"Do you mind if I speak with Faith alone please?" I ask, needing her warm comforting silence more than ever.

"Yeah of course, I'm gonna go to bed anyway. We have a busy day tomorrow and I need to sleep off this booze. See you in the morning, Faithy!" He offers, giving Faith a quick friendly arm rub as he passes her.

"Goodnight Greg," she responds, with the sadness of the day weighing heavy on her voice. She is so beautiful, I can't believe I ever thought it possible she could ever harm anyone. She is too good, too gentle. I don't know how someone can be so fierce yet so delicate at the same time, but she is.

We clear up outside and set out the fire, before heading into Faith and Lorrie's tent. We decide to wash up, seeing as we've been busy all day. There is a privacy screen set up around a small water barrel for us to wash from. I let Faith go wash first, before I head over myself. I didn't realise how much I needed it until I'm clean and in fresh clothes.

I announce myself before I walk into the tent, half expecting Lorrie to be back by now. Faith calls for me to come in, letting me know she's still alone. She immediately pulls me in for a hug. My need to feel her skin against mine intensifies the moment I smell her sweet soapy scent.

I kiss her gently. These slow soft kisses seem to blow my mind, and I can't get enough. They clearly affect her too, as she lets out a soft whimper. That sound is my undoing.

I pick her up and she wraps her legs around my waist, grinding her centre against my already hard dick. I lay her down on her cot and climb on top of her. I kiss her again while trailing my hand lazily down her body, before slipping it into her waist band. I happily find her already wet and ready for me as she writhes and moans with pleasure.

I don't waste any time. I press my finger deep inside of her, drawing a loud gasp from her that I swallow with my mouth. She feels amazing. I add another finger and reach for that sweet spot inside of her. I work it until she's moving against me, needy for more, and it's not long before she comes apart beneath me. It's just as fucking hot as the first time.

Just like the first time she moves to return the favour. Maybe it's the liquor, maybe it's the asshole in me, but when she reaches in and releases my dick from my pants, I don't have it in me to stop her.

She looks down at me hesitantly, waiting for my approval. I place my hand around hers that's wrapped around my dick. Slowly I start to use her hand to jerk myself off, never taking my eyes off of hers. Her cold steel eyes are on fire. Every moment of her intense stare feels like a bullet into my fucking soul, the shattered shrapnel splintering itself under my skin.

Faith is the first to break the connection. After a minute she looks down, looks at our hands entwined together, pumping me slowly. I continue to watch her eyes. They are filled with desire. She likes this, she likes seeing me hard in her hand. She licks her lips, and I remove my hand to allow her to take over, and what a fucking job she does of it.

"What are you doing to me, *Foi*? Just like that, baby, don't stop!"

She increases her pace and I'm fucking done. I throw my head back and close my eyes, pleasure taking over. I'm just about ready to shoot my load when she leans down and puts her mouth on me.

Fuck.

It's so intense I can't even bring myself to make sure this is what *she* really wants. The last thing I want is for her to feel pressured into it, but fuck if I can get any words out right now. As if reading my mind, Faith pulls up.

"Relax, I want to taste you," she says confidently, and puts her mouth back on me. So fucking good. Her lips are so full and pink and her cheeks hollow as she takes me in deeper. It's clear she's never done this before, but it still feels amazing just the same. The fact she trusts me this way makes something ache in my chest. I definitely do not deserve her, or any of this, but I let it go on.

I need it. I need her.

Maybe I will fuck her afterwards? *Don't you fucking dare, asshole.*

I know I'm going to hate myself later, but as the feeling intensifies I lose all self-control. I put my hand on her head, holding it still as I push myself into her mouth. I thrust into her, thriving off of her choked moans. *That's it baby, take all of me.* There are tears in her eyes, but I take what I need. *Just like you used to take from Liv? Just like Shane tried to take from Faith?*

The thought is a sobering one that has me crashing back down to reality. I quickly stop, and let go of her head. To my surprise she doesn't stop, she carries on, taking me as deep and as fast as she can. I put my hand on her head to slow her down.

"I'm sorry, I didn't mean to lose it like that," I swiftly apologise. She still doesn't stop, but she does slow back to her original pace. I stroke her hair and gently run my fingers into it. How the hell will I ever be good enough for this girl.

"Fuck, if you don't stop now, I'm going to cum down your throat!" I consider that fair warning, but when she doesn't stop I take it as an invitation to spill inside of her mouth. I would normally hold a chick's head still, making sure she takes every last drop deep in the back of her throat, but I refrain from doing so to Faith.

Turns out I didn't need to anyway, because she stays down there until I'm done, swallowing it all down. She comes up beaming from ear to ear and kisses me. I taste myself on her lips and it's such a fucking turn on, but I'm to confused right now to do anything about it.

"Aren't you mad at me?" I ask, not knowing what the fuck just happened.

"No, why would I be mad at you? I wanted that, I wanted you. Was I... W-was that not good?"

"Good? No. You were fucking amazing, baby. It's me, I completely lost it. Fuck, Faith I'm so sorry. Everything that you've been through with Shane, and I practically forced myself on you. I'm such a prick!" The truth of my own words stings my soul. What kind of a monster am I?

"Ryan, stop. You didn't force yourself on me, and I certainly wasn't fighting you off. If I hadn't wanted it I would have let you know, and I know that if I had, you would have stopped. I trust you, Ryan."

"Well you shouldn't. I lost it, Faith. I lost control. What if you didn't want it? What if I hadn't come to my senses?" I question, wondering if I could ever forgive myself.

"You didn't lose control, you gave it to me, and it was amazing. Knowing that I made you feel that way, having you give yourself over to me like that, I've never felt so empowered in my life. You're not Shane! Now please stop over thinking, because I've just given my first blow job and we need to appreciate that I'm a badass bitch right now, okay?"

She smiles a beautifully innocent smile at her own joke and I can't help but roar with laughter. This girl isn't Liv, and I don't want to treat her the same way either. In fact, I was wrong to treat Liv the way I did, I see that now. Even if she was down with it, I used her, with no regard to her feelings or her welfare.

It's not that I didn't like her, she was pretty cool, I just wasn't in the right frame of mind to be getting into all the things we were. I make a mental note to message her social media account and give her an apology the first chance I get. Not that she will likely give a shit two years later, but I still feel I need to regardless.

Faith is so very different to Liv. She *should* feel like a badass bitch, because she is one. She definitely has all the power now where I'm concerned. From now on I'm hers, whether she wants me or not. She puts her hand on my face the way I like and I'm done.

"You are so beautiful when you laugh. I know you feel like you don't have much to laugh about anymore, but when you do, it's the best sound in the world to me. I want to make you laugh every day. If you keep me, then I promise I will try."

Faith smiles from ear to ear as she moves into the space between my arm and my body. Honestly, she fits so perfectly I'm starting to think it was always her space.

She's happier than I've ever seen her, and I wonder if it's the relief she got from speaking her truth earlier. I admire them both so much. Not just for the shit they have been through, but to speak so openly about it without fear. Can I ever speak about mine? My Mother, what I've done to Malcolm, any of it?

"I would like that a lot..." I say leaving a heavy silence between us, knowing I have to at least be honest about one thing tonight. "I can't love you, Faith. Not like you want me too, not how you deserve. I'm too broken, and I'm not capable of loving anyone. My heart just doesn't work that way anymore, I'm sorry."

She doesn't move except for her fingers tracing patterns across my chest. "I want to love you, to feel what it's like to be loved by you, but I can't because I'm in pieces now. I'm worried I will never be enough. Not for you, or for anyone. You are so full of light and warmth, but, my pieces, they are all black and toxic, and they will poison you if you get too close."

I try to swallow down my emotions, but my chest aches and my eyes are burning. I've given her an out, but I'll be damned if I let her take it without a fight. She said 'if you keep me'. Yeah right, like I even have a choice anymore. More like if she keeps me.

I expect Faith to get mad at my confession and throw me out. I figure it's not the sort of thing a girl wants to hear after she has just kindly sucked your dick, but she actually does the opposite. She never does what I expect, she's too fucking badass for that.

She moves to straddle my lap and wraps her arms around my neck, pulling my head into her chest. She kisses my forehead, and we sit there in silence as she just holds me and strokes my hair. I feel a tear or two roll down my cheek. How the fuck did they slip out? I attempt to pull away to hide them from her, but she just holds me tighter, and for the first time since my mom died, I feel safe.

My mother always taught me that it was okay for guys to cry when they need to, but my father always taught me that it wasn't. Gotta be a man's man, as they say. I guess when the time came for me to actually need to cry, Mom was no longer around to tell me it was okay. Dad wasn't around much either for that matter, but I knew his thoughts on the matter all too well, so I tried my best to keep my tears to myself. I have done so ever since.

I haven't spoken to anyone about what actually happened that day. None of my friends know the full story, not even Kat. All they know is that I came back to school one fall, and my mom had died over the summer. I never spoke about the details, not to anyone. My father had her medical records sealed, so very few people know the truth about what happened. The truth about what I did.

"Three years ago, my mom died, and it was all my fault..."

# CHAPTER 23

## Ryan

*August 2016...*

"Ryan, come on sweetheart. We're going to miss the bus, hurry up, baby!" Mom giggles, pulling on my hand as she runs toward a bus that's not even close to leaving yet.

It's early. Not even 6 a.m., but Mom is having one of her 'excited' days. She woke me at 4 a.m. with a huge stack of pancakes with marshmallows and chocolate fudge ice cream, telling me she was taking me for a surprise day out. It's not a surprise, seeing as how she's done this every summer since I can remember.

Coney Island.

I don't know why she insists we take the bus, but she always does. She loves it, and says it's all part of the fun. Don't get me wrong, I love spending time with my mom, and seeing the smile on her face makes it worth it. But the fucking bus, man. It's August in Manhattan, so it's hotter than Satan's armpit.

We should be in The Hamptons like any other respectable New Yorkers. We have a large beach house there, but Mom hates all that crap. She's not exactly a socialite.

My mom suffers from bipolar. She was diagnosed shortly after she gave birth to me, and it's ruled her life ever since. The anxiety keeps her housebound most days. If she leaves the house it either means she's having a good day, or she's manic. Today is somewhere in between, let's call it a seven on the mood scale.

Mom was only young when she married my father, at ten years his junior she was barely eighteen when they met, and practically nine months to the day after, she had me. My parents had an arranged marriage, but even so they grew to love each other. My dad is a dick most of the time, but Mom is his world, he would do anything for her.

Unsurprising really, because my mom is beautiful. With her long blonde wavy hair, and freckles across her nose she looks like a mermaid. Think Daryl Hannah, that's her, although my dad is nothing like Tom Hanks. He's more like Richard Gere with his silver hair and debonair suits.

Today, Mom's wearing a white linen dress, with a thick brown leather belt around her waist, and a pair of vintage cowboy boots that she's owned since high school. She gets a lot of male attention, not that she notices, but I do. I stare out any bastard that dares look at her, just so they know what's up. No joke, I will literally fucking kill a dude if he tries to talk to her.

"It's okay Mom, the bus doesn't leave for another hour, we've got plenty of time." I offer her a smile and she puts her hand on my face. I love it when she does that.

"We want to get the best seats though, don't we? Where do you want to sit? Up at the back where the cool kids sit, or right up front with the driver? You always used to love sitting up front. You would talk to the driver the entire journey. Do you remember, Eleflump? You always used to end up with the driver's hat, you'd make me ask for it every time!"

Eleflump was my mom's nickname for me when I was a kid. Apparently, that's how I used to pronounce elephant when I was really little, she thought it was cute, so she used to call me it all the time. I can't remember the last time she called me that.

My mom beams a smile at me, but her eyes are hazy. "Do you remember that one year, when I asked if I could wear it first? You said I could, but your sad little face was so heartbroken, I couldn't bear to keep it from you, not even for a moment! Do you remember that, baby?"

I know her well enough to know she's only half here right now, in the moment. The other half is off dancing through her memories, that's why she used my old nickname.

"Of course I remember. You did that on purpose. You knew I could never say no to you, Momma. Show me anyone that can!" She laughs an embarrassed laugh and playfully pushes me before I pull her in for a gentle noogie. I'm a lot taller than her these days so it's not hard, but I let her escape easily enough.

"Front seats it is then, and just so we're clear, I'm calling dibs on the hat!" I say, and Mom squeals in delight, racing off towards the bus again.

***

It's 4 p.m, and we've been out here all day. We've eaten enough hotdogs, and cotton candy to feed an army. We've been on all the rides, some more than once, and now we are chilling on the beach. This place is corny as hell, but Mom loves it. She can be herself here, she can be free. The city is no place for wild horses.

I watch as my mom dances in the surf. She loves to bathe her feet and dance in the water. She looks at me and smiles, the late afternoon sun illuminating her youthful features. She looks like an angel today in her white dress. Her hair is mostly hanging free, only a delicate braid around her head like a halo.

Mom comes racing back towards me, ignoring everyone else she passes. In her world, they don't exist. Not when she's high like this anyway. Usually, she is a very traditional southern lady. She's well-mannered and considerate of others, but once she gets like this, all etiquette goes out of the window.

Very few people continue to exist as themselves anymore in her world. She actually sees strangers as animals. Like earlier, she pointed out a polar bear to me as if it were the most normal thing to be roaming around Coney Island. She had pointed it out because she said, to be a polar bear was rare. You get a lot of black bears, and grizzly bears, but a polar bear is rare, apparently. Pure.

My mom is a medium, and gives psychic readings to people who come to see her at our apartment. Mostly, she will have dreams in the days before they arrive for their appointment. She tells me it's like puzzle pieces, each one alone is meaningless, but once she meets them, she can put the pieces together and understand them better. She always tells me that I have the gift too, but I've never experienced anything like that myself.

Mom always tells me that she and I are both elephants, which I personally think is pretty cool, because elephants are totally rad. Maybe that's where the Eleflump thing came from? Apparently, my father is a grey wolf. You got that right. But how can an elephant be in love with a wolf? She just laughs at me when I ask that, tells me I'll get it one day when a wildcat steals my heart, whatever the fuck that means.

Sometimes she sees people as demons. I personally think how she sees people matches their souls. Like the animal is maybe their spirit animal or something. She rarely sees demons, but when she does, I bet it's because they are just an evil bastard. Somehow, she just knows, you know.

Whatever. Not everyone believes in that paranormal stuff but it's normal to me, and I understand her when she talks about it. She's so fucking wise, she's the smartest person I know. There is so much truth to everything she says. Even when she's not feeling herself, in fact especially when she's manic, she comes out with some mind-blowing shit that really makes you think.

"You want to ride the roller-coaster one more time, baby? You want to come dance in the water? Ooh do you want another hotdog? We could go to the haunted house?" She rattles off at a fast pace, moving her hands animatedly.

She's over stimulated and is moving up the mood chart. I can usually handle her when she's like this, most of the time anyway. It's when she's at the opposite end of the mood scale and depressed that I don't know what to do. Mostly because that's usually when I've been shipped out, so I rarely see her that way. When I do, it totally fucking guts me, I can't lie. Even so, I wish she wouldn't shut me out. I want to learn, I want to help. I'll always be here for her, no matter what.

I think maybe it's time to call it a day before she ends up running off alone somewhere. She does that sometimes. One time, when I was five-years-old, she left me indoors all day alone.

Shortly after Dad left to go to his office that morning, Mom left the house convinced she needed to find me. She sat me down and told me I wasn't the real Ryan, I was a ghost of past Ryan or some shit. But she told me not to worry because she was going to rescue me, the real Ryan. She told me to be a good boy and sit still, while she looked for the real me.

I remember it as clear as day, I guess even at five I knew something was wrong. I did what she asked though. I sat still and I waited. She walked from our apartment in Lenox Hill, all the way downtown with no shoes on her feet, she even managed to board the Staten Island ferry. It wasn't until the cops picked her up in the middle of a bridge on the other side and took her to hospital, that my father was alerted.

She was in a complete state of psychosis by the time they picked her up. She was screaming that I was going to be hit by a car and taken by God if she didn't save me. She was so hysterical she had to be sedated by the hospital, where she was detained for 72-hours. That's what I read in the report I found in my father's office a couple years back anyway.

It was almost twelve hours later by the time anyone came for me. I was still sitting in the same spot my mother told me to wait in. I hadn't eaten or drank anything all day, but I had wet my pants.

It was my father's assistant, Miranda, who eventually came for me. Not the most maternal of women, Miranda's first instinct was not to be concerned for a small child left alone all day. No, Miranda dragged me up, pulled off my wet pants and spanked my ass. She told me I was a disgusting little brat for wetting myself. When I cried she then told me I was a freak just like my mother.

I never told anyone that. But shortly after, my father had a new assistant. Dad has always been very meticulous when it came to home security. I'm guessing he was curious that day what I had been up to and saw for himself.

After that, Mom was too afraid to be left alone with me, and we had a nanny with us wherever we went. Then, when I was eleven, I was sent to boarding school in London. I only come home for the holidays, but even then, sometimes I'm sent somewhere else.

I spent last Christmas in Scotland with my friends at their family home. I was angry about it at first. Took me a while to figure it out, but I realised whenever they don't want me home it's because Mom is in a bad place. Just lately, that seems to be more and more. Sometimes, like at Christmas, she has even had to spend time at a private facility up in Connecticut. I'm not supposed to know that of course, but I got a good thing going on with the doorman at our apartment building, Martim.

I spotted him running in the park once wearing the Portuguese soccer team shirt. When I saw him next I mentioned that I played, and that I was even lucky enough to see Ronaldo play in the World Cup in Brazil a couple years back. Turns out Martim is a huge soccer fan. It also turns out there isn't much that goes on in the building he doesn't know about, so when I offered to throw him a couple hundred bucks in return for him keeping me informed about my mom, he was happy to accept.

"I'm all good, Momma. It's getting late I think we should start heading home."

She looks at me disappointed, and it breaks my heart. She nods and throws her arms around me, wrapping me in her love.

"Thank you, sweet boy. You always take care of me when I should be taking care of you. Thank you for today, and for every day. I love you so much, with all my heart. Don't ever forget that!" She squeezes me tightly like she's about to say goodbye. The thought she's about to run off twists inside me but I shake it off.

"I love you too, Mom, always. I've had a great day, I love coming here with you, you know that. And you're a great mom, so stop talking shit." My cursing earns me 'the look'. Like a true southern momma, she doesn't need to say anything, just 'the look' is enough. I apologise and stand us both up, and after dusting the sand off, we grab an ice cream, before heading back to the bus station.

"I want you to know, Ryan, that I don't want to leave, but I'm so tired. I hope someday you will forgive me?" Mom says softly as she waits to get on the bus. We have had a long day, and she hates saying goodbye to this place.

"There's nothing to forgive, Mom. I've had a really great day, but I'm tired too. I'll sure be glad to get home and take a shower!" I help her onto the bus and into her seat. She looks out of the window and doesn't respond anymore after that.

The ride home is quiet. It's like a switch has flicked inside of her. She's gone from hundred miles per hour to no gas in the tank. The way she was with me before we left the beach plays on my mind. I worry about her more when she's like this. She closes her eyes, so I let her sleep. I decide to call John, our driver, and ask him to meet us at the bus station. Fuck if I'm going to try and hail a cab. I send my father a text to let him know how she is, but it remains unread.

It's about 8 o'clock when we finally get home thanks to traffic. Mom has been passed out for most of the journey, so I carry her up to her room as soon as we arrive back at the apartment.

"I'm so tired, Ryan." Mom whispers as I lay her down on her bed. "Today was the best day, wasn't it? Promise to keep it with you always. Be happy when you think of it, please? No matter what," she adds, cupping my face with her hand.

"It's okay, Momma. I will I promise, get some rest. We're home now, you're safe". I put a blanket over her and switch on her nightlight, and leave her to sleep. She always sleeps with a nightlight.

As I walk down the hall something doesn't feel right. A darkness creeps over me and I can't explain the feeling of unease. Maybe I need some air? I walk out onto the roof terrace and try to take in the night breeze. Except it's hot and sticky, and there is no breeze. Why is it so fucking hot tonight, I feel like I can't breathe? I try to call Dad but he is out of town on business and doesn't pick up. He still hasn't read his message either.

I hear a loud thud from inside and I instantly run back to my mother's room. I open the door to find her standing at the window, the moonlight the only light in the room. I could've sworn I turned on her nightlight? Mom is afraid of the dark, she always uses a nightlight.

"Hey, is everything alright, Mom?" She doesn't answer. She doesn't turn to look at me, she just sways. Is she dancing? She's always dancing.

"You need me to bring you something, Momma?" Still no answer. I step into the room towards her. That's when I see it. The chair on the floor. The cord that's going up out of the window, snaking down around her neck. She's not dancing, she's swinging.

"Fuck... MOM!" I scream as I run over to her. I lift her up and sit her on the window ledge, giving some slack to the cord. With all of my strength I manage to pull the cord apart from around her neck. It's the cord from her nightlight. Even in the moonlight I can see her neck is heavily bruised.

"Momma! Come on Mom, wake up!" I yell as I pick her up. She falls limp in my arms.

"Wake up, Momma. Please... PLEASE WAKE UP!" a loud sound comes out of me that I didn't realise I could make, that's a mix between a cry and a roar. "It's okay, Mom. It's me, I'm here. Wake up, Mom. Please!" I put her onto the bed and try with everything I have to revive her. Nothing.

I try over and over, and over again. "Come on! Just breathe, damn it!" I do more compressions. I scream at her, I shake her.

Nothing.

I hold her.

I cry out for her.

Nothing.

"It's okay, Momma, it's okay." I repeat over and over as I rock her and kiss her head. I sing one of her favourite songs for her, *Three Little Birds*. Mom loves to dance, and I know she's afraid of the dark. I don't want her to be afraid, especially not now. "You're not alone, Momma…"

I don't know when I called 911, but I must have done, because they arrived pretty quickly. Or has it been hours? Has Dad come home yet? I really don't know. Everything is black.

\*\*\*

I wake up in a hospital room, alone. Why am I in the hospital? Where is my mom? I really don't know?

Everything is black.

I wake up again. I'm not sure I was even asleep because I'm now standing in my grandparents' hall, wearing a black suit. How did I get here? I'm not alone now. My father stands next to me, also in black. My grandfather is next to him talking to someone as they walk through the front door. Was it the funeral already? How long since I last saw my mom? I really don't know?

Everything is black.

I wake up again. I'm in my dorm room. I'm back in London now, but it's okay, I remember how I got here. Time and reality have come back to me now. It's been thirty-four days without her. Now there is nothing *but* time. Tick tock, tick tock, tickity fucking tock.

    Everything is black.

# CHAPTER 24

## Faith

Of all the truths to be spoken last night, the most devastating was Ryan's. I don't think neither he nor I were expecting him to open up and talk about what happened to his mom like that. His poor beautiful momma. My heart aches so much for him.

After he finished telling his story he cried. He sobbed his entire heart out uncontrollably, and I held on to him as tightly as I could. My eyes were burning with unshed tears but I forced them back. This was Ryan's time and he needed me to be strong.

Neither of us spoke another word. There was nothing else that could have been said right then to make either of us feel any better. What Ryan needed was a safe place to let go of all his pain, and thats what I gave him. After three years of bottling his emotions deep inside, this was the release he had so desperately needed.

He fell asleep in my arms, still letting out sobs in his sleep. Only when I knew he was sound asleep did I allow myself to cry my own tears. I don't think I've ever felt so heartbroken in my life. I realised I was crying, not only for all that he has lost, but for my failing relationship with my own mother. Ryan's story has taught me that tomorrow is never promised. I need to air my issues with Lorrie while there is still a relationship to save. Life is too damn short as it is.

I woke up this morning surprised not only to find my mom asleep in her bed, but Ryan is still sound asleep in mine, his arms wrapped tightly around me. There is no way Mom wouldn't have noticed when she got back. Oh biscuits, I bet I'm in trouble now. As if reading my thoughts, she wakes up and gestures with only a look for me to join her outside. Double biscuits.

I manage to unwrap myself out of Ryan's arms without waking him, and although it's already hot, my body screams at the loss of his warmth. I throw on his hooded sweater. He wore it again last night and now it smells of all his yummy deliciousness.

My cheeks flush at the memories from last night. I can't believe I had my first sexual encounter, and it was with Ryan. I've thought about it happening so many times, but I never thought he would ever actually look twice at me that way until now.

The way he kisses me. I've never been kissed before, but I'm sure he must feel the same way as me, from the way he makes me feel. Would a kiss feel that way if he didn't? Is that just how it always is when you kiss someone? Does the world always seem to stop turning? So many questions.

I have no idea where I even stand with Ryan after last night. Am I his girlfriend now? *As if, Faith, seriously? Ryan could have any girl he wants, why would he want you?*

My self-loathing Inner Bitch seems to have taken over inside from the confidence-boosting Inner Brit again. Great. I guess last night probably was just a one-time thing. Or was it though? Does he want to have sex with me? Am I even ready for that? Do I want to have sex with him if he doesn't want to be my boyfriend?

I wonder if I should talk about it with my mom. That's what normal girls do, right? Talk about boys with their mothers? A part of me desperately wants to bridge the divide between us, but the other half of me still feels far too bitter about everything that's happened. I just hope too much of the bridge hasn't been burnt beyond repair.

I head outside, and Mom has made a pot of coffee. She offers me a warm smile that leaves me feeling a little confused. Is she not mad about finding Ryan in my bed?

"Morning honey, how are you feeling today? It's so hard when we lose a little one isn't it? Poor Esther, she's heartbroken." Crap. I had actually completely forgotten about that after everything else that happened last night. I'm a terrible person.

"Oh Mom, it's so awful. I can't imagine how hard it must be. It must be especially upsetting for you too." For the first time in a long time, I offer my mom a hug. It takes her by surprise but she hugs me back all the same, which in turn takes me by surprise.

"I'm fine. I'm sorry I was gone so long, but I didn't want to leave them until the rest of the family arrived. Sam and Remy were able to go and pick up Esther's sister and her family and bring them over," she says passing me a coffee.

"I'm just glad Ryan was here to comfort you, I knew how upset you were. He's a good boy, he didn't need to stay with you like that," she offers with a look I can't decipher. It's almost like pity, but then who does she feel sorry for here, me or Ryan?

"Yeah, he's really great. Wonderful, actually. I kinda

wanted to talk to you about that. About Ryan. See I... Well I... I kinda like him. A lot. More than as a friend I mean. What I'm saying is, well, is that… I love him. Ryan, I'm in love with Ryan." *Not one bit awkward there, Faith. Jeez.*

God, I sound like a moron. I blame her unwanted pity look, for throwing me off key.

"Well I sort of already suspected that, Faith. Your father and I, well we already noticed you had a little crush. Just be careful, otherwise I'm worried you might be disappointed," she says matter-of-factly as she sips her coffee. A little crush? Jeez Mom, I'm not twelve.

"What's that supposed to mean?" My defences immediately shoot back up. Can't we even manage to have one mother-daughter conversation without her pissing me off.

"Well honey, your father mentioned that you used to talk about Ryan a lot back home, but he said he had never come around or anything before? Well, I guess we just thought that it might be a little one-sided, this little crush of yours. I may be wrong, so I just meant, maybe you should be careful. That's all."

Little crush again. She smiles an innocent smile at me like she hasn't just belittled my feelings. The nerve of this woman. I'm about to give her a piece of my mind when I'm interrupted.

"It's not one sided," Ryan offers matter-of-factly from behind us, startling us both. Jesus, he looks so good. His eyes are a little red, but other than that he is rocking that just-crawled-out-of-bed look. With his light grey sweats hanging low on his hips, his white tee fitted like an absolute dream across his lean chiselled body, and his curly blonde hair, sitting messy on top of his head. Wow, he is just hot as hell.

"I'm sorry about last night, it was inappropriate to share a bed with Faith. I only intended to stay with her until you got back but we must have fallen asleep. You should know that Faith is my girl now. It's most definitely not a little crush, and it's certainly not one sided." Ryan offers me the warmest smile and my heart melts.

He said I was his girl. Me, Ryan Scott's girl. Holy cow.

Noticing my reaction Ryan sneaks a wink at me. Why does he have to look so hot when he's smug? Mom, on the other hand, looks stunned. Ryan moves to sit next to me and takes my hand. Mom clears her throat.

"Well, thank you for your honesty, Ryan. Had I known the full story, I don't think I would have been comfortable with you two sleeping in the same bed. Faith is still only seventeen."

Kill. Me. Now.

"Mom, I'm already eighteen!" I snap, praying the ground will swallow me up.

"Alright, barely eighteen! I won't have you sharing a bed again, or even the same tent do I make myself clear? You're not even on the pill!" She adds sternly and I literally want to die of embarrassment. That's what you get for having a gynaecologist and a paediatrician for parents.

I start to hear Inner Brit singing *'Circus'* in my head. I roll my eyes. Oh, now you're back. Well not now B, I'm too pissed off.

"Really? Shall I just tattoo 'virgin' on my head and be done with it?" Ryan's lips ever so slightly curl and I know he is amused at my discomfort.

"Perfectly clear, Dr. Pierce. It won't happen again," Ryan interrupts, and my heart drops. I guess I'm not worth fighting for then. Sensing my hurt, Ryan squeezes my hand. "What I mean to say is, I care about Faith very much and I'm not the type of guy to pressure a girl into things she's not ready for. I know I need to be respectful, and I will be, I promise." Well, I wasn't expecting that.

"I'm glad to hear it, at least one of you is responsible. Faith hasn't had a boyfriend before, so we've not had to have this talk until now. I've always thought she was far too naive to the world to be honest, and no offence to you, Ryan, but I'm not fully convinced this isn't just some summer fling. Until I'm satisfied you are both serious about each other I'd rather you weren't alone together either."

"Fucking hell, Mom. Seriously just stop it!" I can't take this woman's bullcrap any longer. It's like she's deliberately trying to sabotage everything.

"Faith Marie Asher, you watch your language young lady, you weren't raised to talk that way!"

"What, now you care what I do? Now you want to be a parent? What about the last three years when I've needed you, where were you then?" I'm so angry. Of all the times she chooses to try and be a mom, she picks now? "You think I'm too naive to the world, well then whose fault is that, huh? Whose job is it to teach me how life works? Whose job is it to tell me I was adopted? Because it sure as hell wasn't supposed to be a teacher at school. A stranger, who I've never even met before!" I scream.

The more I say, the more I want to say and I carry on, not giving her or anyone else a chance to respond. "Where were you when I found out that my real mother SOLD me to her doctor, and then ran away so I could never contact her again? You were here, that's where! You've never given two hoots about me in my entire life. You've never wanted to be my mom, and you've made that abundantly clear over the years so let's not pretend to start now!"

Mom stares at me in disbelief while Ryan hasn't once let go of my hand. He gently rubs his thumb in small circles, letting me know he's here for me. "I am eighteen. Mom, I love you, but you stopped being my mother when you chose to abandon me when I needed you the most!" I stand up, pulling a hesitant Ryan with me.

"Faithy, I'm sorry. Please don't walk away. Let's talk about this, honey?" Mom pleads, but her words fall on deaf ears.

"No! I've said all I have to say. As far as I'm concerned, what I do with Ryan is none of your business." With that I turn and leave, too upset to look back. I don't know where I'm going, but I walk towards the village. I just need to be away from her right now. I feel sick to my stomach that Ryan had to see that, after he shared his story about losing his own mother last night. God, he must think I'm a selfish bitch.

Before I know it, he is behind me, his strong arms pulling me back and into his embrace, and I selfishly fall into him, allowing myself to cry. There is so much I need to say to Ryan about last night. Ryan blames himself, and he needs to know that none of what happened is his fault. I should be the one comforting him this morning, but yet here I am making it all about me again.

"It's okay, *Foi*. You are allowed to be angry. Your relationship with your mom is yours, it's got nothing to do with what happened to mine. I know you're feeling guilty, I can practically hear your brain working overtime," Ryan offers, having read my mind. I shake my head. I'm so selfish.

"I think you needed to say those things to your mom. You've let it fester inside you for far too long. I know you didn't want to upset her, and it's obvious that you want to fix your relationship with her. I think maybe you need to talk again. Maybe give her a chance to respond and explain her side? Anyone can see that she loves you. You guys just need to be honest about the past and how you feel."

He looks at me with sincere concern, and to be honest it makes me feel like shit. Mostly because I know he would give anything to speak to his mom one more time. I should have let Mom speak before storming off.

"I didn't mean for that to happen, I actually wanted to try with her. I brought up how I feel about you, thinking we could be normal for once, and instead of being supportive or happy for me, she just kept belittling my feelings. She said it was a one-sided crush. It's not a crush Ryan, I'm in love with you. I know I might sound crazy, but it's how I feel. I love you!"

I expect Ryan to run for the hills at my announcement but he doesn't. Instead he gives me a heart melting kiss I feel deep in my core. He doesn't tell me he loves me back, but honestly, I'm okay with that. He explained last night he doesn't feel capable of falling in love anymore, and after the heartbreak he has suffered, it's no wonder he feels that way. He needs time to heal, and I know that I will be here for him if he wants me to be. He can take as long as he needs.

"Thank you for loving me. I'll never deserve you, *Ma Belle Foi*," he says sadly.

"What happened to your mom wasn't your fault Ryan. It wasn't. Neither was it hers, it wasn't anyone's fault. What happened was just a terrible, heart breaking accident that only happened because your mom was sick. She didn't deserve that, and neither did you. I wish with all my heart I could take away some of your pain. I can tell by how you speak about her that she loved you very much."

"I should have taken better care of her, I should have seen the signs. I should never have left her alone. I knew something wasn't right, but I left her to sleep because I didn't know what else to do." He swallows and looks away. After years of practising holding in your emotions, you can't change that overnight.

"You know what I think? I think you did all you could that day to make sure your mom had the best day, and from the sounds of it she really did. It was such a great day, and she wanted that to be the way you remembered her. It's what she asked of you, isn't it? To remember it that way no matter what? From what you said, it sounded like her depression was getting worse over time, and she didn't ever want you seeing her that way. So maybe, I think she must have decided that she would leave on her terms. She would have likely planned it before she did it."

He nods but doesn't speak. I can tell he is fighting an internal battle with what he has always believed to be true and the possibility of what I'm saying being the real truth. "After such a great day with you, that's when she chose to leave her illness behind. I don't think she ever wanted to leave you, and I think she will always be with you in your heart."

I touch his face. He is so beautiful. He looks so vulnerable right now it breaks my heart. He takes in a deep breath through his nose and closes his eyes, and I can tell he doesn't want to talk about it anymore.

"You wanna do something fun today? We are supposed to go with the others, but I'm sure it will be fine if we stay behind? We can go over to the school and say hello, spend the morning there. Then afterwards we can see if we can sweet talk Rems into taking us over to the elephant sanctuary that's a few miles up north?"

Ryan gives me a huge smile. He looks like a kid on Christmas morning.

"Elephant sanctuary, are you serious? Hell yeah, I freakin' love elephants," he beams. "Plus, I am kinda excited to go to the school. I really enjoyed my little soccer game with the kids yesterday. What do you think they will want us to do?" He adds with uncertainty.

"Probably just introduce yourself. Talk a bit about your life, ask the kids about theirs, maybe play a few games. We have a few supplies to take with us, they will love all the new pencils." His face flashes with guilt over that statement. "Look, I'm sorry for giving you a hard time before about not bringing anything, you weren't to know."

"No, don't apologise. I feel like a total asshole, you were right to call me out. But I have arranged for some bits to be shipped over. I think I might be gone by the time they get here though, sadly. But I guess you will still be here though, right? Can you make sure they get where they are supposed to be?" He says casually, or almost hopefully even, as if the thought of being apart doesn't tear him up inside. Then I realise, maybe it doesn't.

I might be his 'girl' right now, but that doesn't mean he wants me as his girlfriend back home. Then again, perhaps Mom was right, maybe I am too naive.

Maybe being Ryan's girl and being Ryan's girlfriend might actually be two different things.

## CHAPTER 25

### *Faith*

The thought of being here without Ryan now, twists in my gut. The thought of him being back at school, while I'm here, urgh, I don't like that at all. He will be with Mia, and all of his douchebag friends, and that makes me feel uneasy. Would he get back with her? Would he find someone else? Would he still be friends with Shane?

I'm almost certain he would have at least a dozen girls make a pass for him the first day back if they knew he was single, and he would be bound to accept one of them. Maybe he would stay single and make his way through all of them?

Could I spend a year apart without him after this? I'm not sure I could. *Dude, you won't have a choice if he doesn't want you around?*

Oh crap. I know I'm falling down a rabbit hole now with all these internal questions, but I can't help it. What if I am just an easy summer fling like Mom said? I'm not sure I could watch him with other girls. It was hard enough watching him with Mia, but that was before. Now I know what it's like to be kissed by him, to be touched by him, to hear him call me his girl. I just couldn't bear it.

Even if by some miracle he did want to be with me officially, it's still a whole year apart. Would he really wait for me? It would be longer if we went to colleges in different states. The University of Michigan is just under seven hundred miles from Columbia. Yes, I already looked it up back when I was just his silent stalker. Pathetic, huh?

I guess I considered for the briefest of moments that maybe I could have a trip to New York and go and watch one of his games, just to be near him. Even back then the thought of being apart from him hurt. Then, seeing as we're being honest, I might have also imagined how we might accidentally happen to bump into each other, and he invites me to go for a drink to catch up, before we fall madly in love.

Told you I was pathetic.

My mother's words of a 'one-sided crush' spring to my mind, but I ignore them.

I guess I could look at colleges in New York. I don't think I could get into Columbia, and even then, it would still mean a year without him first. Not unless I went back. Could I do that, go back to California with Mom?

"Earth to Faith? Hello?" Ryan waves his hand in front of my face and smiles, and I realise I've been staring off into space for God knows how long. "Hey, there you are. Where'd you go? I swear I lost you for like a full minute and half there," He says, pulling me in for a playful kiss.

"I'm sorry, I do that sometimes," I offer hoping he won't delve any deeper into what I was thinking.

"You were over thinking something, that's for sure. Was it about what happened with your mom? Do you wanna talk about it?"

"What did you mean before when you said I was your girl?" I blurt out before I've even realised what I'm saying. He looks at me confused at first but a smirk forms on his face. This isn't funny, dickwad.

"I mean, *Ma Belle Foi*, that you are mine! God help any other asshole who so much as looks at you. Why's that? Don't you want to be mine, Asher?" He asks playfully.

"No… I mean, yes! Yes of course I do. What I mean is, well, what does being your girl actually mean? Does that mean I'm your girlfriend? Because you didn't specifically ask, and I don't want to assume, so…"

Before I can say anymore Ryan picks me up and throws me over his shoulder caveman style. I scream but he slaps my ass and roars with laughter as he strolls back down towards our camp, casually saying hello to anyone he passes. He sets me down outside the camp. He peeks inside his tent and it's empty. Greg must have left with Mom and Sam already. Ryan and I were supposed to be going with them, but I guess Mom didn't want me around.

There is a large town about eighty miles east where they are doing a free children's clinic, offering check-ups and vaccinations. They try to see as many people as they can because they can only spend the day there, so they will be gone most of the day and won't be back until late. It's a little risky driving the journey at night though, especially with medical supplies, so that's why they need Sam to go with them to chaperone.

Ryan pulls me inside and lifts me up again before gently lying us both down on his cot.

"Faith, I know I've been a grade A dick to you in the past. I didn't know you then and I'm sorry for the way I behaved. I think you're fucking beautiful, inside and out. In the short time I've been here, you've rocked my world, and I've shared a deeper connection with you here than I have with any other girl before, ever." He gives me the sexiest smile, like he knows something I don't. "I want to tell everyone I know that you're mine. I want everyone to know how fucking awesome you are, *Foi*!" He says sweetly, running his hand over my blushing cheek.

"I know we are on different paths right now, but I can't imagine my life without you in it anymore. Even if it means I have to write you a letter every day that we are apart; receiving just one of yours back would make it worth it. Nothing would make me happier than to call you my girlfriend, even if we are half a world apart."

I can't help but smile like a Cheshire cat. This the best moment of my entire life, and the sweetest thing anyone has ever said to me.

"Ryan, do you want to be my boyfriend?" *Wooaaahh! Hold the effin' phone. Where did those lady balls come from?*

Ryan throws his head back and laughs a sexy chuckle that has me filled with need. "What? It's 2019, modern women can do the asking!" I say proudly, trying to hide the fact I even surprised myself.

"Yes ma'am, they certainly can! You're a fucking lioness, baby. You can do anything you want, and yes, I really want to be your boyfriend! Do you want to be my girlfriend?" He says as he slips his hand under my waistband and inside my panties.

"Yes, I would love to be your girlfrieeennd… ahh, oh God Ryan!" He lets out another of those sexy chuckles before pressing deeper inside of me.

"Well you better, because fuck if I'm going to let any other bastard have you now!" With that he pulls his hand away, and my body instantly protests. He pulls off my shorts and panties and spreads my legs as wide as they can go. My cheeks instantly heat from being so exposed. I pull the pillow over my face out of embarrassment, but he laughs and pulls it away.

"Don't hide yourself from me, *Foi,* ever. In fact..." He pulls off my tee-shirt and bra, leaving me completely naked and vulnerable. I watch his Adam's apple bob slowly as he swallows, taking me in. He rubs himself through his pants, a look of pure lust on his face. He likes what he sees?

"Now *Foi*, I'm going to do all sorts of things to you until I've heard you scream my name. There's no one around except us, so don't fucking hold back, because I won't!" He teases, as he runs a lazy finger up and down my inner thigh making me inadvertently move to close my legs. He slaps them back open.

"Don't you dare close your legs, not even a little bit. If you do, then there will be consequences, understand?" Holy moley, his alpha side is hot as hell. I nod, not knowing what to say or do. He gives my inner thigh a playful smack with the back of his hand. It stings, but at the same time it feels surprisingly good.

"Use words to answer me, Faith!" He commands. Well hello *Mr Grey.* Tie me up and do whatever the hell you want with me, sir!

"Yes. I understand." I barely manage to whisper. I'm nervous as hell, but I'm more turned on than I've ever been and he hasn't even started. He gives me a dangerous smile before lowering his head and putting his mouth on me. My legs instantly close, trying to relieve some of the pressure. He chuckles against me as if he saw it coming, and when he glances up at me I know I'm done for.

He flips me over on to my front before pulling my ass up in the air. He pushes my head back down and puts his leg in between mine forcing me to spread myself wide. He laughs again sitting back on his heels, and my cheeks are instantly on fire. I'm totally exposed and he is now just staring at me. All of me.

Completely on show for his viewing pleasure.

He lets out a heavy breath before composing himself again, giving away how affected he is.

"Hmm... what to do with you now, *Ma Belle Foi*? I like seeing you like this, all wet and ready for me to do with as I please. You should disobey me more often I think. I told you there would be consequences, did I not?" He says, his voice all sexy and low, showing once more that this is having just as much of an effect on him as it is me. He is trying to play it cool though. "We definitely agreed you would use your words too if I remember rightly?"

"Yes, you said there would be consequences," I mutter, barely able to speak. The anticipation of what he will do has me aching with need. I didn't realise I could feel pleasure without even being touched. Before I even know what's about to happen, a swift hard hand comes down on my ass with a loud smack.

Jeez! Right in the Backstreet's Back-side. Man, that hurt, but at the same time, I weirdly kinda liked it? I let out a whimper, as he does it a second time, and then a third. By the time he smacks me a fourth time I've crossed the line between pain and pleasure and I'm aching for more. I'm so wet and needy I find myself pushing back toward him, silently begging him not to stop.

"*Foi*, you're so sexy you know that. You make me fucking crazy!" He strokes my sore ass gently, admiring what I'm sure are his bright pink handprints against my pale skin. He slips two fingers inside of me, and I moan with pleasure. He pumps them slowly in and out of me whilst peppering small kisses around my sore ass cheeks.

He removes his fingers and flips me back over onto my back and spreads my legs as wide as he can. I couldn't move them now if I tried, his strong arms holding me in place as he lowers his mouth back on to me. He devours me, with relentless strokes of his tongue. His mouth is everywhere, he is biting, licking and sucking, before pushing his tongue up inside of me. I'm in a complete haze of pleasure.

He takes one hand from my leg and inserts two fingers back inside of me, while he continues to use his mouth right where I need him, pushing my body closer to the edge. Every stroke feels like I'm just one more away from falling into oblivion. I'm so hot, I feel like I'm going to catch on fire as I feel my orgasm begin to grow.

"Fuck Ryan, yes!" I scream, just like he said I would.

People say they see fireworks, but I feel like I *am* the firework, exploding into my climax as Ryan continues his assault relentlessly in lazy circles until I am completely spent.

He comes back up and gives me a sexy, dirty kiss. He invades my mouth to have me taste myself on his tongue, and I can't get enough. I pull him in deeper, greedily trying to take more, making him groan in the process. I pull back and smile. I'm breathless as hell but I still speak.

"You, Ryan Scott, are now also a badass bitch!"

# CHAPTER 26

## Ryan

It's extremely hot today, but thankfully there is a nice warm breeze rolling through the truck as we drive up towards the sanctuary. I take a quick minute to check my messages.

**Kat** - Hey, thought I'd send you a private message. I know we joke around on the group chat, but fucking hell I miss you. I hope you're alright, I hope you're living your best fucking life and just being #topwanker, because if the reason you're not responding is because you're not alright, please talk to me? X

Delete. I miss you too.

**Spencer** - You are a fucking arsehole. Don't you give a shit anymore? I'm gonna tell you something that you once told me. I will be your friend forever, no take backs! Please let me know if you are okay? X

Delete. I'm sorry Spence, I just can't.

I feel so awful, because I know she wants to talk to me about this stupid surgery she doesn't even need. Apparently, thanks to her mother's constant pressure about her weight, she is looking into having a gastric band fitted. What the hell? She's not even that overweight, and she's only eighteen. I'm not sure what doctor in their right mind would have agreed to that. I definitely need to call her back.

I look at Faith as she beams back at me, a vision of innocence. She knows that coming to visit the elephant sanctuary is one of my dreams, and she can't hide her joy at being the one to put a smile on my face. Okay, so it's not ideal that these wonderful beauties are in a sanctuary in the first place. It would definitely be better for them to be out in the wild, but just to be near them is a blessing.

Elephants are so wise and loving, they experience a whole range of emotions similar to our own; joy, anger, compassion. Grief. They remember the ones they have lost long after they have gone. The best part about them though is they are also so playful, they are just like children at times.

"Don't worry," Faith assures me. "This place is completely ethical. I wouldn't come here if it wasn't. There are no tourist gimmicks or dick things like that. There is no breeding at the sanctuary either. All of the elephants here are either orphaned or injured, mostly by poachers, sadly."

The thought of my father and his merry band of assholes leaves a sour taste in my mouth.

"Some of the elephants can be released back into the wild after rehab. But most end up staying here. It's not the same I know, but it's a safe, healthy environment for the elephants to live out their days," she says with a sigh. I can tell she cares very deeply about the elephants here.

Faith told me earlier that they accept visitors here but

under very strict rules. Like she said, no staged photo ops, no rides, none of that shit. We get to come here on the basis we muck out, and help with the daily chores of looking after the elephants, and the other menagerie of small animals they have adopted along the way.

"One of the keepers here is a photographer. He takes natural photos throughout the day, which you can buy at the end of the day if you want. Plus, it's a great way for them to make some extra funds for the sanctuary," Faith offers as she continues to tell me animatedly about how one of her photos hangs in the lobby. She tells me that she first came here in 2012 right after her parents bought the Old Farmhouse, and has come here every summer since.

A few summers ago, the photographer apparently took a black and white shot of her with one of the much-loved matriarchs, Habiba, who sadly passed away only a few hours later. She was old and had barely eaten in days. They knew she was dying, and so tried to make her as comfortable as possible while nature took its course.

For whatever reason Habiba, or Biba as Faith affectionately called her, responded to Faith, and seemed to recognise her every year she visited. When Faith arrived that day, not only did Biba leave the stables for the first time in a week, but spent her last day following Faith around the entire time. She wouldn't leave her side. When it was time for Faith to leave, the elephant appeared to cry, and show signs of distress. Faith put her hand on the elephant, and gave her a kiss, calming the elephant instantly.

The precious moment happened to be captured on camera. The sanctuary thought it was so beautiful they decided to enlarge and frame the image where it now hangs in the reception area, as a memorial for Habiba, one of the first elephants to arrive at the sanctuary.

"I can't wait to see it, baby," I say to an excited Faith, whose cheeks pinken at being called baby. The sight sends blood rushing straight to my dick. This chick has no idea how gorgeous she is, and her innocence only seems to highlight her beauty. When I say her innocence, I don't mean the fact she's a virgin, at this point I honestly couldn't have given a fuck if all the rumours about her sex life had been true. I'd still be proud as fuck to call her my girl, and I'd have words with any asshole who had something to say about it.

What I actually mean is her pure heart and her kind nature. How I ever thought this girl could be capable of being a bully I'll never know. I'm definitely a dumbass, that's for fucking sure. I smirk at her reaction to my calling her baby, knowing before I even set eyes on the picture that I'm going to buy a copy.

I can't wait to see her with the elephants, with her kind heart, I just know she will be in her element. At the school this morning Faith was quiet. Don't get me wrong, she was great with the kids, and they all just adored her from the offset. She's such a natural, but she wasn't herself. I could tell she was still upset about what happened earlier with her mom, but also about everything that I shared last night.

Truth is I don't know why I even told Faith about my mom, I was adamant before that I wouldn't. After everything that had been said earlier, I just felt like I should at least say something. Then it was like once I started speaking, I couldn't stop.

It was definitely cathartic though. Whilst the guilt I feel about that day hasn't been alleviated, I do feel better for having spoken the truth out loud. It's like I realise now that by not talking about her last day, I made what happened so final. In reality I know my mom, there is no way she would let a little thing like death be the end for her, no way.

No, she's still here. I feel her around me all the time, and hearing what Faith had to say about it, I know for sure now that I'm not crazy. When I feel her with me, I know it's not in my head. The truth was out there now, it wasn't just a case of my mom taking her own life anymore. Now her story was more than that. Her story was about her life, her beauty, her spirit.

Actually, talking about it all has given me some new perspective. She really did know even back at the beach what she was going to do. She knew she was saying goodbye. Whilst I can still never forgive myself for what happened, I can accept that retrospectively, it's always easier to see what could have been done differently. Hindsight is a wonderful thing, right?

As much as I wish my mom was still here, she wanted to take back control, and I get that now. I can never forget my part in it all, but I am starting to wonder; even if I had done things differently that day, would the outcome still have been the same eventually? Who the fuck knows. It's her anniversary in three days. Three long years without her and it still hurts like hell, every thought of her is another cut to my soul. My whole body burns with anger and pain, and honestly, I can't imagine a day when it won't.

I heard somewhere that you never get over the pain of losing someone you love, you just learn to live with a broken heart. Piece by piece you can slowly put it back together again and try to heal, and whilst it will always be filled with painful cracks, I wonder if you put enough of the pieces back, will it start to beat again?

I've always held on to that with a silent hope that just maybe, I have enough blackened pieces left. I just have to figure out how to fit them back together again. For a long time, I was dead inside. But now? Faith deserves to be loved, I'm going to do what I can to fix myself.

We wave goodbye to a troubled looking Remy who will be back later to collect us. He has barely spoken to us on the ride up here, not that he is very chatty anyway, now that I think about it. He clearly had something on his mind though, I guess I just put it down to the little boy who died yesterday. That hit everyone hard.

We walk into the lobby, and Faith hides her head in my arm in embarrassment upon seeing her photo. It's hard to miss, it's not just a framed photo like Faith made out, it's practically the entire wall. It's stunning, I can see why they chose it as the welcoming backdrop for the reception area. It's the perfect way to greet guests.

They say a picture paints a thousand words, and this is a candid shot that has captured the pure beauty and raw emotional essence of both Faith and of the elephant.

"Well, what do you think? Embarrassing, huh?" She grimaces.

"It's beautiful. I wonder if they still have the shot saved somewhere? I definitely think I need to buy a copy." I say casually.

"Oh God, seriously?" She raises a questioning eyebrow, a nervous half smile hovering across her full rosy lips.

"Most definitely. In fact I think something in this size too, I could just picture a wall like this somewhere at home. "Don't you dare!" She cringes, making me smile a genuine smile back at her. Her quizzical expression tells me she mostly thinks I'm playing, but she can't decide if I'm being half serious. What she doesn't realise is that I'm deadly serious, as she bites her bottom lip, before walking away unsure of what to say next. Fuck, I am definitely going to bite that lip myself when I get the chance.

Faith goes to the desk to check us in while I go take a

closer look at the memorial plaque to read Habiba's story. I'm shaken to my core when the first thing I see is the date she passed away. It's the date the picture was taken. It's dated 5th August 2016.

"Everything okay, you're as white as a ghost?" Faith asks as she comes over from the desk.

"Do you believe in fate, *Ma Foi*?" I ask, knowing already that there is no way a girl like Faith doesn't.

"Yes, I really do", she says, confirming my suspicions. She takes my large hand in her small one, and fuck if it isn't a balm to my soul. "When we got to the village that year, Mom was really busy every day and she said she might not be able to bring me here. I was so angry with her, I told her I hated her. I regret that badly. Mostly I was angry about being shipped halfway around the world to go to school." She says sincerely, guilt written all over her face. "Mom eventually brought me on the last day, and I guess it was fate we came the day we did. I would have never forgiven myself if I had missed my chance to say goodbye to Biba on her last day. It was meant to be!"

I kiss the top of her forehead.

"My mother was an elephant," I say matter-of-factly. I sound fucking batshit I know. Surprisingly, *Foi* doesn't bat an eyelid at my statement like it's the most normal thing in the world to say. I feel like she gets me, I can be myself around her and she wouldn't run for the hills, and that makes something in my stomach flip over.

"Mom used to say it all the time that she and I were elephants, and now, never have I ever been more certain of fate than I am at this moment," I say boldly, knowing Faith will get it. Instead, she offers a confused smile, waiting for me to elaborate and I realise I've left out a key detail. "The date. The 5th of August 2016? It's the same date, Faith!" I offer as I point to the plaque. Faith's expression turns from bewildered to shock as she connects the dots.

"That's when your mom died?"

"Yes, and I believe with all my heart that the two of them were connected spiritually somehow. Mom, she believed in all that stuff, spirit guides and such. She was a psychic medium, and she literally saw people as their spirit animals. I know you must think I'm crazy. I don't know why, but I just know it's true!"

"That's amazing Ryan! Do you think they are together now?" Faith asks sincerely. She seems genuinely open minded about what I'm saying, just like I knew she would be. I swear my mother would have loved her, just like I do. *Wait, what?*

"Don't you think I'm crazy? Do you think it's just a coincidence?"

"No way, of course not! Ryan, there is so much about this world that we are yet to fully understand. There are millions of people who believe there is more to life after death, more than the eye can see! No one knows the answer, so how could anyone tell you that you are wrong. Some people choose to believe in coincidences, and others choose to believe in fate. This is so wonderful Ryan, you were clearly meant to come here today. I didn't realise it was her anniversary so soon though, I'm sorry," she says squeezing me tightly.

I pull her face to mine for a gentle kiss. If I think about what Greg said last night, maybe there is a difference between being alive and living? When I am with *Foi*, I do feel like I am alive again. I'm not a zombie when I'm with her, and that's a start.

All I know, at this moment, is that this chick, this beautiful, powerful lion heart, will be my undoing. She already owns the last black pieces I had left, that's for sure. She will either nourish the fire back to life, or destroy them down into nothing but ash.

Either way, my fate is now tied to hers, I've never been more certain of anything.

# CHAPTER 27

## Faith

Today has been one of the best days I've had for a long time. Being here with the elephants and with Ryan was just a dream, one I don't think I will ever forget. After mucking out at first, we spent most of the late afternoon playing with the two babies that recently came here, Coco and Mabel. So. Much. Fun.

I don't think I could have imagined myself ever feeling so happy like I have been today, but I've honestly not laughed this much in a very long time. Seeing Ryan so carefree and full of life today made my heart feel whole. It's like I didn't even know that there were parts of me missing until now.

He was so playful, he was like a kid on Christmas morning. I'm pretty sure this was definitely a glimpse of who the real Ryan is, without all the grief, without all the pressures of familial responsibilities, and without all the anger. This was just him.

He even sang to Mabel as he bathed her in the lake. It was so sweet and unexpected, I couldn't help but stop and watch him. After a minute he looked at me, giving me a devilish wink asking if I 'saw anything I liked', when he caught me staring shamelessly at his body. Of course, my cheeks were scarlet in an instant. Truth is I did see something I liked, because damn this guy is some hot sauce.

I'd seen him take his shirt off on the field a couple of times after a game, but this was the first time I'd seen him shirtless up close. I couldn't help but watch as droplets of water slowly drip down his lightly bronzed abs. The waistband of his navy-blue *Ralph Lauren* swim shorts sat dangerously low, making me instantly think of what was inside. My thighs clench together at the memory of last night. I gotta admit I kinda liked it when he went all '*Fifty Shades*' on my ass.

Although he smacked me, it was nothing like with Shane, everything Ryan did was for my own pleasure, and I trust him completely. The thought of taking the next step with him has me both nervous and excited. I want him, I do, but what if I'm not enough? What if he moves on to someone else right after?

It was at that moment during my line of internal questioning that he'd caught me eye-banging him, so I wasn't able to fall down too much of a rabbit hole like I usually did. It was such a beautiful and innocent moment that made me fall even more in love with him than I already was. Him singing to Mabel that is, not him calling me out for being a perv.

I was bathing Coco, who didn't hesitate to bounce off into the shallows and splash around like a pro. Ryan had to hold back for a bit with an unsure Mabel. He could tell she was nervous but he was so patient. He gently reassured her, but also waited as long as she needed for her to decide when she was ready. He didn't once try and push her into it.

When she finally braved her first steps into the water he delicately started to sponge her. He then started to sing, and it was simply magical. *'Three Little Birds'* by Bob Marley & The Wailers. I'm not sure what I expected his voice to be like, but his alluring Bieber-esque falsetto was hella' sexy. This boy, honestly.

After that, just like most girls, Mabel was putty in his hands. Splashing and playing, following him wherever he went. We spent the rest of the afternoon in the water, and I'm not sure who enjoyed it more, us or the elephants. We were just four big kids having fun together.

When it was time for us to say goodbye to the elephants, Mabel was clearly saddened. I'm not sure if he meant for me to hear or not, but I heard Ryan tell her that she was his beautiful girl, and he promised her he would be back to see her again soon. The thought he might come back here, with or without me, made my heart swell.

Now we have dried off and freshened up, and we are just relaxing in a hammock waiting for Remy to come pick us up. It's not cold, in fact it's still pretty hot, but I have Ryan's hoodie back on. It just feels too good on for me not to wear it.

He has been showing me pictures on his phone from back at school in London with all of his friends. I wasn't surprised when he told me he had only had two girlfriends before Mia, and that none of them had been very serious. I'd always assumed he was a player, having his pick of the girls. Why would he want to settle down when he could have any girl whenever he wanted?

I could already hear Inner Britney in my head singing *'Womanizer'*. I wonder how many girls he's been with? I could feel the questions brewing inside of me, so I was definitely surprised when he later told me that he wasn't all that popular with the ladies back in London.

"I dunno," he shrugs, "I guess I wasn't all that interested in girls that way when I was young. All I ever wanted to do was play soccer. When girls did start to pay me attention, they didn't really seem to like the fact that two of my best friends were chicks," he muses, brushing his fingers gently through my hair. "Tom and Alex, they didn't really seem to have that problem because, well Tom was related to Kat, so she was never a threat where his girlfriends were concerned, and Alex? Well he had a pretty 'big reputation' if you catch my drift. He had already fucked half the school by the time he was sixteen, including a faculty member!"

I'm not sure what to do with that information about his friend's junk, but I am curious about what he meant about Kat being a threat.

"So, would Kat have been a threat to one of your girlfriends?" I ask, hating the fact I am being openly jealous of a girl I know nothing about. *She was smoking hot in the pictures though, it's not like anyone could blame you.*

Crap, now that thought officially makes me one of *those* girls.

"No, she wasn't a threat." He smirks, clearly liking my jealous side. He puts his large hand on my waist and teases his fingers just underneath my clothes to brush them across my tummy. The skin-on-skin contact sends electric waves right through my body. This bastard knows exactly what he is doing too.

"She was my best friend, that's all. Don't get me wrong we fooled around once. We were both single, and we both agreed it was just fucking weird, so it never happened again," he adds, and even though it twists in my stomach, I do appreciate his honesty.

"What about Spencer? Did you ever fool around with her? Were girls threatened by her too?"

"No, we never fooled around. I gave her a kiss once. My

first kiss actually, but that's all it was. Let's just say she was going through a lot of personal shit, and she was bullied a lot. But she had me. I guess I just needed to show her that I was there for her, and well, a kiss seemed like the right thing to do at the time," he admits, and I'm a little intrigued as to why it stopped at a kiss.

"Spencer is so beautiful inside and out, it's just taking the world a little longer to catch up on that," he offers, and whilst it didn't clear anything up, I still appreciate his honesty again. I think I'd like to meet these girls. I wonder if they would like me? Would they be protective over Ryan? Probably.

I look around and see that we are alone, so I slowly turn on my front so we are chest to chest, and I give him a far from PG kiss. This time I take control, entering his mouth with my own tongue to claim him as mine. He groans into me as he squeezes my ass firmly.

"What are you doing to me, *Ma Belle Foi*?" He says breathlessly in between kisses. "I'm going crazy for you; do you know that?" He runs his hands under my shirt, up my back and the warm feeling of his touch is setting me on fire.

"Are you really?" I ask innocently, my best attempt at flirting, whilst still hoping to get a real answer from him. A big part of me thinks that he just says things like that in the moment. How could I drive anyone crazy?

"I've never wanted anyone so much. I would fuck you right here if I could!" He says, getting hard beneath me as he continues to kiss me into oblivion. Heat soars through my entire body at his confession. He moves one of his hands around the front and finds my bra, and makes short work of pulling it down to access my breast and tease my nipple.

"I want nothing more than to eat your pretty pussy till you come hard on my mouth." Holy shit. I can already feel my cheeks redden. "Then I want to slide my cock as deep inside you as I can possibly get and fuck you until you swear to always be mine!" His dirty words turn me on more than I would have expected and I let out a breathy moan. I can't help but focus on that one word.

Always.

Forgetting we are in a hammock I move far too quickly to straddle him and instead we both come rolling off onto the floor, literally bringing us crashing back down to earth. After laughing so hard I actually snorted, making me laugh even more, Ryan helped us both up, a look of angst sitting on his face.

"I'm sorry, I got a little carried away," I grimace, feeling more than a little bit embarrassed about my snorty laugh, now that the moment has gone. *Real lady-like, Faith.*

"It's fine, so did I," he says in a tone that sounds a little bit like regret. *I guess he is just a caught-in-the-moment kinda guy after all.*

"We should probably make our way back down to the lobby, Rems will be here soon anyway," Ryan suggests with a sad smile, his gold flecked eyes offering no hint to what's going on inside. I try not to read too much into his sudden change in demeanour. Neither of us is ready to leave the perfect bubble of today. Reality just seems to hurt too much at the moment.

"I'm just going to use the bathroom before we leave, I'll be out in just a minute," Ryan suddenly says as we are halfway out the door. I can't help but feel a little weird. I know I'm needy as hell, but I need reassurance right now. *Not just right now, babe. You always need reassurance.*

"Okay, I'm going to wait outside for Remy," I say, not having the lady balls to speak up. He pulls me back into him for a quick kiss. He smiles his brilliantly gorgeous smile at me.

"Talk to me, *Foi?* I can practically hear your thoughts

again, they are so loud?" He says, making me cringe. Am I that obvious? *Yes!*

"Stop overthinking. I said I didn't want to rush you and I meant it. I'm just pissed at myself for saying those things just then. Not because they aren't true, because they fucking couldn't be truer. I want to do all those things and more to your fine ass, I won't lie about that. But all in good time. I don't ever want you to think I can't wait, because I will gladly wait as long as I need to." He gives me another soft kiss before releasing me. "You good?" He asks and I nod back, embarrassed about being caught out by my insecurity.

Again, as if still hearing my thoughts he raises an eyebrow. Is he a freakin' wizard or something?

"I know you have every right to be insecure when it comes to me. I haven't exactly given you a reason to trust me, and thanks to the people I used to call my friends, you haven't exactly been treated how you deserve by any guy for a long time. But trust me, if those assholes hadn't made up those lies about you, then I can tell you now, you would be having your pick of guys at that school," he says confidently. Yeah right, sure.

"I'm not sure that's true, but thank you anyway." His kind words embarrass me, but that doesn't stop me wrapping my arms around his waist. He feels so warm. It's like I've finally found my home. Safe.

"You're so fucking beautiful, Faith. You are on fire and it kills me to think that I'm part of the reason you don't see that. But fuck if I'm going to ever stop trying to make you believe it from now on!" Ryan leans in and kisses my neck, before pulling back, but he takes my hand in his. "If you ever need reassurance from me, Faith, then ask. You can ask me anything you want, I don't mind," he offers with a sincere smile.

For some reason, just by him saying that it makes me

feel more secure than I did before. Could this really be something real for us?

"Thank you! I guess I just get a little caught up in my own head sometimes. I end up worrying about stuff that may never even happen, and I feel like an idiot, but I can't help it," I say sheepishly, biting my bottom lip. Why do I feel nervous admitting to that?

"That's called anxiety, Faith. Growing up around my mom, I totally get it, trust me. Don't be embarrassed, and don't ever apologise for it either. Finding out you were adopted the way you did? The bullying? The awful things that *I've* said and done? It's no wonder you have all this doubt. I promise, you can say anything to me. I would never judge you or get annoyed about it, no matter how many questions you have to ask. Ask me the same question every day if you have to, I'll do whatever it takes. Whatever you need, okay?" He offers, with a kindly wink and I nod feeling a little less worried than I was.

He slaps my ass and I head out the door, bringing yet more memories back from last night. We haven't been able to keep our hands off each other all day, but I know he intends to keep his promise about waiting.

I check my phone to see if Mom has sent a text or anything, but there is nothing. She hasn't even been online all day to check if I've messaged her. I don't know if that pisses me off or if I honestly don't blame her, after the things I said. I don't know how I feel anymore, but I do know that my mom and I have a lot to talk about when we get back. I need to at least hear her out because I need answers.

Don't get me wrong, I know she loves me in her own way, but does she love me like her daughter, or just as someone who she became fond of over the years? If it's the latter, fair enough, but please don't pretend to be my mother any longer.

I knew when I asked Ryan here it would not only be

the perfect escape from my own issues with Mom, but I also thought that maybe it might be a brief respite from all of his grief, and after seeing the way he was today, I can tell that it was desperately needed.

It doesn't surprise me when I see him through the window, staring back at the photo on the wall. What he believes about his mom and Biba being connected means a lot to him, and I respect that. I decide to give him some privacy and walk over to the opposite wall so that he is no longer in my line of sight.

As well as showing me some photos of his friends, Ryan showed me a bunch of photos of his mom. She really was as beautiful as he says. Ryan definitely has her genes that's for sure, he looks just like her. From her unruly wavy blonde hair, and her golden-brown eyes, they look so similar. She had a very bohemian style, and from the way he described her she was also very in touch with her spiritual side too.

God my heart aches for him. He loves her so much, it's been three years and he is still hurting as if it were yesterday. Can a person ever get over losing someone like that? I want to hold him so tight, so that he knows I will never let go of him, ever. I think about what he said to me earlier about me promising to be his, always. I don't need him to fuck me into saying that, it's already been promised.

I'm not sitting in my new spot for more than two minutes when I'm pulled from my thoughts by Remy pulling up in the truck. I notice his mouth pressed in a hard line. He wasn't really himself earlier either, now that I think about it.

"Hey Rems, how's your day been?" I greet him and he offers me a weary smile. Something pools in the pit of my stomach and I'm not sure why, but it feels like dread. "What is it, what's happened?" I ask bluntly and the look Remy gives me says all I need to know. Something *has* happened.

Remy shakes his head.

"I think we should wait until Ryan comes out." Oh God. If he wants to wait for Ryan this must be bad. My mind rushes through a million scenarios a minute.

"What is it Remy? I'm not a child, please just tell me?" I half shout, barely able to contain my fear. I'm shaking.

"Hey, why are you upset? What's going on?" Ryan says sternly, walking towards us with a cold look on his face to match his tone. Ryan's icy stare is directed at Rems. He's pissed before he even knows what's wrong. His eyes are black, and he is ready to kill someone, he just doesn't know who, or why yet.

"Remy, talk. Now!" he commands authoritatively, a look of murder in his eye.

Remy and Sam are both in a pretty serious gang, the same one Ade used to be a part of. That's how they have access to guns. My parents don't agree with what they do, but they are generally good people, who are always on hand to help chaperone and keep us safe. They always help Ade to make sure all the medical supplies reach the clinic's secure store room without interception, as a lot of what we store here could fetch a high price on the black market. It's the bigger picture that allows my parents to turn a blind eye.

Ade told us that him getting out of the gang was a fluke. Usually, you're recruited as kids, mostly orphans, or kidnapped from parents living on the street. Some are even sold into it. You're handed a weapon, and a job to do, and that's it, you're in for life.

With all that in mind I'm surprised when a guy like Remy appears to heed Ryan's unspoken threat.

"Listen, try not to worry there could be a number of explanations," Remy tries to reassure but he is just making this worse. "It's the others. They didn't arrive for the pop-up clinic, they haven't been seen since they left this morning and all of their phones are disconnected!"

## CHAPTER 28

*Faith*

It's been fifteen hours. No one has been able to reach them all day. While we were at the sanctuary, Remy had driven out to some nearby villages along their route to see if anyone saw them passing through. Nothing.

I was told to 'get some sleep' by an authoritative Ryan, who has been outside, obsessively ringing Greg's number over and over in the hopes that the next time he will get a different result. I can't sleep, so I'm just lying here waiting and overthinking. My head won't stop replaying this morning's scene with Mom over and over.

The past few years have been so strained between Mom and I, and I can't help but feel saddened by all the time we have lost. I also feel a tremendous guilt deep in my soul when I think about how Ryan has spent the last three years wishing he could have just one more day with his mother, while I've spent the same time avoiding mine. God, I feel like such a brat now.

I spoke to my dad. Ade is away with work, but he is headed back to go get my dad so they can come here and join the search. Rems and some of the local guys have set up a patrol around the village. They moved our camp inside the perimeter just as a precaution. The country is troubled by extremists and civil war. Entire villages have been taken hostage in recent years, and when someone goes missing, especially aid workers, it's hard not to fear the worst.

I hear Ryan's phone ring outside and he is on it in an instant. My nerves are shot to pieces waiting for him to reveal who's on the other end.

"Hello... Yes, we're fine, just waiting for news... Well of course I am keeping her safe, I'm not a total asshole... How did you even find out?... Is that really necessary?... Okay, well Dr. Asher should be here tomorrow night, if that's what he thinks is best, then of course I'll do as he wants..."

I listen to every word of this one-sided conversation intently, trying to make out who it is on the other side, but I can't take anything in. There is a long silence, I assume the other person is talking. Ryan takes a loud breath in and out of his nose.

"You know you missed my birthday... Yea whatever, I'll guess I'll see you when we get back... Goodbye, Dad!"

I'm so highly strung at this point it isn't until he actually says the word 'Dad' I realise who he is speaking to. Did his dad really forget his birthday? The thought breaks my heart. Even my mom hasn't ever forgotten my birthday. I feel the need to hold him after this revelation, so I get up and go back outside to join him.

Ryan is sitting with his face in his hands. He sits upright at hearing me come out and frowns at me. God, even when he is brooding he is gorgeous as hell. His hair is even more wild than usual, he has most likely been running his fingers through it all night with stress.

"What are you doing awake you're supposed to be sleeping, *Foi*?" He questions, but still opens his arms and gestures for me to climb onto his lap. He wraps his strong arms around me tightly and I hear him breathe me in. As usual, I instantly feel safe, like there is nowhere else I'm supposed to be. I know there is definitely nowhere else I'd rather be than wrapped in his arms, that's for sure.

I breathe him in too, the romantic scent of Pacific Ocean sunsets filling my nostrils. How is it possible he still smells so good like that after the day we've had? My California dream.

"Did your dad really forget your birthday, baby?" I ask, unable to hide the sorrow filling my voice. I'm also acutely aware of the word 'baby' that just slipped onto the end of my sentence like it belonged there. *You luuurve him, you wanna kiss him...*

Ryan can't hide his pleasure at hearing the word escape my mouth, with a devious smile sneaking across his face, but as quickly as it arrives, it leaves, and he is back to frowning again. I begin running my fingers through his untamed curls, being sure to tickle his head as softly as I can. He responds with a heavy breath, showing me he is relaxing a little.

"I knew he would. It's been that way every year since, well, you know. I meant it when I said I haven't celebrated a birthday for a while now. I don't know if he forgets or just simply ignores it, but I presume it's the latter. Either way it didn't seem right to celebrate, so I kinda get it," he shrugs nonchalantly, but his beautiful sad eyes can't hide his true emotion. I understand a little more now why he was so overwhelmed by our surprise on his birthday.

I offer him a kiss, which he reciprocates gladly, dominating me with his tongue inside my mouth, leaving me breathless. He pulls me over so I'm now straddling his lap. His hands grip my ass as he continues to kiss me into a semi-coma.

"It's a good job I made you that lame ass cake then, huh?" I tease when I finally break away for some air. He smiles and rubs his nose playfully against my own.

"That cake was the second best thing I ever tasted, *Ma Belle Foi*," he teases in return.

He begins rubbing his hand up my bare thigh, where the bed shorts I'm wearing are riding high up my leg. My cheeks begin to warm, not just at his less than subtle innuendo, or at the thigh rubbing, but also at *Ma Belle Foi*.

My Beautiful Faith.

He has called me that a few times now, does he think I'm beautiful?

"I liked it when you called me baby, by the way," he adds before gently sliding down the strap to my vest and placing open-mouthed kisses on my shoulder. I can't help but let out a soft moan and he deliberately presses himself up between my legs applying pressure to my core with his hard erection. Again though, as fast as a moment of lust took over him, he quickly regained his composure.

"Seriously though, how are you doing?" He asks, his playful mood now gone. At first, I'm a little confused with him killing the mood like that, but then his question sinks in and I'm filled with guilt that I allowed myself to forget all that's happened for a moment.

"I'm so worried, Ryan. About all of them. What if something terrible has happened, what if we never see them again?" He brushes his hand up my thigh again but this time it's more of a reassuring gesture.

"I know it's hard, but we have to stay positive. Like Remy said it could be a number of reasons we can't reach them. Let's try not to panic until we have more information. At first light Rems and a couple of local guys are going to drive out and take the same road the others would have taken. I wanted to go with them, but there is no way I am going to leave you alone, and you are definitely not going. So, I'm going to stay here with you and we are going to go to the school as planned and keep things normal until we hear otherwise okay?"

Before I can protest he gives me a stern look, the kind that says 'don't even think about it', and I gotta admit I'm really starting to like this alpha side to him.

"Faith, I trust Remy, he won't leave a stone unturned. That is his brother out there too, remember?"

"Oh God, I actually didn't think about Sam being Remy's brother, I was so worried about Mom. Sam is Ade's cousin too, and what with Greg being missing as well, Ade must be beside himself. Wow, I'm a self-absorbed asshole. Talk about a shitty friend, it's no wonder I don't have any!"

I stand up from Ryan's hold, not feeling very deserving of his comfort right now, and wrap my own arms around my middle.

"Faith stop, okay. Don't worry about it. That's your mother out there. I'm pretty sure no one is judging you right now, they know you care. Besides, the reason you didn't have any friends is because some jealous witch decided she was going to take them from you. But you have me now, I'm not going anywhere." He stalks over to me and takes my hand. "Come on, let's go and lay down. You need some rest," he commands as he leads me back inside.

"Will you lay with me? Please?" I ask unashamedly. I'll beg if I have to, I need him right now. He takes a deep breath and closes his eyes, fighting an internal battle.

"Okay. I'll lay down with you, just for a bit till you fall asleep," he offers, taking his place on the cot. I lay beside him snuggling into the space under his arm that feels like it's always been waiting for me. *My safe place.*

"What was your mom's name?" I ask after a few minutes of silence, realising only now that he has never mentioned it. He smiles like he is in on a joke I'm not privy to.

"What else would a true southern belle of the Pelican State be called, huh?" He says in his best Louisiana accent. "Why, Magnolia of course! Magnolia Louise Ambrose-Scott to be exact, but she always had everyone call her Maggie," he smiles again innocently as if remembering her for a moment.

"Magnolia? That's really pretty. She didn't like it?"

"No, she hated it, but my father refused to call her anything else. He said she was far too beautiful not to be called Magnolia. She wouldn't let anyone else get away with it though, only Dad. Well, him and Gramps, he did name her after all." I've heard him speak about his grandpa before. I wonder if his grandparents are still around?

"She loved the tree though, it was her favourite. My dad, he always promised her that one day they would move down to Louisiana, where she could have a garden full of magnolia. It never happened though. Funny thing is, he couldn't move fast enough when it came to making Melody happy. Now he lives somewhere warm, but there isn't a magnolia in sight. Too much fucking glass and metal in that monstrosity of a house he built!" He shakes his head in disgust.

I've never seen his house in person, but I've seen pictures of it on gossip pages. Plus, there was a mini-series on TV, *'Christmas At Home, with Melody Scott'*. It was basically a TV crew filming her making and baking different Christmas stuff like she was Martha freakin' Stewart or something.

It was filmed inside their actual home, and in between her making stuff, there were all these Kardashian-esque type scenes where she was enjoying the holidays with family. Well

I guess I might have been guilty of watching, hoping to catch a glimpse of Ryan. He was in a few scenes, he never looked particularly happy about it, but now I know him better, he was probably just being his usual brooding bastard self.

Of course, him being so gorgeous, his appearance on the show increased his already high social media following to about two million, and he doesn't even post that much. The last post he shared was way back on Valentine's Day, when he did the generic three photo slide of him and Mia enjoying their date, complete with a huge hat box of roses, and a Tiffany Bracelet. So basic. *Yeah okay girl, you don't sound one bit jealous.*

"Mom would have hated that house, it's not her taste at all. It's not even Melody's taste either, so I can't blame it on her. It's like he deliberately chose the exact opposite of what she would like just to erase everything about her from our lives," he says sadly, his voice etched in anger.

"How about Melody? Do you like her?" I ask, realising he hasn't really mentioned her much either until now. He smirks again leaving me intrigued.

"She's actually pretty cool, I guess. I know she's an actress, but what you see is what you get with her. She really is exactly how she comes across on TV, that's not fake, so it's kinda hard not to like her when she's like an adorable bunny rabbit all the damn time," he says shrugging casually. His response leaves me a little confused.

"So, what's with the smile before? Has something happened between you two?" I ask, even more intrigued, although I'm not sure I wanna know the answer. There is no way in hell I can compete with a Hollywood actress. He laughs through his nose, as if he was expecting my question.

"No. No way. It's just, most people expect me to either say I hate her and that she's a gold-digging bitch, or they think that I might be trying to fuck her on the side. I can't say I ever felt either way about her. I mean, anyone who wants to put their junk where their own dad has dumped his load, is just fucking gross. Trust me, that was never on the table," he grimaces at the thought and honestly so do I, hearing him put it that way. He smirks again at my reaction.

"Get it now? It's bad enough I've seen photos of her online. Fucking assholes at school are always sending me shit. I need some fucking bleach or something to permanently erase those images from my brain," he screws up his face like any other boy would at the thought of seeing his step-mother naked. I guess being a famous actress doesn't make the slightest bit of difference. To him, she's just his dad's wife.

"I never really thought of it like that, but eww!" I say, feeling a little guilty about being one of those people he spoke about.

"It's cool. Besides, Melody is actually rich enough in her own right. Not like my family is rich, but she is worth a few million all on her own. Whatever she sees in my father, it was never about money for her. It just makes me laugh, as if there is a rule that people are supposed to hate their stepmothers. Then, if I say 'yeah I think she is great', people think I must be boning her. I can't win either way, so I usually let people draw their own conclusions. It's fucked up, but I don't get anywhere denying either assumption, so I stay quiet."

I shake my head as I cringe again. Society is pretty fucked up sometimes.

"Sure, when I heard my dad was getting married again, especially to someone practically my age, I was angry at first. It seemed way too soon. I met her and she was nice enough. She has never tried to replace my mom or anything. It's only my father who seems to wanna forget she existed. I just wish he would show some fucking sign that he misses her, or that he even cares that she's gone. He doesn't talk about her, he doesn't ask me how I'm doing. Nothing. But that's my issue with him, it's got nothing to do with Mel. Plus, she's gonna be my little brother's mom, which is awesome, so I haven't got any issues with her."

He actually smiles at the mention of his new impending brother, and it lights up his entire face. His sad eyes seem to sparkle, if only for a moment.

"You know what, I think you will be a great big brother, I can tell!" I say sincerely. I can see how much he already loves him, and he's not even met him.

"Thanks! I fully intend to be the best big brother there is. They have already decided his name, it's going to be Dexter. Pretty cool, huh? Little dude's not even born yet and he's already fucking rad. I'm so buzzed to meet him, I can't wait!" He says beaming from ear to ear, warming my heart.

"Well, I guess it's a good job you had to repeat after all then. At least you will be in California when he is born," I say, but notice how he frowns. "Why did you really agree to repeat junior year anyway? I'm calling bull on that stuff about different grading systems. You totally could have fought that?"

He shrugs. "I could have, but I really didn't care enough at the time to try, and my father didn't seem bothered. In hindsight I probably should have, because now all my friends are off to college and I'm still stuck up in high school." he frowns.

I run my fingers gently across his chest. "I found out that it was actually Shane's father, Daniel Frost, who demanded I join as a junior. Guess he just wanted his son to be associated with a Scott or some shit, I don't know. I can't think why else he would have said it, but he makes all the decisions at that school. You have a scholarship, right? It would have been him who chose you. The school has a board, but he is the only one with any say as to what goes. It's weird as fuck really because the school is really old, but the Frosts have only been in town since just after Shane was born. Daniel isn't even an Alumni, it makes no sense," Ryan shrugs again.

"Shane's dad gave me my scholarship? Could that be why Shane hates me?"

"I honestly don't know," he frowns. "I actually have more than enough credit to graduate now if I want. I don't really have to go back I could just ask for my diploma," he shrugs casually, offering no further explanation as to why he doesn't just graduate and apply for college. "Anyway, surely it's my turn to ask the questions now?" He says with a mischievous smile before I can continue with my inquisition.

"Okay, what do you wanna know?" I ask hesitantly, deciding not to press the issue about college for now.

"What do you want to do with your life? You've told me what you don't want, but what you haven't told me is what do you want? Do you actually want to go to Michigan or did you just randomly pick? What do you wanna do there?"

"Well, I havent decided for sure. Like I said, I chose Michigan mostly because it wasn't any of the schools my parents were pushing for, and it was just somewhere new. I've looked at Portland, and a few others. I even considered NYU, but I soon vetoed that idea. I would actually cross the line to full on stalker if I followed you right across the country!" *Jesus Faith, please stop talking.*

I laugh awkwardly, but he just frowns, making me nervous about what else I'll admit to with my word vomit. I decide to move swiftly on, before he can think too much about my confession.

"I help out at a soup kitchen, back in L.A. There are so many vulnerable young people living on the streets, too scared to go home, nowhere else to go. The system doesn't care about them once they turn eighteen, even some younger ones slip through the net. Well, I want to help them. I don't know how yet, but I was thinking about maybe taking some social care classes, maybe psychology? I guess I need some direction from the guidance counsellor?" I shrug.

I don't know what reaction I'm expecting from him, but the steaming hot kiss that follows is not it. He sends blistering heat coursing through my entire body. His hands are everywhere, burning like a poker, branding me with his touch.

Ryan rolls on top of me, making his way from my mouth to my neck and collar bone, where he bites and sucks me hard enough I'm sure it will leave a mark. I moan out. I'm not sure if it's from pain or pleasure, or both. When he is satisfied with his handy work he comes back up to my face, our noses barely an inch apart.

"You're so beautiful, Faith Marie Asher, do you know that?" I blush at the compliment, but I know I'm not actually beautiful.

Not knowing what to say I don't reply, I just give an awkward smile. "Tell me more. What else do you want, *Foi*? Tell me all of your dreams!" He looks down at me, his expression set in what seems like admiration, making my tummy flip with butterflies. Does he really think I'm beautiful?

"Well, you might think it's dumb, but all I've ever really wanted is a house. A home really. We have moved around so much, I've never really had somewhere permanent that really feels like a home. I want the *cliché* white picket fence, a tyre swing on an old tree in the yard, a love seat on the deck. I want a family to fill it. Kids, dogs, cats, and maybe even some alpacas?" I smile as he raises a questioning eyebrow.

Ryan is the son of a billionaire. He is used to so much luxury, I can't even begin to imagine what his dreams are like. I'm guessing by the look on his face they don't include any alpacas.

"I want Christmas where everyone comes home to the house. I want summer barbeques where all our friends show up with their kids and their dogs. I want water fights, I want snowball fights, and I want silly fights over nothing, just so we can make up again." I realise I'm probably scaring the hell out of him right now. I mean he did ask, but I think he probably meant more of the immediate future, not a life story. What the hell is wrong with me? He's going to freak now for sure.

"How many kids do you want? I'm definitely down for a few, at least enough for a five-a-side team. Dogs I can do, I fucking love dogs. Big dogs though, not those pathetic little ones. I'm not sure how I feel about alpacas, I'd have to give it some thought, but it's not off the table. I draw the line at cats though. Not my bag, sorry," he says, shrugging casually, his response confusing the hell out of me. Is he mocking me?

"Erm, a few would be nice. Not sure about five? What's wrong with cats?" I laugh nervously.

Maybe he does want the same things I do? Does he actually see a future with me or is he speaking rhetorically? Why are boys so damn hard to read?

"Well let's start with three then, see how we go? But I'm aiming for five just so you know. I mean, If I'm open to alpacas, you gotta at least agree to three? But cats give me the creeps, especially white ones. They look like little fucking ghosts, and don't get me started on the ones with no fur. The fuck is that about?" He says faking a shiver, but I see the corners of his mouth turn up ever so slightly.

I actually can't believe we're having this conversation at all. Could he really want all that with me?

"Well of course I do? I said forever, didn't I?" He answers the question I thought I'd asked in my head. Sweet Britney Jean, did I ask that out loud? Kill me now.

"I mean, I gotta take care of business first, you know college and shit, but in the future, I absolutely want all of that with you, including the fence. Where do you want this house anyway? I know you said you want snow, but I'm hoping that's up for debate, because you know I got a magnolia tree to plant? You down? Because if you are, I'll probably even swing for a naked cat, if that's what you really want?"

I'm not sure what I'm agreeing to, the warm climate, the Magnolia tree, the five kids, or the naked cat, but yes, I'm down. I nod my head, excitedly smiling from ear to ear.

"Yes! Yes, I'm down!"

He fist pumps the air. "It's you and me, baby. Ride or die! Plus, we gotta see the world first, before any of that. Where was it? First stop Lapland for Christmas, then Paris for New Year? Although, no one quite does New Year like the Scottish, so actually let's put Edinburgh on the list? Then of course London straight after so you can meet my crew. They will love you by the way. Then, it's on to Paris, maybe a summer in Italy? Then after that we can talk white dresses, yard swings and alpacas, deal?"

I'm at a loss for words. Wait, did he just talk about marrying me some day? I pull him in for a kiss, but we are interrupted before our lips even touch. His phone buzzes with a text. He quickly pulls it out of his pocket to check it straight away in case it's news. He doesn't attempt to hide it, and whilst I don't mean to read it, I can't help it. While he is reading, more come through one after the other, all from the same number.

**Spencer** - Please just say something.

**Spencer** - Anything?

**Spencer** - I can see you're reading my messages Ryan!

**Spencer** - I'm sorry I've been harassing you, but I just have so much to tell you. I didn't want to tell you this over text, but I've got a date for my surgery. I wish with all my heart you were here, no one gets me like you do and I need you. I know you are hurting, please don't shut me out, not after you promised me forever. X

He quickly closes out of it, without replying, a pained expression on his face. I swear for a minute his eyes glass over, but he blinks away his emotions. He doesn't try to explain it, even though I'm certain he knows I saw it, leaving me with a whole bunch of questions. What does she mean, he promised her forever? Did he lie to me about there being more between them?

"Is everything okay?" I ask as he seems lost in his own world. I don't get an answer though, because a commotion outside has us both rattled. There's a lot of shouting, and we can hear a lot of footsteps running, and I'm sure I can hear drumming.

"Stay here!" He says jumping up, throwing on his sneakers, before I've even had a chance to find mine. "I mean it *Foi*, stay here!" He warns again sternly as he quickly runs out to go see what's up.

Stay here? There is no way I'm just going to stay here. I throw on some joggers as I'm currently still just in a vest and bed shorts, and grab my shoes. Shit these are Ryan's pants, how did they end up in my tent? They must be from after he washed up last night. They are too big but I decide they will have to do. I have to roll the top over a few times.

How did he get his shoes on so fast? I'm still putting my sneakers on when he runs back inside, panic written all over his face.

"Faith come on quick, it's them! They're back!"

# CHAPTER 29

## Ryan

"Yo, what the hell man?" I ask a weary looking Greg. Faith is still holding tightly onto Lorrie, I guess they have a lot to talk about. Is it wrong I can't stop thinking how fucking hot she looks wearing my clothes right now? Although ironically, all I want to do is rip them right off of her, but that will have to wait.

"Mate, you won't believe the bloody Jeep broke down. Sam couldn't fix it, and I know Jack shit about cars. Shocking, I know. Sam being the fountain of knowledge that he is, called a repair guy. Don't ask me how he knew who to call, but he did. Friend of a friend, he said. Be there in a jiffy, he said. Well, I don't know who this friend is, but Sam wants to have a bloody word!" He shouts the last part, giving Sam the stink eye, but I can tell by his tone he doesn't really blame Sam.

"We waited nearly two bloody hours for that twat to show up, but instead four ruddy great big fellas showed up in an armoured bloody van. They had these massive bloody guns and took the lot, our phones, the supplies, our cash, the bloody

Jeep, everything. They even took my watch and the bloody thing doesn't even work. Not surprising, I only paid a pony for it. Got it off some dodgy bloke in some boozer one night, so jokes on them really!" he says, his British timbre making it seem like it was more of an inconvenience than anything.

I can't help but smile. This guy is so laid back, I wonder what it would take for him to actually lose his shit for real.

"We ended up having to walk back. Luckily, I had my bottle of water on me, but that's all we had between the bloody three of us for forty miles!" he adds, at the same time as I'm passing him some more much needed water. He takes it and gulps it down entirely, so I pass him another. I guess this place teaches you to really appreciate every drop.

"... And before you say it, I realise I said 'bloody' more times than necessary, but you seem to manage to fit more 'fucks' into one sentence, than anyone else I've ever bloody met!"

He's not fucking wrong.

"Fuck man, that's fucking crazy. You're lucky that no one was hurt or worse you could have been kidnapped! Everyone here was really worried, bro. Faith especially."

It is crazy to think how lucky they were, things could have been a whole lot different, and the pensive look on Greg's face tells me he knows it too, he's just letting off steam. I mean I get, I was pissed *Foi* made me walk a half a mile, fuck trying to walk forty in this heat.

Remembering the look of satisfaction on her sassy face that morning sends blood rushing to my dick. Fuck she has no idea how sexy she is. What did Greg call her again? A salty potato? In America, to call someone salty would mean to call them bitter or jealous, but I've heard the expression in London before and basically, I think it means that they are hot as fuck, and Faith is one salty ass potato.

"Yeah, well let's not dwell on that, ay! I didn't want to say too loudly in front of Faith, but the bastards tried to snatch Dr. Pierce. It was only that Sam and I managed to pull her off of the truck as it went to drive away. Otherwise they would have taken her," he says grimacing. "It was bloody scary for a minute, I tell you. One of them was screaming in Sam's face 'where's the girl', or some shit like that. Then they just grabbed Lorrie. I actually got a punch in to another one though, he was just standing there like a lemon. Someone's gonna have a black eye at least!" He says casually, as if an attempt to kidnap Lorrie is something to easily be brushed off.

Flabbergasted, I stand there silently like a moron.

"Anyway, all's well that ends well. How *is* little Faithy by the way? Noticed you didn't come back to your own bed last night, you sneaky little bastard. Is that why Lorrie had a face like a slapped arse this morning? Catch you shagging, did she?" He says, raising his eyebrows suggestively.

It's a good job I've spent so much time around British people, otherwise I wouldn't have a fucking clue what this asshole was saying half the time.

"We fell asleep, and before you ask we were both fully clothed!" Only a white lie by omission. He doesn't need to know the intimate details of our love life. *Love life? Dude. That's the second time you've used that word.*

"Faith and Lorrie had some words. I think she had a lot to say to her mom after everything she shared last night, but they didn't really get to clear the air. I think we should give them some space tonight to let them talk."

Greg shrugs, and slaps my back as we head off, back toward our own tent.

"Fine by me, mate. Now, I need real fucking drink after

the day I've had. Did we finish the tequila last night? 'Cause it's that, or Sam told me there might be some moonshine around the village, but trust me, that shit will royally fuck you up!"

"Time to get royally fucked then, boy!" I respond, recognising his need to feel that familiar burn. Fuck if haven't felt it myself today.

Greg was right last night, loss is loss, he gets it. Whoever they were to you, however they went, you can't compare anyone's story to your own, but neither person's loss is greater than the other. If your heart is broken, it's broken. All you can really do is be there for each other.

Whilst talking about grief may be cathartic for some, it doesn't lessen the pain. It doesn't take the soul-sucking demon from above your head. The ache in your chest is still there. As time goes by, sure, you can ignore it, forget that it exists. Like today, with *Foi* and the elephants, but it's just pretend. A dangerous placebo, temporarily fooling you into thinking you're okay again, but the darkness is always there. It lingers, waiting for the right moment to consume you all over again.

So tonight, we moonshine, and boy does that shit royally fuck you up. Just what I need. We drink ourselves into oblivion, until yet again, everything is black.

\*\*\*

It's late Friday afternoon when we arrive back at the Old Farmhouse. Even though the others were all fine, when I spoke to my dad the following day he still demanded I return to the clinic. Malcolm apparently shared my father's views and insisted Faith also return, but I have a feeling that had more to do with Lorrie almost being kidnapped.

Anyway, seeing as we were now a Jeep down, there was no way for us to be brought back by anyone without leaving the others stranded. There wasn't even room for all of us in the truck that we had left, what with all of the gear and supplies. We had to wait until Ade could come up and collect us, but by the time he arrived here it was Thursday afternoon, and it was too late to head back the same day.

Lorrie and Greg decided they would pack up, and that all of us should head back together at first light. We were supposed to stay until Sunday, but because they were worried about how they would get everything back even with Faith and I out of the equation, we all left together. Sam and Remy took the remaining truck and all the supplies, while Ade drove the rest of us.

So here we are. Mom's anniversary, and I've been sat in the back of Ade's mini-van all fucking day sweating my balls off. Lorrie took the seat next to *Foi*, and Greg sat up front with Ade, so I've been in the back on my own, with just my demons for company.

Faith keeps looking back at me. She wants to know I'm okay, but I can't talk right now. Opening up to her the other night was a huge step for me, but I still feel like I'd rather spoon my own eyes out than discuss it with anyone else. I haven't shared that it's her anniversary with anyone else, and Faith respects that. So instead, I've been alone, stuck in my own fucking head all day, and by the time we pull up, I'm in my familiar full-rage mode.

As soon as the van comes to a stop I open the rear escape door and jump out without looking back. I can't deal with anyone right now, Faith included. I just need to be alone.

I slam the door to the cabin shut and lock it. I hear knocking on the door but I don't need to look to know that it's Faith. I go straight to my bag to find one of the other bottles I swiped from my dad's place. I know I'm being an asshole, but better a silent asshole than the hurtful one I'll be if I start talking.

I drink. I drink some more, and I drink some more after that. Faith's incessant knocking was replaced by a light tap every so often. She's letting me know that she's here. Go away, baby girl, while you still have a chance. I'm fucking poison.

My phone vibrates and it's Kat. Her unanswered call is quickly followed by a text.

**\*\* Kat -** I hope with all my heart that you are okay, babe, although I know that you're not. I wish I was with you. I'm telepathically sending you all of my healing vibes right now, I hope you can feel them. I'm always here, whenever you are ready. Love you always my Fresh Prince. X

There are various messages from the whole crew, one is just a single 'X' from Spencer. She's mad at me, but she's still here for me, like a true friend. Yet here I am so self-absorbed in my own shit I can't even be there for her when she clearly needs me. I don't deserve any of them. There is a message from Melody as well, to say that she's thinking of me and she's lighting a candle for Mom tonight. It's nice an all, but whatever. There is nothing from Dad. Not a single word. Fuck him! Fuck. Him.

I throw my fucking phone and it hits the wall, smashing the screen. I drink some more. I punch the shit out of something, I'm too drunk to know what it is. I throw up a couple of times, and then I drink some more.

Everything is black.

*\*\*\**

*Tap, tap. Tap, tap.* Tick tock, tick tock. *Tap, tap. Tap, tap.*

How can time fly by in the blink of an eye, yet at the

same time feel like it's been a hundred years with each day that passes. You know that excruciating feeling that comes right before you open your eyes, when you realise it's another fucking day to get through. Another day to learn how to breathe all over again.

*Tap, tap.*

The fuck is that? I'm used to tick tock. I can handle tick tock. There's always a tick tock.

*Tap, tap.*

What in the fresh fucking hell? Why can't everything just be black all the fucking time. I like the black. In the black there is nothing. No pain, no anger, no fear, no guilt, no shame. Nothing.

Outside of the black everything is cold and harsh, and everything hurts. Outside of the black, I'm consumed with guilt and anger. Fear burns through my soul like fire and ash. Outside of the black there are consequences. Outside of the black, there is no more you.

Then again, inside of the black, there is no more *her*. Which is worse?

I hear a tap, tap, again. My now fully lucid consciousness realises it's someone tapping at the door. I instinctively look at my phone, but the screen is fucked. I can still make out the time and it's late, it's 3 a.m. Or it's early, depending on your perspective. I wonder if it is Faith knocking? I splash some water on my face and open the door.

Her eyes are red and puffy. Her cheeks are stained with tears. Her lips are trembling. She stands there, she doesn't move or speak. She is hurt. Yet again, I have hurt her. Yet again, I am responsible for her tears. My stomach knots at that thought. I tug at my hoodie that's wrapped around her body, pulling her into the cabin. I wrap my arms around her, keeping her close to me as I close the door behind her.

It's dark, only the moon's ethereal light fills the cabin. Even shrouded in darkness, her silhouette is beautiful. Her warmth, her soft skin, her clean soapy scent, it's like a beacon calling me home.

Home. A safe haven.

I feel safe when I'm with her, like I'm not alone in this world anymore. She is my home. So why the fuck have I been avoiding her all night? I'm such a dumbass sometimes. How did I not know that this was all I needed. I feel her pull back and take in the sight of the room. It's a mess, completely trashed. Fuck. Did I do that?

Instead of telling me off for wrecking her room like I expect, she does the complete opposite. She pulls at my shirt and tugs it up and over my head, revealing my bare chest. When Faith and I have been intimate, I've always remained fully clothed, so this is new. She runs her small hand delicately along the lines of my abs, down to the waistband of my shorts. She pauses for a moment waiting for my approval. I don't give it, but I don't deny her either. I let her decide.

Faith takes my hand and leads me to the bed, where she sits down, her face now level with my dick. I'm already hard, my cock straining against my shorts to be released. I watch as she swallows, and slowly starts to pull down my shorts, and my underwear, leaving me completely exposed, just as I did to her.

She swallows, taking in the sight of my naked body so close to her. With only a slight hesitation, she looks up at me and starts to remove her own clothes, one painfully slow item at a time. Once we are both naked she starts breathing deeply, her eyes closed. It takes me a moment to realise she is practising her breathing exercises that she showed us last week.

Fuck, was that only last week? I breathe with her.

In for five, hold for five, out for five.

We do this for a few minutes, and I can't deny how much more relaxed I begin to feel. Especially as she's still running her fingers gently around my torso. My dick is still hard as a fucking rock though, begging to be sucked by those pretty pink lips. She has her eyes closed, but fuck if I'm going to miss a moment of her being naked in front of me, even if it is in the moonlight. She's so fucking beautiful.

I honestly feel like such a prick for wasting so much time with her. I can't help but wonder who I would be if I'd pursued her after that first day. Being around her is a balm to my soul, and I know if I had, I would be a different man to the miserable bastard I am now. If only I'd realised she was mine back then?

When Faith does open her eyes, a fire ignites in them as her gaze connects with mine. I don't make any attempt to move. This is all on her. She takes my hand and moves back to lay on the bed, her stony grey eyes are a glow of silver, hinting at the fire burning inside them. She gestures with only a look, giving a silent invitation to join her, so I move to lay next to her.

I know what she's offering, but there is a big part of me that's well aware she is here trying to comfort me. If this is what she wants, it needs to be because of her. It needs to be because *she* needs it, not because I do. Fuck, do I need it, but I will wait as long as I fucking have to.

I hold her gaze as she looks at me expectantly. Her gunmetal eyes are now ablaze with need, but her face is full of worry. She wants this, but she's nervous. It's at that moment, I know that this is all for me. It might be for her too, but it's mostly for my benefit, and as much as I love her for that, I won't take advantage of her. *As much as you love her? Third time now. Wake up, man.*

Do I love her?

How is that possible? I pull her close and kiss her, her full breasts gently brushing against my chest. She moves closer still, her soft body now firmly against my dick.

"Not tonight, baby girl," I whisper in her ear. I feel her tense a little, feeling rejected, so I kiss her some more. She's so perfect, so innocent, so fucking mine.

"I'm fucked up right now. I just need you to hold me, please?" Funny thing is, that statement isn't far from the truth. Right now, I'm not sure I could give her what she needs even if I wanted to. I'm exhausted, emotionally and physically. The thought of spending the rest of the night lying next to her is enough. She makes me feel like it's safe to fall asleep.

"Shh, it's okay, I got you," she whispers softly, wiping my cheek. Am I fucking crying? What the hell is wrong with me? "I got you, baby," she says. Her calling me baby again, making something inside my chest warm.

She wraps her arms around me pulling my head into her chest. She runs her fingers through my hair and down my back, and then back up again, repeating the motion over and over. I'm not sure what spell she's casting, but the next thing I know, I'm deep in the most restful sleep I've had in a very long time.

# CHAPTER 30

## Faith

Waking up naked, entwined with an equally nude Ryan has my tummy flipping in all sorts of new ways. We have somehow managed to go from me holding him, to him now spooning me. He has a lean muscular leg wrapped around me, as well as a strong possessive arm. I'm not sure if I could move right now even if I wanted to.

I can feel him getting hard at my back. I already knew guys got hard in the mornings, I know it doesn't mean anything. Last night I was ready to take the next step, but he said no. I gotta admit I felt a little disappointed, but I understand his reasons. I'm not sure if he really wasn't in the right space, or if he was just trying to protect my innocence. *Maybe he just doesn't want you that way?*

I silence Inner Bitch. I know she's wrong. The big hard dick in my back right now was equally present last night. I could see in his eyes that he wanted me. Being naked in front of him doesn't terrify me like I thought it would. The way he looks at me, like I'm the most beautiful girl he has seen, makes me feel all kinds of confident. He looks at me like I'm a woman. A sexy woman.

I feel like I could have my usual barrage of insults thrown at me, but with him looking at me the way he did last night, I wouldn't hear a single word. I feel almost certain that if he wanted me to go back to school with him now, then I would.

The feminist in me objects at my needing a boy's validation to feel confident, and especially making serious life choices based on a guy's opinion, but it is what it is. I'd follow him anywhere if he wanted me too. Hell, there's a chance I would follow him even if he *didn't* want me to. School is a different matter though. I can't face it there alone, not anymore.

Last night was one of the worst nights I've had since finding my dad on the kitchen floor. I knew as soon as Mom sat down next to me in the van that Ryan was disappointed. He needed me, although he would never say so. I desperately wanted to reach back and hold his hand, to ask him how he was, but I knew I couldn't.

I could see he wasn't doing so good from the moment I laid eyes on him packing up the tents with Sam. His angry silence was deafening. Greg had pulled me aside to ask what was wrong, he could see Ryan wasn't himself. 'Why does lover boy have his fuck-the-world-and-his-wife face back on again? You have a tiff?' He had asked. Not that I really understood a word of that British-ness, but I knew what he was asking; Was Ryan pissed off because of me?

I just shrugged and didn't answer. If there is one thing I've learnt about Ryan, he would not want me to draw attention to his grief. He struggles with it desperately. He doesn't understand it, he doesn't know what to do with it, and he certainly doesn't want to talk about it. I wish his father would get him some sort of help, or just be there for him himself. Why hasn't he noticed his own son is dying inside? It breaks my damn heart.

When we pulled up back at The Farmhouse, I thought it would be okay, that Ryan and I could sneak off somewhere. I thought he would let me comfort him, maybe he would even talk about it some more, if it was just us. But I was wrong. He looked right at me and I saw his beautiful honey brown eyes were dark, and filled with something I've never witnessed before. It was as if he was looking at me, but saw someone, or something else. He was afraid.

He shot out of Ade's van like a bat outta hell and locked the door to the cabin. Everyone looked at me like I was crazy, chasing him down, banging on the door. When he didn't answer, my dad told me he knew it was a special day for Ryan, and perhaps we should give him some space if that's what he wants. I don't know how Dad knew it was his mom's anniversary, but he doesn't know the full story. There was no way I was leaving, so I sat outside and waited.

After hours of silence, there was suddenly a lot of noise. He was throwing things, punching things, screaming out in pure rage. I desperately tried to knock on the door but he couldn't hear me. I was screaming his name, begging him to open up. Greg and Dad came out of their cabins when they heard me shouting. Greg had also tried to get Ryan's attention, calling out to him, but he just couldn't hear us. It was as if he was possessed.

After about fifteen minutes it stopped, but we could still hear him crying. Again, my dad said it's probably best to leave him be for tonight, that he deserves some privacy. Greg promised he would keep an ear out, only being next door, so with a heavy heart I went to bed. I couldn't sleep though, I was just too worried.

I snuck back out. Although I was seen, I didn't care. Greg

was outside with Ade, apparently doing some sneaking around of their own. They had been arguing ever since Ade arrived at the village to pick us up. Ade had gotten into some sort of altercation during his work in the city, and had a bruised face. Greg was worried he had gotten himself into some sort of trouble with his old gang, but Ade swore it had nothing to do with them.

Something was off between Ade and his cousins too. Samuel and Remy were both involved in the same gang as Ade when they were younger, and whilst Ade had gotten out, the brothers were still very much in. I don't know what was going on between them, but I didn't like it, and Greg was right to be worried.

We all silently acknowledged each other and resumed our business. I was tapping at the door for about a half hour. I was just about ready to give up when Ryan unexpectedly opened it and pulled me inside.

The sadness on his face made my heart ache. His eyes were red, and he had clearly been drinking. He had vomit on his shirt, and the entire room was smashed to pieces. I did the first thing that came to mind, and that was take his vomit stained shirt off, but once I did that, I needed to take everything off. I had a sudden urge to see him. I needed to know that my Ryan was still here.

Once I did that and he was naked, a different need took over me entirely. I took my own clothes off and expected him to make a move. That was my mistake I think. I should have been more confident, I should have made the moves. Maybe I should try again?

I turn around so we are face to face, and uh, body to body. I'm suddenly very aware of my potential morning breath but it's too late now, I've committed.

I brush his unruly hair out of his eyes, and place a chaste

kiss on his forehead. He lazily moves his hand over the curve of my ass, and squeezes, with his eyes still closed and a large grin on his face. I reach between us and take hold of his hard shaft, gently rubbing up and down. He giggles at the unexpected hit of pleasure, but soon composes himself. I can't help but smile at his moment of innocence.

"*Ma Belle Foi,* you are a devious little minx aren't you? You should stop now while you still can, because if you carry on a minute longer, I'm definitely going to fuck you," he purrs dangerously, still smiling, but now his eyes are wide open, and filled with desire.

"W-what if that's what I want?" I ask nervously. Stop it, Faith. Confidence is key. I don't give him time to answer before I begin to rub him a little harder. He takes in a sharp breath.

"Is that really what you want?" He says in a low voice, not attempting to remove my hand. I take his lack of action as an invitation to continue, so I go from my slow suggestive movements to a more rhythmic pace.

"Yes. It's what I want," I barely manage to whisper, my eyes locked on his. He removes my hand, but only so he can roll over on top of me, nestling in between my legs. Oh heck, is this really going to happen?

He kisses me. It's soft but playful. He grinds himself against my core, teasing me. He smiles down at me before pushing up onto his hands. Supporting himself with one hand he moves the other in between us, between my legs. He lets out his usual growl of appreciation at finding me already wet for him, before sliding his fingers inside of me.

"Is this what you want, baby girl? Or do you want more?" he asks in a sexy as sin, deep voice, pumping his fingers in and out of me hard but slow.

"Oh God, Ryan!" I feel my orgasm building already as

he lowers his head to suck on my nipple. "I want more Ryan. Please, I want to feel you inside of me."

Ryan pulls up from my breasts and looks at me. His eyes stay locked on mine as I come undone. He continues to thrust his fingers into me while I ride out my unexpectedly quick orgasm. When I'm done, he gets up off of me and walks off into the bathroom, and I'm left feeling more than a little hurt at his continued rejection. He knew what I was asking for, and now he has just left without saying anything? I get up and cover myself with the sheets, before looking around for my clothes.

"Fuck, I don't have a condom," he says coming back into the room. "Wait, are you leaving?" He rushes over to me from the bathroom doorway.

"I thought... When you just left I thought, maybe you didn't want to?" I say, sheepishly. He pulls my face up to look at his. He is still stark naked and still hard as a rock between us.

"I want to!" He says enthusiastically. "I just went to look for a condom real quick, but I can't fucking find one, I'm sorry. I just, well it's important to be safe you know. I should have said that before I got up. I can see how that looked, especially after how I was last night. I'm such an idiot sometimes."

"I have one!" I interrupt excitedly. For some reason I feel shame creeping in at that admission. I don't know why I feel embarrassed to admit that, maybe it's because of all the rumours before. What the hell though, I shouldn't feel like that. This is the 21st century, girls can and should, carry their own condoms. Safe sex is nothing to be embarrassed about. After all, isn't that the exact message we teach at the clinic?

"There is a whole stash in the clinic. I may have borrowed a couple, you know, just in case," I cringe.

"Well then lead the way, beautiful," Ryan smirks at me and gestures for me to return to the bed. I grab the condom out of the dresser drawer, and pass it to him before lying back down on the bed. He climbs back on the bed and tears the golden packet open with his teeth. Okay, why is that sexy as hell?

He tugs himself for a bit before he rolls it over his hard length, and I can't take my eyes off him. I'm completely memorised at the sight of him touching himself that way. It's not until I watch his hand move up and down his shaft, I appreciate how impressive he really is. Now I'm wondering how that's going to fit inside of me?

He moves back in between my legs and gives me a devastatingly wonderful kiss. He pours his whole heart into it, and whilst he hasn't told me how he feels about me, this kiss is showing me.

"I love you," I say out loud, breaking our perfect kiss. He smiles at me, and kisses me again.

"You are so beautiful, *Foi*. After this, you will always be mine." He kisses me softly on my neck, just behind my ear, driving me crazy. Why does that feel so good?

"*Tu es à moi. Tu seras toujours à moi, Ma Belle Foi!*"

It's hard to focus, what with him peppering these tiny kisses over my neck, but I'm pretty sure he said something like '*you are always mine*'. Ahh I don't know, I can't even think straight. He could be telling me my breath smells like a baboons' ass right now, and it would still sound hella' romantic.

He kisses me on the mouth again. Another soul binding, heart melting kiss. In fact, he kisses me for a few minutes not attempting to do anything else. It's only when I'm completely relaxed, not even thinking about anything except how wonderful this moment is, he enters me. Sweet mother of...

I take a sharp breath, and he pauses waiting for me to adjust to the sudden intrusion.

"Are you okay?" He asks, looking down at me with concern. I nod. Unable to breathe let alone speak. Wow, that hurt, and he's not even properly in yet. He kisses me some more, before starting to move in deeper, he keeps going until he meets some resistance. Tears begin to fall down my cheeks, but he kisses them away.

"It's okay baby. I got you, I promise," he soothes. He pushes in, a little more forcefully this time, until he is all the way in, and I'm unable to hold in my gasp.

"I'm sorry. I'm sorry baby... My Beautiful Faith," he reassures me, continuing his assault of delicious kisses. My Beautiful Faith. It sounds just as sweet on his lips in English as it does in French.

"I'm okay," I smile back at him through my tears. I'm not a virgin anymore, and I've shared this special moment with Ryan. I'm more than okay. I touch his face. "I love you, Ryan," I can't help but repeat my earlier sentiment.

I don't expect him to say it back, but I can't seem to hold it in. I need to say it, whether he loves me back or not. Ryan looks down at me and that's it, that's the look. His face is filled with pure wonder, like he can't believe that someone could love him.

When he looks at me, it's like he isn't the most popular guy who could have anyone he wants, and it's like I'm not the girl that everyone despises. Instead he looks at me like he is the luckiest guy alive just to be with me. His smile tells me he wants to cherish me, and in the only way he can manage with his broken heart, he does love me back. I don't need to hear words right now, that look is enough to steal my heart.

"It's okay, I'm okay," I try to reassure him again. In this moment I know, no matter what happens between us, I will never regret sharing this with Ryan. He is mine. My elephant heart.

"I'm going to move, okay? It will hurt at first, but not for long. I will take care of you, I promise."

I nod, offering him my silent consent. He kisses me again before slowly starting to move in and out of me. It does hurt, but as he continues to kiss me, he begins to change his movements a little. He starts to grind into me with every push and soon my body begins to relax. It still hurts, but less and less every time.

As the pain starts to give way to pleasure, I realise that I am now moving with him, slowly meeting his gentle thrusts with my own. My body knows what it wants. I let out a soft moan as I wrap my legs tightly around his waist, a sudden need to feel him deeper taking over me. He lets out a low growl of his own.

"You feel so good *Foi*, so fucking good," he says hazily, his eyes filled with lust. He begins to push a little harder, but still keeps his movements slow. He pushes himself up onto his hands and looks down at me. He wants to know I'm alright with this change of rhythm. I smile at him and pull his face back down for another kiss, and at the same time, I decide to be cheeky and squeeze his ass possessively, like he does mine.

"Mine," I say into his mouth, repeating his own words back to him. Apparently, that was all the invitation he needed. He pulls back up and wow does he look gorgeous right now. He smirks a playfully devious smile at me before doing exactly what he promised he would. He fucks me.

He pushes into me deeper than he was before. I didn't realise it was possible for him to go any deeper. I let out a loud moan this time, unable to contain it. This only seems to spur him on as he pounds into me harder, but still at the same punishingly slow pace as before, grinding his body hard against mine at every push. He lets out another masculine growl, as his movements start to become more erratic. He must be close.

"So fucking perfect," he says in a low sexy voice. He pushes himself into me, deeper still, hitting a spot where I didn't know I needed him. He hits it just right, again and again.

"Fuck Ryan, oh fuck yes!" I scream breathlessly. He moves harder, faster, driving into that sweet spot every time. Our bodies are soaked in sweat, but we can't stop, we can't slow down. We need each other more than we need air to breathe right now.

"I'm so fucking close. Come for me, baby. I need to feel you come!" He commands, and just like a slave to him, my body answers, as the most intense orgasm washes over me like a tidal wave. He pounds into me wildly, chasing his own release, which quickly follows my own.

He kisses me uncontrollably. It's raw, with no rhythm, as his tongue possesses my own. He is lost in the same haze as I am. After what could have been hours but was probably only a few minutes, he rubs his nose to mine, before he pulls out of me and rolls off.

"I'll be one minute," he says before he goes into the bathroom. I hear the water running, before he comes back out with a warm wet towel. He puts it between my legs gently, giving me the relief that I didn't realise I needed until now. Shit, there is blood all over my legs and over the sheets.

"Are you okay?" He asks, his face etched in concern. He looks so handsome right now, more so than he ever has. He looks different, softer somehow. His gorgeous curly hair is messier than ever, and I can't help but playfully rustle it.

"I'm great," I smile back at him, and he offers me a knowing smile in return.

"Not just physically, I mean are *you* okay? Are you happy?"

"Yes, I'm so happy, are you? Oh God, was I okay, was

it not good?" I ask, suddenly panicking that it wasn't. *So now you're that girl, huh?*

"Good? It was fucking perfect, *Foi,* you are amazing! Faith, do you have any idea how crazy I am about you? I'm just so sorry I hurt you."

"It was always going to hurt, Ryan. I'm just glad it was with you."

Ryan pulls me into his chest not giving a crap about the bloody mess between us. He holds me, drawing lazy circles around my back with his finger. We lay there in silence and within a few minutes we have both fallen back to sleep.

# CHAPTER 31

## Ryan

It's late Sunday afternoon. Faith and I have been swimming down at the lake, but now she's just showering up while I made her something special for dinner. I figure after I basically ruined our last dinner, I definitely owed her a do over.

We've been together the entire weekend, and while we haven't had sex again, we have made out a lot. In fact, we haven't been able to keep our hands off each other, in the PG sense anyway. Holding hands, touching legs, cuddling at every opportunity, and of course some dry humping here and there.

It's been fucking amazing.

I'm not used to things being this way. It's like I've never really done the whole dating thing, like taking things slow, even with Mia. She made her move at a party the first weekend after we met. She took me up to a spare bedroom and sucked me off, and to be fair to her, it was a pretty decent blow. The next night she invited me to her house, and I fucked her in her bedroom while her parents watched *Long Island Medium* re-runs downstairs. I fucking love that show.

After a couple more weekends of the same, she started wearing my number to games, and telling people we were dating, and I never really corrected her. I mean, I did take her out on actual dates. I'm not a total dickwad, but only after I'd already fucked her a dozen times.

Same with Liv, even though that was mostly about sex, we did hang out too. I'm not a complete asshole that I didn't take my girl out from time to time. Things moved very quickly though with both girls, and there was no excitement or anticipation, everything was always on a plate.

*Foi* on the other hand is very different. She's very tactile, but not in an obviously flirty way, and she's all about talking, getting to know each other. She asks so many questions and seems genuinely interested in what I have to say. It's as if she wants to learn everything there is to know about me, and honestly, I want to know every fucking detail about her.

I want every inch of her, mind, body, and soul. The thing I want more than anything is her heart, even if mine isn't worth giving her in return.

This girl is so perfect I can't even deal. Her body is a fucking dream, she's so soft I've never known anything like it. Running my hands over her curves has my dick hard as a rock, especially the curve of her ass. I can't wait to explore her body some more.

When we woke up yesterday morning and I realised we were both still naked, I knew it was game over. Or game on, however you choose to look at it.

I don't know if it was the great night sleep, or just waking up next to Faith, but things felt very different in the morning than they had the night before. She was so much more confident and so fucking beautiful. I know it's cheesy as hell, but she seems to get more beautiful every day.

The worry on her face from the night before had completely gone, and I couldn't help but think she had the same reaction to our night together as I did. Does she have nightmares too?

The soft sunlight was kissing her porcelain skin, and her messy bed hair only encouraged me to want to mess it up some more. With her soft dark hair against her light milky skin, she looked like *Snow White*, waking up from her slumber. She was stunning. As soon as she began rubbing my dick I was gone. I needed to be inside of her, feel her soft body beneath me. I needed her to be completely mine, and she made it very clear that's what she wanted too.

I'd never actually been with a virgin before so I wasn't sure what to expect. I knew it was supposed to hurt a chick the first time, so I tried to be as gentle as I could. I swear it was the hardest thing I've ever had to do though, because she felt too fucking good. All I wanted to do was fuck her hard, but instead I held back to take care of her.

Faith was giving me a precious gift, and I intended to cherish every moment of it. So, I took it slow. So fucking slow, but actually so good. I had no idea that slow-mo sex could feel like that, I've honestly never fucked that way before.

After washing up, and changing the sheets, we spent the rest of the day back in bed. Like I said, nothing happened we just chilled, but it was the best fucking day I've had in a long time. About dinner time Lorrie came and knocked at the door. I gotta say that had me worried as fuck. I'd promised Lorrie I wouldn't share a bed with Faith again, and I'm about sure Malcolm would probably wanna kick my ass if he suspected we'd been up to anything.

Anyway, Faith told me to chill and that her parents weren't mad that she was with me. Apparently, Lorrie had said that we could go have dinner with them, or Lorrie would send some over. We chose to eat by ourselves, so Lorrie's only stipulation was that Faith come back to her own bed in their cabin by eleven.

Reluctantly she left, and although it wasn't quite the relaxing sleep I'd had the night before with her in my arms, I wasn't plagued by my usual insomnia either. Normally I'd be awake going over shit in my head till at least two or three in the morning, but I drifted off relatively easy. *He* was still here though, the soul sucking demon that lives above my head. Like I said, happiness is a dangerous placebo. By 3 a.m. I was jolted awake by my usual nightmares.

*A misty bridge, the screams of a young child. Then there's the guy in some giant pink floppy eared bunny rabbit suit hopping around with no fucking clue what his involvement is supposed to be. As always, I ask it what it wants from me. It never talks, just jumps in the air, and shrinks so small it lands in my hand and appears like a child's toy. I hold on to it as tightly as I can, with no idea why? Maybe it belongs to the screaming kid? Where is the screaming kid?*

*I want to leave this place, but I can't see what's beyond the bridge, it's too misty. One end is a dark, pitch black abyss. It hurts my heart the closer I get to it. It feels like there is nothing there, but I hear voices begging, pleading with me to continue on towards them, and not to give up.*

*At the other end is a light so bright it's not even white, it's just nothing, but it's also everything at the same time. Does that even make sense? It feels safe, it doesn't hurt to come this way, in fact I feel more untouchable with every step toward it. This has to be the right way?*

*The voice coming from that end disagrees. A woman's voice, pleading with me not to join them. Turn back before it's too late. Wait, is that my mom? I've never recognised her voice before. Why wouldn't she want me to go to her?*

*Then it comes, the searing pain through my chest like a flaming sword. There's blood, so much blood. I feel my demon hovering above me, choking me, taking life from me. I can't breathe, I can't move, all I can see is the pink floppy bunny in my hand.*

Right before what feels like I'm about to die is usually when I wake up. Usually. Last night was different.

Last night, right before I almost died, I looked to the dark side of the bridge. That's different.

Hearing my mom, that was different.

Out of the darkness stepped a grey wolf, and a honey coloured rabbit. Not a cartoon rabbit like the one in my hand, no this was a real rabbit. Different.

There is only one grey wolf I know, and that is my father, and I instantly recognised the rabbit as Melody. Why didn't I see that she was a rabbit until now? Out of my hand, the little pink bunny finally spoke. Different.

"One day, you will have to choose which way to go, you know that right?" it said, in a little girl's voice I was not expecting. She's no longer the creepy ass bunny suit guy that haunts me at the beginning of the dream, nor is she the soft toy I held tightly in my hand. She's now an adorable, soft, real rabbit that looks exactly like Melody's rabbit. Well, except for she's cotton candy pink and small. She's beautiful. My heart warmed at the sight of her. Different.

That's when I woke up. Fucked up right? I have no idea what any of it means. Not that I had any idea what the fuck it meant before, but now I'm even more confused.

Anyway, bad dreams aside, tonight I'm making dinner for *Foi*. I had to ask Lorrie to do me a solid and help me with sourcing the ingredients. In exchange I offered to make extra plates for both her and Malcolm. It served a purpose, because while they are all enjoying their meal they won't be spying on us.

I'm making Cajun chicken, with rice and fried beans. It's not quite the same as what I'd make back home but I'm pleased with it. I've set up the table down by the lake, and Malcolm even had this pop-up mosquito dome thing to go around it. It's actually pretty cool, it's about 12ft wide and about 8ft high, so plenty of room for two people. I've put up some candle lanterns for light, and I have laid some cushions and blankets on the floor so we can chill out after.

I've not got any really smart clothes with me, so I've dressed in my smartest navy chino shorts and a light linen shirt. I told *Foi* this was going to be our first date, so I will knock on her door like a proper gentleman should. It's not the first date she deserves, but it's all I can give her right now.

So here I am, outside her parents' cabin. Greg apparently found out about our date and both he and Charity are standing at their doors watching me. Blessing and Ade are both here too. Great. Let's invite the whole village.

"You gonna eventually knock, mate? Or you just gonna stand there looking like a lemon?" Greg teases.

"A rather handsome young lemon," Charity adds, fanning her face with her hand.

"Ry-man, you got a little mark on your shirt... Ha! Made you look!" Ade jokes, howling with laughter as I check for marks. Tool.

"Hey dickhead, just knock on the bloody door will you. Your girl is waiting for you," Greg pushes, smirking over at me.

"Alright, alright, just give me a damn minute. I'm nervous as fuck, man," I admit honestly. I am nervous, and I have those stupid ass butterflies again. I don't know what it is about this girl, but she drives me crazy. "Even my palms are fucking sweaty."

"This is Faithy's first date, so make it a good'un. Our gal deserves the best!" Ade reminds me. Fuck, I hadn't even thought of that. I was so wrapped up in it being our first date together, it didn't even occur to me that this might be *Foi's* first date ever.

"Don't you think I know that, asshole?" I snap, but I'm not pissed off. He has Faith's back, and that's all that really matters. Besides, I know they are all routing for me really. Greg wouldn't have kept what he overheard that day about how badly I've treated her in the past to himself otherwise.

Shit on a fucking stick. I hope this isn't a disappointment. Shit on a stick? Where did that come from?

Anyway, like I said, it's not what I would have done if we were back home. But it's too fucking late now either way. So with my sweaty hands, I flip Greg and Ade off, before knocking on the door.

# CHAPTER 32

## Ryan

What a fucking dream. My girl looks amazing tonight. She is wearing a light denim shirt dress that's tight at the top and all flowy at the bottom. The skirt goes down to her knees, and she's teamed with a tan belt around the middle, and a pair of sandals. It's a pretty casual look by most girls' standards, but Faith is making it look sexy as hell.

The sleeves of the dress are short, and she's left a few buttons undone, so every now and again I'm getting a glimpse of her amazing cleavage. She's wearing a bit more makeup than usual, but it's still a natural look, and she's styled her hair even wavier than normal. She looks like one of those real glamourous chicks from the old Hollywood movies, like Elizabeth Taylor or Vivien Leigh. That thought instantly warms my heart as I know my mother would approve. *Scarlett O'Hara* is of course, the ultimate Southern Belle.

Knowing Faith, I'm quite sure she wasn't trying to be sexy, but fuck if she isn't looking hotter than I've ever seen her tonight. I've only ever seen her wearing a dress once before, which tells me that just wearing a dress would take her out of her comfort zone. The fact that both times were for my benefit makes my heart swell, especially seeing as how I don't fucking deserve anything from her.

"This is so amazing, Ryan. I can't believe you did all of this for me," she says as I lead her into the dome.

"It's not much, but it's the best I could rustle up I'm afraid. You deserve better," I admit nervously. She does deserve so much better. Better than this shitty dome, and better than me.

"No, this is so perfect. I love it thank you so much!" Faith adds sincerely, beaming at me like a Cheshire cat. Her smile is so contagious, and I can't help but offer her a smile in return. She's right, it is perfect. She's my girl, it's our first date, what more could any guy want.

"I can't believe that you're mine," I say, pulling her in for a kiss now that we finally have some privacy. Her parents wanted to take photos of us before we came down, like we were off to fucking prom. I get it though, after everything they have been through the past couple years as a family, I get it.

"Mmm, thank you. That was a really nice kiss," she purrs, sending all my blood rushing south.

"I mean it, *Foi*. I hate the fact you don't know how beautiful you are. You look amazing tonight," I tell her as I run my hands down her hips. Faith blushes, and I can't help but follow the pretty pink trail down to her chest. As she breathes her chest rises and falls giving me a hint at what's inside her dress. The thought of ripping open all those buttons, unwrapping the present inside, has my dick screaming to come out and play.

"I'm really happy, Faith. You are the best thing that's ever happened to me, and I feel like such a tool for not realising that sooner. I know I've been with girls before, but I want you to know that what we shared together yesterday, was just as special to me as it was for you." It was too, I've never had sex with a girl I've been in love with before and it was fucking amazing. *Wait, what?*

Fuck, am I in love with her? I keep thinking that maybe I am, but how can I be? Can a broken heart start beating again?

I pull out her chair so she can sit down. I've already brought the food down and it's all covered up, hopefully it hasn't gotten too cold. I begin to pour her a glass of water.

"Yesterday was amazing, I'm so happy I shared it with you. All of this, no one has ever done anything like this for me before. Could you believe a couple of months ago that we would be sitting here now? It's crazy, but I am so happy things worked out how they have," she says, holding her glass waiting for me to finish pouring mine.

"Cheers! To my beautiful girlfriend, and our first date," I offer as we clink glasses, and take a sip.

***

"You know, I can't really cook, so you are probably going to have to cook for me now for the rest of our lives," Faith says with a smile after dinner.

"What about that awesome cake you made, huh?" I tease.

"Oh, baking I'm good with. Cakes, bread, cookies, all the fat girl stuff. It's just actual meals, nuh-uh, that's all on you now buddy." I frown at her use of the term 'fat girl'.

"Hmm, well let's make a deal then. For every wholesome meal I feed you, you'll let me eat my fill of your sweet dessert," I say playfully, smirking at my own innuendo. I give her a wink.

She always blushes when I wink and I just know she's clenching her thighs too.

"Well, fair is fair I guess. I suppose it's a good job I'm not wearing any panties right now then isn't it," she smirks back at me smugly, her statement surprising the fuck out of me.

"*Foi*, the fuck are you doing to me? You better not be teasing me right now. Because if I check now, and find panties, then there will be consequences," I warn, keeping my voice low and my face as serious as possible. Fucking hell, I don't know what I want more, for her to be wearing panties or not.

"No, I'm not teasing. Although now I'm slightly disappointed that I'm not," she giggles, I can see the anticipation on her face. She wants me. It's definitely risky, who knows if anyone is keeping any eye on us, but for some reason the danger of being caught has me more turned on than I'd expect.

"Show me," I command, keeping my expression stony. "Pull up your skirt, and open your legs for me." I keep my eyes on hers, not letting my need for her show on my face. She pushes out away from the table so I can see her clearly. She moves painfully slow, gently teasing her dress up, lightly brushing her inner thighs as she moves.

Faith is facing the lake, I'm facing the track so if anyone is watching, no one will see her but me. She gets her skirt to the top and I can see that she is bare. To my surprise she isn't embarrassed, she confidently opens her legs just as I asked.

"Wider," I command her again, unable to take my eyes from the sweetness between her legs. She obeys, and opens herself up to me even more. Slowly she runs her hands along her thighs and delicately begins to touch herself.

Fuck. Me.

This is hands down the most erotic thing that's ever happened to me, and my dick is already straining against my shorts. I swallow hard as she releases a soft moan of pleasure at her own hand. I can't fucking take it anymore.

"That's enough, *Ma Belle Foi*. Stand up and put your hands on the table," I growl out, not being able to hide my arousal anymore. She does as she's asked, her cheeks a little pink from pleasuring herself.

"Good girl. Now pull up your skirt and show me your pretty little ass!" Again, she does as I ask, but I notice a flicker in her eye. She's getting nervous now. I deliberately take my time clearing the plates off the table.

"Do you trust me, *Foi?*" I question, not really wanting to hear the answer. She shouldn't fucking trust me, I'm a liar, but fuck if I'm going to let any of those thoughts cloud my head right now.

"Y-yes. I trust you," she admits, as I gently stroke her bare ass. Her hands are still holding her skirt up, so I push her face down towards the table. She instinctively moves her hands towards the table but, with my other hand I smack her peachy ass.

"Hands back on the skirt!" I demand, not able to hide my pleasure at her yelp.

"You know, it's a shame you weren't wearing any panties, because now I don't have anything to gag you with," I say seriously as I smack her ass again. This time she lets out the most delightful moan that I can tell is all pleasure.

I actual have no idea where this boldness is coming from with me, but I feel like I can be more myself when I'm with her. I was never this way with Mia, and with Liv, well that was just plain disrespect on my part. With *Foi*, this is different. Watching her ass pinken under my touch turns me on a lot more than I would have thought, and don't get me started on her reaction to it. Fuck, if she likes it, then I'm all for it.

I bring my hand around her front, and as usual, when I find her wet for me I lose all my composure. A loud, guttural sound rips from deep within my chest.

Mine.

I've barely touched her and she's moaning in pleasure, pushing against my hand, needy for more. My other hand comes slamming down against her soft creamy skin, and she immediately comes over my fingers, moaning out my name breathlessly as she does. Hot. As. Fuck.

I'm not through with her yet, in fact I've barely even started. I pick her up caveman style and carry her around the table. I put her down on it, pull her forward so she's barely on the edge, as I spread her legs. I drop to my knees in front of her. She's still a little dazed from her orgasm, and probably partly from immediately being hauled upside down. She smiles down at me and giggles, her rosy cheeks flush with post orgasm glow.

"What are you doing, baby?" She asks playfully, knowing all too well what's coming next. I have a sneaking suspicion that she also knows what hearing her call me baby does to my dick, because she immediately glances down at the tent in my shorts, her eyes black with desire.

"Later. Now it's time for dessert," I purr. I take a long slow lick of her, relishing in the soft moan that escapes her lips. I begin to draw circles with my tongue as I move down, right from her clit to her ass, where I remain, continuing my assault of lazy circles. She lets out a gasp that's half pleasure, half being scandalised at having her asshole licked. I move back up to where I know she needs me, as I slide two fingers inside of her, and pump them over and over hitting that sweet spot until she comes undone for a second time.

"I need you Ryan, please," she begs, and fuck if I'm not all too happy to oblige. As I'm just over 6ft the table is a little low for me, so I carry her to the cushions I laid out, which I'll admit was half in anticipation of what's to come. The same reason I packed a gold one in my pocket, there was no way I was getting caught short again.

She lays back on the cushion lazily. I slowly undo her buttons, needing her naked. I kiss and nibble every inch of her neck and chest, relishing in the small gasps of pleasure that escape from her lips. Her full breasts bounce free as I tug down her bra. I take one in my mouth, enjoying the feel of the other in my hand.

She tugs at my shirt, needing me as naked as she is. I remove my clothes and take out the condom. She watches intently as I tear open the foil. I give myself a few tugs, and her chest rises and falls quickly. I watch as she licks her lips taking in the sight of me.

"I want to watch you ride my cock, baby," I say as I pull her up. I sit back on the cushion myself and pull her across my lap. I line my dick up with her entrance and slowly she lowers herself on to me, gasping as I fill her completely.

"I don't know what to do," she says nervously. I pull her in for a kiss. I intend for it to be reassuring, but the selfish bastard in me can't help but possess her mouth. She needs to know that she's mine.

"Just move your hips so it feels good, your body will do the rest," I manage to get out in between kisses. She slowly starts to move her hips, grinding herself into me. I meet her with my own gentle movements, matching her pace, until she gradually starts to find her rhythm.

"You feel so fucking good, baby. I love the feel of your body in my hands," I tell her as I grip her hips harshly, relishing the little pink marks I leave behind. She moves slowly up my cock before slamming back down. I can feel I'm getting close so I hold her in place. I thrust up into her, over and over, pushing myself deep inside of her until she throws her head back in ecstasy.

Faith lets out a loud moan, before quickening her pace. Her perfect breasts bounce and jiggle in my face with her every move, only encouraging me to fuck her harder. I let out a low growl, before quickening our pace even more, my need to watch her come like this taking over.

She lets out another moan and I know she's close, with one hand I reach between us, finding that sweet spot of hers. I use my other hand to hold her still. I pump up inside of her fast and hard, pushing myself deep until she cries out my name.

"Fuck Ryan, fuck. I'm gonna come!" I continue my relentless pace through her orgasm, chasing my own release.

"So fucking sexy, baby. Fuuuuuck!" I roar as my own climax takes hold.

When I'm done, Faith rolls off me, and we both lay back on the cushions completely spent. I honestly don't think I will ever get bored of that. She lays next to me, naked, and glowing. I can't believe she looks even more beautiful than she did earlier, but she does.

I have no idea how this is going to work. We have a week left before I have to head back. I know *Foi* is coming back to school for three weeks, but after that, who the fuck knows what will happen. The thought of being apart from her flips my insides. The selfish bastard in me wants to beg her to stay for senior year, but I know I can't ask her to do that, not after everything she's been through there. *Yeah, no thanks to you, asshole.*

We just need to make it work somehow. It's not like I'm not used to being a half a world away from the people I love. First my parents, then my friends, now it will be Faith. It's also not like I don't have the money to come see her on the holidays either. I know we can make it work. We have to, because she's mine now, and I'm not giving her up. Turns out I didn't really need to worry about that when *Foi* finally speaks.

"So, I'm not sure how to say this, but I've made up my mind. I want to come back to California for my senior year. Only if you want me to, that is?" She says looking away from me nervously.

"Faith, how can you be so confident one minute, and small as a fucking mouse the next? You come here with no panties on, and gladly spread your legs for my viewing pleasure. You lay here naked with me, not one hint of the shame I saw that afternoon I caught you dancing, but then the next minute, you can't even look me in the eye when you talk to me? What's that about, huh?" She moves to pull on her dress, making it clear that I've killed the mood.

I don't want to upset her, but I hate seeing her make herself small like that.

"Honestly, I don't know? When I'm with you, I feel confident. You make me feel sexy, the way you look at me, the noises you make when you see and touch my body. You make me feel like I could be beautiful, you know. But, well, I guess a part of me can't help but feel like maybe this is just a here-and-now thing. Like you've always known it has an expiration date, so why the hell not?"

"Is that what you really think? That it's just a here-and-now thing? Is that how you feel about it?" I ask, suddenly feeling a little vulnerable myself. I reach for my own clothes, now everything's awkward as fuck.

"No, of course not. That's why I want to come back to school with you, I wouldn't want to be there without you. Not anymore. I just didn't want to assume that you'd still feel the same once you got back home. Everyone will know you're single now, and there will be a lot of girls who are interested. Girls who *are* actually beautiful and sexy, and I... well I wouldn't stand in your way, if that's what you wanted," she says sadly, looking away again.

"And why the fuck not, huh? I'm supposed to be your guy right? So what, you'd just give me up without a fight?" I say defensively. I stalk over to her and get right in her space. I gently wrap my hand around her throat. She could easily get out of my hold but she doesn't. Clearly, she wasn't lying when she said she trusts me.

"You should know that I would not offer you the same courtesy. Some fucking asshole wants to try his luck with you, he can damn well kill me before I'd give him his shot, and even then, I'd haunt the bastard for the rest of his fucking life. There is no way in hell I'd stand by and let another guy fucking touch what's mine. You. Are. Mine." I scowl, running my thumb up and down her throat.

"Mark my words baby, I have no intentions of giving you up. Not now, not when we get back to California, not ever."

# CHAPTER 33

## Faith

After our date, Ryan walked me back to my door, gave me the best kiss goodnight any girl has ever had, and then gave me a gift. His elephant necklace. He said I was his lion, and he was my elephant.

At first, I didn't want to take it, knowing the significance of the elephant for him, but he insisted he wanted me to have it. I knew that it was his way of reassuring me that he wanted to be with me, and I felt confident now that there wouldn't be any other girls when we got back to school. He was my boyfriend, but I doubt I'd ever get used to saying that.

The whole night was amazing, and I was even more smitten with him now than I'd ever been. I didn't want the night to end, and even though he was just a couple of cabins away, saying goodnight was hard. So, after my parents went to bed, I decided to sneak out over to his cabin. He wasn't one bit surprised to see me when I crept into his bed, he just wrapped me up in his strong arms and held me until we both fell asleep.

I'd had to set an alarm to wake up of course, so my

parents didn't realise I'd spent the night with him. It went off just before 5.30 a.m. The sun was coming up, and after giving me yet another orgasm, Ryan suggested we go for a quick run before work. I knew if we got caught it would make my whole I-woke-up-early story seem more legit, so I reluctantly agreed. Luckily most of my stuff was still in Ryan's cabin, so I could get dressed without having to sneak back into my own.

I'm not the fastest of runners, so Ryan kept pace with me. We only ran a mile out, we weren't going far, but when we got to our turn point to run back we saw Greg sprinting towards us coming back from his run. He said it was just the twenty miles for him this morning; he couldn't manage the full marathon distance he was aiming for. Ha! What a wimp.

Coming back with Greg also made our story a lot more believable, as my parents were already up and at work early before we got back, but neither seemed to think anything of us all arriving back together in our workout clothes.

It was our last week before Ryan, Mom, and I would be heading back to California. Albeit on separate flights of course as his dad and associates were all still in Kenya on safari. Ryan would be taking a small chartered plane back to meet them on Friday. Then on Saturday, they would all be flying first class to Paris, and from there, they have a private jet to take them back to L.A.

Mom and I on the other hand, would be flying in coach. We have a stop-over in Istanbul, and a stop-over in London, before an eleven-hour flight on to L.A, with a total travel time of forty-four hours. Eff my life. Although Mom and I would leave first on Friday, we still wouldn't arrive in L.A until half a day later than Ryan. I guess being a billionaire really has its perks.

"So Faithy, when are you gonna tell me about your date? I noticed the new little trinket you're wearing. Pretty sure Ryman has one just like it," Greg teases as we sort out the new supplies. Greg is on the laptop taking inventory while I stack everything away where it needs to be.

"Loverboy give it to you for keeps this time, or is it just another loner like the jumper?"

"He gave it to me, and if you must know he also gave me the sweater, he just borrows it back from time to time," I smile back at him. I'm still on cloud nine after our date, and I haven't been able to stop smiling all day.

"You better keep it safe then. It might look simple to the untrained eye, but I can tell you now, that would have cost a pretty penny," he warns, looking at my necklace.

"What do you mean? It doesn't look all that expensive? It means a lot to him, and he gave it to me to show me that I mean a lot to him too. If it's really expensive I'd rather just give it back," I say, worried now that Ryan has given me something I have no business wearing.

"Just keep it covered up when you leave this place, okay. That's all I'm saying," he says smiling, holding his hands up submissively. I realise he isn't going to elaborate, so I throw a pack of paper towels at him.

"Hey! Take that, you little shit!" He says throwing them back, but I catch them.

"The date was great, like so, so good. I really like him, Greg. I've told him that I want to go back to school to be with him," I admit, but Greg frowns on hearing my words.

"Faithy, please don't make any rash decisions. That's what the first three weeks were for wasn't it? I know you like Ryan, but remember the reasons why you didn't want to go back. Will anything be different just because you're with Ryan?" He cautions, but of course they will be. Ryan promised me they would be different.

"I was alone before. With Ryan, everything will be better. He will make sure of it," I say, trying to sound confident.

"Whatever you say, princess. I like Ryan, he's a solid bloke, but from what I've overheard he doesn't have the best track record where you're concerned. So just promise me you won't make any decisions until your three weeks are up, okay?" He says raising a concerned eyebrow. I nod silently, and carry on shelving the supplies. We carry on like that for a while, and of course I end up down yet another rabbit hole of internal questions.

"What in the bloody hell?" Greg shouts from behind his laptop, making me jump out of my skin, dropping a bag of bandages. "That sneaky little bastard!" He continues, getting up from his seat and walking out the door.

I have no idea what's going on but I follow him. He storms into the small kitchen where Ryan is making some tea. I always find it funny, at half three on the dot he comes out here to make tea. He can be more British than Greg sometimes.

"Oh, hey man, I just made you a brew," he says, unfazed as he spots Greg marching towards him like a man on a mission.

"Twenty grand? What the bloody fuck?" Greg demands. Not forgetting his manners, he still nods in appreciation as he accepts the tea. British people and their tea, honestly. Heaven forbid anything interrupts tea time!

"It's no big deal, it's a great cause," Ryan shrugs as he passes me a coffee, and yet again, I have no idea what's going on.

"No big deal? Mate, I know you got a silver spoon up your arse, but twenty grand is a lot of bloody money to anyone. Do you even have that sort of money, or just access to your daddy's bank account?" Greg snarks before sipping his tea.

"It's my money, asshole. My mom left me my own money. I can't access the bulk of it until I'm twenty-one, but I get an allowance, and I've spent fuck all over the summer, so like I said it's no big deal. If she had met you she would have done the same in a heartbeat," Ryan says defensively. Wait, has he given Greg twenty thousand? Is that dollars or pounds? Not that it matters, it's still a helluva lot of money.

"I mean thank you, so much. It's so bloody generous of you, and it means the world to me that you've done this honestly, but I can't accept it. This money is for your future, Ry. I can't take that from you!"

"Well it's a good job it goes straight to the charity then, doesn't it," Ryan smirks casually. "It's done. Don't sweat it man, it's cool. Just make sure you smash it out there in that desert and give me my money's worth," He adds, smiling from ear to ear.

It melts my heart seeing him so happy. I always knew he had such a kind heart. I can't help it, even though Greg is right here, and technically this is his moment with Ryan, I put down my coffee and rush to plant a steamy kiss on Ryan's lips. He apparently isn't bothered by Greg's presence either, as he immediately puts down his tea and picks me up, wrapping my legs around his waist.

"Oh, for fuck sake. Is that really necessary?" Greg says walking out, I hear him mumbling on as he walks down the hall but my focus is completely lost on Ryan and yet another delicious steamy kiss.

***

The rest of the week flew by pretty quickly. The first couple of days Ryan spent out in the town doing home visits with my dad, so I didn't see much of him during the day.

Nights were a different story, each one filled with at least two orgasms. I dont think there is a part of my body that he hasnt kissed, bitten, or smacked for that matter.

He is so strong too. Last night, after he arrived back from a long day, he immediately stripped us both naked, before picking me up like I weighed nothing and fucking me against the wall, like a wild animal. It felt as though he couldnt control his need for me, like he had been thinking about me all day. It was the sexiest I've ever felt in my life. My cheeks warm at the memories.

Everyone here just loves Ryan. Dad has literally spent the week raving about what a great down to earth guy he is, and how much the local kids all seem to love him. Ryan seems to really like my dad now too, especially as Dad appears to have taken a sudden interest in soccer. I don't know if their new-found bromance is for my benefit, but it makes me really happy he and my dad are getting along so well.

Ryan also seems to have developed a little dude crush on Greg. I mean, Greg is cool and all, but he's also a bit of a nerd. However, he appears to have become Ryan's idol overnight. One day Greg was wearing a *Blink 182* band shirt, and it turns out they apparently have a shared passion for '00s American punk rock. Who knew?

They spent the afternoon harmonising their way through *'Enema of the State'*, when Greg announced that he used to be in a band that covered British indie rock classics when he was at college. Well that was it, Ryan was smitten. Greg is definitely the big brother Ryan never had, and for Greg, I guess Ryan fills a void left by his own brother. If their friendship will help them both find a way through their grief, then it can only be a good thing.

It's our last night, so Dad arranged a little bon voyage

party. Nothing too fancy, just everyone from the clinic for dinner and a bit of music. Although he hasn't been around much this week, Ade somehow managed to get hold of a guitar so that Greg could play for us.

"He is actually pretty decent to be honest," Ryan says, speaking to Ade. It's so great to see them actually getting along now, although Ryan still looks like he wants to break every bone in Ade's body everytime he comes near me.

"He definitely has the look of a rock band front man, that's for sure," I add, smiling from ear to ear when I notice Greg wink at Ade. Anyone else around who may have caught it would likely assume he was probably winking at me. Ade hasnt taken his eyes off Greg, nor has he responded to either statement. "You like him a lot, don't you?" I say giving him a friendly nudge in the ribs.

"He is okay, I guess. A bit of a diva, but then so is your boy too," Ade teases, and Ryan rolls his eyes unamused.

"You got that right," I add playfully, and Ryan can't hide his smirk.

A part of me is desperate to hear Ryan play. I know he can sing, and his voice is a dream. When Greg finishes his song we all cheer, and I take that as my opportunity to try and get Ryan to play.

"Did you wanna play something?" I ask hopefully.

"Do you play, Ry-man?" Ade asks. Ryan gives me a devious smile that makes me feel like he is hatching a plan.

"A little bit. I'll play if you want me to?" He questions, and I nod my head excitedly. "Yo' bro, this isn't the Greg show, man. Hook me up!" He says, jumping out of his seat towards Greg. With a raised eyebrow Greg passes him the guitar.

"Take it away, little brother. Show us what you got." I

don't know why hearing Greg call him little brother makes my heart leap, but it does, and so does the way Ryan beams with pride when hears it too.

"So, firstly I just wanna say thank you. All of you have made me so welcome, even when I didn't deserve it. You have all made me feel like family, and I have honestly learned so much. Not just about this place and the people, but about life, and about myself. It's corny as fuck, but I definitely think I've found myself on this trip. So thank you, and uh, sorry about all the cursing." He smiles and he reminds me of a little kid being scolded by his kindly old Grampa or something; he's not one bit sorry, but he has too much respect not to apologise.

"... Anyway, I used to sing this song with my friends. It was our song. An anthem, for when we had to spend our summers apart. I've been thinking about it a lot lately, because honestly, I've not been living up to the words. I want to be the kind of guy who his friends know they can count on. I feel like I've made some friends for life here, and I promise from now on I will be the kinda guy in this song." He swallows back his emotions and clears his throat.

He begins playing the chords, and even before he starts singing I recognise the song as Bruno Mars *'Count on Me'*. He has changed the arrangement slightly, it's a little slower than usual. It's a beautiful song, and his dreamy voice makes it sound so romantic. There isn't another sound, just his voice and the guitar, and I can tell everyone else is equally enthralled by him.

The song finishes and he immediately goes into a second song. An upbeat acoustic arrangement of *'... Baby, One More Time'*, and my Inner Brit squeals with delight. I mean, to be fair she's always been Team Ryan, but maybe Inner Bitch might start coming around now too?

I don't know why I suddenly feel like all eyes are on me,

but my cheeks blush with embarrassment. God, did I actually squeal out loud? Ryan sends a wink my way and I swear I almost come right then and there. Had it not been for the fact we are surrounded by people, including my parents, I would legit be getting naked right now.

Everyone cheers, and it seems like everyone feels very emotional as the reality that the summer has come to an end, hangs in the air. As Ryan talks to Greg, I feel the need to give Ade a big hug. I am definitely going to miss his rascal charm. I'm also worried about him. In the past week, he has hardly been around, and when he did finally show his face he was covered in even more bruises.

Ade refuses to talk about what happened to him, he just insisted it was a misunderstanding that's now been resolved. Sam and Remy went straight back to the city, so I haven't been able to ask either of them if they know anything. I know Ade is going to London soon with Greg, and a part of me feels like it will be the best thing to happen to him.

"Are you okay, baby gal?" Ade asks as I probably held on to him for a little longer than I should have.

"Everything is changing. You've been my friend here since day one, but next time I come back, you will be gone. You and Greg will be living in London, and who knows if you will ever come back. It breaks my heart to think I may never see either of you here again," I admit sadly.

"Faithy, this is my home. Of course I will be back, you think my aunts would allow me not to?" He gestures over to where Charity and Blessing are having an animated discussion about something, before they both roar with laughter. "They would probably write to the Queen of England, demanding my return. Plus, you always said you wanted to go to Europe. You can always come and stay with us in London?" Ade offers, and I feel a little better about the situation already.

"Maybe Mom is right, maybe it is time to move on from this place? I just don't think I can, not permanently anyway. I'm not sure I could ever fully close the door on this place, and I know my parents feel the same. It engrains itself in you. It will always be in my heart, thats for sure," I say, giving Ade another squeeze.

When I discussed with my parents about staying at St. Edmund's for senior year, my dad suggested maybe I should board there. He doesn't want to go back, and although my mom had originally said she wanted to return to California, it turned out she only said that because she thought that was what I wanted, and she was trying to fix our relationship.

Although she and I still had some work to do, things are better between her and my dad now, and I didn't want to split them apart again. So, at first, I suggested I could live on my own. I am already eighteen, so it's really not a big deal. They weren't having any of it though, and apparently its board at school or come back here. I have three weeks to decide what I want to do, but honestly, right now, I can't see myself choosing anything else except being with Ryan.

Ryan catches my eye and gestures for me to follow him. Ade notices too, and jokingly raises his hands in a submissive gesture toward Ryan, who playfully flips him off in return.

"That was amazing, you have such a beautiful voice. Can you please sing to me every day?" I ask, as Ryan pulls me behind the cabins for a quick kiss. He looks serious, the playful smile from before has gone, and his eyes are fixed on mine with an intense stare, sending heat soaring through me.

"What is it? What's wrong?"

"I don't want this bubble to end, but at the same time, I can't fucking wait for life to begin again. Literally Faith, I was dead before I came here, but with you I can breathe again. You bring me to life. By the time we get back to school, every person in that place will know you're mine. I swear, if those assholes have anything to say about it, they will regret the day they were born."

I bring him to life? It's as if he took the words from my mouth.

He kisses me again, this time it's full of urgency, as if he is afraid it's our last kiss. I mean, it's probably our last one until we get back to California, but it still feels like a more permanent goodbye. *Stop over thinking things Faith.*

"Ryan! Ryan, are you back here?" Mom yells as she comes running out to join us behind the cabins. Busted. "Ryan, sweetie quickly, it's your father. He is on the phone, it's urgent!" Mom says, hastily passing him a phone.

"Dad, what's up..." He says into the phone. There is a moment of silence before he speaks again.

"Shit is she okay, what about the baby?... No of course, you should go back, I'll be fine. I'll make my own way back with Faith and Dr. Pierce. I'll be there as soon as I can, okay!" More silence. He says goodbye and hangs up the phone and hands it back to my mom.

"I've gotta go, I need to get to the airport, I have to try and get home as soon as possible. Melody has been in a car accident, they've got to deliver the baby!"

# CHAPTER 34

## Ryan

Faith and Lorrie rushed with me to the airport. After months of radio silence on my end, I rang my buddy Alex, told him what was up, and within an hour he had it sorted. No questions asked. He made one phone call, and had somehow managed to get us all on a flight to Addis Ababa, where we boarded a helicopter, which took us to a private airfield where a private jet waited to take us to L.A.

The jet didn't even belong to the Wests, so fuck knows whose it was. The chopper was part of their own extensive fleet. The Wests are some of the richest people in the world, thanks to their diamond fortune, so it doesn't surprise me they had a helicopter and a random luxury jet waiting at the click of a button.

Both *Foi* and Lorrie had originally expressed concerns about how ethical The West Diamond Company business was. I told them that whilst historically some of their original fortune was accrued in ways that were a little shady, they have since totally banned the sale of conflict diamonds. I can't speak for all of the West family, in fact, Alex's father is more of an asshole than mine, but Alex is good people. That reassurance was apparently enough for *Foi* to say fuck you to the forty-four hours in coach they originally had planned, and happily leapt onto the jet and into my world of luxury.

"Holy Moley. This is insane. How can a plane have two bedrooms? Bedrooms. On a plane. Insane right?" *Foi* yells animatedly. She's a little tipsy off the free-flowing champagne, and I gotta admit, I like seeing her so carefree. I was surprised Lorrie was so chill about us both drinking. I guess it had been a long and stressful day for everyone already, without the long journey ahead. Lorrie had said we could have a glass each before she went to lay down in one of the cabins, leaving Faith and I alone. Of course, that meant we had already finished off a bottle and a half already.

"It's pretty rad, huh? I mean I've been on a private jet or two, but this is another level even for me. Still, not quite as impressive as the actual West jet though, that shit is fucking crazy," I say, accepting an enthusiastic Faith onto my lap. She gives me a soft, closed mouth kiss on the lips before laying her head on my chest. Within a few silent minutes, Faith is almost asleep. I put down our glasses, and carry her to the empty cabin and lay her on the bed.

"I'm awake, I promise," she says lazily. "No joke, this bed is comfier than my actual bed. The sheets are so soft and they smell amazing." They do smell amazing, like jasmine and lavender, but it will take more than aromatherapy and a thousand thread count sheets to get me to sleep.

"I can't sleep at the best of fucking times, *Foi*. Don't worry about me. You should get some rest," I say, my voice sounding more than a little frustrated.

"No, not just yet, let's talk for a bit. Please?" She says softly, and with her brushing her fingers gently around my chest, the selfish asshole in me doesn't deny her.

"It's funny, I have this fucked up dream all the time. Same thing happens on repeat, over and over. Then last night, it was the same dream, but different. Out of nowhere Melody appeared in it, and for some reason her baby was a little girl. I don't know what the fuck it means. But it's weird that I dreamt that, and now this happened. You think it's supposed to mean something?"

"Dreams can definitely mean something, although I'm not sure I'm the best person to try to interpret them. I have no idea, sorry," she frowns, clearly annoyed she wasn't more helpful.

"It's okay, I'm just talking shit anyway. Are you okay? Are you nervous about going back to school?" I change the subject, brushing my hand through my messier than usual hair.

"No, I'm fine. I'm sure it will be fine," She lies, looking away from me, making it clear she's anything but fine.

"Faith, you're a fucking powerful lion, stop doubting yourself! From now on, you don't look away from anyone, especially not me, you hear me?" I tell her off. My girl needs to know what a badass she is and stop with this mouse bullshit. "I told you, everyone will know you're my girl. No one will dare say a word to you, I promise. Any one of those pricks sends you one more text, they are fucking dead!"

I haven't told her, but all the graffiti about her has already been removed. I made a point of sending an email to Mel, telling her all about how the school stood by for three years while a young girl was subject to countless acts of sexual harassment and bullying. Melody, being Melody, quickly contacted the principal, letting her know if it wasn't completely removed by the time we returned to school, she would start a campaign online, naming St. Edmund's failures in protecting its young students.

The graffiti was confirmed as completely removed within two days. Guess having a world-famous actress with nearly eighty million followers as a stepmom, has its rewards.

"I'm sure it will be fine," she repeats softly, before yawning and closing her eyes. I can't help but think she just doesn't want to have this conversation, but she is clearly tired, so I pull her into me and I hold her until she drifts off, and surprisingly, so do I.

***

We touched down about two hours ago, but traffic in L.A meant that we've only just arrived at the hospital. I had tried to call my dad, but as usual he didn't answer. All I got was a text to say Melody and the baby were okay, and to come straight to the hospital. I could barely read the text as my screen was still a mess from throwing my phone, but I was able to make out the room number at least.

As we walked past the gift shop I immediately noticed a small fluffy pink bunny sitting in a basket of new baby items that looked exactly like the one I was holding in my dream. I was compelled to buy it.

"I thought Melody was having a boy? Don't get me wrong I'm totally down with kids' toys being gender neutral. I definitely think more boys need to play with dolls and learn how to take care of their babies. Actually, I think a pink bunny for a boy is pretty cool, now that I think about it," *Foi* questions, smiling supportively.

"She is supposed to be, I dunno. After my dream I can't shake the feeling she's had a girl. I'm just being stupid. Maybe I should grab a blue one?" I ask, questioning my own sanity right now. Faith picks up a blue one, takes the pink from my hand and lays them both on the counter.

"I say we get both. You can keep one, and baby keeps the other. It will be like a sweet sibling thing, you know. That way, when you go off to college, you can still be connected," she says, offering another beautiful and innocent smile back at me.

I give her a small, delicate kiss, and put the money down on the counter. The assistant puts the toys into a paper bag, while I shamelessly give *Foi* another kiss, but this time, it's anything but gentle. I claim her mouth with my own, relishing in the little whimpers she makes in return.

This girl is a tourniquet to my broken soul, halting the demons that course through my veins. Forgetting for a moment, the worries of the past couple of days, and where we are, I lower my hands around to feel the curve of her body. She feels too good in my hands. The assistant clears her throat, and Faith immediately withdraws, giving the assistant an apologetic grimace. I on the other hand, snatch the bag from her, annoyed at her interruption.

"Thanks a lot!" I add curtly, my usual good manners refusing to fall completely to the waste side, even when I'm pissed.

We head upstairs to the room my dad told us to go to. We decided Faith should wait in the family room, thinking now wasn't really the time for introductions. The door is slightly open but I still knock before going in. Last thing I want is to walk in and see Melody feeding the baby or something. I know it's natural, but fuck if I haven't already seen way too much of her naked already. I'm fucking scarred for life.

"Come in son, we have someone for you to meet," Dad says as he appears at the door, his cheery demeanour slightly freaking me out. As usual he offers up no physical form of greeting, not even a handshake, so as usual, I walk past him without even an acknowledgement. I notice the frown on Melody's face and what appears to be a silent exchange between her and my father. I ignore it, knowing all too well she wants to play peacemaker.

Melody seems to spend all her free time trying to build bridges between the two of us. Her pleas fall on deaf ears as far as I'm concerned. If he isn't the one making the effort, then I don't wanna know.

"Hey Mr. Big Brother, it's so good to see you," Melody offers sweetly from the bed. As much as she wants us to fix things, and she is my dad's wife, she doesn't ever take sides and I respect that a lot.

Melody has a few cuts and bruises on her face, but other than that she looks okay, thankfully. She's cuddling the baby in a white blanket, and I can't really see much so I go towards her.

"Hey Melly, congratulations! How are you feeling?" I ask, offering her a kiss on the cheek. The baby is beautiful, and I can tell right away that she is a girl. She just has a girl's face, you know. I don't know why this makes me happy, because I was totally psyched to have a brother, but it does.

"I'm okay, thank you. A little sore, but I think that's more from having a baby than from the crash. God, this minivan just came out of nowhere and slammed into the side of me. It was almost as if it was deliberately aiming for me, but that's ridiculous. Then my waters just broke, right there in the street," she says, giving the baby a gentle kiss. "The cops said the other driver died, it's awful. It was pretty scary, but baby is fine. Do you wanna hold her?" she adds, beaming from ear to ear.

"It's a girl!" Dad blurts out excitedly, smiling like a fucking Cheshire cat. I honestly cannot remember a time when he smiled that way before in my whole life. Who even is he right now?

"A girl? No way, how'd that happen?" I direct back to Melody, yet again ignoring my father's lame attempts to start a conversation. Talk to me about what happened to my mother someday, and then maybe I'll give a shit about what you have to say, asshole.

"I had a feeling you know. When they told me it was a boy, I was like, are you sure? Because all I've ever pictured was a girl, and here she is. Our perfect little princess, Dexta-Rose. With an 'A', not an 'ER' though" Melody swoons.

"Dexta-Rose? You still went with Dexter? That's so cool. I guess after months of talking to her calling her Dexter, it would feel weird now to call her anything else."

"Rose was my Grammy's name. It suits her though, right?" she asks, passing me my baby sister for the first time.

"Hey Dexta-Rose, I'm your big bro," I whisper to her, and I know immediately that I'm bound to this tiny person forever. I can already tell this little bunny is going to have me wrapped around her finger, always.

I put the paper bag down on the bed with my free hand and take out the pink bunny.

"This is for you baby girl. It's a talisman that I've filled with what little love I have left to give. It's not much, but it's all yours little bunny, forever," I say honestly.

How is it, that even with a heart as black and scorched as mine, there are still tiny pieces to be found that haven't been burnt. This amazing little girl, *Ma Belle Foi*, my friends. All of them deserve more than I have offered them. But can I ever be enough?

"That's beautiful, Ryan. How did you know to get a pink one?" Dad asks, completely ignoring the fact I just introduced myself to my little sister as a heartbroken chump. I toss him the paper bag with the blue bunny inside. I don't explain the sentiment, I just continue to coo over my precious little sister.

"She's so beautiful, Melly. She definitely has your looks!" I say, continuing to ignore my father's presence, even though guilt and anger rip through my chest like acid. I keep my mask in place.

"I don't know, I think she has your father's nose," Melody says diplomatically as she takes baby Dexta-Rose back. My arms ache with the loss and my heart immediately feels empty. For a split second I picture a future where *Foi* is the one in the bed, and she's holding what could be our baby, and this image warms my insides more than it should this soon into a relationship.

"So son, how are you? How was the clinic? I've heard some good things from Dr. Asher about you," Dad says, snapping me out of my vision. Wow, an actual question about how I am, fucking hell. I decide to answer this time considering he actually decided to pay an interest in my life for once.

"Yeah it was pretty awesome actually. Dr. A isn't who I thought he was, and you were right he's actually a pretty decent guy. They do some great work there, you should definitely think about becoming a sponsor or something. His daughter Faith, she's my girlfriend now. I'll bring her by the house so y'all can meet her." A look flashes across his face at that revaluation that I can't decipher.

"Oh, what happened to the Chase girl?" he asks, another unusual look sitting heavy on his face. Whats with all the questions right now? He is being so weird. "You know her father is running for Senator?"

And there it is. The real reason he is interested. Everything is always about business.

"We broke up," I say bluntly, offering up no further explanation. Fuck him. "Oh, and by the way I went to your condo, have you ever actually been there? That place is like wearing a Rolex to go serve at a soup kitchen. Like seriously inappropriate considering half the people living nearby don't have access to clean water. The whole resort needs burning down."

"I haven't been, but I'll definitely look into that. Your mother would be so proud of you, son," he says sadly. The fuck? Hasn't mentioned her in three fucking years and now he decides to bring her up?

"Don't." I say through gritted teeth, my usual anger now sliding firmly back into place. Most people would long to hear that their mother is proud of them, but I know different. She wouldn't be proud of me, not after everything I've done, she would be ashamed.

What I can't work out is, am I pissed off with him, or at myself? Probably both.

"Ryan, I..." he starts but trails off. This guy. So fucking pathetic.

"Whatever man, I gotta go." I shrug, keeping my face indifferent, even though my stomach is in knots.

"I hope you are well enough to come home soon, Mel. It was really good to see you and meet little Dex, she's amazing." I say honestly. I notice Melody frowning at my shortening her name to Dex, but I don't give a fuck. Boy or girl, she was always going to be Dex to me.

"It's really good to have you home, Ryan. I'm excited to meet your new girlfriend, you bring her round as soon as we are home, okay? No offence but that last one was a total cling-on," she says, smiling knowingly. Melody was always super nice to Mia, she's nice to everyone, but I know she didn't really like it when Mia came by.

"You'll love her, I promise," I smile at her sweetly. I walk towards the door, giving my father one last acknowledgement in the form of a shoulder barge as I pass by him, but I receive no response. No retort. No putting me in my place. No reminder of who's boss.

My blood burns yet again with a familiar rage, although why I'm angry my father *didn't* tell me off, I don't know?

He can go fuck himself. I guess I was right. My Mom was easy to replace, and apparently, so was I.

# CHAPTER 35

## Faith

Ryan didn't go home at all after we left the hospital. After going to buy himself a new phone, he came back to our house where he stayed until Sunday afternoon. I couldn't believe how chilled Mom was about him staying with us, although she did make him sleep in the guest room, and told us that under no circumstances were we to have sex under her roof. I could have died of embarrassment during that awkward mood-killer conversation, but Ryan being Ryan, he took it in his stride and assured her nothing would happen.

He meant it too because he never once tried to break her rules. In fact, he seemed to be avoiding me at all costs, making me wonder why he chose to stay with us in the first place. I could tell instantly he wasn't himself when we left the hospital. He was pissed. He didn't say much about the baby, only that she was a girl, and that they had called her Dexta-Rose. Trying to get much else from him was like getting blood from a stone.

At first, I put it down to lack of sleep on both our parts,

but even the next day, the mood was still sour. It was like those first few days at the Old Farmhouse all over again, where I'd try to talk, but he either didn't answer, or he was short with me.

I tried to cuddle a few times, and although he always cuddled me back, he seemed permanently distracted by his new phone. It was constantly going off with messages, and he would always read it and reply straight away, aggressively punching out his responses. When I thought about it, I had never seen him respond to a single message while we were away, and on the rare occasions he ever did get his phone out, he would just take a quick glance at it and that was it.

I had wondered if it was his dad messaging, and maybe whatever the issue was between them, that was the reason he didn't want to go home. I tried to ask what was wrong, but he told me he was fine. I outright asked why he didn't want to go home, and after at first getting pissy with me about me not wanting him there, he then made up some story about giving his dad and Melody some space to settle in with the baby. It was clearly bullshit, but he apologised for getting angry with me at least.

When we said goodnight last night, he pulled me in for the most amazing kiss. It was so intense and full of emotion, it took me by surprise, and my whole body ached for more. I honestly thought he would try and sneak in my room once my mom was asleep. I waited awake for hours but he never showed. Inner Bitch had no trouble in showing up though, filling my head with my usual insecurities.

I decided to throw on my big girl panties, only figuratively of course, and go down to the guest room, only to find the bed empty. I'd actually worn my sexiest pyjamas, which weren't all that sexy really, but they were satin at least. I couldn't ignore the sting of finding his bed empty. Obviously I called him, but he didn't answer. In fact, the asshole sent me to voicemail after three rings. Not wanting to be *that girl*, I decided not to try again. He would call me back when he was ready.

Like a chump, I stayed and waited in his bed until he finally crept back in, drunk, at 3 a.m, offering up no explanation as to where he had been. He hadn't even noticed I was there until he got up and announced he was going for a run.

By Sunday afternoon, the silence between us was deafening, and I'd had enough. I was about to confront him, when he said he was going home to get ready for school the next morning. I asked again if everything was alright and he tried, but failed, to reassure me it was all okay.

Reluctantly, I let him leave, even though Inner Brit was screaming at me to fight for him to stay and explain himself. After he left, I gotta admit I was pining after him. Inner Bitch on the other hand, was scolding me for being too much of a wimp not to say what I wanted to say. She was also telling me that he must've gone to hook up with someone better. Mia probably. Shit on a stick.

So here we are. After trying to distract myself by organising my homework stationary, I decide to call Ryan again to see how he was. He doesn't answer. Yet again it goes straight to voicemail after only one ring this time. I was desperately hoping his mood might have lightened, I needed my Ryan back before tomorrow, otherwise I didn't know how I was going to face it there alone.

I wasn't even sure if he was still coming to pick me up. I sold my car before going back to Africa, so I would have to get up early to catch the bus without a ride. He had originally said that he would get me, even though I'm right out of his way, he insisted. But now, after the way the weekend has gone, I wasn't expecting him to show up.

He'd sent me to voicemail? Twice. I'd had enough of this

bullcrap. I was about to type out the word 'Asshole' and send it to him but before I could. My phone immediately buzzed with a message.

**Ryan-** I'm too tired to talk, I'm sorry. I'm just going to go to bed. I'll see you tomorrow morning.

No kiss. Well of course you're tired, douchebag. You were out until three in the morning!

** **Faith -** Are you sure everything's alright? I know I keep asking, but I'm worried about you. Are you still giving me a ride tomorrow? It's okay if you're not, I just need to make sure I'm up early enough for the bus. X

I read my text back, and jeez I'm such a wimp. Why am I practically begging for this guy's attention? Urgh. I wait. I must have fallen asleep because it's a full four hours, and the middle of the night before a response comes in.

** **Ryan -** Goodnight Faith.

Faith. And again, no kiss. He didn't actually answer my question either? Everything about this seems wrong. What the hell was he doing for four hours? I guess he was probably asleep, he did say he was tired? *Doesn't explain where he was last night though, does it?*

It takes a while for me to fall back to sleep again because I'm sucked down another excruciating question rabbit-hole, filled with fear and self-loathing. When I finally fall back to sleep, it's anything but restful.

*I dream that I'm on a roller-coaster without any safety harness. It's climbing to the top, and there's that click clacking sound as it moves painfully slowly to the highest point. I know what's coming. It's about to drop down the other side, fast as lightning.*

*Loop the loop, twist and turn, and I know I'm gonna fall out...*

*I do fall out, but I don't come to a crash on the ground, instead I'm just floating into space. The whole world just falls from beneath me. I scream but no sound comes out.*

*I try to grab hold of Ryan, but he doesn't reach back for me. He wears that same look of satisfaction he wore the night of the pig incident.*

*He wants me gone.*

*I'm drifting out into the darkness, alone and afraid, and I know that there isn't a damn thing I can do about it.*

# CHAPTER 36

## Faith

I wake up early, last night's nightmares playing heavy on my mind. After yoga, I check my phone for any more messages, but there is nothing from Ryan.

**Greg-** Have a great first day, and don't let the bastards get you down! I see Loverboy was out having fun last night. I hope those aren't the same friends who bullied you, Faithy? Because where I'm from that's not cool.

He has sent a selfie of him and Ade pulling silly faces. God, I miss them both already. Wait, Ryan was out again last night? I immediately check the socials to see what Greg is talking about, and I'm not one bit prepared for the barrage of photos that fill my screen. There was a beach party, and Ryan has been tagged in a lot of photos. There is one of him with some of the soccer team. That's not so bad I guess? I mean, aside from the fact he lied to me.

Then there is one with a few of the cheerleaders. I'm instantly pissed when I see Mia's little minion Madison with her hand on Ryan's chest. He's laughing, not even trying to remove it. That's my place. She has her hand in my place.

I scroll through the pictures, each one annoying me more than the last. The next one I see leaves bile in my throat. Ryan is standing there, Levi on one side, and Shane on the other, smiling with his arms wrapped around both their shoulders. After everything I told him about what Shane has done to me, he still wants to be friends with him? God, the guy had sex with his girlfriend and yet Ryan is acting like nothing happened?

I can't even look at them any longer, as tears burn my eyes, and acid burns in my stomach. I shut my phone off and grab my school things. Guess I'm getting the bus after all, because every part of me is screaming at me to wake the hell up. Ryan isn't coming for me.

***

I arrive at school and Ryan's truck is already in the lot, just like I knew it would be. I can feel the cracks beginning to form in my heart. Why is he doing this? *Come on Faith you always knew he would drop you when school started.*

I did expect this to happen. I expected his car to be here when I got here, so why does it hurt so much?

What I wasn't expecting was for Mia to get out of the passenger seat. Mia McBitchface. My tormenter, Ryan's ex, is getting out of his truck wearing Ryan's jacket, with a smug look on her face that tells me all I need to know.

I've been played.

This whole time with Ryan wasn't real. Was it a game? Was she in on it?

Ryan looks at me as he steps out of the truck, a pained

expression of guilt sitting heavy on his face. He looks at me like he is begging for forgiveness and for a split second I believe him. Something doesn't fit in this picture, but I can't put my finger on it. Then I remember he lied to me. I remember how he was supposed to be picking me up this morning and yet here he is, riding in with another girl. The worst girl.

I don't know what comes over me, but my first reaction is to flip him off. Ha! Take that, you lying dickwad. I give my cutest smile that I hope screams 'I don't give a shit, baby', when in reality I'm dying inside. Shit on a stick, his betrayal hurts so much. Why did I trust him? Why did I let this happen?

I'm such an idiot.

My heart begins to crumble to pieces as Mia laughs her usual high-pitched squeal, flipping me off in return. I wrap my arms around myself in an attempt to stop myself falling apart. Ryan smirks at me and shakes his head, and I know at that moment that my Ryan is gone. This isn't the boy who sang to comfort an orphaned baby elephant. The boy who took me on my first date, or donated twenty grand to a friend's charitable cause like it was nothing. This isn't my mystery boy.

This is the boy who threw me to the pigs.

Mia whispers something in his ear, touching his face as she does. He laughs, before wrapping an arm around Mia's shoulders, and walking off in the opposite direction, taking my heart with him.

"Well, if it isn't Pork Chop herself, back for another year of fun and debauchery," says a slick voice, as a heavy arm wraps around my waist. The smell of cigarettes hits my nose as I feel his hard chest press against my back. Shane.

I'd been so caught up in Ryan, that I hadn't even thought about where he might be lingering.

"Come with me, miss piggy, before I choke you out right

in this carpark," he says in my ear, his hot stale breath assaulting my senses. Ryan is about to head into the hall with Mia. Look back, Ryan. Please look back. I don't know why I'm hoping he will rescue me, but surely if he sees Shane he will help me? But he doesn't look back. Instead he puts his hand on Mia's lower back and guides her into the hall, holding the door open for her like a gentleman, as she glides in like the royalty she is around here.

"Faith Asher, you're wanted in the Principal's office," an older woman's voice says from up the steps, breaking my attention from Ryan. Shane loosens his grip on me but keeps his arm in place. I look up to see Mrs Trent, the school guidance counsellor. She looks at Shane's arm that's still wrapped around my waist.

"Excuse me young man, please keep your hands to yourself this is a school not a nightclub. Young women have the right to come to school without fear of being groped and leered at, now take yourself off to class before I report you to the principal!"

"This isn't over, Pork Chop!" Shane whispers as he digs his fingers down into my skin. It hurts but I don't dare show it. "Relax lady. I was just giving a friend a hug, isn't that right, Faith?" he stares at me straight in the eye, but doesn't wait for me to respond. "See you later, baby," He adds with a knowing grin, before turning and walking away.

"Was he bothering you? Because the school takes allegations of assault and sexual harassment very seriously, should you wish to report it," Mrs Trent asks with a concerned look on her face.

What the name of Shania Twain is happening right now? Three years at this school and I've been openly groped, harassed, bullied, and had obscenities yelled at me as I walk into class, and not once has a teacher asked me if I was okay?

I have no idea why anyone would be showing concern now, but I know full well that any complaints I made about Shane would never be taken seriously. His father is on the school board, and a serious investor. If what Ryan said about him calling the shots around here is true, I'm pretty sure I'd be the one kicked out of school if I were to report Shane.

"I'm fine," I lie. Mrs Trent looks me up and down, frowning.

"Very well. Principal Meyers is waiting in her office for you," she says as she begins stomping back up the stairs. Her low kitten heels are click clacking on the tile, reminding me of the roller coaster from my dream. I follow her up and head down the hall towards the principal's office. I expect Mrs Trent to leave but she stays and knocks on the door.

"Come in..." we hear from inside. Mrs Trent opens the door and follows me in, making me wonder what all this is actually about. I thought it was just about my decision to finish in Africa but now I'm questioning if there is something more going on.

"Come in, Faith. Please have a seat," Principal Meyers offers kindly. When I take the seat on the right, Mrs Trent takes the one next to me on the left. This is so weird.

"Faith, there have been some very serious allegations made against you, that I am most concerned about."

"Allegations? What kind of Allegations?" What in the fresh hell is going on now?

"Allegations about drug use and prostitution, Miss Asher," she announces sternly, a frustrated huff coming from Mrs Trent.

"Faith, a complaint was made by one of the parents that a female student was being sexually harassed by male students. Complaints were also made about offensive graffiti that was rife in the locker rooms, and the bathrooms. Whilst I was saddened and shocked to hear of these complaints, I have to say I was also extremely concerned at the content of what was *repeatedly* written on the walls. Of course, we have removed the graffiti, but I am under pressure from the PTA to investigate these rumours to the full extent. Our reputation at St. Edmund's is one of superior excellence, and we have a zero tolerance for that kind of behaviour here," She says, sounding exasperated. I wonder who made the complaints?

"Faith, are you sexually active?" She adds, her tone full of accusation.

"I'm not sure that's appropriate," Mrs Trent interrupts.

"Wait, you want to investigate me?" I ask, confused as hell.

"No Faith, what Principal Meyers is saying is we need to be clear on exactly what has happened here," Mrs Trent says, trying to remain diplomatic.

"Faith, what I'm asking is, are there any truth to these allegations, and if there is, are any of these rumours about you true? We need to know so that we can investigate the matter fully." Principal Meyers stares at me expectantly.

"Let me get this straight. Someone makes a complaint that I'm being harassed, the evidence of which is right here on the school walls, and has been there for three years, and instead of looking into who might be responsible for that, you want to investigate if I'm actually sucking dick for drugs?" I yell angrily. "What in the actual fucking fuck?" Principal Meyers looks at me gobsmacked. I don't swear very often, and I've never sworn in front of a teacher before. My lady balls are kicking off right now.

"Of all the crappy things I've had to deal with at this school, this takes the bloody biscuit!" I continue, gathering my things and preparing to walk out. I can't believe I just said 'bloody biscuit' as well. I've been around Greg too long.

"Miss Asher, please sit down. No one is pointing blame here, I'm just trying to establish the facts. When I received Mrs Scott's email I was very concerned, and I assured her that this was likely just some teenage prank that got a little out of hand. She didn't seem to be aware of the exact content of the graffiti, but I'm sure she would be interested to know? I'm also sure she would be very interested to know how many times *numerous* people have said the same thing about the type of girl her stepson is associating with? There is no smoke without fire, Miss Asher?"

Why does she keep calling me Miss Asher like my name offends her? How on earth does she know about Ryan and I? Wait, Mrs Scott? Melody Scott made the complaint? That means Ryan must have said something?

"Well I don't know Principal Meyers, exactly what type of girl do you think I am? Please tell me, because I would also be interested to know?" I say, but im actually not one bit interested in waiting around for her response. I grab my things and walk out., leaving both the principal and guidance counsellor calling after me.

The bell hasn't gone off yet so I rush to go and find Ryan. I know exactly where he will be, in the quad. A small outdoor section of tables surrounded by walls on all four sides, you have to go through a door to get out there. This is where all the popular kids hang out, and normally I wouldn't dream of going out into the lion's den, but today is different.

Today I need answers, and I intend to get them.

# CHAPTER 37

## Faith

I rush out through the door, ignoring the heckling Ryan had promised would no longer happen. A guy grabs his junk and shakes it at me. Eww. I can't see Ryan at first but I do see Levi. His twisted smile tells me he has seen me too, and he struts towards me with a gleam in his eye. I don't have the patience for this A-hole today.

Levi has always been the lesser of two evils where he and Shane are concerned, he doesn't normally get involved when the others are being dicks to me. In fact, he used to send me messages all the time asking to hang out. He even used the word date more than once. I didn't reply. He must be some kinda moron if he thinks I'm ever going to hang out with him when he stands by and lets his friends repeatedly bully and hurt me. Also, I'm pretty sure he had a girlfriend too.

His requests to date soon turned into requests for sex, and when I didn't respond to those either, he eventually started to act more and more like Shane.

"What's happening, Porky? You looking for your boy?"

Levi quizzes knowingly, blocking my path.

"Yes, as a matter of fact I am. Now can you move out of my way please?"

"Well I'm not sure *he* will be very pleased to see you. In fact, I'd say he's more than a little caught up right now," he says stepping aside so I can see what's going on. Ryan is sitting with Mia. Or should I say, Mia is sitting on Ryan's lap, her arms draped around his neck. He looks distant and unamused, but she is rambling on, talking in his ear.

"Those pesky little *Ex's and Oh's*." Levi teases. "I have no idea what Wonder Boy Scott said to make you finally give it up, but I guess now you really are used goods."

His words sting. Ryan told him about us?

My heart hurts as I wonder exactly how much Ryan has shared about our relationship. I ignore Levi and continue to watch Ryan and Mia. He looks like he would rather be anywhere else then with her right now, so why is he?

"Yo' baby, you come to give daddy a quick blow? I'm a little short for cash but I'm sure you'll throw me a freebie, right?" Some random guy yells, drawing Ryan's attention toward me. He looks furious as Random Guy grabs me, pulling me into his lap. "Come on babe, I know you like to party," he says gripping my arm tightly, running his hand up my skirt.

"Get the fuck off of her, you filthy limp dick prick!" Ryan rages, dragging me off of Random Guy.

How did he get over here so fast?

He moves me to the side before he grabs Random Guy's face, squeezing his cheeks harshly, pulling him to his feet. Random Guy clutches at Ryan's hand, but he is so furious he doesn't let go. No one moves. No one would dare challenge Ryan, especially with all of his friends around.

"Touch another fucking girl without her permission again, and I will end your sorry little life!" he says shoving the dudes face away so hard he stumbles back. "That goes for all of you fuckers! If any of you touches what's mine again, I will slit your fucking throats!" Ryan rages.

People already have their cell phones out and have begun filming. Shane has a look of pure hatred on his face, but from where I'm standing, it's aimed at Ryan. "Fucking little bitch," Ryan adds as Random Guy goes scurrying off back to whatever hole he came from. Ryan stares at me. Confusion and annoyance etched upon his face.

"What's she doing here, Ryan? You promised me it was over?" Mia whines, coming to stand at his side. Ryan closes his eyes and takes a deep, frustrated breath.

"I said I would deal with it!" he seethes.

"Deal with it?" I interrupt. "That's how you're referring to our relationship? Because as far as I'm aware, we are still in one?" I can't help but yell, my anger boiling to the surface. Ryan smirks at me, but it's gone as quickly as it arrived.

"What? You didn't get the message this morning?" he says dryly. "Me giving my ex a ride when I was supposed to collect you, that's not enough of a hint?" He steps into my space, leaving Mia wide eyed and smug behind him. "Is me sitting here with another chick in my lap, not giving you a clue something's up? How fucking dumb are you, Faith? Or are you just that desperate for more of my dick you don't give a shit who else rides it?" He spits angrily and the whole crowd laughs. He ignores them, staring me right in the eye.

His beautiful warm amber eyes are now cold and full of sadness. If I hadn't spent the past few weeks with him, I'd believe this bad guy charade he is putting on. But his eyes can't hide his truth. He doesn't want this. But if that's true, why is he doing it? None of this makes any sense.

"Why are you doing this?" I ask quietly, not wanting to fuel the fire forming around us.

"What, you actually thought all that shit was real? You really believed you were my girlfriend? Ha! You were a fuck. A conquest. Everyone here knows you aren't really a whore, just a frigid bitch who thinks she's better than everyone else. I fucking hated you, just like everyone else here, but when I found out you were a virgin, I couldn't help myself. Nothing quite like popping a cherry, especially one that's so hard to get." he says cruelly.

"You don't mean that. You just said I was yours. You said I was always going to be yours. Please don't do this, you promised me," I beg, clutching at the elephant necklace he gave me. He glances down at the necklace and swallows. The bell rings, but no one makes any move to leave.

"A trinket. It means nothing to me. Keep it, sell it for crack, whatever. *You* mean nothing to me. I said that you were mine because you are. Mine to use whenever the fuck I feel like it. As if you fell for that boyfriend crap. Why would I ever want someone like you, when I could have any girl I want? You're nothing but a good blow. A pair of lips to take my dick, and if you're lucky, I may even let you swallow from time to time," He says brutally, stepping away from me as he looks down at the floor. Shane looks furious, but why would he care?

"I know you don't mean that. If you didn't care about me then why did you ask Melody to speak to the Principal about me? Why did you have the graffiti about me removed?" I question, not missing the anguished look on his face. He stares at me, wondering how I would know that he did that. "I came here because I thought you would want to know that I'm actually getting the blame for that. Apparently, there is no smoke without fire and victim shaming seems to be acceptable at this school."

Ryan looks pissed. I can tell he wants nothing more than to storm into Principal Meyers office and trash it. He wants to burn the entire school to the ground with all of my enemies in it. He wants to kiss me, tell me this was a mistake. It's written all over his face. But he doesn't. Instead he steps back to Mia's side and puts his arm around her shoulders.

"No one cares, Pork Chop. Go find someone else to bore with your pathetic pity party." I see it the moment the words leave his lips. Regret. He knows that was the bullet; the one thing that would make me walk away. Pork Chop.

I warned him he would never get away with that again, and he knew I meant it.

"Looks like you put on a few more pounds over the summer, Porky. No wonder there are starving kids in Africa with you over there eating all the food. Please go and shove your fingers down your throat and come back when you're 30lbs lighter," Mia snarls, before pulling Ryan into a kiss which he obliges.

A howl of laughter comes from Levi, as Mia breaks her kiss to begin chanting 'Go puke Pork Chop', over and over and pretty soon everyone in the quad is joining in. Ryan grabs my hand and drags me to the entrance of the quad, before shoving me through the door so forcefully that I fall on my ass. He grabs the door, frowning at me as he slams it closed, right before I hear a huge cheer coming from the other side.

Tears stream down my face but I force myself to get up off the floor. I don't want to still be here when they open the door again.

For the second time, Ryan Scott, has thrown me on my ass and broken my heart, and for the second time, I have no idea why.

# CHAPTER 38

## Ryan

It's funny how you always think life is gonna go a certain way. Like the path that you're on won't ever deviate from its course. You wake up each day, carry on with the mundane tasks, working towards your goals and ambitions. Things in your life seem like certainties, and you take for granted that they will always remain the same until the day comes when you want to change them. Then, one day you wake up and bam! Your whole world has been flipped on its ass.

My world has been tits-up since the day my mom died. It's hard to imagine any certainties anymore when you live in a world of self-inflicted chaos and destruction. But there she was. My one certainty. My light, my warmth, my home.

*Ma Belle Foi.*

We were supposed to be together, of that I was certain. She was mine, of that I have never been more certain of anything in my life. Fate on the other hand, has other ideas. Fate, or my fucked-up self-preservation instincts, either-or.

When I left the hospital, I was pissed. The more I thought about how my dad was acting, the more pissed I was getting. How can he be so happy about a new baby, when he has never showed me an ounce of affection in my life? This, the guy who lays down the law at every fucking turn, reduced to a stumbling idiot who could barely get his words out. I've been here for eighteen years, and he has only ever seen me as his protégé to be moulded, never a son to love or to be proud of.

Don't get me wrong, I want nothing more than for Dexta-Rose to have a much better father than the asshole I ended up with, but I can't deny it fucking stings that I was clearly never good enough for him.

Messages started coming in thick and fast from the guys at school. Apparently, Faith and I were photographed leaving the hospital together holding hands, and it was posted on a gossip site that had broken the news that Melody had given birth to her baby. I didn't tell Faith. I knew she wouldn't like the photo, seeing as how we were both sleep deprived and in desperate need of a shower. Not that she didn't still look beautiful, but girls are weird like that.

At first, I had tried to ignore the messages assaulting my inbox. But then a name popped up I couldn't ignore.

Mia Chase.

I immediately changed her name to McBitchface on my phone, and laughed to myself as I did it. When she didn't get a response, she sent screenshots of messages between us discussing what I had done to Dr. A, telling me if I didn't go meet her, she would send them to Faith. So, like a pussy I went.

I had every intention of telling her to go fuck herself, I was actually glad to have an outlet for my earlier rage. I met her in the parking lot of some highway diner, like we were in some ridiculous fucking spy movie. She was always one for dramatics.

She came wearing heels, a slutty dress, and a full face of make-up. I on the other hand had my old hoodie on, that now belonged to *Foi*, and a pair of old sweats that were a completely different shade of grey to the hoodie, and that had a hole in the knee. To be honest, I looked like a homeless person, but fuck if I was making an iota of effort for this weasel.

Mia lay all her cards out on the table, and kudos to her, she had a lot of shit against me. The messages, photos of my bloody clothes she told me she would destroy but apparently kept, as well as photos of the night of the pig party.

One photo, taken in series, shows Shane trying to pull down Faith's panties, while she lay bound and gagged on the floor with a bag over her head. The next shows me pulling him off her. The next shows me fumbling around trying to pull her panties up again. But then she deleted the first two. Now if you look at the remaining photo of me out of context, it looks like I'm the one pulling down her panties. Lev and Shane have been cropped out of the shot, and my truck is clearly visible in the picture.

Mia threatened not only to go to the police with the evidence against me in Dr. Asher's attack, but also with the image of me pulling at *Foi's* panties. She said she would tell them that I was a jealous boyfriend. That I had found out he was her gynaecologist and I was angry about it, and that's why I attacked him. She would also tell them I repeatedly hurt her, and that she had always been afraid of me.

Mia threatened that she and Shane would swear the fact that the pig party was all my idea, and that I'd said it was only fair I got to look at his daughter the way he looked at my girlfriend. Couple all of that with the fact that Melody reported a girl was being sexually harassed in school, and there was now a mountain of shit against me. I don't even know how Mia knew about that, from Shane's father I guess, he is on the school board?

Mia actually seemed to know a lot about it. She knew that Melody didn't actually name *Foi*, but that it had been assumed because she was named in the graffiti. Mia being the vapid bitch she is, said that she would come forward as the victim and name me as the person responsible.

Mia seemed convinced that she would be believed, as Shane had already made sure his father cast doubt over the fact that Faith was an innocent victim. He encouraged Principal Meyers to be more concerned about the truth behind the graffiti, rather than the truth behind the allegations. Apparently, Mia also has several members of the basketball team ready to swear they have all paid to have sex with Faith, and she has someone who will plant drugs in her locker, making sure they are found.

It was then that she delivered her ultimatum; finish with Faith, and make sure she goes back to Africa for good, and go back to how things were with she and I for senior year, or she will not only destroy me, but she will make sure Faith's reputation is in ruins by the time she's finished as well. Oh, and the cherry on top was that I had to attend the end of summer beach party with her the following night, or she would post a naked photo she had taken of Faith in the showers after swimming once. She had photo-shopped it of course, making her a lot fatter than she is.

What I couldn't work out was why? Why did Mia go to all this trouble? Was it just to be a bitch or was there more to it? And why would Shane want to help her when a few weeks ago he was telling me that they were a couple now?

Afterwards when Mia left, I did what I thought was the best thing to do. I went and got wasted. Why do I always think that's the best solution? It never fucking helps, but for a couple of hours it's takes me back to the black. In the black there is nothing. I like it in the black.

I don't even remember going back to Faith's, or getting into bed, but reality hit me like a ton of bricks when I woke to find my little wildcat asleep in my bed. She looked perfect, and so beautiful. Wait, wildcat? Didn't my mom used to tell me I was destined for a wildcat? Wow, turns out she was right all along.

Faith was wearing some sexy as hell pyjamas that were modest and classy, but knowing her, I know they would have made her feel naughty. They were a pretty dusty pink satin, with a lace trim on the bottom of the shorts that gracefully grazed the bottom of her ass as she slept. I had never imagined she might own something like this, let alone wear it for me. I would never deserve her.

The satin looked exquisite next to her creamy skin and I desperately wanted to run my hands all over her. I wanted to kiss every inch of her, and as corny as it sounds, I wanted to make love to her. For the first time in my life, I actually thought about sex as an emotional connection, rather than just a physical need. But as much as I wanted to, I didn't do anything.

My stomach was in knots with guilt. Knowing *Foi* came to find me, dressed like a sexy goddess, even after I was a moody asshole to her all day made something wretch inside of me. Even worse, I wasn't there when she got to my bed, so she would know I snuck out.

I decided to get up and go for a run, even though that was the last thing in the world that I wanted to do. While I was out, I decided it was time to call Alex and say thanks for hooking me up. He answered on the first ring.

"Well if it isn't the Fresh Prince of Ruddy Arseholes! How was the flight back? Is everything okay at home? How's the baby brother?" he shouts loudly.

"It's a sister," I say, but I can tell he doesn't hear me. I can hear a lot of background noise, and I realise it's probably late

Sunday afternoon in London which means the guys must all be at the pub. Fuck, is he with them?

"Yo' Alex, is that Ryan?" I hear Tom ask in the background. Fuck.

"That sneaky bastard! Where the fuck has he been all this time?" Kat screeches.

"Put him on loud-speaker so we can all talk to him!" Spencer demands. Fuck me, please don't.

"Will you lot shut the fuck up for a minute. I can't hear what he is saying!" Alex orders, not that anyone ever takes him seriously. "Ryan mate, you alright?"

"No. I'm not alright. I haven't been okay for a long time. I've fucked everything up, Alex. I'm a bad person," I say honestly.

"What did you say? We're at the Dog and Duck, it's happy hour and the place is rammed. I can't hear fuck all in here. Listen, I'm putting you on loud speaker, hang on."

"No Alex, don't! I was just calling to say thanks for helping me out, I'll speak to you soon, okay." Like a coward, I hung up before he could respond. My phone rang a few times where they each tried to call me back, before I switched it off.

I knew what I had to do. So, with a heavy fucking heart I left *Foi*, and went to the beach party. I put on my best fake smile that I had gotten far too used to wearing nowadays, and I acted like nothing was wrong.

Shane bizarrely, also acted like nothing was wrong. It was as if I hadn't caught him dick down with my girl. Like he hadn't told me they were together now and to deal with it? He didn't even acknowledge anything had happened? I would under normal circumstances be pissed as fuck, but in the midst of all this bullshit, that told me all I needed to know.

Whatever was going down with Mia, Shane was clearly in on it like she said. I decided to play along. I'd have my revenge on both of these cunts soon enough, but I needed to play my cards close to my chest. For now.

I told myself that I was doing it to protect Faith. I honestly believed that was true. It is true, isn't it? When I saw the look in her face when I called her Pork Chop, I knew then I'd fucking lost her. What good was protecting her if I was hurting her anyway? How else can I get us both out of this?

I could tell she didn't believe a word I was saying, she knows me too fucking well. She sees me like no one else, as if she has a window into my blackened soul. There was only one way that I knew I could get her to accept it was true, and I took it. The disappointment on her face when I broke my promise to her, yet again, was unbearable. When Mia started chanting and Faith's eyes went glassy, I knew I had to get her out of there. I couldn't bear for Mia to be the one to get Faith's tears. Mia does not deserve her beautiful tears.

I swore I'd hurt any bastard who put tears on her face again, even if that person was me, and fuck if I don't intend on paying for my sins. First things first. I intend to raze this school to the ground, with every single one of these assholes in it.

# CHAPTER 39

## Ryan

I type out message after message for Faith, but delete every one without sending. I want to beg her to forgive me, tell her it's all part of my plan, but to what end? If I tell her I'm faking it, she will want to know why, and if I tell her why, I will lose her anyway. It's not like I even have a plan, I don't even know what the fuck I'm doing. All I know is that I'm completely fucked.

I lay on my bed and put in my earphones. Fuck, I'm so tired, and not just physically either. I close my eyes for a bit, knowing I won't fall asleep. How could I have said all of that to *Foi*? How could I disrespect her like that in front of the very people who I should be protecting her from?

I told her that my elephant necklace meant nothing to me. I even told her to get rid of it too.

Fuuuck!

What was I thinking? My friends gave me that necklace after my mother died, and until I gave it to Faith I had never taken it off. That necklace was my most cherished possession, but I gave it to her because I knew that she was going to be mine forever.

Sentimental value aside, it's also worth a lot of money too. The stone alone is worth over a half million. It was gifted to me by The West Company, compliments of Alex. Each of the guys designed a different aspect of the necklace and without even telling me who designed which part, I already knew.

Kat would have chosen the elephant. She is the only one who knew the significance of an elephant for me. Kat loves all that spiritual stuff too, and even used to speak to my mom on the phone for spiritual guidance. She would always get me to take personal items back home so Mom could connect with her through them for a reading.

Mom used to say that Kat is in fact, contrary to her name, a dog. A Golden Retriever to be more precise. Gentle, loving, loyal to a fault. The best friend anyone could have, and that I should keep her close in my heart for all time. That thought rips through me like a tornado.

Then there is Tom. He would have chosen the circle. It's simple, masculine elegance, and it's Tom all over. The guy is like *James Bond,* even at school he just had an air about him. Sophisticated, suave, breaker of hearts.

Spencer would have chosen the black rope; a rather significant talisman to our friendship. The night we shared our first kiss, she was in a really bad way. Ironically, I found her just minutes before she was about to take her own life. I know right? I'm like the angel of fucking death or something.

She had wrapped a black tie around her neck and was in the process of tying the end to the door when I walked in unannounced. The girls always yelled at me for not knocking, but this time I was happy I didn't.

I pulled it off of her, and spent almost three hours just holding her in my arms. When she finally stopped crying, I asked her why she would do something like that. We all knew guys were picking on her from time to time, calling her fat, making snide comments about her appearance, but regretfully we had let a lot of it slide.

It wasn't until that night though, that I learned the full extent of the things she had gone through, and it was awful. None of us had any idea it was so bad. Even worse was the constant pressure to lose weight, coming from her parents. She began putting herself down, saying that no one would ever want her, that she was disgusting, and so I did the first thing that I could think of. I kissed her.

It was sloppy as hell, being both of our first real kisses, but it was nice nonetheless. Afterwards, I took the black tie, and wrapped it around our hands, binding them together. I told her that we were connected now, forever, and I would always be there for her. I promised I wouldn't let anyone treat her that way again.

I've never told anyone that story, and as far as I know, neither did Spencer. I just made sure I kept my end, and went ham on anyone who tried to bully her again. Luckily, the rest of the crew all followed suit, no explanation needed. I made damn sure the boys both treated her like a queen too. She needed to know she was beautiful.

Anyway, last of all, Alex would have chosen the stone. It's a very rare, flawless, Fancy Vivid Blue diamond, from his family's personal collection. The ethereal, almost ghostly stone represents the moon.

Some people believe elephants worship the moon, did you know that? In the wild, their different behaviours at night appear to be in correlation to the moon's cycle. However, Alex choosing the moon wasn't significant to the elephant at all, that was just a coincidence. For him, the moon is a reminder that there is always light, even in the darkness. Alex gets it.

He lost his own mother when he was only a year old to cancer. He knows that after a loss like that, then darkness will always follow you. It doesn't matter that he barely had a chance to know his mother. It doesn't matter that he doesn't even remember her. He still feels the darkness.

It would be a safe bet for people to see the elephant and assume that it represents my mother. I imagine that's what Kat had in mind when she chose it. But when I see it, and when Alex sees it, we know that's not the case. You see, *I'm* the elephant. The moon is my mother. She looks down on me, shining her light, constantly helping me find my way through the black.

For a long time, the moon was my only light source. That is until *Foi* came into my life. That's why I knew I could give her the necklace. *Foi* isn't just the light, she's the fucking sun. A magnificent star that shines brighter than all the rest, pulling me into her orbit.

My light, my warmth, *Ma Belle Foi.*

I'm broken from my thoughts and scared out of my fucking skin, when I'm suddenly whacked in the face with a pillow. The pillow gets pulled back and for a split second, I catch a glimpse of Faith raging at me before the pillow comes crashing down on my face again.

"... then you can kiss my fat ass!" She yells when I only catch the end of her speech as I pull out my headphones. She's wearing her usual yoga pants and a baggy slogan tee. Today's one says '*Livin' la vida yoga*'. Christ.

"What are you doing here, *Ma Foi*?"

"Don't call me that! You ended it, remember? We are done, finished, broken!" She snaps, throwing her hands around animatedly. She is so hot when she's pissed. *Not the time, dude.*

"Faith, I'm so sorry. I shouldn't have ended it the way I did, I shouldn't have treated you that way, but I had no choice." Shit, I definitely did not mean to say that. Hopefully she doesn't pick up on it.

"What the hell does that mean? Why wouldn't you have a choice?" she demands. Fuck. I shake my head, silently refusing to answer.

"Ryan, why can't you just be honest with me for once? You keep on lying to me, over and over. If you really are breaking up with me, don't I at least deserve the truth? I know that whatever's going on with you has something to do with Mia. I know she has something over you? It was so obvious you didn't want to be anywhere near her, you kept looking at her like she repulsed you! What is it, Ryan? Tell me? Whatever is going on we can work through it together, but I can't help you if you aren't honest with me?" *Foi* pleads with me, her cold steely eyes begging me to let her in.

"Just don't, Faith. Just please go home okay, I can't do this with you. It's over, just accept it!" I snap back at her. What the hell is wrong with me?

Here she is, my perfect girl, and she's fighting for me even after everything I've done to her. Here I am, I can't even find the fucking balls to fight for her and admit what I've done? I am a coward. A pathetic wretch who has no business even dreaming of being with this girl.

"Just accept it? How can I just accept it, when only last week you were telling me I should fight for you, that you're my guy. That I was yours and you were mine. Mine! Not Mia's, not anyone else's. You're mine, Ryan. Mine!" She yells passionately, claiming me as hers, like the fierce lion she is.

*Foi* moves to put her arms around my neck and I immediately pull her off. She gives me a look filled with shock, like even now after everything, she was still expecting me to hold her and tell her everything was going to be alright. Fuck, I really want to do that.

"What's changed? Tell me what's changed and I'll leave?" she says bitterly. "I can't leave if I don't know why I'm being sent away," she adds, barely whispering now, hugging her waist protectively. Back to the fucking mouse.

What am I supposed to do? All I can think about are Mia's threats to ruin us both, and I need to protect Faith above anything. At least, that's what I tell myself as I do the one thing that I know will drive her away for good.

"Nothing changed, Faith. I meant what I said, you were nothing to me. A meaningless fuck and a means to an end. I wanted revenge on Mia and I knew fucking you would piss her off. As if I'd actually want you? You disgust me," I brutally lie, as I rip the elephant necklace from her neck. She stumbles back, gasping in shock, rubbing the spot where the necklace used to sit.

She looks utterly heartbroken and all I want to do is scream at her not to believe a word I'm saying. I want to beg her forgiveness until the end of time but like I said, to what end? I know now that it's far too late for that. It was already too fucking late the day I put her father in the hospital.

I can see in her eyes that she is questioning me now. She was so confident I was lying before, but now she's unsure. She is beginning to believe the lie. I mentally remind myself one more time that it's all for the best. It is for the best right? *She's better off without you, asshole. You're toxic remember?*

I am fucking toxic. Broken, bloodied, and bound to repent for my sins. But like I said, first things first. I will make her enemies pay for what they have done, if it's the last thing I do. I will drag every asshole down with me. Anyone who has ever hurt *Foi* will answer to me now, starting with that bitch Mia Chase, and her stooge Shane Frost.

Whatever it is they are up to, whatever their agenda is with *Foi*? I will find out, and I will make sure it's dead and buried along with the pair of them. Before I can do that, I need to protect Faith, and if that means chasing her away back to Africa, then so be it.

"How many more times do I need to say it. Get the fuck out of my house! Even better, go back to Africa and get the fuck out of my life. We. Are. Done!" I keep my face impassive, but I swear my voice might have croaked a little at the end of that outrageous lie.

If it did, *Foi* didn't notice. She shoves me to the bed, with a loud frustrated scream as tears begin to slide down her cheeks. She stares at me. She doesn't say anything, she just stares. She hates me for doing this. I fucking hate myself.

"So, I'm supposed to fight for you, but yet you won't fight for me? I'm not worth it?" She questions sincerely. How can you think that, baby? You are precious to me. *Maybe because you're not fighting for her? Face it you're only saving yourself.*

Fuck. Is that really what I'm doing? I was dead before she came into my life and I'm throwing her away? I've been a fucking idiot, I can't lose this girl.

My realisation comes too late as Faith is already halfway out of the door. I know I'm fucked. But I can't bear for her to walk out like this without knowing how I really feel. She will hate me one day, but I'm praying that day won't be today, because I'm just not ready to lose her just yet.

"Keep your fucking secrets! I just hope they are worth it!" She rages, and storms off out of the room, yet again, slamming the door behind her.

Shit on a mother fucking stick.

# CHAPTER 40

## Faith

I race out the door, but he follows me and grabs my wrist. Ryan slams me against the wall and kisses me like his life depends on it. Or maybe mine does.

"*Foi*, I'm sorry. I'm so sorry, I didn't mean what I said. I didn't mean any of it," he pleads desperately. "Please don't go baby. I love you. I should have said it before, and now I have I honestly don't know why I couldn't before, but I love you!" He adds, stroking my face tenderly.

"Please don't, Ryan. I can't do this not now, not after everything else you've said today," I beg, looking away from him. Yet another tear trickles down my face and Ryan watches it silently as it rolls to a stop near my lips, before he kisses it away.

"You wait until now, right when I'm walking away, to finally tell me how you feel? How is that fair?" I whisper in his ear while he peppers soft, beautiful kisses over my neck that hit me right in my lady parts.

Well now, how on earth is a girl supposed to stay strong when he does this? He said he loves me. What am I supposed to do with that now? Yet again, I hear the lyrics to *'Toxic'* playing over in my head. Is our relationship toxic?

"It's not fair, I know that. I'm an asshole, and you still have no idea to what extent. The things I have done..." he shakes his head, making his golden strands fall loosely across his eyes. My weakness. "I *should* let you go, that's why I said what I said. I'm no good for you. Faith, I'm a demon. I'm fucking Medusa. Anyone who even looks at me turns to stone. If you stay with me, you will be reduced to nothing but dust, because that's what I do. I breathe poison until everything around me is as dead as I am!"

He looks at me sadly. Does he really believe that? What more could he possibly be hiding? Is this about what happened to his mother?

My heart breaks inside for him. I still have no idea what a loss like that must feel like, made a million times worse by the horror of being the one to cut her down. The guilt eats away at him every day, and I don't think he will ever be able to love me the way I wish he could. Not until he gets help with his grief that is.

Then I remember that there is more to it. Whatever happened today happened because of Mia, that much I am certain. McBitchface has a hold on him, but what could it be?

"Ryan, I promise I will help you. Whatever it is, I will be here for you. This thing with Mia, we can work through it together? Please just tell me what's going on?" I plead, desperate to understand why he keeps hurting me this way.

"I can't, Faith. I just can't. I'm sorry, but I swear to you that I will sort it, okay. I won't take Mia's shit anymore. I will fix it," Ryan promises, though the pained look on his face suggests he doesn't have any idea how he is going to keep that promise.

I shake my head. Why does it have to be this way? Why can't things ever just be easy?

Ryan inhales deeply. In for five, holds for five, then out for five, just like I taught him. He repeats this several times until I join in with him. After a few minutes I wrap my arms around him and he does the same to me. A tension seems to leave his body that I don't think even he realised was there.

He smells so good. Not as coconutty as usual, in fact there is also a hint of vanilla creeping in now too, making me wonder if he is still using my soap. Why does it feel so good in his arms? *It's a lie, Faith. He will just keep on hurting you, over and over again. When will you learn?*

Jeez, I can't keep getting caught up with him like this, my heart can only take so much. Inner Bitch is right. If he can't even respect me enough to tell me the truth now, then he will always think it's okay to lie to me. As much as it hurts, we can't be together like this.

That's why I came over here, to tell him that I'm going back to Africa. I thought we would be in this together, but he couldn't even stand by me for one day, and I just can't do it alone. Ryan says he loves me and maybe he does, but he needs to deal with his demons, and I can't stick around to be his verbal punching bag.

I know it's wrong, knowing what I need to do, but I kiss him, and this time it's all me. It's so raw, and there's a part of me that wants him to know that it's the last time. My efforts are mostly in vain though, because he retaliates by kissing me as if he's never going to let me go, and damn it if it doesn't tempt me to forget everything and stay.

He picks me up, and my traitorous legs wrap around his waist without hesitation. We continue kissing each other in our unspoken battle of make-or-break, as he walks us back into his bedroom and kicks the door closed behind us. He lays me down on the bed and all too eagerly I am pulling off his shirt. Oh crap. This wasn't part of my break-up plan?

What the hell. These abs are too delicious to ignore. We both frantically undress each other, resenting every second we have to break from kissing. Barely taking a breath, our need for each other grows, but it's as if he is holding back tonight. Normally his kisses are possessive. Normally, he completely loses control, dominating my body with his desire for me. Tonight, is different. His actions are all gentle and deliberate, like he wants to prove to me that he really does love me. It's as if he believes this is the way for him to show me how he feels. He just doesn't get it.

I don't need him to be gentle to prove that he loves me. If anything, I can already see that in the way he looks at me, like I'm the most desirable girl in the world. Like I belong to him. Doesn't he realise that it's his passion for me that makes me feel alive? What I need from him is for him to be honest. What I need is for him to come to bat for me like he was going to do that first day. The day that he was just my mystery boy.

Although, that being said, I can't deny that this, right now, feels so good. Too good. God, this boy knows every button to push. Ryan chuckles, his laugh vibrating against my neck sending goosebumps down my body. I cringe, realising I said that out loud.

"I need you, Ryan. Please," I beg unashamedly. Ryan pushes himself into me, giving me what I asked for, while continuing his assault of deadly kisses.

Ryan makes love to me. He worships every inch of my body, every kiss and tender touch, bearing the weight of his apologies. He takes his time, making sure I feel every moment until I come undone, and even then, he relentlessly continues, pushing me further over the edge than I've ever felt in my life. It's not until I'm coming again, and he reaches his own climax that I realise we haven't used any protection. Oh crap.

"Ryan, I.." Shit on a stick. It's no use. I can't even get my words out. My body feels like it's made of mush right now. I realise mush is not an actual thing, but heck I can't even think straight. The mush feels so good.

"*Foi*, listen…" he starts, a frown forming on his beautiful face. Here we go again. This asshole better not ruin my mush moment I swear to God. "I'm so sorry, I know I keep on doing crap that I need to apologise for, and you keep on giving me chance after chance that I don't deserve, but I need you to know that I meant what I said. I love you. You're so beautiful, I swear I won't ever behave the way I did today again."

He kisses me, and it's wonderful. It's so wonderful, my heart aches knowing that I'm going to leave him. Can I really leave him, after what just happened?

"Please say you believe me?" he begs between kisses. It's so hard to stay focused when he is being so sweet like this. Every part of me wants to accept his apology and forget the hurtful things he has said and done. It would be so easy.

"I believe you," is all I can say as I kiss him back, my heart breaking inside my chest. He holds me in his arms tightly, and I tickle his back gently until he falls asleep. He looks so peaceful. His beautiful messy blonde hair falling across his eyes.

I manage to unwrap myself out of his strong arms without waking him up. I throw on my clothes reluctantly, as every bone in my body is screaming at me to climb back into bed and try again, but I know I can't.

I sit at his desk. He has some really beautiful stationary that has the geek in me giddy and jealous in equal parts. Albeit only for a moment, as the reality of what I need to do sinks through my stomach like lead. I quietly take a couple of sheets of paper and a pen, and I begin to write him a letter. The moon is shining so brightly through the window, it's as if she knows how much I need her comforting light right now.

I know I am a coward, but I know if I try to say these things to his face, then I wont be able to leave. Looking at him now, alone in the bed, he seems lonely somehow. Like his heart already knows what I'm about to do. He is going to hate me when he wakes up, and that thought rips through me like acid in my lungs. I take my letter and I leave it on the pillow next to him. I know I'm a total weirdo, but I also take a photo on my phone of him sleeping. He is so painfully beautiful, I need something to remember that he was once mine, if only for a minute.

I grab the necklace he ripped from my neck and put it back on. After all, he gave it to me, and if he really wants it back then one day, he can come and get it.

# CHAPTER 41

*Ryan*

'To Ryan,

My sweetheart.

My elephant.

My love.

I know you are hurting.

I know you are grieving.

I know you regret the things you have said. I know you have always loved me, even if you could never say it.

I know you didn't mean any of the nasty things you said to me. I know you never really mean to hurt me, but you do, over and over again.

I know you find it hard to say how you really feel, instead you push people away with hate.

I know you have your secrets, and you have your reasons for keeping them from me. I know you have repeatedly hurt me just to *protect those secrets.*

*I know with all my heart that this isn't who you really are, which is what makes what I'm about to say a million times harder.*

*I'm leaving California for good. I know I promised you I would be there for you, but you've hurt me with your cruel words too many times. I swore to you that you would not get away with calling me a pig ever again, and I meant it.*

*You called me your lion, and told me it was forever, and I believed you. I was yours, you were mine.*

*I promised you that whatever your secret with Mia, we could get through it together if you would just trust me, but you made your choice, and you chose her and your secrets over us and our future. For whatever reason, I don't know, but now you will have to live with the consequences of your choices.*

*Whether you meant it or not, you told me to go away and leave you the fuck alone, so I will.*

*I know you are a good person. I know you have a beautiful heart. I know you have a lot of love to give, and I know that you think that you don't. I know that you think you're broken. I know you think you don't deserve to be loved. I know all of these things, but I want you to know this.*

*I love you.*

*I have loved you from the moment I met you and you will always have my love, whether you want it or not. Always.*

*You have been consumed by your grief. So much so that you now take comfort in the demons that haunt you, and instead you fear the people who want to love you.*

*You fear the light.*

*You have become afraid to live, and now your fear controls you. It darkens you, it keeps you bound in chains.*

*I know you will not be expecting this letter, especially after last night. I know there is a chance that you won't forgive me for leaving, and if that's the case, then I accept that. I know if I don't leave, you will never get better. I am deeply sorry, and I am quite sure I will regret this decision the moment I close the door behind me, but right now it's the only one I can make that will save us both.*

*I will always dream of our life together, our yard swing, our five kids, and our bald cat neither of us wants. Until you get the help you need to deal with your grief, then we can never have that.*

*I've taken back the necklace. You did give it to me after all. I know it's expensive, and I know how special it is to you, so I promise to keep it safe, and cherish it always. If you still feel like you want it back, then you know where to find me, but if you meant what you said last night, then I guess someday you will come for it anyway, and hopefully you'll be coming for me too.*

*Whatever the future holds, I wish with all my heart that you can find peace and happiness, and most of all love. You deserve to have love, and if that's not with me, then so be it. Just please find it, and cherish it.*

*Beautiful Ryan,*

*My first,*

*My always,*

*Foi x`*

What. The. Fuck. It's been two weeks, but I still read it over and over again. When I woke up to find her gone, this letter in her place, I rushed straight round to her house. Lorrie was there, but she told me Faith had already gone to the airport hours before. I debated the big movie scene gesture of showing up at the airport, but I knew it would be too late by the time I got there. Besides, isn't this what I wanted?

Once Faith was gone, I told Mia to go fuck herself. Without *Foi* in the picture she didn't have any leverage over me anymore. She continued to threaten to out me to the cops about what happened to Dr. A, but she never followed through. I realised she knew that if I was going down, I would pull her snake ass along with me. What she didn't realise is that I was biding my time. Her father is running for Senator after all, a detail I will use to my advantage when the time is right.

Faith was right, I did need to sort myself out, and I knew that meant I would eventually need to atone for my sins and come clean about everything I have done. I was going to turn myself in to the cops, but I had a few things to take care of first, revenge on Faith's enemies being high up on my list.

First things first though, I needed to sort shit out with my crew, starting by being completely honest with them about everything I've done, even what happened to my mom. I sent an S.O.S on the group chat, and not even twenty-four hours later they were all touching down in L.A. No questions asked, no further explanation needed.

Yet again, Alex only needed to make one phone call and the whole crew were on a private jet halfway across the world. That boy could rule the world if he wanted to, but that's the thing, he doesn't want to. He doesn't even want to take over at The Diamond Company until he absolutely has to, and even then, I'm not convinced he won't just break it up and sell it off soon as he has the chance, just to spite his father.

See, his father wasn't supposed to be running the company. His older brother Nathan West was first in line, right up until he was murdered in New York about eighteen years ago.

The West's have always been pretty archaic in the way they inherit the family fortune. The oldest son will inherit the lion's share, if no sons, then the oldest daughter will inherit, so long as she's married. Then any spares, as other children are often referred to, will inherit a much smaller annual allowance.

With Nathan not having any children of his own, the baton passed to his younger brother, Alexander West Senior, who instead of tracking down the assholes who murdered his brother and avenging his death, ran away to London and lapped up his new position of power. He was more interested in running the company, and the whores and cocaine that came with it, than he was in taking care of his dying wife and new born son.

See, I told you he was an asshole. At least my father was always faithful to my mother.

The guys arrive, and Melody had the guest house made up for them to stay, so we had some privacy to catch up. She told me to have fun with my friends, but to make sure no one was drinking any of the booze in the mini fridge, because while we were old enough in London, here we were under age.

The guesthouse is always left closed down when no one is staying here, so I know for a fact she had the fridge stocked before they arrived. Particularly as she stocked it completely, all with McGowan Brewery owned drinks. Her not-so subtle attempt at being cool, but with plausible deniability.

"Wanker!" Kat screeches, as she literally throws herself into my arms. I pick her up from her waist and spin her around, and she squeals in delight. She's even more beautiful than I remember, but there is still nothing romantic there. I put her down and she slaps me hard across the face. "Don't ever bloody worry us like that again, you hear me!" I rub my face and she cringes, her face apologetic from the slap that was clearly harder than she'd meant for it to be. Seeing as how I deserve it though, I offer her a wink and smile in return.

"My man! What's happening, brother?" Alex says enthusiastically, offering me a fist pump. I grab him and pull him into a hug. I've been away from these assholes for too long to just fist pump. "Alright, alright, don't hog me for too long, the ladies will get jealous!" he says, feeling awkward but I just hold him tighter. He relaxes, sensing I'm not fooling around, and gives me a tight squeeze in return.

"I dunno about the ladies getting jealous, but I'm getting well jel here, let me in on this lads," Tom says, wrapping his large arms around us both. Although he is Kats twin, they have their differences, the most obvious being their hair. Tom's hair is a lot darker than Kat's. Where she is a proud fiery redhead, Tom's hair is more a chestnut brown. Neither of them has any freckles, in fact they both have flawless milky skin, very similar to *Foi's*. Fuck, the thought of her hurts my heart.

"... Na-na, na-na, hey!" I realise the boys are chanting soccer songs as they dance around me like cavemen. I have no idea how, but they already have beers in their hands, and Kat is already on *Uber Eats* ordering pizza. A beer is thrust into my face by an angry looking Spencer.

"Dickhead!" She says, walking away without so much as a hug. She takes a seat on the couch facing away from all of us. Away from me. Fucking hell, my heart aches at that now too.

Here I was thinking my heart was dead, but oh no, apparently it's still very much a-fucking-live. I let one person in and now I'm a fucking *Carebear* or something.

"Give her a minute," Tom says seriously, his instincts to protect her now fully engrained. I appreciate that. I nod accepting that I owe these guys a lot, and the fact Spencer has even come here to hear me out means the world to me.

"Okay Fresh Prince. We've been here for about ten years already and you haven't even said a bloody word. We didn't come all this way just to look at your ugly mug, now spill," Alex says, now standing in front of Spence. Another show of solidarity towards her. I trained these guys well.

I take a deep breath.

Here goes…

# CHAPTER 42

## Unknown

*Two weeks earlier...*

"It's done, she's gone back. What happens now Pakhan?" I ask my father as he sits back in his antique green leather chair, behind an endless stream of papers and photographs scattered across his walnut desk. His office is dark, and full of stale cigar smoke. A large photo of The Church of the Saviour on Spilled Blood in Saint Petersburg, hangs behind him. Behind me, above the door, is a replica of Our Lady of Kazan, watching over us and all our wicked deeds.

As Bratva, we have always known our lives were destined for sin, merely a journey on our pathway to hell. We just hope to say enough Hail Marys, and earn enough money to bribe our way out again once we're there.

"Now, we wait. Let's hope our little spy at the clinic has learned his lesson this time and sticks to the plan in future. We were so close last time, it was the perfect plan, until he went and messed up the snatch." He slams his fist on the desk and I notice what appears to be a recent photo of his lifelong obsession.

Lena Lewkowicz.

"He said Faith wasn't there. The crew tried to grab the mother instead, but the British doctor got in the way."

"He assured me she would be on that truck! If he messes up again, he will be thrown back into the slums we dragged him from. Let the lions have their way with him! We need to get that girl to the compound, it's the only way to get to Lena. She will never show her face in L.A, because she knows we are here. However, she will come out to play if we have her daughter," he says with a gleam in his eye.

"Lena has been seen in Africa by the asset, all over the summer. She follows the girl and the good doctors around. He can't get close to her, so Lena must know he's working for us. She's probably the reason Scott dropped his son off there. We just need to draw Lena out of hiding for good, and the girl is the key."

"Why didn't you just have Faith snatched while she was here in L.A? She's been here for years, you could have taken her to the compound yourself?"

I'm so over this bullshit. He has been trying to track down Lena for as long as I can remember. The bitch stole something and got away with it. Whatever it was, sent our family into hiding. My entire life we've pretended to be people we aren't and I'm sick of it.

"Because it's not so easy to go under the radar if you are kidnapping girls on your own doorstep. Eamon Scott would soon point the finger at us, and the cops cannot know who we really are. I can't risk the other families finding out where we are either, and we cannot draw attention to the girl. The Morozov family are the only ones who know of her true lineage, and I have kept it that way until she becomes of age."

"She's gotta be eighteen already?" I ask knowing all too well that this will never end, not until he has Lena.

"She won't inherit until she is twenty-five. Her real father was the heir to one of the most powerful and richest families in the world, and I intend to cash in when the time is right. Besides, if we had taken her in L.A, the Scott boy and his father would have been a problem. I thought that having that ex-stripper bitch run off the road would bring him and his father back, away from the girl! I didn't realise he had started slipping her his dick? You said he hated her, but yet he brings her back with him? She was supposed to be staying in Africa, that's what the asset said."

He pours two large glasses of straight vodka over ice. slides one over to me and I gladly take it. Just the mention of that asshole Ryan's name has my fists curling.

He touched what's mine.

Faith, or Vera as her Polish whore mother named her, has always been promised to me and I made sure she stayed a perfect little virgin until I was ready for her.

"He took what was meant for me, and now he will pay. Meyers is the one who told her to come back for three weeks. Stupid bitch thought we wanted her back." I add bitterly. I hate that old hag almost as much as I hate Ryan.

"Don't worry Slavik, she will be dealt with. I will make sure she is buried right next to that bitch coach who spilled about Vera's adoption. But all in good time. Meyers is not our priority, and while the Scott kid is still at the school, she is useful. Just make sure that Mia keeps him occupied and in Los Angeles. We must make sure he stays away from Vera if he is going to go back to New York after graduation. The last thing we want is for the girl to follow him there, out of our reach."

I nod in agreement. My father was exiled from New York

by the other families. If Faith goes to New York we won't be able to get to her there, and if the other families find out who she is, they will take her for themselves. I still don't fully understand what all of this is about, but I know all of this started with that bitch Vera and her whore mother, Lena.

My father, the great Daniil Molotov, grandson of the greatest Pakhan of all time, now reduced to hiding in the shadows like a miserable wretch. He was next in line to take control of the five families, but whatever the situation was with Lena, it ended up seeing him banished. The heads of the other families had called for my father to be presented to them for judgement, and when he wasn't, my grandfather was slaughtered for his mercy, and replaced with a usurper.

We still have a degree of wealth, and to some extent power. In L.A we rule the roost, albeit covertly. Those still loyal in New York keep us informed, but our power and wealth is nothing compared to what is rightfully ours.

"Lena Lewkowicz was seen leaving Eamon Scott's office just under two years ago. The next thing he remarries, packs up his entire life, and enrols his son in the same school as Lena's daughter? Keeps him back a year? That is not a coincidence, and I intend to find out exactly what he knows."

My father is right, Eamon Scott is shady as fuck. He was the one who insisted his son repeat and start as a junior, then made out to Ryan that it was all Meyers. It must have been so he would be close to Faith, but why? What's his involvement in this?

"And Lena? Will you keep her alive if you find her? What exactly did she take anyway?" I ask, knowing full well he won't tell me. He never has.

"That's none of your concern. All you need to know is that she stole from me. I *will* find her, and I *will* deal with her my way. No one steals from Daniil Morozov and lives to tell the tale." Yeah, yeah, so he keeps saying. Yet here we are eighteen years later, living like dogs.

"What about Vera? What happens to her when you get to Lena? Vera is mine." I ask, the real question burning in my head.

"Relax, I only want Lena, her offspring is not my concern. You will have her as promised, she's yours to do with as you please. Fuck her, keep her in chains, whatever you want, but when she turns twenty-five, you will marry her, and she will give you a son. Then Slavik, my son, you will have the legitimate heir to The West Diamond Company fortune, and The Morozov family will finally return to power!"

***

To be continued...

# USEFUL CONTACTS

For more information about suicide prevention in the United Kingdom, please contact:

**Samaritans**
116 123 www.samaritans.org

**Anxiety UK Helpline**
03444775774 www.anxietyuk.org.uk

**National Suicide Prevention Helpline UK**
0800 689 5652 www.spbristol.org/NSPHUK

If you're experiencing a mental health problem or supporting someone else, you can call:

**SANEline**
0300 304 7000 (4.30pm–10.30pm every day). SANEline

**NHS**
111 www.nhs.uk

# AUTHORS NOTE

Dear Reader,

For as long as I can remember, I have had a number of strangers occupying space in my head. I could never understand why I spent so much time thinking about imaginary peoples' lives, and become so invested in what might happen to them. It wasn't until I started reading books that it occurred to me that these were my people, and that they were crying out for their stories to be told.

I hope with all my heart that I have done Faith and Ryan's story some justice, and I am looking forward to finishing this journey with you all in their second book, Bring Me to Love.

Thank you all for reading.

# ACKNOWLEDGEMENT

Thank you to my Stuart, for always supporting me in everything that I do, even if an American high school, enemies-to-lovers romance is not for you.

Thank you to my whole family, for being the absolute best there could be.

Thank you to Frankie, for being my inspiration to get this book started, and to carry on when I thought that I couldn't.

Thank you to Brooke, for always answering my random grammar question texts without ever wondering why I was asking them.

Thank you to Laycie, who once told me that you never get over the pain of losing someone you love, you just learn to live with a broken heart - These words still resonate with me ten years later and I knew I wanted to incorperate them into this book.

Lastly, thank you to Sarah, for your continued words of encouragement, especially when I have doubted myself.

**xoxo**

Special thanks to Britney Spears for her wonderful music, without which Faith would not be the girl she is in this book.

# BACK TO LOVE DUET

## Bring Me To Life

## Bring Me To Love

Coming Soon

# Charlotte Frances

Printed in Great Britain
by Amazon